A GRIM REUNION

Polijn knew what dead bodies looked like in all their phases, from the moment of realization that it was all done to three years after that. She was not on her knees for the novelty of it.

The woman had been stabbed at least twice, that she could see, by someone who had twisted the knife well to be sure. And her hair was mussed . . . Polijn reached out and smoothed a few locks back into place.

"Mother?" she said.

Ace Books by Dan Crawford

ROUSE A SLEEPING CAT
THE SURE DEATH OF A MOUSE
A WILD DOG AND LONE

A WILD DOG AND LONE

Dan Crawford

ACE BOOKS, NEW YORK

This book is an Ace original edition,
and has never been previously published.

A WILD DOG AND LONE

An Ace Book / published by arrangement with
the author

PRINTING HISTORY
Ace edition / March 1995

All rights reserved.
Copyright © 1995 by Dan Crawford.
Cover art by Bryant Eastman.
This book may not be reproduced in whole or in part,
by mimeograph or any other means, without permission.
For information address: The Berkley Publishing Group,
200 Madison Avenue, New York, NY 10016.

ISBN: 0-441-00183-1

ACE®
Ace Books are published by The Berkley Publishing Group,
200 Madison Avenue, New York, NY 10016.
ACE and the "A" design are trademarks
belonging to Charter Communications, Inc.

PRINTED IN THE UNITED STATES OF AMERICA

10 9 8 7 6 5 4 3 2 1

*This book is dedicated to TIM CRAWFORD,
who hates buying fantasy series novels*

PROLOGUE
Sielvia

THE day was damp. Everyone in the Palace Royal was stickily hot and damp, save for a privileged few, like those in the dungeons, who were cool and damp. Sielvia was one of the cool few.

The little room was filled with exotic damp smells: the not quite nice aroma of stored flesh, the earthy, common odor of damp living flesh. Under it all was the cold smell of old stone. The room was ancient beyond imagination; the smells told you that. Sielvia shifted on the plank under her legs. She supposed no one living could recall when the nicked, initialed wood had been new.

"Any more?" called a woman at the door.

Sielvia leaned way over, shivering a little as her hand vanished into the shadow. Of course, nothing so large as a spider would lurk in the darkness of Forokell's vaults. It wouldn't dare.

"Coming!" she called, as her fingers touched crockery. She fastened both hands around the precious pot of goose liver and handed it along to the woman on the ladder, who passed it to the woman on the floor, who sent it along the human chain up the stairs and out to the wagon.

The youngest, smallest member of the goose liver brigade had earned top spot by virtue of the fact that she fit onto the shelves. But she was tall enough that, by stretching, she could reach the length of each shelf and clear it of the little stone jars. This saved moving the ladder every few minutes, an efficiency that Forokell, the First Housekeeper, appreciated.

Lying flat on her side, passing goose liver along to the ladder, Sielvia could see out the door and up into the drill yard, to the end of the goose liver chain. A tall man in blue and brown was whispering to the woman packing the little crocks into a wicker case.

The woman straightened and gave the man a push in the chest. "Get away! Berdais!"

A robust, red-faced woman who had been walking up and down the line of liver handlers turned and lunged for the wagon. The man backed off, holding his hands up in defense and apology. The kitchen guards, their swords drawn to discourage pilfering, did not move. Sielvia assumed the man was one of the amber merchants, too rich to be maimed for a minor infraction, even on such a steamy day.

The merchants from Falastur were waiting around the Palace to join the caravan when it trekked north. They hoped their valuable cargo would be safer in this company, though it was really just as much at risk parked within the walls of the Palace Royal as it would have been in the bandit-infested territory around the lake.

Talking fast and low, the man seemed to be making peace with Berdais. Some of his companions followed his progress; others called suggestions to Iranen's slaveys, grunting and glistening in the sun as they loaded wheels, barrels, and wheelbarrows onto another wagon for the long trip. A few more stood at the platform where Rabioson Sausagefinger was practicing. Those massive hands had delicately directed the huge axe to the same spot on the practice block sixteen—no, seventeen now—times in a row. There was to be an important exhibition for him before he, too, set off for the north.

Colonel Kirasov shoved among the crowds and paused, breathing hard as he surveyed what was usually the archery range. Slapping one hand on a wagon stave, he clung for support as half a dozen guard and hunting dogs dashed past him. The head treasury guard regained his equilibrium in time to direct a booted foot into the midsection of the last dog. This, as it happened, was a hunting dog, and belonged to a man trying to catch up with the pack. He abandoned the chase and took Kirasov by the collar, screaming invectives up the taller man's nose.

Four kitchen guards turned to look; the fifth spied a hunched figure sidestepping up to the wicker crate. "Back, there!" roared the guard.

The flat of his blade caught the man's bare arm, slashing off a collop of flesh. Head down between his shoulders, the man dashed off cursing, more from the embarrassment of being caught than pain. The guard took out a bandana to wipe his forehead and then his sword. To add to the gaiety, someone screamed, "Hoo hoo! Hoo hoo!" at the top of his lungs.

Sielvia, cool and recumbent in the vault, reached back and found yet another row of crocks. Mijan was nobody in particular, and no one would have avenged him even if the whole arm had been cut away.

Up the stairs, Berdais had been joined by Forokell, who had somehow worked her farnum chair through the confusion. The venerable housekeeper studied the goose liver chain with distaste, or perhaps she was looking beyond it at Mijan. The goose livers were, some of them, as old as Sielvia; packed in their own fat, they kept for years, the flavor and price increasing with each month. The kitchen guards, therefore, were alert for would-be thieves. The would-be thieves were watchful in the background.

Technically, Sielvia was not one of Forokell's underlings, but she handled the pricey livers all the more carefully because of that. Ten years old, too young to be attached to anyone's staff, she could still see the benefit of making a good impression on the First Housekeeper. Besides, Berdais would have flayed her for any mistake.

Forokell had wheeled as close to the stairs as she dared. "All of them!" she called. "All! We'll need every one up north!" Turning to Berdais, she repeated her description of the staff at the Summer Palace as thieves and incompetents. All the stores left carefully packed last fall were undoubtedly eaten, sold, or riddled with vermin by now.

The disruption in the regular disorder of the Palace Royal was a result of the King's annual parade north, to wait out the heat of the season in the Summer Palace. Usually, the commotion was finished up in the last cool days as spring bleached into summer, but the heat had attacked early this year. People were fairly irritated about it. Some, in fact, had set off north already, either to see that things were made ready there, or just to lay low for a few days.

Worse than the commotion was the competition. A very few of the highest officials of the court had a choice, whether to stay in the Palace Royal and relax (or plunder) or to move north with the center of things. Most did as they were told, but all tried to change the orders before they got any. North, with the King, was the only way to go.

Sielvia had never made the decision. Like her sisters, she had always accompanied her father, and he always went north. Staying behind might be interesting, she thought: finding out what the Palace Royal was like, two-thirds empty, or what life would be like without her parents and older sisters.

She hardly ever mentioned this; no one ever understood. Even little Polijn, usually so careful not to exhibit any unrehearsed emotion, had looked a little shocked when Sielvia said something about it. She supposed she wouldn't really stay behind even if she were given the choice. It was traditional, the whole family going up to the great cold lake for three or four months.

Sielvia frowned. Only they wouldn't be together this year. Cidre was out west, on the border with her husband. (Husbands were not easily come by; one didn't desert them to go swimming.) And her next oldest sisters, Jolor and Ysela, had not been told by their superiors whether they'd go north. The smart gossip said General Ferrapec and his wife would be snubbed, left behind, so Jolor, in Lady Raiprez's retinue, would probably stay. That was a pity; of her three oldest sisters, Sielvia liked Jolor best.

Ysela was leaning against one of the wagons now, listening to a merchant who was holding a bit of amber out to her. Sielvia wrinkled her nose. That had to be fake.

Whoever it was was still screaming, "Hoo hoo! Hoo hoo!" Sielvia saw more than one person looking around, fingers curled as though already around the man's throat. Kirasov's head jerked toward a corner of the yard Sielvia couldn't see, and marched off.

By now, several members of the colonel's staff had caught up with him, and they all followed, except for one—it looked like Trobosh—who had to cut wide around a mob of little kids, naked or nearly so, screaming their way under the crowd, in pursuit of a brown ball. Forokell wheeled her chair around and was among them in seconds, calling the ragamuffins to attention and informing them in words of greater force than length that anyone who would play ball around a wagonload of crockery was just as clever and less useful than a cracked chamberpot. Trobosh surreptitiously kicked the ball back to one of the boys, who sat on it for safekeeping.

Then Trobosh strolled across to Berdais and made some murmured remark, pointing at the boy. Sielvia saw something white change hands.

"Any more?" called the woman at the door.

Sielvia rubbed the back of her neck and extended her reach. Her fingertips brushed stone and nothing else. "Next shelf!" she shouted, and eased back to the ladder.

The woman there stepped down a few rungs to give her room, and she mounted up to the next level. Positioning herself securely on the old wood, she wiped her hands on the front of her apron before beginning anew. She glanced back at the next link in the goose liver chain. The woman nodded at her.

"Sielvia!" snapped Berdais, at the door. "Are you just sitting?"

The attack was unexpected: Sielvia had no answer. "I . . . I . . . Mother!" she said, pointing to the empty shelf below.

"Don't talk back to me, girl!" Berdais ordered. "Come here! Mataquin, you take her place!"

"I was just starting the new shelf," Sielvia protested. Sitting up there was her job, and she had been doing it all morning. "My hands were wet. You don't want . . ."

But by this time she had come all the way down the ladder. Berdais took her by the shoulder and hauled her off the bottom rung. With a free hand, her mother dashed up her skirt in the back and, releasing the shoulder, dealt her a swat that echoed through the chamber. All Sielvia's suspicions were awake at once. When Berdais hit someone, the desired effect was pain, not sound.

"Get out!" Berdais went on, ushering her daughter out onto the drill yard. "As though I thought you could be any help!"

Sielvia found a piece of paper being forced into her left hand. "To your father," Berdais whispered, low and fast. "Nobody's to know."

Sielvia's eyes sparkled. She wrenched free of her mother's grasp. "All right!" she yelled. "I didn't want to squat around here all day anyhow!" She pressed her advantage, spitting and adding, "You buncha rat traps!"

Her mother swung at her and missed way wide. She hurried off to the sound of Berdais's promise of a much redder backside later, young lady, and Forokell's shouts that everyone could get back to work now so hand those crocks down, take it slow and easy, and be quick about it.

Sielvia did not have to look to know she was being watched. Some were waiting to hear if she thought of something juicier to call her mother, while others were betting on whether Berdais would come after her. And there were no doubt those who had not been fooled by the little drama, and wondered what it was all about. Sielvia closed her fist a little tighter around the note, and slid between two sagging wagons.

On the far side, she brushed against Iranen's chief assistant, Aoyalasse Smoketail. Severely reddened by the sun, the woman snarled and aimed a spread hand at Sielvia, who was already ducking. The slap went around and caught the crock that Sirsten had just laboriously worked out through a hole in the side of an unobserved wicker case. The little pot hit the wheel of the cart and shattered.

Sirsten's knife flashed out. Iranen's slaveys were not permitted weapons, so Aoyalasse snatched at one of the larger fragments of pottery. Sielvia tried to dive clear, but stepped in goose liver at the same time Aoyalasse did. They fell together, but the older woman had her eyes on the knife, and kicked up at the arm that held it. The blade flashed past, snicked through a rope, and lodged between two staves of the nearest barrel.

The rope snapped free, welting two women Iranen had ordered to pile more cargo onto the overburdened wagon. "I'm killed!" roared Sirsten, as barrels and women started to crash around him. "I'm killed! I'm killed! And I hurt my foot!"

Unloading itself in much less time than it had taken to load, the cart sent barrels and cheap, everyday dishes across the yard. Two women waited for Iranen's permission to dodge, and were crushed to the ground. Mijan, who had taken what he thought was shelter, jumped over a stack of bowls, collided with two kitchen guards, and landed facefirst in the goose liver. A worried cooper, seeing a month's worth of overtime being turned into kindling, jumped over him, only to be sent sprawling by one of Iranen's bodyguards. Iranen herself was in the thick of the confusion, knife in one hand and whip in the other, seeking not to end chaos but to prolong it.

The cooper, trying to rise, caught hold of an ankle. A rumbling cough made him look up. The cooper fainted.

"Lady Iranen!" called Forokell, whose ankle it was.

Even the barrels seemed to stop rolling. Iranen looked up.

"Clean this," Forokell ordered, and turned her chair away.

Iranen licked the point of her knife thoughtfully. Numerous combatants recalled urgent appointments elsewhere and, helping erstwhile foes to their feet, slipped away. Iranen's bodyguard came up around her, bringing her sun canopy. (Iranen had designed it herself so that none of the nude men who bore it would ever feel any shade.)

Aoyalasse was sprawled on the ground, cursing and tugging at her hair, which had been caught under a wheel when the wagon lurched. "Well!" said Iranen. It was a syllable of solid satisfaction.

Sielvia peeped out from under a less eventful wagon. People in songs, she knew, would have pushed through the carnage to deliver the message with their dying breath. But if she had done that, she'd have missed the trip north, and she had a new swimming ensemble, after all.

Three of Iranen's bodyguards had raised Aoyalasse, without bothering to shift the wagon. Bracing one leg vertically, they brought the other up perpendicular to its mate. Ambermongers and idlers pushed in, clearing a path for Sielvia toward the Palace Royal. She didn't need to watch, having seen Iranen in action before.

She did glance back when the onlookers, who had been jeering advice, fell into awed silence. Aoyalasse's scream rang out in the hush, full of pain and shame and fury.

"Will you look at that, then?" whispered one of the merchants, wiping his forehead.

"Don't know if I can stand this for two days more," murmured his companion.

"Oh, they'll never be ready in two days."

Sielvia staggered to her feet from all fours. Maybe Aoyalasse would know better next time. She doubted it, but she'd never liked the bossy little redhead anyhow.

She didn't pause until she reached the vast, shady passage that led to the main courtyard. There was always a little breeze in here, and she stopped to catch her breath and let herself dry a bit, shaking sodden skirts away from her legs. If it got any hotter than this, she'd have to go north or melt.

The stairs up into the Palace itself were a struggle. Aoyalasse's screams still ripped through the air, and traffic was moving in the direction of the drill yard to find out what was new. Sielvia decided to take the message the long way around, by way of the hall past the dungeon entrance.

She was not the only one eluding the crowds, Aperiole was slipping along next to the wall, carrying a bucket. Sielvia assumed there was food and drink inside, for some private conference in a sheltered nook. Aperiole had only one underskirt on, to judge by the way the gown was caught up behind, and the features that had earned her the nickname "Dragonthighs" were easily discernible, every muscle showing under the sweat-soaked muslin.

She was trying to be inconspicuous and exude an air of mystery at the same time. There had to be an air of mystery about everything she did. Yearning to be elegant and sultry and mysterious, she had so far achieved little more than sullen and greasy.

Sielvia stepped up behind her, yanked the skirt out of the crack, and yelled, "Boo!" Then she ducked as the bucket swung past her head.

"Brat!" shrieked her sister.

Sielvia dodged the backstroke as well. "Who're you off to now? Your black eyes are running."

"Oymanung!" Aperiole dropped the bucket and scraped at the blue dripping from her artistically shaded eyelids. "And keep off!"

One heavy foot slammed down on the lid of the bucket, just missing Sielvia's fingers. Sielvia withdrew to a safer distance. Aperiole had violent spells, and was ferociously jealous of her younger sisters, who associated with the King. They would have an inside shot at the good jobs and/or husbands, while Aperiole had to work for anything she got.

"If you're so lintik interested," Aperiole went on, "you can carry it for me."

"I am SO sorry," said Sielvia, with a sweet smile. "I have official business in the Council Chamber."

Aperiole turned a little redder without artificial coloring. "Get back here, you laplicker!"

Sielvia delayed just long enough to suggest Aperiole explain to their mother the significance of the agate she wore in her navel. Aperiole responded that though all her sisters were ugly enough to tree a wolf, only Sielvia could scare a mule with all her clothes on. After an exchange of finger salutes, the sisters marched their separate ways.

Around the next corner, Sielvia pulled aside for a ragged sorcerer who wore a dried bat across his chest. Aizon of the Bat was not going north, but, as Royal Exorcist, he was required to rid the royal wagons of any evil ghosts that might have taken up residence during the winter. Otherwise, he would have been sequestered in his tower room, studying. He hardly ever ventured down; her father said of Aizon that he was too busy amassing power to enjoy what he already had.

Aizon passed her without a word. She knew those tiny black eyes had spotted her, though: his lip curled. The rest of his face was stiff, two angry red spots decorating the cheeks. This was his normal expression. Had he been genuinely displeased, he would have looked exactly the same, but his assistant would have been more solemn.

"Hi, Siel!" called Karabari. He paused, as if to chat, but a snarl from his mentor sent him trotting along. Aizon had no use for females, less from personal preference than because they distracted Karabari. His quest for extended life having been stymied, Aizon had become particular about assistants not wasting their time, so they could study his accumulated wisdom, lest that perish, too.

His wisdom was doomed. Karabari Banglebags had more than seclusion in a tower library on his mind. He knew by name every female in the Palace Royal. Bright and chipper, with hair that grew off his cheeks into fuzzy epaulettes, he was a great favorite, undaunted by the glares of husbands or lovers. For a sorcerer, he was harmless enough, and very ornamental. Today his light summer robes of blue and white were hung with colored ropes and an array of gems, tacked here and there about his person. The stones twinkled in the light as if they were alive. He had never parted with a one, though rumor said they were pledged to various loves of the moment, who paid for them over and over, only to be disappointed at last.

Sielvia waved back as he disappeared around the corner she had just turned, and then looked ahead to the Council Chamber. The usual gaggle of hangers-on clustered at the painted door. The door was closed, but unlocked. Only overcrowding and the heat kept most of the onlookers out of the room. The Council Chamber was not closed to most inhabitants of the Palace, which Sielvia thought far more civilized than those governments run in exclusive and rarified rooms of aged dukes, no matter how much their ambassadors sniffed at the crudeness of Rossacotta.

Sielvia nodded to the guards on duty, who nodded back. One reached out to pull the door open. A hand gripped his arm.

"You're letting HER in!"

Sielvia glanced up at Adimo, a burly man with a thick beard and bushy black hair. A fierce frown wrinkled the swarthy forehead and shadowed the hook nose. He was sweating heavily for someone who had been just standing there; water trickled down his temples. His robes were heavy, dark blue with black velvet trim, and, Sielvia knew, unpaid for. His former position in the Regent's retinue was now filled by a younger man from Braut, and, as Adimo no doubt knew, he was being gradually deported.

"Yes, sir," said a guard, smirking in a civil way. "SHE is permitted to enter."

Adimo's hand drew back, "But I'll put in a good word for you," said Sielvia, stretching her mouth to bring out the dimples. "I'm sure everyone really wants you to come north."

A general laugh greeted this. There had been no doubt that the Regent's former lover would go north. There was also no doubt that he would not be back in the fall. Adimo glowered.

Adimo could get as mad as he liked. Everyone knew who Sielvia's father was, and that she was among the King's Companions. This double shield held the world at bay.

But Adimo had not achieved his post through common sense. His hand went to one of the knives at his belt. Sielvia didn't move. She carried a knife, but had never yet had to use it for anything but eating.

A dozen hands gripped the ex-favorite. He vanished, and there was a sound of blows back in the crowd. With a nod to the guard who had opened the door, Sielvia trotted inside.

The noise and smell was worse than in the kennels. Nearly a hundred people were packed into the Council Chamber: those councillors summoned to the meeting, plus all the backers, bodyguards, and assistants each could muster. It had been easy enough to muster them. Several important issues would be discussed, in faint hopes of coming to a resolution before the trip north. And, if one was needed in Council, one's spouse could not possibly expect one to help with the packing.

The cadaverous Regent, Kaftus, sat at the head of the massive table. At its foot perched a black bird on an empty chair. Important councillors had seats along the sides of the table, with lesser lights sitting behind them and nobodies standing along the wall. Competition for chairs was fierce, but no one cared to dispute Mardith's possession of a choice seat.

"Missy don' fool, no!" spat the black bird.

Mamouthi, a jewel merchant from the city, grinned at having made the bird lose its temper. Had the bird's mistress been present, he might have kept his satisfaction to himself.

Garanem smiled, too, but a moment later frowned, pulling off his orange wig to wipe sweat from his forehead and under his arms. Rossacottan fashion made its point through sheer weight and number of garments, an advantage during the harsh winter but a drawback in the heat of summer. The

general tossed the sodden wig back to one of his underlings,
while another offered him a glass of wine. After a couple
of swallows, he passed the drink on to a favored aide to
finish, and scratched at his beard, dyed three colors to amuse
the King.

Not many of the councillors present had enough servants
on hand to send out for refreshments. Another who did was
Laisida, chief among the King's Minstrels. He had a seat right
against the wood, too, and his retinue formed a brightly colored
wedge in the crowd behind him. Bodyguards, servants, former
apprentices, and anyone else identified with the minstrel's
causes wore some arrangement of orange and black, Laisida's
colors. Most also wore his badge as well, the metal circle
bearing the mystic image of the man-hawk.

"Need I point out that many officials," he was saying,
running one hand through his hair, "particularly at the outset,
will need the guidance of this governing body?" He shook the
hand to indicate the Council, spattering Arberth, who sat to one
side. Arberth just wiped the moisture away, saying nothing.

Under the table, at Laisida's foot, sat a thin girl with dark,
shifting eyes. She held a tambourine and wore a tight summer
costume that covered her most where she had least to hide.
Laisida was busy, so Sielvia crawled under the table and patted
little Polijn on the thigh. Polijn nodded back. There was too
much noise for any other greeting.

Council meetings were very structured: no more than six people were allowed to talk at once. "A site in North Malbeth . . ."
Mamouthi began.

"Ach, Amànamin!" exclaimed Haeve, apparently in des-
pair.

"Foreign learning must be balanced against foreign influence," boomed the bass voice of Kaigrol Frogshead. General Kaigrol was very old, and very deaf. He probably didn't
know anyone else was talking. To do him justice, he probably
wouldn't have cared.

Sielvia leaned against her father's wooden leg, to let him
know she was there, and unfolded one corner of the message
against her own. Sielvia was no great reader, but she could see
in a second that this gibberish was code. How vexing! She
might have to sit down here among the squatpots for who

knew how long, with only the possibility of a fight breaking out for entertainment.

Laisida liked to keep his family up-to-date, so Sielvia was able to follow the gist of the debate, And, since these debates never really reached an end or a conclusion, she knew pretty much what speeches would be redelivered and which arguments reintroduced. The Council was planning the University of Malbeth, a center of learning to show the rest of the world that Rossacotta was not a land of barbaric illiterates. The scheme was older than Sielvia, and had never even been considered worthy of discussion, much less argument, before her uncle, Morquiesse, took it up. Even then it had been dismissed by the Council. But Morquiesse had died this spring, at the hands of sorcerous traitors. As a martyr, he had more power than he had had as King's Painter. Thus his plan for governmental reorganization was implemented almost immediately, despite the necessity of fulfilling the prophecies of several people who had said it would pass only over their dead bodies.

The idea of a university was even more radical. Literacy was still regarded subversive by conservatives, and the army regarded the University as a direct threat. Kaigrol led the opposition by means of his favorite tactic: to leech the enemy's strength in small skirmishes rather than risk all in pitched battle. A dozen niggling points had arisen, all of which, the general constantly assured the Council, had to be settled before one could start a project of such magnitude.

At Laisida's end of the table, the debate centered on location. Should the University be built in Malbeth itself, for easier communication with the Palace? Or would there be more room and less trouble placing it in a remoter and less developed area, say, North Malbeth? A score or more of volunteers were willing to set off north right now to investigate.

Around Kaigrol, down the table, size of the student body was under discussion. It made no sense, said Grandfather Frog, with foreign affairs in a state of flux, to be taking a considerable number of young men out of circulation to make librarians and minstrels of them, and providing university chancellors with a private army so they could foment rebellion in safety. Substantial eddies in the torrent of argument concerned foreign students and faculty (infiltrators or merely traitors), the lack of manpower in the Palace Royal if the University were started at the same time troops were sent to the wars in the Northern Quilt, and, by the way, were the troops going to be sent or would they stay home to twiddle toes and blow bubbles through another summer?

"Borrum did well on border inspection," said General Gensamar. "I've a mind to see him brevetted colonel. He can lead a party to North Malbeth now. While he's checking sites, he'll also serve as an additional advance scout on His Majesty's Route."

There was a stir behind him as someone stood up. Sielvia recognized General Ferrapec's legs; his thick robe hung to his ankles. Old Polishlocks couldn't afford to have his robes altered to the shorter, cooler style favored by the King. Besides, it covered the patches in his hose.

"Borrum?" he demanded. "That sprig lead an expedition?" His left foot slid forward. "I see no reason to send anyone north, least of all a youth of thirty-one winters. If His Majesty were allowed to take a safer route, there would be no need for scouts, while as for this business of North Malbeth being a fit place for . . ."

A boot that Sielvia did not immediately recognize shot up against the speaker's nearer shin.

"That is," Ferrapec Tattercuffs went on, belatedly recalling the party line, "when we send a party north to seek suitable North Malbeth sites, it should certainly be headed by a man of experience, a man we all can trust."

His tone suggested that some arcane logic had led him to place himself in that category. Sielvia knew perfectly well that he and his whole family had been ordered to stay in the Palace Royal for the summer.

Snorts came from several people who also knew this. Mardith, from his perch, croaked, "You got you already maybe a swimming suit, ha?"

Sielvia heard Ferrapec laugh at this, but he was tapping the toe of one boot hard on the stone floor. "What is North Malbeth?" he demanded. "Not Malbeth. What is Malbeth? Not North Malbeth. We need a man who knows both, a man of vast experience, a man who has seen something of the world.

Before coming to any decision, gentlemen, for these are modern times and we do not rush into things without taking aim, we need proof. Not documentary proof, by people who can write, and may well write anything, but reliable testimony, from eyewitnesses. What the eye sees can never be replaced by what the pen scratches."

He paused for acclamation. It was a brief pause.

"Documentary evidence could lead us down many paths," Ferrapec insisted, as Orna stooped and lifted one of the pots on the floor for Haeve. "Take the so-called proof in the case of the twelve missing Ykenai. All this documentary evidence has not proven their existence. No doubt there are those who would point to the deaths of Lound or Linter this past week as proof of their presence."

Ferrapec had the fortune to inject this during a lull in the debate at the other end of the table. Any mention of the suppressed Ykena sect was bound to draw attention, much of it hostile. Sielvia felt her father lean back, as if bored. Remembering the message, she slid a hand up his thigh. Laisida glanced down and pulled the message up, spreading it out on his knee. Handwriting in the Palace was very idiosyncratic, and even the literate would have had difficulty making out someone else's words at that distance. But Laisida was trained, and could do it without even moving his lips.

Sielvia could have left now, but things were getting interesting. From this angle, she could see three councillors near Ferrapec reaching for knives.

"Yet, what real proof can we have?" the general demanded. "Who has seen, or said to have seen, or dreamed to have seen, a Brown Robe? Not a robe that is brown, of course, but a member of that frequently maligned . . ."

He was losing steam. No one tried to shout him down; maybe it was too hot.

"Er, you see what I'm saying?" he said, sparring for wind.

"We might," noted the Regent, "if it were a bit brighter."

The general had not, apparently, known Kaftus was listening. "Um . . . ah . . . I am but a humble soldier," he said. His feet shuffled toward each other.

"Well, you may be a soldier," agreed the Regent.

Ferrapec rallied. "I am a soldier," he said, planting his feet firmly. "It is no wonder, therefore, that my remarks are not accorded more respect. I will say nothing about the redundance of a University when the army exists to train men. It is no doubt futile to point out the decreasing respect shown by every part of the population, so I will not refer to this. No unpleasant accusations should be allowed to upset this Council at this busy time. Therefore I will not even suggest that this business of the twelve Ykenai is being shuffled under lesser concerns for the benefit of certain people. I will ask only that my objection to the unwarranted promotion of an inexperienced officer be noted, and then I will take my seat."

But a boot jerked forward and took his seat away. Ferrapec dropped with a thud, his bodyguards pulling back and to one side so he wouldn't fall on THEM. A knife popped out of its belt sheath, and skittered under a chair. Ferrapec looked for it in the wrong direction, and it was retrieved by someone else.

The general straightened his tunic and glared around the knees of his colleagues. There were plenty of targets, but none he could attack, even if he hadn't lost his handiest knife. His retinue was too scant to risk an attack on any of them, and everyone else outranked him or was accompanying someone who outranked him.

He stood up. "Now I must be about my duties and check the, ah, men on the drill field." Two of his bodyguards followed him from the room. The third slid closer to Colonel Umian.

Conversation had resumed before Ferrapec reached the door, none of it having much to do with anything he had said. In moments, Orna was on his feet, bellowing at Pammel, General Kaigrol's son, who pounded on the table and bellowed back. Both men were just trying out new arguments which, once broken and saddled, would be used by their mentors in Council meetings to come.

Orna had dashing sideburns and an elegant swagger and, besides, Pammel had white hair and grandchildren. Sielvia leaned over to little Polijn. "My mouth against yours that Orna wins."

Polijn glanced up at Laisida, who disapproved of gambling among his dependents. The minstrel was following another argument, leaning forward, ready to throw his weight on the

Tutor's side, if required. Polijn nodded.

"All the Turinese are liars!" roared Pammel. "They're born smiling!"

Sielvia felt a hard knuckle rap her just where her hair was parted. When she turned, a piece of paper dangled before her face.

"Loser carries this to Malaracha," said Laisida.

Sielvia sneered at him. "They're right about minstrels: always listening in." He rapped her once more, and she snatched the note back.

CHAPTER ONE
Polijn

I

THEY could see she was trying to get out from under the table, but she figured it was too hot to be polite. Polijn sat back on her haunches and studied the legs of the crowd, shoving her copper armlet up higher, where it would be tighter. When Balimon stepped forward to give Jok, across the table, a piece of his mind and all of his hand, she darted forward. Head down, she jumped over an ankle thrust in her path, grazed a cheek against Protuse's ornamental eared dagger, and put one shoulder against Ulorin's pouch.

Farther from the table, the crowd was denser, as minions not directly involved in the debates clumped to pass around the newest gossip.

"Oh, Hedoras gave her the green gown that afternoon."

"Thought she looked a mite queasy."

"Say, Chymola was saying it was Berdais slipped it out, but my money says Chymola had that Fausca do it and then tried to tack it to Berdais."

No one moved to let Polijn through, but she was not fooled into thinking she was unobserved. Those eyes were on her as she lunged and ducked through the uncooperative mob. There was speculation in all eyes, as well as calculation. Life in the Palace Royal was livable only if one kept tabs on where one stood in the scheme of things. People were climbing up and slipping down ladders all the time. To understand one's own position, everyone else's had to be taken into account.

The lowest rungs of the ladder were mired in the Swamp, the lowest, ugliest, most dangerous spot in the city of Malbeth. In the world, said some. Polijn had started there as a thumb girl, advertising inexpensive services with her thumb in her mouth. She had thought, at four, that it was a pretty funny way to make money. By the time she was six, and old enough to work a regular route every night, it had lost its drollery. But she had learned the first rule of the professional: do what you're told and don't waste time complaining about it.

This had served her well. In the ensuing six years she had been a paid companion, a jester, and a chambermaid. Now she was apprenticed to the most powerful minstrel in Rossacotta, and a frequent companion of the King. Working conditions were better and the work less physically demanding: never before had Polijn given so much lip service by merely talking.

So she knew the crowd was not watching her for visual gratification. (She had been told, repeatedly, as a child, that she was of hideous aspect and ungainly body, of repulsive personal habits and little grace. This was to keep her from getting too proud to work.) No, these were eyes that had watched her jump from Swamp to Palace, and wanted to know how far up the ladder her next jump would take her.

Polijn had never, in fact, jumped anywhere; she was always pushed. Her concern was only the job of the moment. And at this moment, that was getting a piece of paper to Malaracha.

Outside the Council Chamber, hangers-on without the personal clout to squeeze inside did part to let Polijn pass. Some of them even bowed slightly and murmured, "My Lady," as if in practice for the day when they'd be required to say that. Polijn did not notice this so much as she noticed that the crowd was also parting for someone else. She thumbed the message inside her tambourine. The hand not on the instrument slid down her body to a dagger.

Whoever was behind her would probably not attack. Everyone knew Laisida took an interest in his belongings, and one did not risk lightly the displeasure of a King's Minstrel. On the other hand, it was hot.

The main problem was that she wanted privacy to peek at the note. Laisida's sense of humor was such that he could very well have written, "The bearer has been gambling in the Council Chamber. Smack her soundly." But it was one thing to peek at the note herself, and another to let someone else get a look at it.

Pretending not to notice anyone behind her, Polijn worked free of the mob, keeping a tight grip on the tambourine with four fingers, and easing the paper open with her thumb. Once she felt she had put enough distance between herself and any witnesses, she risked a peep inside.

The lintik thing was in code. It was a code she knew, for Laisida had taught it to her, but it took time to translate. She couldn't sit down here and puzzle it out. Less than a fourth of the court could read, but everybody knew by now that little slips of paper could mean big trouble/big money. And Polijn, Swamp-bred though she was, wouldn't be too hard to overpower.

Booted footsteps came behind her. But everyone had three places to go at once this week. He might just be walking along in her direction.

She sped up and risked another peep into the tambourine. The name Janeftox met her eye. The message could hardly have anything to do with her, then. She folded the paper over and paused. The boots paused behind her.

Well, as long as they did stay behind her, she was content. Now, where could she find Malaracha at this hour? Easy enough to find people like Aizon, or General Jintabh, who stayed in their little rooms, but Malaracha could be any-where.

She turned toward Laisida's suite. If Malaracha wasn't there, chances were he had been. The tall minstrel had been Laisida's first apprentice. Now attached to the retinue of Mitar, he still frequented his former master's rooms, out of habit or to consult Laisida's library. And it was the nearest of the three places he was most likely to be.

Polijn shook out her hair and pulled her damp tunic away from her body. The dank, unseasonable heat was the most common explanation for the sudden upswing in Palace murders.

The cooler weather of North Malbeth would be kingsgift. The second most common explanation of the latest murder craze was that everyone who had died had been intended for the northern excursion. Those not selected were taking one last shot at it by making vacancies in the caravan.

Polijn would be headed north, as some slight compensation to Laisida for his daughters Cidre and Jolor, who were staying behind. She had never been part of so vast a relocation. Changes of address in the Swamp were a matter of grabbing up your possessions and making a run for it. Here, the process involved a little work, a lot of sitting and watching, and a surplus of screaming at people to stop sitting and watching, and get back to work.

A door pulled open at her left, admitting a fox-faced man with an eyepatch. Polijn was dismayed. First, she had no desire to stop and chat. Second, she had assumed this was the man following her.

"Why, Polijn Dwillindiel!" Carasta exclaimed, sharp eyebrows leaping up. "Where away, my dove? Do you need an escort?"

Polijn said nothing. "Hotter than the bone today," he replied, running a finger inside his red-and-gold collar. "Ah, but to think that I came north to escape the heat!"

News of the infant University had prompted an influx of consultants, most uninvited, from across the continent. Carasta came from the School of Minstrelsy in Gilraën. He was uninvited; the Council had decided no one from an institution of that stature would bother with Rossacotta. The oldest school of any kind in the known world, it was known simply as The School. Lesser institutions might call themselves for their locations or patrons. This was the original.

Polijn's awe of it was diminished by its having Carasta as its representative. The swagger and eyepatch gave him a raffish air, and his appetite for women was voracious. His songs were studded with lightly veiled references to recognizable and even more lightly veiled Palace inhabitants. These could be effusive or satirical, depending on how susceptible to flattery the woman in question had turned out to be.

His taste was wide-ranging and unpredictable, as shown by his recent decision to turn his compliments on Polijn. (To earn the title Dwillindiel, Polijn would have had to complete the equivalent of three years' training in music and history.) He was probably trying to use her to rake favor with Laisida.

Fortunately, he did not have time to flirt just now. "Alas, I must hurry away," he sighed gustily. "I must take my seat on the balcony ere someone else does, and I meet the same gruesome fate, e'en, as Ferrapec."

He lowered his face to hers and added, "But you must meet me under the balcony some time. I can teach you a few dances even Laisida doesn't know."

He strode away, whistling. Polijn watched him go, just to be sure he did. A growl behind her made her turn her eyes toward the ceiling. It was Timpre, another of her improbable conquests. Glowering at the older man, he muttered threats that Carasta fortunately did not hear.

She sighed again. Timpre wasn't the one following her either. He was barefoot, and even shod he wasn't heavy enough to have made those steps. Like Carasta, Timpre wanted Laisida's attention more than anything she had to offer. He was inclined to minstrelsy, with a distressing tendency toward romantics, languishing for love of his unattainable heart's desire. Polijn was handy, so he had chosen her to be the heart's desire.

There was no escaping him, either, for he was the son of Laisida's sculptor brother, Morafor. But he was more easily abashed. If she hurried away with enough of an air of importance, he would accept the rebuff. She nodded at the boy and turned away sharply. Something hard pressed into her hand, nearly knocking the tambourine out. Polijn didn't look down. It was another of the boy's practice paintings, on a shard of one of his practice sculptures (he was equally execrable at all the family trades): one more picture of Polijn, surrounded by references to the great beauties of song and story, scribbled in wherever there was not quite enough space.

Traffic was sparse in the halls, with people either in Council or working in the courtyard. Polijn encountered no one else who was inclined to bother with her. No passerby hailed her follower, either, but a footfall now and then assured her that he was still there.

With one hand on Laisida's door, she felt safe enough for one glance backward, covering the motion by wiping sweat from her chin. He pulled back into the doorway that connected the tower with the corridor. Polijn's chest heaved with relief. That was surely Janeftox. She knew him well enough to talk to. Besides, he was set up with Laisida's second daughter, and had a legitimate excuse to come this way.

She walked back to confront him, but found no one there. She shrugged. Laisida might have sent him to see her as far as the door.

Inside the apartment, Fiojo was trimming the wick of a lamp held by one sculpted boy to the toes of another. Morafor had designed this lamp especially for Laisida, and sold it to him. Polijn tugged at the chambermaid's skirts. "Is Malaracha here?"

The larger woman leaped into the air, nearly rolling the lamp into a desk. "Lintik blast you, child! No!"

Fiojo was always jumpy, and not dangerous, but it was hot and she had a knife in one hand. Polijn pulled around to the far side of the lamp before asking, "Has he been here, though?"

"I don't know," moaned Fiojo. "Ask them." She jabbed the knife toward the far door.

Laisida was important enough to have a three-room suite on the King's Floor. Polijn found the second room silent, but the third sounded occupied. The door was closed.

When she opened it, the room really turned noisy as four women jumped up, two of them thrusting garments under furniture in case Berdais should see. Lotyn, who had been changing, caught up her clothing and held it in front of her, doing this in such a way that the majority of the cloth hung harmlessly over one arm, and that arm was supporting her considerable bosom.

Her shy, startled glance dropped as she announced, "Oh, it's just Polijn."

"Oh, it IS!" cried Lauremen, dashing over to gather her father's apprentice in a damp embrace. Polijn was alert at once, and she caught the motion as Irisien stooped quickly to shove something a little farther under a chair cushion. One leg of the little garment, and the monogram M, were recognizable before it vanished. Laisida's daughters had somehow latched onto a pair of Maiaciara's controversial thigh-hiders.

Lotyn gulped something from a pewter mug, and explained, "We thought we'd try our swimming ensembles one more time, to be sure they fit right."

"Yes," Irisien agreed, wiping her long neck with a bandana. "Lotyn keeps expanding." She jabbed one long finger at Lotyn, who dodged.

"You must come over here," said Lauremen, one arm still around Polijn's waist. "Tell me if you like the black or the yellow on me."

"What's Polijn going to wear?" Irisien demanded. "You don't have a thing her color."

Lotyn shrugged. "Something of Sielvia's. They're much the same size."

"Oh." Irisien was one of Kirasov's daughters, and the best friend of Lotyn, who was the same age. This was all they had in common. Lotyn was chubby, cheerful, and lazy, while Irisien was long, rangy, intense. Lotyn lolled; Irisien's usual aspect was standing, a hand on one hip, the left foot forward. She had a great deal of energy that needed an outlet, and was always scheming. No doubt she had stolen Maiaciara's underpants.

Or perhaps Jolor had borrowed them from her mistress. She took no part in the conversation, staring out the window at the whipcrackers. They would be in charge of crowd control during the journey, and were practicing on prisoners to see how close they could come to an ear without the whip actually slashing it off. Her gaze was wistful; she bit a red underlip.

Jolor was not going north this year. She waited on Maiaciara, who liked the way Jolor's masses of pure white hair contrasted with her own raven locks. Jolor's man Janeftox, further, was one of Maiaciara's father's remaining bodyguards. Since Ferrapec was unwelcome on this trip, Maiaciara would certainly not be a part of it, and naturally neither would Jolor or Janeftox.

This had upset her sisters, briefly. They got used to the idea. Lotyn slid the top of her swimming ensemble down a bit and studied the effect in a mirror. "Bare shoulders are very much the item down south," she announced. "Carasta said so."

"I'd never get away with it," said Irisien. "Daddy's been so cranky."

"Mnmfmf," said Lauremen, who was stuffing tissue paper behind an already fleshy lower lip to improve her pout.

Polijn knew every one of them had things to be doing elsewhere. Competition for jobs in the Palace was bitter, but these girls saw no need to compete. They played a ding-ding harp (practicing was bad for the nails) and the only other talent they had from their father was graceful walking, so they could strut to an audience. Polijn didn't understand them; they were like cattle who had never heard of butchers. What would become of them if Laisida died? Their remaining uncle would have no use for them. Jolor and Cidre, their older sisters, were established but didn't have the status to help them. And the Palace Royal always had a surplus of unemployed women. Sons had an out: everyone needed guards and soldiers.

But Polijn admired both of Lauremen's swimming ensembles, and sat on a little wooden chest set against the wall. She held the tambourine carefully so none of the girls would sit on it. It was a memento not only of Arberth, but a gift: a rare phenomenon in her life. In the Swamp, you worked for everything you got, and sometimes you didn't get it.

On second thought, she rose and set it inside the chest. If someone had followed her, and saw that the tambourine was missing, he might assume the message had been left behind with the instrument. She took out her deck of cards, and slid the paper among these.

"Have you seen Malaracha today?" she asked.

"No," Lotyn told her. "Try upstairs. Wait a bit and I'll come, too." She looked around the room, seeking out garments in the tumbled assortment.

Shrieking, she launched herself at her little sister. "Lauremen, you're sitting on my hat!" Pudgy fists hammered on a bare back. Her sister grabbed up a pillow and flailed at her.

Polijn slipped out and headed for the stairs, Malaracha's room was only two flights up. If he was not there, it would have to be the Royal Library, clear across the Palace. This carrying messages was no easy trade. In the Swamp, you didn't have to walk so far to get somewhere.

She was wet and panting by the time she reached the top of the second flight, and nearly went rolling down again. Two boys, wearing very little and grabbing to tear away what little each had left on, charged past her, screaming in glee.

Polijn caught her balance and then flattened against stone as they pushed past on their way back up. "Ha!" one panted, "My father could cut your father's arms and ears right off!"

This had to be answered, The boy in the lead spun around and brought his face up against the foe's, at the same time pushing down to keep the other's hands away. "My father could pull off your father's ears with just his hands!"

Bony hands came down and knocked the two heads together. "All you or your putative fathers will ever be good for is decorating the Regent's bedroom. Make way for your betters, brats."

The boys wrenched out of the man's grip. Hot words died on their lips as they saw someone their fathers couldn't, and wouldn't, take on. Colonel Umian stepped farther onto the landing, three of his black-jacketed New Guard behind him.

"I . . . I'm sorry, sir," said one of the boys, as both backed toward the stairs. "We were only playing, sir. We didn't mean to get in your way, sir." He glanced back to see how close he was to the top step.

A New Guard caught his wrist. "Maybe you'd like to play with Acknock and Arina," suggested the colonel.

The captured boy's eyes grew round and damp. His mouth fell open, but no sound came out. His companion came up and put an arm around his waist, which Polijn thought rather daring. Expendable children with little or nothing to wear were an enticing resource; Acknock and Arina had gotten up a little game involving them. Arina had been reprimanded for using someone she had no way of knowing was the son of the youngest of Colonel Kirasov's cousins. Ironically, it had been Colonel Umian, always demanding more civilized behavior in the Palace Royal, who had argued for a stiff sentence. Acknock and Arina would not be going north. This did not bode well for any children also left behind.

Polijn was pretty sure what Umian thought of her, so rather than try to get past him as he lectured the boys, she went up another flight and then down by the down spiral, which left her at a landing opposite the one where the colonel was still holding forth. Fortunately, Malaracha's room was handier from this landing.

Which helped only if he was actually inside, of course. She raised a fist and thumped the door.

Something thumped back from inside the room, and fast, angry footsteps followed. "What . . ." demanded Malaracha, looking out and then down.

Polijn fanned the deck of cards at him, forcing the folded paper forward. Malaracha knew what it meant when Laisida entrusted a message to an apprentice rather than a servant. "Ah!" His hand came down and the paper shot up into his sleeve.

"If you're going back down," he said, "tell him I've just about got that torn chording figured out. I can't talk now, though."

Polijn nodded. Malaracha had a song to finish for the lunch entertainment. She did feel he could have offered her a drink, though.

She paused on the landing to push prickly hair off her shoulders. One eye caught at a figure pushing through Malaracha's doorway. That couldn't be Janeftox again, could it?

Polijn stepped back into the corridor and listened for a fight. Laisida would be upset if anything happened to Malaracha. Though she all but put her ear to the door, she made out no sounds. She shrugged and headed for the stairs.

II

LIFE, thought Polijn, would be simplified if Janeftox could be transplanted to Malaracha's retinue. Quite the step down, of course: Malaracha was nobody compared to a general—any general. But stepping down was no disgrace if you did it to duck a punch. All Ferrapec's retainers knew the punch was coming.

She leaned against the stones of the wall. Malaracha's message was not urgent; it could be delivered any time. What time was it? No sunlight penetrated to the tower stairs. Anyway, Polijn had never mastered the daytime trick of estimating time by available light.

It must be getting on, though: the debates had gone on forever. If she went down to Laisida's rooms now, she might be able to skip the big luncheon on the balcony. But Berdais might catch her there and set her to work. Which was worse: sitting with the King, in the sun, or packing food in the larder vaults?

She tottered down a few more steps. An angry voice exclaimed something about the Council. Umian must have finished haranguing the boys and started for the Royal Balcony. She moved a little faster. It was entirely too hot to run into Umian twice in one day.

"That business of Borrum," the colonel was saying. "Don't

you understand how much easier this would be if we got him out of the Palace?"

"But to promote him!" cried General Ferrapec. "That tonguetail! And to send him north, deliberately passing over more. . ."

"That was an excuse, dolt!" snapped Umian.

Ferrapec's voice was cold, superior. "You forget yourself, Colonel."

Polijn reached the fourth-floor landing. No one here: the men's voices came from below. She glanced at the corridor. She could go out, take a right, walk the entire length of the Palace Royal, and come back around after descending to the third floor via the stairs in another tower. She shook her head.

"General," said Umian, "only wait until we're in charge. Then you can reduce Borrum to evening duty in the dungeons."

The general's voice blazed with shock. "Dungeons! Evening duty! That's Treasury's responsibility! You can't seriously think an army . . ."

"Why do I talk to you?" Umian demanded.

"Oh, you're the expert," snarled Ferrapec. "You and your New Guard can turn the trick all by yourselves. You know what they say about those Blackbonnets in the . . ."

"Wait until we solve the murders," Umian replied. "Let me tell . . ."

"Ho!" said Ferrapec. "Four of the New Guards are dead themselves. What is it: investigation by attrition?"

"It is part of the campaign," the colonel answered. "I promise you there shall be more to laugh at when we reveal the culprits at . . . the highest levels."

"Highest . . ." Ferrapec's voice dropped. "Do you mean the . . ."

Someone was coming down the stairs behind her. Polijn looked back at him. "I thought I had seen you come this way, My Lady," the man panted, stopping one step above her. Polijn slipped one step down, unobtrusively, she hoped.

Adimo was a large, muscular man, always looking for some job where mass and muscles were unnecessary. He had, however, obviously been exerting himself lately. A fog of recent sweat radiated from him, but this was minor compared to the torn overtunic and swollen black eye.

It wasn't just the bruised face that surprised Polijn, though she knew no one would have touched him last month. That "My Lady" was also a clue. Had he spoken to Polijn even a week ago, his language would have included no references to ladies.

But his fate had been recorded and certified the day Soedol refused to open the door for him, without rebuke from the Regent. Inferring a withdrawal of Kaftus's protection, Adimo's rivals had been swift to improve on Soedol's example. Adimo, a man of moderate intelligence and no subtlety, had complained bitterly to the Regent, hoping for action. He got it. By royal decree, Adimo was no longer allowed to enter any room occupied by the Regent or the King.

"Losaigon is under the same ban," Adimo told Polijn, "and he'll be on the balcony, same as you, just because he's in Morafor's bodyguard. If you could . . ."

"Lord Laisida has enough bodyguards, so far as I know," said Polijn, easing down one more step. "But I can ask."

"No!" He came down two steps. "That is, er, My Lady Polijn, I don't have that time. I wouldn't worry about that Losaigon if Lord Kaftus could see us side by side. But I can't get onto the balcony. You will be there, however."

Not if she could help it. And if she was there, she did not intend to jeopardize her own position by mentioning Adimo's. He was far too massive to be told that, though, so she said, "I doubt Lord Kaftus would have time to listen to me."

The former favorite shook his head. "No, that's all right." He held out his hands to her. "See, you're . . . one of the King's Companions. No one would complain if you took a bodyguard of your own onto the balcony."

Polijn raised her chin and stared into the square face. Was he seriously offering his services?

"I don't take up as much room as you might think," he told her. He flexed one arm and covered his grimace of pain with a quick smile. "And I can be useful . . ."

"What's all this about?" General Ferrapec had left Umian and continued up the stairs. "Here, we can't have your sort accosting ladies. Be off, you lump, and go lock windowsills."

After one hopeful glance at Polijn, Adimo backed away. Ferrapec was still a general in the Rossacottan army, certainly outranking one who had no official identity at all. Polijn was not sorry to see him go. Interesting to think of starting her own personal retinue, but there was no sense starting with a bodyguard no one was afraid of.

Ferrapec's hand was on her shoulder, preventing escape as he called some more suggestions to the retreating favorite. What did the general want, now? Was he looking for Janeftox? Had he guessed who had stolen Maiaciara's expensive underwear? Polijn knew he couldn't afford to make an outright accusation against one of Laisida's daughters, but he couldn't afford the loss, either. His own clothes showed a hundred mends, and there were suggestive little tunnels through the padding at the calves of his grey hose.

"You shouldn't encourage that filth," he said, turning Polijn to face him. He attempted a warm, paternal smile. "I know that at your age one cannot always control one's urges, but these handsome young yoke oxen can only do you harm. A woman your age needs mature guidance."

Polijn knew what guidance he had in mind, from the way he stepped back to look her over and then moved closer, guarded approval on his face. In a detached way, she felt sorry for the face, being able to see what it had been before it sagged and fell. He maintained the dashing curl in the center of his forehead, but this left him very little hair on the rest of his skull. Some lingered around the ears, brushed back into fetching wings. Hair was the foremost field of fashion; it was cheaper than cloth.

He drew her down the stairs with him, pointing out that his offer was not only inspirational, but her duty. Polijn was uninspired. Half the Palace had hinted at similar offers, betting on the chance that she would turn out to be The One eventually chosen by the King. To have been The One's lover might mean something for the moment and, in the end, might mean everything.

It was easier back in the Swamp, thought Polijn. You knew no one was pretending to like you because they wanted something. They either had a use for you or they did not, and they let you know which it was by the most direct means. Here they went through a lot of wheedling preliminaries, for weeks sometimes, before coming to the point.

This was the first general to stoop to wooing her, but she knew Ferrapec was buried up to his knees. When his father, the Count of Bonti, died, he would be sent off to rot in Bonti, or forced to accept a court overseer, putting him and his land under the thumb of the Regent. To avert these fates, he had to find a way back into the inner circles. For that, he needed a miracle. Somehow he had decided Polijn was that miracle.

Just a week ago, after the King's compliment on her rendition of an old war song, Polijn had been stopped in a corridor by sleek, elegant Kodva. Ferrapec's civilized mother paid her only a few passing compliments in a voice of gentle condescension. But Polijn had found herself thinking, almost blasphemously, "What is this woman trying to sell me?"

The next day, Kodva's equally fashionable daughter-in-law had taken the time to chat with a lowly apprentice minstrel. "We have not had a good songstress in our household for simply ages," Raiprez had said, rolling those big, glowing eyes. "When the general is bowed by the cares of office, nothing cheers him like a stirring tune. Would you consider a change?"

She had put it so casually, and been so unoffended when Polijn declined, that Polijn could not help but be suspicious. And ever since, after every performance, there would be a compliment from Ferrapec's wife or Ferrapec's mother. Even Maiaciara occasionally deigned to smile in her direction.

Maybe they just liked her voice. Their taste was notoriously faulty: didn't they keep telling Ferrapec he was the bravest, brightest officer in the Army? The general did not dispute this. No war had been vouchsafed him so that he could prove it, which was dreadfully unfair, but true worth would always shine through. (In the days when he was still Somebody, there had been no more vehement antiwar voice on the Council.)

He liked to play that he was still Somebody. "If those about the King knew what I know about the Ykenai . . ." He tapped one grey temple with his free hand. "Ah, but you perhaps know nothing about such things. No doubt His Majesty's friends don't worry him with such matters."

If he was digging for information, he was to be disappointed. Polijn would not have repeated the conversations of the King even if she ever listened to them. Getting mixed up in the business of subversive religious cults like the Ykenai or Neleandrai meant involvement in politics and sorcery, either of which would only make life here the more precarious.

Ferrapec stepped down onto the next landing and propelled Polijn ahead of him into the corridor of the King's Hall. Her mind raced to find some excuse that wasn't too obvious. Stony silence had done her no good so far, and her expression wasn't helping because he never looked down at it. He couldn't do much to her if she simply broke and ran; Laisida would see to that. But he could hiss next time she performed, and nothing was more deadly contagious.

The general's hand slid down to the small of her back as he toed open the door to his suite. His family was assigned to a drafty sixth-floor tower apartment, but like many an ambitious courtier, he rented rooms on the King's Floor, paying an extortionate rate to the assigned tenant.

"Do come in," he said, combining a caress with a push. "No one will see. They're all out on the balcony."

He was probably right, lintik burn him. "I, er, I should be there as well, My Lord."

Pulling back got her nowhere, but the general did pause. His brows dipped together but as suddenly relaxed. "You needn't worry about Lady Raiprez," he said, his tone understanding. "She is certainly on the balcony and, in any case, she said, just yesterday, it would be a fine thing if someone were to take you in hand."

Polijn reached one foot tentatively to the doorjamb to see if she could brace herself against it. "But I was commanded to attend the ceremonies. His Majesty will be annoyed if he sees I am not there."

She realized it was the wrong thing to say as thin lips drew together. No one would have missed Ferrapec. "Don't fill your shirt with air for me!" snapped the general. "One insignificant child will make no difference in that crowd!"

He followed this with a yank that pulled her off her feet. With resource born of practice, Polijn kicked at the door, knocking it wide open. As long as she could see the outside face of the door, escape was a possibility.

But Ferrapec was no stranger to the struggling of prisoners. Polijn rolled her head forward as he dashed her against the door. A long hand darted in under her chin to hold her throat while the free hand drew back.

"There is so a lake monster!" somebody screamed.

The blow did not fall. Ferrapec and Polijn turned toward the corridor.

"Is not!" came the indignant reply.

"Is!"

The Royal Party was proceeding to the balcony. King Conan III, at the head of the mob, was magnificently robed, all in green and gold, the only incongruity a blue, stuffed whale he dragged behind him. The Ladies of the Wardrobe had dressed him for show; an emerald etched with a portrait of his mother sat in a gold circlet at his neck, and jewels rattled on his boots as he stamped his feet. "Is not!"

"Is!" cried Merklin, his whipping boy.

"Is not!" roared the King, trying to convince his opponent by volume. "It's in the song! Magien went to the lake and banished him!"

"Is so!" countered Merklin.

"Magien was really brave, wasn't he, if he did that?" injected Argeleb, a smaller boy walking behind them.

Neither the King nor Merklin had time for any peacemaking nonsense. "Is not!" screamed His Majesty.

Merklin opened his mouth. "Do not presume to argue with His Majesty," ordered a tall, broad woman farther back in the assembly.

Every child in the group drew a head back between hunched shoulders at the sound of Nurse's voice. So did several adults.

"Is!" whispered Merklin defiantly.

The King raised his toy whale as if to swing, but slid his eyes back to Nurse. A delicate little girl with wide eyes, though hugely enjoying the fight, glanced around too and caught sight of the open door.

"Oh, it's Polijn!" she shrieked. "Just in time!" She turned to the King. "She has to come along, doesn't she, Your Majesty?"

"Who?" the King demanded. Ferrapec removed his hand

from Polijn's throat just in time. "Oh, Polijn! Yes, oh, yes. Of course?"

He glanced back at his retinue for verification. At the very rear stood his Chief Bodyguard, Nimnestl, followed by two members of the New Guard who looked as if they wanted someone to guard them. She wore a gown of darker green than the King's, but its thickness proclaimed its value. The insignia of her office, shining high on her chest, was pure silver.

The marks of her office that garnered the most respect, though, were the scars on the polished, muscular arms, and the nicks in the head of the hammer that hung from her belt. She smiled at Polijn and nodded. "If she doesn't mind getting into bad company."

Stroking her throat, Polijn left without a glance at Ferrapec, and took up a spot between Argeleb and Iúnartar. The general showed his upper teeth. No one had even glanced at him.

As the group passed him, he found Nurse at hand. "I have no patience with these girls who engage their betters in vulgar, uncivilized flirtation," he growled. "I am amazed at so forward a creature being allowed among the Companions."

One of Nurse's thick, heavy hands landed on Polijn's right shoulder. "His Majesty may invite whom His Majesty wishes," the older woman said, sniffing and waving away imaginary flies.

The King glanced up, a little surprised, but dutifully agreed, "Oh, yes. Any of Lord Laisida's family is welcome at any time."

Possibly the little monarch did not know how much that stung. The general bowed, his eyes wide and his teeth set. Nurse proceeded, and the little group moved on at her pace. The New Guard followed at a cautious distance.

Iúnartar, one eye on Nurse, moved over to Polijn. "Was . . ." Something rattled on stone.

A black dagger sheath lay on stone. Ferrapec had stooped to pick it up and return it to its owner, not thinking.

"What's the matter, General?" hooted Iúnartar. "Can't you afford to buy one?"

Even Polijn never expected the general to lunge at the girl. "Brat!" he snarled, groping in his tunic for a knife of his own.

The New Guard, including the owner of the fallen sheath, parted before him, but the King's usual attendants were more decisive. A black blur whizzed between Ferrapec and his target, screeching for attention. The general jerked his face up and then down, to try to avoid mutilation.

"Will Your Majesty accept the general's apology?" Nimnestl inquired, as blood spurted and Mardith came around for another pass.

The King waited for the second slash to say, "I may."

Ferrapec straightened, blood dripping down his chin. "I most humbly beg pardon, Your Majesty. I forgot myself." Mardith came up behind to peck at the general's bald spot.

"You may go," the King informed him.

Disgrace complete, the general bowed and backed away. Polijn's heart was around her ankles. Ferrapec couldn't let this go unavenged. Of Mardith, the King, Iúnartar, and herself, she knew which was the easiest target.

At least Nurse let go of her. The big, broad woman was neither wet nurse nor dry nurse, nor yet a mere rockster, but Mistress of the Nursery, a position of some clout. She neither liked nor trusted Polijn, though this did not excuse the criticism of a mere general poking his nose into Royal affairs.

Iúnartar moved in as Polijn eased away from Nurse. "Was that old bristle-balls making up to you? I like to died!"

"You never have that problem," said Merklin.

"Of course I have," sighed Iúnartar. The girl was the House-keeping Staff's chief candidate for Queen. Some court handicappers were giving very good odds on her, as she had six times been allowed to comb His Majesty's hair at bedtime, a signal honor.

None of which weighed with Merklin. "Not in summer," he said. "At least, I never seen anybody with a clothespin on his nose."

"Pig!" said Iúnartar, letting go of Polijn to give him a shove. "Piglet!"

Polijn pulled farther away. Unlike Iúnartar, who had been raised here, she could not forget she was in hallowed company. It wasn't just the King and his awesome protectors; even his companions, Argeleb, Merklin, and Masalan (not Iúnartar, of course), seemed to her so far above her as to be legendary. So she walked a bit behind and to one side, in case they should want to dissociate themselves from her.

It was safer that way, too. The King had taken advantage of this diversion to stick a foot between Argeleb's ankles. Argeleb caught this in time, though, and, with a smile, turned to pat the King on the cheek. The King patted back, a little harder, and Argeleb returned that with interest.

"Very pretty this will look in the Diary, I must say," noted Nurse.

The children hunched their shoulders again. The King's doings were recorded every day in the Court Diary, often with Nurse's editorial comments. Merklin was the first to recover and, with resolute dignity, started to march for the balcony. The King, catching on, assumed the same expression and a little more than the same pace. Argeleb followed.

They fooled no one; Polijn wondered why they even bothered. "This is not a race," Nurse announced. "Proceed with kingly steps."

The boys grimaced. Merklin and the King had to attend a dancing master to learn how to walk in public. Argeleb's parents occasionally required him to attend as well. The Council was opposed; vigor and aggression, not grace, were required of a King. On occasions like this, Polijn felt Nurse had the right of it.

Polijn had fallen back almost to the New Guards, when Merklin recalled her existence. "Hey, Polijn!" he shouted, cutting into Nurse's definition of proper kingly speed. "Do you know about the lake monster?"

"There isn't one, is there, Polijn?" called the King.

Everyone turned and waited for her to catch up, which gave her just enough time. "I know the story," she said. "Of course, in any case, it wouldn't be in the lake now. Your Majesty knows, certainly, that on the first of spring and the last of summer, the spirits of evil move to different homes. That's when their strength is at its height."

This was obviously the opening of a story; everyone pulled in around her, moving at her pace toward the balcony. Polijn saw Nurse glare at the Bodyguard, who simply shrugged in reply.

III

IRANEN was roasting potatoes in a brazier. Slaveys stood around her, sagging, sunburnt, mouths open to inhale any cool air that got so far. Three or four were allowed to sit; they had been disciplined in such a way that standing would have been a relief. Aoyalasse, trying not to moan too loudly, was propped up between Imidis and Loy, two of Iranen's bodyguard.

Sharp little eyes checked the potatoes. "That one is done," said Iranen.

It was forked out of the coals and brought to her. She split it deliberately and poured a thick, steaming garlic sauce inside. Salt was poured on top of this. She gestured to Aoyalasse.

"For her," said the Housekeeper. "And feed it to her. She's a bit shaky, the poor puppy."

Fiejin took the potato, but got the tip of one thumb into the hot sauce. Imidis charged down to catch the potato as she jumped.

"Do sit down," Iranen purred to Fiejin. "Right up here. I do like my favorites near, and the next potato is for you." Fiejin sat down right next to the broiling brazier, and shivered.

One or two people betrayed a moderate interest as Aoyalasse choked on hot bits of potato; it was something to beguile the time until the luncheon began. Polijn and the King's Companions were now in place on the balcony, but the King had been held back to make a more regal entrance, as King, and not as the center of a gang of noisy children: Nurse's suggestion.

Polijn was curled into her spot near the Royal Footstool, her knees pressed to her chest and her chin on them. This stretched the fabric of her summer costume to maximum, but if anyone was interested in the display of her thighs, Polijn didn't care. It was cooler this way and, anyhow, providing diversion was part of her job.

"More coals!" ordered Iranen. "Do you want the fire to die?"

Courtiers unlucky enough to be posted at that side of the balcony glowered, but none were senior enough to suggest moving the brazier. Those who were either sat far enough away not to care or were old enough to be glad of the heat.

"On my artery, it's going to be a hot one," Iúnartar declared, wiping the spaces between her toes with a bandana.

Hot as it was here, Polijn could see things were worse in the courtyard. The common people—"Cotton Robers"—had assembled early to be sure of a good vantage point. Hot and thirsty, they were easy prey for the wine and food vendors working through the mob. One in ten of the vendors was legitimate; the rest had come emptyhanded and were now selling what they'd snatched from wagons on the parade grounds.

Here, at least, there was room to wave a fan or a handkerchief, both considered highly civilized and the peak of fashion. Aperiole sauntered through the assembly looking for a vacant seat near a likely male, eight fans dangling from one of her belts. The more accessories you could pile on, the more beautiful and civilized you were, even if you died of the heat. Nobody moved to make space for her; they were watching the prisoners being moved into place under the platform below.

"Getting a little thick these days, eh?"

"Around the waist, you mean? She was always a little thick."

"They do say Noquiere will be killed but at the last minute the Regent will let Acoson off with whipping and exile."

"I'll be bound she paid to get it. Money's the best antiseptic."

Aperiole nodded to Carasta, over in the knot of foreign scholars, but the one-eyed minstrel had that eye on Sobaquillo,

weaving feathers into her hair without being conscious, perhaps, of what her clothes did when she raised her arms. To
display her wardrobe and still maintain ventilation, she had
simply hung the garments on ropes tied at strategic spots on
her body.

That leisurely touch-up of her coiffure finished, she rose and
strolled away on the arm of Wengefrid, whom she had chosen
to be her next husband, though he didn't know it yet. Oldest
son of the Manager of Palace Mare Milkers, Wengefrid was an
excellent catch. He was also exceedingly civilized, rivulets of
greased hair trickling to his shoulders from under an imported
silver hat.

Polijn could see the regret in Aperiole's eyes at not having a
shot at Wengefrid. But this did open up a seat. Aperiole started
toward it, smiled at Colonel Umian, and walked on. No fun for
her there: Umian's face was little more than a battered wedge
of scars, his eyes dark in the pit of concentrated crease that
was a permanent scowl.

Instead, she aimed for the spot Argeleb vacated, to sneak
closer to Polijn and the King's seat. The boy had orders to stay
among the older children, but he had been a bit overindulged
by his father, and could not be denied. The seat among the older siblings of the King's Companions was more to Aperiole's
taste than his.

"Froduin bought that roan of Nipzah's," Ziant was telling
Mields.

"That'll eat more than it'll run," Mields replied.

"What a warm day!" injected Aperiole, by way of announcing her arrival. "I declare I didn't know what to put on!"

"Well, it might be a runner, once it gets enough to eat,"
Ziant said.

Aperiole looked around for some other seat, but the only one
she saw was way over among the unfashionables: merchants
from Malbeth and those out of favor. Raiprez was there, with
her whole family (excepting only her husband), and looking
very civilized, too, but Polijn was willing to bet Aperiole
wouldn't want to be seen with her.

Or with Veldres, who sat with a woman on his lap, her hands
tied over her head to a rod that extended from the back of her
collar. "Oh, yes," the merchant said to Torrix, "Your palace

executions are much the better spectacle."

Polijn turned away from Aperiole's dilemma at the sound of trumpets. The King was being allowed at last to make his entrance. The crowd rose hastily, pushing this and that behind them so it would not be spotted by those entering, or by those in the courtyard watching them enter.

IV

THE King was accompanied by only the essentials: the cadaverous Regent, the muscular Chief Bodyguard, and the sinister black bird, Mardith. Not a few spectators pulled over toward Iranen to keep out of their way.

After a few seconds, the New Guard stepped onto the balcony as well, trying to act as if they were part of this entrance, and not trying to maintain a safe distance. Even those who stood to benefit politically from this company's competition with the Royal Bodyguard had trouble keeping their faces straight, except Colonel Umian, whose face would take no other position.

The focus of all this bustle stepped in a practiced manner to his high seat, and sat down in a move that had taken him two days to perfect. He adjusted his robes, noticed the silence, and looked around the crowd. A smile came into view and disappeared as quickly; his right shoulder dipped. "They may sit down," he whispered.

"His Majesty grants that all may be seated!" cried the Senior Herald.

Lady Maitena had a drink poured for His Majesty, and set it on a credence for the Royal Taster. No one else moved until the Regent had moved to his place on the balcony. Kaftus raised an eyebrow at them, but said nothing.

In the courtyard, the first prisoners were prodded up toward
the stage. Only half a dozen were to be punished at a time; the
rest waited below, among coffins that were suggestively small
and oddly shaped. Most were naked. Since clothing was a sign
of status, nudity was a sign of none at all.

Guards everywhere from the palace gate to the balcony
curtains took a new grip on their weapons and studied the
crowd. Attempts were occasionally made to rescue a prisoner
from the gallows, most of them token efforts to satisfy some
half-recalled vow over a bottle, or to appease one's in-laws.
These were usually easily repelled; none had proven fatal to
any minion of the law for over a year now.

Seuvain stepped up behind the row of prisoners. Sobaquillo
strolled past the throne, flashing open a gap between garments.
The King was not gratified; she was blocking his view. A
gesture, and she moved on, with a faint sniff.

The crowd roared and stamped its feet as Seuvain held his
ceremonial dagger over each prisoner in turn, announcing the
crimes for which they were to be damaged or destroyed.
This one had killed no one but her husband, but lacked a
protector to overrule her brother-in-law's complaint to the
Council. She was not important enough even for the attention
of Lord Executioner Rabioson. His apprentice, Averyx, known
as Squire Averyx because he had terminated nobility, would
preside over her demise.

"Illefar says she'll bleed before she'll scream," murmured
a man not far behind Polijn.

"Two plows says she don't."

The prisoner was carried to a working table and stretched
across. Her fellow prisoners watched her, but also kept an eye
toward the crowd for stones, hot potatoes, and other missiles.
Apathy hung on most, but there was an air of relief about
others. Some prisoners awaited trial or punishment in the
dungeons; a few had been waiting for half a dozen years.
The gallows at least meant an end to the waiting.

"Ooh!" said His Majesty.

Five servants were carrying in a tray, not so much heavy as
awkward, for it had to be tipped at just the angle that would
display the contents but not spill them. An immense gilded
cookie, nearly as tall as the King, sat on the tray: a mighty

stag with blue stones for eyes. The King's eyes were nearly as shiny; he would gladly have tackled this with both hands. As he leaned forward on his chair, though, Nurse whispered to him.

The King frowned, but then drew himself to his full seated height (what there was of it). The frown gave way to his most earnest expression, and he lifted the knife that was brought to him. The Royal Tutor leaned forward as His Majesty began to divide the cookie.

"What is this?" Merklin demanded. "A feast of state?"

The King lifted his nose. "Certainly, villain. Be silent."

As a Royal Companion, Polijn had sat in on some of the tutoring sessions, though what use all this information would ever be, she wasn't sure. The King needed to know the proper forms and procedures for carving venison at a feast of state, and assigning each cut of the meat to the person of proper status. Polijn doubted this would ever be one of her duties. But it might come into a song some time. Laisida said you couldn't waste anything you learned; eventually, you'd find a use for it.

Other Royal Companions had had the same lessons, to more purpose, and watched intently. Merklin, completely disregarding his sovereign's demand for silence, kept whispering conflicting advice. Fuming, and trying not to giggle at the same time, the King forced the knife in and out. Straight lines were almost impossible, between the soft cookie and the hard gilding, and the form of the cookie was nothing like that of the stuffed toy roast Haeve used in teaching. As Merklin cheerfully pointed out, venison seldom came to table with hooves and antlers attached.

"Here," said His Majesty, taking one antler between knife and fork. "Take this and . . . We, er, provide this for you."

Polijn nodded at his recollection in time of the proper formula. A second passed before she realized that the shining antler was being poked at her.

"Er," she said, having to bring the proper response to the top of her memory. "Your Majesty is ever beneficent." He shook the antler at her, and it nearly slipped away from the knife, so Polijn had to take it.

The King could turn back to his chore; Polijn held the piece of cookie and tried not to look around at the balcony crowd, which had been following the division and distribution, both to see how His Majesty did, and who got the most prestigious cuts. The award of an antler mystified them as much as it did the King, and the ramifications were tossed back and forth in whispers almost too low for her to catch.

"Near the head; it's a sign."

"The p'ring it is. They always start with the Royal Fool."

"Horny."

"Who got the other?"

Who had gotten the other? Eru, it was Merklin! He'd given her the same part he'd given his best friend; she'd never hear the end of this now. Polijn broke off one branch of the antler and offered it to Iúnartar, who didn't take it. The smaller girl was either ignoring the whole thing, or had been distracted by events on the gallows.

With the first death well under way, Lord Rabioson had taken Acoson in hand. She was to be whipped and exiled for helping Nulidad in his assault on Loyois. She looked a different person, shorn of the layers of brocade and strung up for the whip. Apprentice executioners bustled to prepare a display table for her, angling it so that it would receive direct sunlight, and be the hotter when she was stretched across it after the Lord Executioner was done.

Iúnartar was the only person on the balcony who seemed to be interested. Pedophilia was technically treason, which called for a very complicated death, but Acoson's reprieve meant that real entertainment would have to wait for some later prisoner.

Polijn was neither particularly interested in the whipping nor especially hungry. Tucking the antler into the neck of her suit for future reference, she shuffled her cards together and began to run them. This should be enough to distract her from the sounds of prisoners in pain, and the gossip of courtiers, since running the cards took concentration even if you didn't pause to interpret the auguries. She counted to herself as the cards sped by, plucking out those that fell to the numbers.

She had not seen them fall so fast in a long time. Good and bad cards dropped from the deck, especially the axes, all under the supervision of the two of axes. That was not especially good, but at least the death card was not the prevailing influence.

A loud clearing of a throat attracted her attention just a second before Iúnartar jabbed a sharp fingernail into her thigh. "His Majesty was addressing you, girl," said Nurse, with an expression designed to remind her that she was here to attend on His Majesty.

"No, no," said a higher voice. "That's all right. Let her finish."

Polijn looked up. The cookie had been distributed and the King, at least, had finished eating his proper portion. Now a large bowl of flavored snow, imported from the north, sat on the little table; he was offering her two fingersful.

"When you're done," he said, "do you want to run my cards for me?"

The crowd whispered some more. Polijn took the snow, but the shiver that ran through her was not from that. His Majesty had made another minor error of protocol: he had official soothsayers to run his cards, and this was the second time he'd singled out Polijn for notice. It was not, however, Polijn's place to point this out to him.

"That would be a great honor, Your Majesty," she said, and sped the cards under her fingers. The deck had to be finished properly so as to be stable for the King's fortune. Her attention was not fully on the numbers, though; her eyes went to Haeve, to Nurse, to anyone she could see without straining herself. The Regent's expression was unreadable, which was the way he liked it. The Chief Bodyguard's face seemed to hold hostility, but Polijn wondered if this was just because she was expecting to see hostility there.

"Are they singing?" someone demanded.

Eyes turned to glare at Jintabh, who had spoken too loudly. The Duke of Bonti, Hero of Southgate, Jintabh was just a husk of a human being now, unequal to everything and unwelcome to everybody, fiddling and fussing his way through the remains of a world he could barely see, hardly hear, and understand not at all. "I never wanted to be an old thing," he used to say, back in the days when he had one foot in the grave but was still using the other to kick out at everyone else.

The women around him whispered something fierce. They

had dragged him out on the balcony simply because he was the only reason they were allowed there themselves.

He was not to be quieted. "I thought there was to be singing. You told me there'd be singing. Didn't you tell me there'd be singing? Isn't she singing?"

Some kind of seizure had broken him down in early spring; he talked faster now, even louder than before. Or he sat silent for hours, his wooden face propped on a feeble hand. He knew something had happened to him; he commonly spoke of "the days when I was alive," but he maintained his aristocratic dignity. He sat erect, proud, sturdy, utterly senile.

His wife, daughter, and granddaughter simultaneously tried to explain the sounds, not entirely unlike singing, coming from the gallows. They were not getting through. The senses that brought in mental stimulation—sight and hearing—were all but gone. The mind had turned inward in search of sustenance, and was eating itself away.

His family shushed him again, apparently pointing out the royal presence. "The King?" demanded Jintabh. "The King? What? Oh, yes. His mother was afraid of me, poor poppet. My beard was spiky."

Nurse pointed a finger, and two members of the bodyguard started for the Count. "No!" ordered the King. "Don't stop him. Bring him here so he can talk to me."

Polijn moved back to make room. It was one of the King's weaknesses: memories of his parents were rare. He had not known them at all. Neither had Kaftus or Nimnestl. He read the Annals and Diaries constantly for stories about them, but courtiers were tentative about talking about the subject. Admitting there were any Kings prior to the current incumbent was considered bad form—except when monarchs of legendary eras were discussed—because this was to admit that Kings died.

Jintabh had very few inhibitions left, though he was also too far gone to be thrilled by the honor shown him. His women nodded, and accompanied him up to the King's place, trying to behave as if they hadn't considered the Count obsolete up to a minute ago.

Polijn pulled way back; if the King forgot about her and her cards, maybe the courtiers wouldn't hold that against her. She found a seat nearer to the foreign ambassadors, who would have less motive to pick her up and drop her off the balcony.

In fact, they weren't paying much attention to her at all. Rabioson had moved on to the next prisoner, who was to die by the knife basket. For this method, a basket of knives, honed to their sharpest, was brought to the Lord Executioner. Each knife was decorated with a picture of some part of the body. Rabioson drew these, apparently at random, and threw them twenty feet, to land in the body part indicated. For a fee, of course, friends of the prisoner could insure that the heart knife was drawn early in the demonstration. But it couldn't come first: enough of the others had to be thrown to give a good show.

A number of the foreign envoys were watching intently; some had been sent by their governments specifically to research new ways to kill traitors and assassins. Rossacotta was an honored name in refined cruelty; it was said, "Rossacottans never burn anyone at the stake: they think it gives the prisoner a chance." Rumor had it that Rabioson knew ways of killing that he was paid never to use even in exhibition.

Other ambassadors were amusing themselves not by watching the show, but by studying the reaction of their wives to it. Some countries, more civilized, separated their women into other galleries. Rossacottans were not inclined toward that level of sophistication.

That had brought barely disguised sniffs of contempt from some foreign visitors. Others, though, had found themselves fitting easily into life in the Palace Royal. Lord Arlmorin, for example, could plot and scheme as if he'd been born here. Lord Nasarem was an intimate of Veldres and Torrix, though officially this was a deep secret. Nasarem carried a cane, but never used it for walking. His nostrils flared as he watched Veldres kiss the captive on his lap, pointing to something being done on the platform.

"Where's Polijn?" a voice demanded. "Where did she go?"

Jintabh's ramblings had apparently proven a disappointment, and the aged Count was being shuffled back to his seat. The King was leaning out of his seat, looking all around. Polijn rose, chewing the inside of her upper lip. Did he have to do that? He could have sent a nice, quiet message by somebody. Now Lady Forokell and the rest of her staff scowled, and the enmity of that formidable old woman could not be compensated for by the grins of Laisida's retinue.

Of course, every female member of the Royal Playmates who had been allowed on the balcony was smiling. They always smiled, smiled as though good teeth were the prime consideration in the breeding of future Kings.

The Royal Playmates who had been allowed into the King's immediate vicinity made room for her. She knew she was not really one of them, or a future Queen, for that matter. Polijn saw the Royal Playmates for what the group really was: a miniature court, a baby court that would grow up to be the real one in a decade or so. Within that court she aspired to nothing higher than—what had the man said?—Royal Fool. That or King's Minstrel would do; anything higher was far too exposed.

"I thought you were going to run my cards," said the King. He sounded peeved. When the weather was this hot, and he was weighed down under all that cloth, he could be very difficult.

"La!" cried Iúnartar. "Where's there room to run? Even for a card?"

They laughed at that. "A sad romp," said Forokell, shaking her head but remembering to give Lynex's protégée a mild smile. Everyone was very nice to Iúnartar, just in case.

Polijn could see why. The current leading contenders for Queen had to be Iúnartar and Masalan, the only girls allowed to sit with the King today (leaving herself out of consideration, which she was only too happy to do). Iúnartar excelled at these state swarmings. Her voice cut through the buzz, and what she said hardly mattered, since everyone was saying vacuous things.

Masalan was quieter, appealing to the King's nobler side, which was growing at a ridiculous rate. Her gratitude, when he saved her from humiliation at the hands of the Neleandrai cult, was so vast that he regarded himself as something of a hero. Masalan had a face like a horse's, surrounded by waves of chestnut hair, with an appealing expression of appeal that always seemed to ask, "You really do like me, don't you?" Well aware of the uncertainty of her position, she kept busy

carrying food, tidying up odds and ends, and just generally doing things for people who liked to have things done
for them.

Why couldn't the King pay attention to them instead of to
someone with lank hair, damp clothes, and no desire to be
noticed?

As she sat down, though, Lady Maitena furnished a distraction by bringing in cooled wine. An even better distraction
came from a member of the New Guard who came up to the
credence table as though intending to double-check the wine
after the real Royal Taster.

Biandi, a member of the Royal Bodyguard, raised one nostril. The black-clad guard stepped back and glanced at his
chief. Colonel Umian looked displeased, and waved him back.
The guard took another step away, but Umian repeated the
gesture. The man's head fell, and he started off the balcony.

He collided with a soldier at the entrance. Hot, humiliated,
he reached for a knife. The soldier waited, expressionless. The
guard's hand hung on the knife for a moment. When the soldier
failed to show any interest in meeting this threat, the member
of the New Guard pushed past, cursing.

The soldier continued onto the balcony, walking straight
into Umian's glare. He met it, and returned the same blank
face he'd given the New Guard. Umian fumed, glared, and,
finally, turned away.

"Wow!" said Iúnartar, who had missed not a twitch of this.
"That Gilphros has it!" The soldier found a vacant seat among
the Army contingent, where there had been no seat a moment
earlier. Umian seemed to be chewing on something.

Ambitious, Umian had decided he would never make general by quality alone, and had turned to religion. His new sect
was known as the Closed Robes. Among their crusades to civilize Rossacotta was one to end all prostitution, unsanctioned
sexual connections, and "all manner of other lascivious acts
which create an atmosphere not conducive to the creation of
saints." The creation of saints seemed to be a major concern
of his. He had gravely offended all the most fashionable wom-
en in the Palace Royal by coming out against immoral garments, particularly underwear. "Covering those parts," he had
preached, "enhances unavailability, awakening desire. Each

man will wonder, 'Does she?', causing great inconvenience to each woman."

A rare literate in the Army (probably one reason for his slow advancement), he had written a tome of warning against vice that was so thoroughly detailed that scribes were busy day and night making copies, to keep up with demand. Those with less money and/or patience could purchase a set of the illustrations alone.

His son, currently head of the Ewe Service in the Sheep Office of the Manager of Stud, regarded his father with some amusement, not unmixed with fear. But there were those in the Palace Royal who followed the colonel, hoping the novelty of the movement would lead to promotion. Chief among these were the New Guard, a company of would-be Royal Body-guards who sought, without success, to insinuate themselves into the jobs held by Nimnestl's men.

"Wine, Polijn?"

Polijn took the cup with proper deference. She preferred beer, particularly the excellent beer available in the Palace Royal. Where she came from, the worst beer was generally better than the average wine. People were glaring at her again, especially Umian.

Umian's movement opposed the intellectuals who supported the University, and Polijn, because of her apprenticeship to Laisida, was considered one of these by everyone except Polijn. She tried to stand clear of any party, though she had occasionally done some odd jobs for the Regent and the Bodyguard. Few knew about these; she was happy to keep it that way.

Umian's chief opponent was, as it had always been, his superior officer, General Torrix. Some of Torrix's indulgences had probably inspired the Closed Robes' policies. A Swamper, and friend of Veldres, the general was watching the gallows dreamily. Everyone knew the purpose of the overstuffed stools in the general's quarters, though no one knew for certain who supplied his victims. There was always a surplus of children in the Palace Royal; no one really cared. Those who were old enough to wield a weapon had a slightly better chance, but not much, against a general with support. If daughters of marriageable age, and younger sons, disappeared, it relieved some of the competition.

"Polijn," said the King, "do you think you'd like going along on the parade tomorrow?"

She sipped the wine and looked around. When the King asked something like that, someone had already made the decision, and he simply wanted to know whether it was going to be all right. Polijn could see no clue in any faces as to what the decision had been, and so could not pick out the safe answer.

"I don't know." She turned to Iúnartar. "Would that be fun?"

But the little girl's attention was suddenly fastened on the platform, where Oigeron, a former apprentice of the sorcerer Aizon, was being fastened to a ladder preparatory to a beating.

"It's just that you know the Swamp," the King went on, with a shrug much too high for real carelessness. "You'd know where to go and what to look at."

"Yeah," Merklin agreed. "Tell us where we'll see some real action."

On the gallows, Oigeron raised one hand. A glowing ball rose from his palm. Rabioson looked at it with some reproach, and knocked it away with the iron rod that hung at his belt.

The King's departure from Malbeth was to be a grand procession, which the Regent had announced would pass through the Swamp, so as to impress all the inhabitants there. The Council had objected, on considerations of safety. Whereupon the King, on his own, had decided to hold a preliminary parade through the Swamp, both so that the proposed route could be checked, and to perhaps awe the Swampites enough to keep them quiet when the full procession passed.

Not a landmark in the Swamp occurred to Polijn as fit for the King. Fit for Merklin, perhaps. But the monarch had gone on to other concerns.

"Where can I go so the most people will see me?" He looked to Polijn, but as she was starting to open her mouth, he hurried to assure her, "So everyone will get a chance, I mean. What will they think about me coming down there?" He came forward a little in the chair, as if to make it easier for her to deliver the answer. "I'll be handing out candles, but they won't think I'm just being nice because I'm raising taxes, will they?"

There was no way to tell him that everyone in Malbeth knew he had nothing to do with raising the taxes. "We might put the University there." He searched her face for ayes or nays. "It would give the people something to do. They might not think the Swamp was so bad, then, and they'd start to act civilized."

Masalan swung a fan toward His Majesty, and donated, "People come to the Swamp and . . . and there they are. But why don't they behave themselves?"

Nothing, as far as Polijn could see, was going to change the Swamp and, insofar as it was her home, she didn't know if she wanted it to change. Then, too, much of its revenue derived from the Swampers, courtiers who visited down there simply because it was not civilized.

"We could think about that on the parade," her sovereign went on. "Maybe there's a building there where the University could start." He pushed his face toward her again, encouraging comment.

Polijn looked to Laisida, who smiled in sympathy but offered no hints. Her hint came from the intent expressions of those around the throne, reminding her of the danger of seeming to influence the King one way or another.

She flexed her fingers. "Let's see if the cards have any counsel," she said, riffling the deck.

"No," said the King, "that takes too long. I think . . ." He didn't seem to notice the people leaning in, but all the same, he stopped. His right thumb angled in toward his mouth, but he lowered it again just as it came up to his chin.

"Sing us a story," he said, slumping back in the chair.

The courtiers relaxed. So did Polijn. All she had to do now was think of some story that wouldn't seem to be a kind of veiled hint. The court, accustomed to having to live on the expectations raised by a wink or a nod, could find hints in anything.

She winced at the click of a bone from the gallows. The sounds were a bit like combat. The tale of Ostrogol might fit in here.

She announced nothing; no need to turn the eyes toward her again. Anyway, Ynygyn, one of her first teachers, had told her,

"Don't call for silence when you begin. If you're good enough, they'll listen. If not, why draw attention to it?"

Polijn sat up straight and, taking a key that would not clash with the shrill screams in the background, started the tale of the man in the mound.

V

"GIVE us that song you gave the King: a good choice, but it would have been better had you chosen one you've practiced more."

Polijn rolled her eyes. Lotyn and Lauremen laughed.

But she brought her feet up onto the seat with her, crossed her ankles, and propped the ficdual against one knee. She was expected to play not only for practice, but for the entertainment of her master's guests.

"In the dirge key, mind," Laisida went on, "and in the lesser time. Remember, child: faster rhymes with disaster."

Polijn obediently plucked out the first notes of the overture. The King's Minstrel picked up a wax tablet on which he had been making notes. "That reminds me, Celeron. Have you finished that fair copy of 'Warrior on the Field' for the King's Book?"

"Not yet, Master," said the minstrel's copyist.

Laisida looked up from the tablet, his eyes huge. "I gave it to you a year ago, man!"

Celeron shook his head. "All those words!"

"You prefer pictures, of course." A few guests, knowing how much Celeron was making from copies of Umian's book, snickered. The minstrel raised one hand with the fingers spread. "Come, man, is there nothing I can offer you to encourage speed? Ah! I'll award you one of my daughters."

"Threats will avail you nothing, Master."

A loud laugh was followed by a louder splash. Lauremen had been settling into the tub, not noticing that Lotyn, who had just climbed out, was emptying the kettle from the hob just behind her.

"You asked for more hot!" called the older girl, shaking with laughter as Lauremen leaped out, steaming in more ways than one.

Pink fists thudded against pink flesh. "It's bad enough I'm last, putting on a show for the whole lintik . . . you let go!" Lotyn had ducked in back, taking one of Lauremen's wrists and pulling it up her spine. The sisters stepped back onto a greasy pewter platter someone had left on the floor.

What looked to develop into a promising wrestling match was interrupted by the sound of fingernails tapping on a wooden leg. "Do not beat each other," their father called across the room. "There are those present who will gladly do that for you."

Lauremen snatched up her robe and started to wave it over the tub, growling, "Liked her best . . . her and her fat breasts . . . layer of grease on the water . . ."

Lotyn took her robe and retreated from the hot metal tub to a corner of the room farthest from her parents. "Who's winning?" she asked the little group around the game table, thrusting an arm into one sleeve and searching for the other.

Two outer rooms had to be penetrated to reach this inner chamber, where the family received guests. Only the most important and intimate guests made it that far, because those outer rooms were filled with Laisida's servants and bodyguards, playing cards and screening callers.

Laisida's hospitality was well known, and, besides, he was to be very important in setting up the University, which some courtiers felt might become as important a means of advancement as the Treasury or Ministry of State. So once Laisida had finished his evening bath, and sat polishing his leg, the influential and ambitious surrounded him. One could sip cool wine, make policy suggestions, and bathe in the family tub, too, if so inclined. No one was inclined tonight: the bath clothes were packed away, and few in the Palace Royal were as addicted to hot water of an evening as Laisida and his family.

As far as Polijn could see, though, the scene was much the same as usual: lots of people sitting on low stools, trying to dry off. The heat and humidity had diminished only slightly after dark. The little seats were always scattered throughout the three chambers; wherever Laisida settled, he'd want somewhere to prop his leg. The Royal Tutor and some other University officials (as well as a number of hopefuls) sat around him, to the left of the window, while Berdais's circle chattered to the right.

The minstrel was also keeping an eye on Lotyn and Lauremen, in case of delayed revenge. But Polijn did not assume he had forgotten her. Laisida could keep his mind on three or four things at once; that was what accounted for his rapid rise in the court.

"Umian," he told Haeve, "seems to feel the University can be tucked into North Malbeth and be forgotten."

"Umian," the Tutor replied, "is a fool. The University will become a power anywhere."

"True, no doubt," said the minstrel, sighting down his leg for spots. "But I would be grieved to lose your company. Intelligent conversation is always to be missed, even if the other person is completely wrongheaded on virtually every subject."

Haeve gave him a thin smile. "Of course. I should miss the entertainment of some people's stubborn stupidity if I had to relocate. And I think Orna will require some assistance with His Majesty. I would NOT miss Nurse." He tightened his voice in imitation. "I do not expect that you will behave with the wisdom demanded of a monarch, but you MIGHT think for one moment about your attendants, who had a great deal of work to do, ALL for you, and retire early enough for them to take SOME rest and . . ."

Laisida padded his hands together in silent applause, "However," he pointed out, "her vigilance at least affords me a few early evenings, to rest in the bosom, or bosoms, of my family."

His eyes were on Lotyn, who was pulling up an empty plant stand with a slanted top, the better to watch the game between Malaracha and Ysela. She sat down and stood again quickly. "Ooh! That's cold!"

She had neglected to notice that the stand was solid marble. "No, don't get up," Malaracha commanded, raising a hand. "I feel I shall be inspired to an ode on romps who set their rumps upon ramps."

"Huh!" Lotyn stripped off her robe, rolled it up, and shoved it beneath her, using her free hand to gesture her opinion of Malaracha. The man laughed, and reached to move a piece on the game board. The little group immediately started to discuss his strategy. Polijn raised an eyebrow. Lotyn's exposure, or even Lauremen, stark naked, bending to check the temperature of the bath water, attracted fewer eyes than the game, or Ysela, setting one lapel aside to draw the back of her left hand down one breast. That was visible only from the proper angle, and was thus a private peek, producing more interest than the general show. The same principle allowed Laisida's daughters to wear as little here as Iranen's slaveys wore in the courtyard, without incurring the loss of prestige that accompanied the latter.

She shrugged. To display yourself that recklessly in the Swamp, except by way of advertisement, was to invite disaster. Perhaps it was the same here. But, of course, Laisida's daughters would be immune, since everyone knew their father took an interest in their welfare.

Her mind went back to her own first bath here, a few months ago. She had had no idea what to make of that big metal tub with cloth draped in it. Bathing in the Swamp was limited largely to thunderstorms, falling in the river, and games of "Who Plops in the Trough?" The first thought that struck her was that her apprenticeship to the country's leading minstrel, a ridiculous idea from the outset, had simply been a ruse, and that she had been acquired for the purpose of sacrifice in some secret rite.

"The world is a cold, dirty place, Polijn," Laisida had explained, while Berdais and Aperiole hauled her to the steaming water. "This is your opportunity to repair its wear."

She had eventually developed a taste for the habit, if not for the display that followed. Tonight she had been fortunate enough to draw high card, bathing just after Laisida and Berdais, and before most of the guests arrived. She now sat in a soft pink robe (rather too large, but it covered the tattoo that had once told other Swampites that she was under Chordasp's protection) and her striped stockings. These were the first stockings she had ever owned, and she liked to keep track of them. Besides, they were more covering. She attracted entirely too much attention, as a newcomer, and her underfed frame, with much leg and protruding hipbones, made her conspicuous among Laisida's more cushiony daughters.

Polijn checked the crowd. No one seemed to be watching her right now. Irisien was sitting on a little rug next to the tub, peeling sunburnt shoulders and chattering four miles to the minute with Lauremen, who was flipping the soap. A little nothing-trick, unworthy of a minstrel's daughter, but Polijn had never gotten the hang of it. Beyond them, Malaracha was executing some masterful move on the gameboard. Those of the crowd who were paying attention drew long breaths.

But at least two spectators had their minds elsewhere. They wore tall, cylindrical, feathered hats, a fashion that had oozed in from the south and now hovered between chic and ridiculous. They would not, in Polijn's opinion, turn out to be acceptable. They indicated too clearly where the wearer was looking.

The curtain in the book niche ruffled as Aperiole slipped between it and the urn in what she no doubt considered an inconspicuous manner.

She and Eneste had nearly made the door when her father reached one hand in her direction. "I see that my daughters are loath to leave the world unpopulated."

Aperiole pulled her robe a little tighter and raised her chin. "I was just going to check the courtyard."

"Not dressed that way," her father corrected her.

"Colaniss's father says . . ."

"And who," the minstrel inquired, "is Colaniss's father?"

The crowd snickered; Aperiole heaved. But then she had a thought, and smiled. Gliding behind her father's chair, she leaned forward as if to address him, letting her breasts just caress the top of his head. "Well, it is so boring tonight," she tried to coo, "talking politics instead of telling us your interesting stories. What was it like, in the old days?"

"Very much like today, only younger. Sit down, girl. You know I hate cajolery."

Berdais laughed out loud. Laisida didn't look up. "That isn't better disguised. Ah, if chastity belts were to be legalized, I'd have to buy a dozen."

"There aren't twelve of us," Lauremen pointed out.

"They'd melt." The minstrel gestured Aperiole to a vacant seat at the game table. "Now, sit down and stop heating up the chamber. You're as bad as your sister and that son of Kimian's."

"I am not!"

Ysela also objected. "We aren't like those two at all. We just respect each other's singing."

Laisida sniffed. "I'd respect your judgement more if you were only . . ."

"Cikits!" Aperiole had started away, not noticing where her father had set his leg. She rose from the floor, straw sticking to her face and scattered in her hair.

This vision brought a little laughter, but no comment; one had faith that Aperiole would always land on her face. People had more pressing things to consider.

"Ghosorky will sell that bay of his to anyone that's going north," Ziant told Mields. "I've got a mind to take him up on it."

"You've got a knucklebrain if you do," Mields replied, "with those three white legs."

Lotyn slid up the sloping seat to be nearer. "I never have understood about the white legs," she said, leaning toward them. "What does it mean?"

"Oh, how does that go?" Mields demanded. "One white leg, buy him. . . ."

"No, no," Ziant answered. "Starts with no white legs. 'White legs none, he's the one.' "

Polijn knew the whole poem, but her attention was drawn by Laisida's waggling finger. "Slower, Polijn, slower." He turned back to the man at his left and said, "You'll have to ask Lord Haeve about that; he's to be Chancellor."

This group was so much more literate than the circles Polijn had been accustomed to in the Swamp. Polijn could read when she came to the Palace Royal, but only just. This had improved under three teachers, though her handwriting was still a scrawl. As chambermaid to King's Minstrel Ynygyn, she had learned some of the basics of her profession. Becoming assistant to the jester Arberth, she had picked up more pointers, particularly on how to duck projectiles from the audience. A good-natured soul, Arberth had made her feel safe enough to offer suggestions, so that he improved a bit under her help, too. That he had noticed these, and resented them, had not occurred to her until Laisida had mentioned he'd like an apprentice. Saying, "Well, I can always claim I gave you your start," the jester had sent her off that very night, with a tambourine and all his good wishes.

Laisida had been without an apprentice for nearly a year, and he had quickly started loading Polijn up with the songs and techniques of the great minstrels of history, from the legendary Galfa right down to Baradon of Thurth, whom Laisida had actually met and worked with thirty years earlier. Not to mention Laisida himself, which it was always best to do. Laisida was the self-ordained, self-anointed Master-of-Music-For-This-Generation (And-Though-I-Would-Not-Like-To-Boast-Probably-A-Dozen-Generations-On-Either-Side-Of-It). There was nothing he would not do for an apprentice who properly fed his self-esteem. Since he was genuinely good, and since any apprentice would expect to do the same for any master, probably with less reward, Polijn had no difficulties with that.

His wife, Berdais, was a little more difficult to get around; years of working with her subordinates and daughters had left her suspicious. Polijn looked to where she stood before the tall narrow window, her robe hiked up in back in hopes of a breeze. Berdais was a plump, genial soul who had not an enemy in the world. She had seen to that.

Berdais had all the ruthlessness that Gloraida, Polijn's mother, lacked. What would they all be doing right now, at home? Of course, if everyone was home at this hour, it would be because the weather was too bad for Gloraida to report for her show at the Yellow Dog, or for Polijn to go out. So Ronar would be in a proper snit.

"Don't break the skin," Gloraida would say. "The customers won't pay as much."

Ronar would glare, the rod or strap or whatever he had handy poised above Polijn. "Some of them," Gloraida would say, taking a step back. Ronar would start forward.

"Not all," Gloraida would continue, getting back behind the table.

And Ronar would drop the twisted wrist of Polijn and growl, "That's right." Then would come the lecture on how she should be making more money, combined with a little noncontroversial kicking. Gloraida wouldn't object to that, or to anything else for the rest of the evening. Ronar was her protector, not Polijn, and her manager.

Gloraida's chief asset on stage was an ability to look like a naughty little girl in need of the firm hand, among other things, of an older, wiser male. She had a whimper men paid good money to hear, and no one on any stage in the Swamp could look more helpless or confused. Perhaps because the offstage reality was not so far different.

Just off to the side of the room, a man was locked in combat with what appeared to be a hat. The hat was winning. The women around the game table stretched for a good look.

Which combatant was the target of Laisida's scowl was hard to tell. Then the minstrel sighed, "Polijn, could you oblige?"

Polijn shifted key and mood to a snappy little dance tune called "The Virgin Unmasked." (She knew all the words to this, and to the alternate version called "The Virgin Unasked.") The hat dropped to the floor, and the pixy underneath danced through the air to the musician.

Polijn had always considered the pixies touching: the male ones particularly. This was a grey-and-yellow male known as Porkribs. He darted up to kiss first her upper lip, and then her lower.

"Let's you and me race north, Fluteface," said the fist-high creature. "You dance and I'll fly, and I bet we're both in the exact same place every night when you undress for bed."

"Oh, fly away somewhere." Polijn was not in the habit of giving orders, but it could do her no harm here, because pixies never paid any attention. She had wanted to see whether Janeftox had looked at Malaracha at all as he entered.

Porkribs showed no sign of departure, settling onto the top of her head, but then spied the bathtub. "Oh, it's poor baby!" he squealed, and zipped over to straddle Lauremen's chin. "Tell me how badly everyone's treating you!"

Lauremen did not hesitate. Polijn glanced over toward the door, but by now Janeftox had crossed the room, smiling bravely in response to his chosen father-in-law's glower, to talk to Berdais. Berdais was more amenable to this prospective addition to the family, having come from a military family herself. (Her mother had denied critical arms to the rebels of oh-one and been rewarded with a permanent position in Weapons.) Laisida turned to make some comment, but his wife got in the first shot with, "Is Polijn quite in tune, love? She sounded a bit sharp when she changed songs."

"You'd better retune," the minstrel told his apprentice. "And don't make that face. If you live to be eighty, you'll have spent sixty years tuning up. By this time next year, you'll be able to tune all the strings while doing an overhead leg kick and landing on one hand."

Polijn suspected he'd given her all the instruments hardest to keep in tune, just for the learning experience, and said so, as loudly as was consistent with prudence. He heard her anyway, and held up three fingers. "You can be this good, but if you don't have this . . ." He raised the remaining two fingers. "It's nothing."

Laisida always urged her to strive for omnicompetence and perfect pitch: that is, his level. "I don't suppose everyone has decided on the security men for the University," Polijn remarked, not looking at Berdais.

Berdais would have liked very much to get Janeftox out of the Army and into the new branch of government, to be headed by the new post of Fifth Chief Housekeeper (which might be Berdais). This branch would include the University and all artists previously included in Iranen's department. The number of professions demanding to be considered arts was legion. Laisida sneered, but turned to consult Haeve.

"Psst!" called a voice. "Polijn! Come on over!"

Sielvia and the younger crowd were playing cards with Lauremen's deck, which was distinguished by illustrations of an intricate and highly amusing nature. Sielvia was dealing a card to each player to open the next hand; the players would take on the identity of the card dealt, though no one was required to find a partner and assume the positions depicted.

Argeleb, who had called, went on, "Someone else can sing now. He won't notice you're gone."

"Ho ho," said Polijn.

She saw the shift of Laisida's eyes, but no one else did. "You're always watching, and never joining in," complained Marista.

Polijn had received similar complaints. Girls who hadn't noticed her all winter, when she was Arberth's assistant, now were offended if she failed to reply to any saccharine greeting in the corridor. "Thinks she can dance across the honeypond," more than one had muttered.

Sielvia considered her father's apprentice, the grave, dark eyes moving up and down. "You know," she said, "he'd sell us before he'd sell you."

"Huh," said Lauremen, from the tub. "I like to think that's because he'd get a better price for us."

She yowled as Irisien jabbed a finger into her tender mid-section. "Well, there'd be no lack of buyers for some of you," noted Laisida. "General Ferrapec has been showing interest in Polijn. Of course, he's approached Masalan as well."

"He probably thinks he won't look so small to itty-bitty women," returned Lauremen, shaking water, and Porkribs, from her hair.

Everyone had a bit of a laugh at that, except Janeftox, but her father waggled a finger at her. "You show proper respect for generals, my dolly, or I shall report that to Ferrapec. He will then complain to Colonel Umian, who will have his New Guard spank you silly."

"She's silly to start with," said Porkribs, zipping away to where Bersidis and Tipap, the minstrel's grandchildren, were playing some incomprehensible game with marbles.

"Then you won't be able to sit down any more than Ferrapec can," Irisien pointed out.

Polijn looked over to see how Janeftox took that, but Fiojo passed in front of her, inquiring in a whisper whether Lauremen had finished bathing. The girl climbed up out of the tub, and Fiojo beckoned to two of Laisida's bodyguard, who carried it into the outer room where the servants bathed. It was one of the hazards of working for the minstrel, but better than working for Lady Iranen, to be sure.

Lauremen buttoned all three buttons of her robe and checked the mirror to see how it looked on her, front and back, when she bent over. Her opinion was indicated in the way she went to the bed to join the card game, and immediately dropped her cards on the floor.

Sielvia looked across to Polijn and sniffed. "I saw that, you moonfaced brat," said her sister. Bersidis and Porkribs ran squealing between the bed and Laisida; Sielvia took advantage of the distraction to reach behind her and reveal a corner of the stolen pair of panties under a pillow. Lauremen swallowed, and relinquished her hold in her sister's hair.

Polijn felt the move was hazardous; Laisida had been distracted, but Janeftox could have spotted the M monogrammed on the garment. But Sielvia was not cautious by nature; she had never known a time when her father wasn't in the ascendancy.

Fortunately, Janeftox had been moving across the room, easing past the big family harp, covered on its stand, to join his contemporaries at the gameboard. He was overdressed for the group; most of the men there were topless, and those women who were not wearing the damp, nearly transparent bathgowns were displaying the same superficial availability in a minimum of cloth. Sobaquillo, though she was not hampered by much of anything in the way of garments, was having so much trouble painting her toenails that Wengefrid, a flower clutched between his teeth, finally felt it was necessary to put his hands over hers and take over the job.

Lotyn took a puff on her little amber elf pipe. "He said I'd make a good whore, and offered to give me my start," she was saying. She squeezed one breast in the crook of her elbow as she put the pipe back in her mouth. Kester looked as if his hands hurt. He glanced at Laisida. Laisida glanced back. Kester looked in another direction entirely, disowning all interest in the players at the gameboard.

Lotyn was a plump white berry, juicily ripe for harvest. Blondes were rare in Rossacotta; she would have less trouble finding mates than her redheaded sister Aperiole, who was pointing out to Malaracha all the advantages of marriage. Malaracha smiled a lot, but obviously didn't see it that way. Other listeners had less patience; Kester finally plucked at the rivulets of damp hair between Aperiole's breasts and, under pretext of patting them into place in front of her ears, pasted two strands across her mouth.

"You look sudsy with a mustache," called Porkribs, easily dodging a marble tossed by Tipap, which plopped into Laisida's wine. The minstrel shrugged and went on discussing university security, but his eyes were on the gameboard group. Polijn knew he hoped to establish all his older daughters in secure households, as a byproduct of the university organization. He was very important and visible now, so the market was in his favor; a fall could come at any time.

"Hey, what's the difference between Sobaquillo and the Palace Royal?"

"What?"

"The Palace Royal has secret entrances!"

Polijn decided that one was worth remembering. It brought a nice laugh, spoiled a bit by the entrance of Sobaquillo's father. Colonel Kirasov had not, apparently, heard the joke; his hands were not on his highly decorated eared daggers. One of the men at the gameboard quietly collected a few garments and slipped out of sight.

But Kirasov walked on over to Laisida's chair. "Evening, minstrel," he said. "I've come to see Argeleb and the girls back."

Berdais raised her eyebrows. Kirasov was not known for showing an interest in the women he had begotten.

"Don't let me interrupt, young one." Polijn had reached the point in the song where Ostrogol cut off his hand and tossed it out the window, in hopes that if he failed to gain revenge on Epax, his hand would. "That's a fine song, a perfect piece of singing. Just the thing for His Majesty."

Polijn nodded in acknowledgement. The colonel liked the songs of the nobler, simpler days.

"May I offer you a cup, Colonel?" Laisida asked his guest.

"Not for me," Kirasov replied, holding up both hands. "Lord Garanem's been hosting Aizon, whether Aizon wanted to be hosted or not, and I'm overflowing." He moved over toward the fireplace.

Sielvia nudged Timpre and pointed to a chamberpot, but the Colonel was already taking care of the excess wine. Sobaquillo, turning bright red, put two fingers of each hand over her eyes. "I swear he does that just to humiliate me," she seethed. "He is SO old-fashioned."

"Remind him he's important now," suggested Jolor, "and has his own private garderobe."

Laisida took no notice of this breach of civilized manners, but nodded to Haeve. "Here's the man we need, if you want to talk security," he said. "He's been guarding Morquiesse's paintings in the Treasury for months now."

"Hmmm?" demanded the Chief Treasury Guard, adjusting his garments. "Morquiesse? Oh, um, yes. The man could paint a piece of wood and make it look so much like stone, it sank."

Haeve smiled, less at this compliment to the late artist than at the man making it. Kirasov lacked any interest at all in painters, and had very little more for minstrels. But it was hardly politic to say so. For that matter, the honored founders of the University, Haeve and Morquiesse, had never had any use for each other until after Morquiesse died.

"How goes it with the University?" the colonel inquired, his eyes moving around to check the locations of his children. "Ready to dazzle the world with it yet?"

Polijn knew no more than anyone in the Palace Royal why Colonel Kirasov chose to support the University, which was opposed by his chief, Lord Garanem. Her own guess was that it was either a desire to score off the Army (always a major concern of Treasury officers) or a hope for alliance with the currently powerful minstrels. If he could arrange for his banished son to marry one of Laisida's daughters, for example, he might be able to bring the young man back from exile.

"Well, now," the colonel responded to a query from Haeve, "that depends a lot on how much of the Royal Library you plan to transfer."

Bersidis, meanwhile, had sneaked up on her tiny cousin, and tickled him. Tipap emitted a shriek so high-pitched that even Polijn could barely hear it, and wrapped himself around Kirasov's leg for shelter.

"Faff!" The big man leaped, swinging his leg against a table. It was not a move meant to dislodge a child, but to maim or kill a foe. Fortunately, he had hit the gate-leg of Berdais's newest acquisition. The leg slid back, dumping a heavy silver bowl of flowers, but saving Tipap a broken spine.

Polijn counted nineteen knives out and clear before the bowl had stopped bouncing. Even naked people kept weapons at hand. Laisida's bodyguard came bustling in, with one or two members of the colonel's retinue.

"Ah, well," said the minstrel, waving them away. "Beget in haste, repent at leisure."

He brought his wooden leg into position, gave it a twist, and fastened it down. Then he reached for his crutch. His guests looked around for their discarded garments.

"Say, now, I don't mean to break up your evening," said the Colonel, ignoring Ysela's apologies. "The little assassin just startled me a bit."

"No matter," the minstrel told him. "I have a long day ahead, and I was trying to think of some way to shoo all these animals off to bed without encouraging what they'll probably do anyhow." He caught at a long linen napkin and tossed it over Lotyn, who was still studying the gameboard.

"The market's closed," he told her. "You needn't display your peaches again until tomorrow."

"Oh, no," Berdais was telling the colonel, who still wanted to apologize. "It's not as though you drew steel on him, after all. He has to learn these things."

Tipap had not regained full control of his breath yet, but was preparing a good bawl for when he did. Sielvia caught up a large, heavy cookie from a tray on the bed and forced it into his mouth. Between surprise and sustenance, Tipap forgot his grievance.

"Thank you, Flower," said her father.

Jolor picked up the game pieces and returned them to their cupboard on the wall, as Janeftox repinned her robe where it had fallen open a bit. Invitations to the cooler tower rooms, or simply choice spots on the roofs or down in the yard, were whispering around the room.

Aperiole stretched forward and yawned, touching the tips of her index fingers to the top of her head, waiting for an invitation that didn't come. She bared her teeth at the sight of Lotyn shaking her head to a young acolyte.

Colonel Kirasov had assembled Argeleb, Marista, Irisien, and Sobaquillo, and was marching them out the door, declining all invitations for them. Polijn saw Berdais frown, watching them. This was not like the colonel at all. His children, particularly Argeleb, generally did as they liked.

In fact, this was a fairly rare tableau: the colonel with all his family, excepting only his wife, and Anrichar, who had years of exile to go in payment for his insult to the Regent on the King's Birthday. That might be it, thought Polijn; exile was at the top of every Rossacottan's fears, surpassed only, perhaps, by the Chief Bodyguard. Other nations dreaded and detested Rossacottans so much that any who left the country were believed to suffer fates worse than those available on the gallows. The banishing of Anrichar might have encouraged Kirasov to take care of what he had left.

The general bustle of the departing guests had alerted the servants, who were moving their tub out to the front room. In winter, the household congregated in and around the big feather bed. Come the hot season, though, Laisida shooed everyone but his wife out of the room with the window, claiming, "Girl children are such intolerably noisy little chipmunks."

Apprentices generally slept in the antechamber, with the servants, but Polijn had been unofficially adopted as a semi-sister. So, after laboriously retuning a bit, to provide cover as Sielvia stuffed Maiaciara's panties under her robe, she moved on out into the middle room. Aperiole unlocked a little chest in a corner and drew out three hammocks.

"Siel's got the cards," said Lauremen. "A quick game of Monarchy?"

"It's too hot," said Lotyn, winding the hammock lines around a torch bracket and then down to a spike on the floor. "Let's just draw."

Sielvia shuffled. Aperiole cut the deck. In spite of this, Lauremen drew the high card, and went dancing around the room. This gave her the hammock nearest the door, where she would sleep alone. Only three of the five original competitors took part in the second drawing, the winner getting to take the corner hammock with Polijn, who took up less room and didn't sweat as much as the others.

"No fair!" cried Aperiole, pointing at Lotyn. "That cow sags right down to the floor!"

"Why, I never heard of such a thing," said Lauremen.

"It's only when those two fat calves join me," Lotyn agreed.

The cards in the preliminary drawing had never yet come up so that Polijn slept alone. She knew, though, that this was not so much a matter of affection on the part of the sisters as it was of their being too old for a stuffed animal and too young to attach a man. Give even Sielvia a chance at a husband, and Polijn would be sleeping on the floor.

Well, her own sister would have been the same, if she'd lived. Polijn tested the tension of the hammock, and jumped up.

CHAPTER TWO
Nimnestl

I

THEY padded silently along the walls, beyond her reach: five men with large hammers, just watching for an opening. Nimnestl stayed right where she was. Let them wear themselves out in this heat, if that was the extent of their ambition.

The men were uncertain, confused by this lack of action. The tall, dark woman might have many surprises stored away. Her simple yellow knitted garment might or might not be just that. Was it really worth one's head to move in and try to find out?

One, bolder than the rest, took a step closer. The man had a neck like a tree trunk, and his face bore the tattoo of a snarling wolf. With no war cry to serve as warning, he took five more steps and swung his hammer in at the level of her chest. The Chief Bodyguard knocked it up with her own hammer and pushed her dagger in at him. He jumped away.

When he came at her again, the hammer sped in at her face. Nimnestl accordingly watched for the man's dagger; the hammer was meant only as a distraction.

Nimnestl was willing to lay down her life for the King, but she would have to be shown there was no other way; she would not let herself be killed in some trivial cause. She would also die for Kaftus, as he was necessary to Conan. It was really the better measure of her devotion that she would admit the Regent was more important to the King than she, and would sacrifice herself accordingly, at need.

There was no such need here. She parried his dagger with hers and, when his eyes shifted there, swung her hammer hard against his ankles.

The other men had pulled back to watch a single combat. So, as her foe hit the floor, she sheathed her dagger and set the hammerhead on the floor behind her, leaning on the hammer for rest. Hot as the bone today.

She saw his eyes come up. This was something she had taught her men: encourage the foe, let him think there's a chance. That way, he would try nothing drastic, nor go to cover. If the prey holed up, you had to go in after it, and that could be dangerous.

He came at her full speed, springing up from the floor. But he was too far away. Nimnestl swung the hammer up from behind her, her arm fully extended.

One man said, "Eru!" Two others sat down hard on the floor.

The man halted, a little surprised himself, but then resumed his attack, knowing the momentum of such a blow must carry her around. Nimnestl let the momentum do so. The man's own momentum had been interrupted, and she knew where he would be when. And he wasn't fast enough.

By the time he got there, she had come completely around. Her hand was higher up on the handle of her hammer, the head of which came up into his elbow, sending his dagger free. Then the head was the least of his problems, as the handle jerked back against his throat.

Nimnestl considered letting him go, to recover again, but twice was too many. She had, in her youth, occasionally fought for the fun of it. Now she just tried to get it over with.

Her opponent, not quite through, tossed his hammer experimentally over one shoulder. That did not work. The audience gasped as he scrabbled in his belt for a second knife. Nimnestl did not raise an eyebrow. She did raise a knee.

He had no breath left to complain, but he did have spirit enough to aim his knife into that knee. His aim was so wobbly, though, that Nimnestl had pity. Saying, "Done," she released him.

The other four men waited for a second after he hit the floor. Then, seeing him try to sit up, they dropped their hammers and came forward.

"To think I volunteered for this," he whispered, as eight hands hauled him to his feet.

"You're still trying to use the hammer like a saber," the Chief Bodyguard told him, unlacing the leather pillow around her hammerhead.

"You made her sweat, anyhow," murmured one of the other bodyguards.

In this weather that was no surprise, but Nimnestl supposed a few words were in order. The men did think, after all, that these training sessions were to train them, not herself.

"You've done well this morning," she told them, "though I suggest you stick to blades for a while yet. This afternoon, put your men through the emergency drills, particularly cart-to-cart movement. The rains will be on us before we can get away, and if the procession is stuck in the mud, we will need to be as mobile as possible. There may well be people fighting for the right to protect the King. That right is yours alone."

Koroyke, who had been with the Royal Bodyguard since the days of Queen Kata, nodded. Biandi started picking up the discarded hammers and setting them into their rack, but glanced up with a little dismay as the Chief Bodyguard went on, "This evening, be on alert, even if off duty. The number of petitioners to His Majesty will increase, with the excursion coming up tomorrow, and these people must be watched. The King, I may mention, has expressed admiration of your work." She set her head to one side. "His Majesty has expressed the opinion that any five members of the Elite Bodyguard could arrest ten of the New Guard and bring them in alive." Her head tipped back a bit. "I agreed with him."

Eyes twinkled; no more had to be said. This would be a nice setback for Colonel Umian.

"Koroyke," she went on, "check with the infirmary and see that they've made the necessary arrangements for Dilathys to accompany us to the north. He was injured in the line of duty, and deserves no less."

She nodded to them, and they moved to finish the tidying of the training room, discussing in undertones where the New Guard was vulnerable, or the state of Dilathys's health. Nimnestl had, in fact, already checked all the arrangements with the infirmary. But it was good for them to check, too, and know they would be looked after in case the expected occurred.

She reached down to the stack of overclothes she would have to put on to be presentably prestigious outside. Even as she dressed, though, she had a knife ready when Culghi and Bonti started toward her. The Elite Bodyguard consisted of some sixteen men she had chosen herself. She had trained them to command the rest of the Royal Bodyguard, and to do a little spying on the side. They had uncovered a good many plots, and reported even more. They were men she could trust as much as she trusted anybody.

But she couldn't trust anybody, and knowing this had helped her survive. Just because she had ended the training session did not mean they had agreed to quit.

"Ma'am," said Bonti, "did you want us to do any looking on the murders of the people going north?"

"None of our business." (She hoped.) "Just Offhand." There were four degrees of investigation. Offhand meant you kept your eyes open for things that passed. Looking meant you went out of your way to find them. The next degree up was Asking; questions started rumors, so you did that only for matters of genuine interest. And then came Telling, as in, "You're coming with us to the Chief Bodyguard."

"A lot of people are worried," Bonti noted.

"They're allowed to." The murders were genuinely none of her business, except that the King felt she could do something about them. He thought she could do anything.

"There haven't, Ma'am, been rumors of . . . strangeness in the killings?"

She raised an eyebrow at that. "There have been all kinds of rumors, as usual. So far as I know, that is all they are."

The big man turned a little red. "No stories of, well, something unnatural?"

Nimnestl looked past him to catch laughter in Biandi's eyes, shut off as soon as Biandi saw her gaze on him.

What kind of joke or trick was this? "Something unusual?" she demanded. "About murders in the Palace Royal?"

It was no laughing matter to Culghi. "No rumors of, um, bears?"

Nimnestl's face went totally blank. "Bears?"

"Ah, somebody's got to say it." Biandi punched his partner in the shoulder. "The great looby thinks we've got a werebear loose in the place."

Culghi was now bright red, and the wolf tattoo stood out sharply on his face. "It's just . . . it's just that . . . there were big pawprints around Prabeo's body."

"Pools of blood," snorted Biandi.

"And there was the smell of a bear in the hall," Culghi retorted, more to Biandi than Nimnestl.

"And where would a southern brat like you learn what a bear smells like?"

Biandi was a native of Malbeth, but Culghi had been recruited during a drive among southern peasants five years ago. Their bickering friendship sometimes erupted into open combat, and was none the worse for it, but Nimnestl did not feel like letting it go so far in today's heat.

"And if it is a matter of werebears," she said, angling a shoulder between the two men, "what measures should we be taking?"

Culghi looked as mystified as she had been when he asked about bears. Fighting and spying were his trade, not policy.

"Well, er, we'd need to know who it is." His chin came up. "We could serve wild onions and honey at supper, and see who refuses it."

"I would, for one," said Biandi.

"You!" snapped his partner. "You're no werebear. You're a . . . wereworm!"

"Enough," said Nimnestl, raising a hand. "I will bring it to the attention of the Regent, who can test for it." Kaftus had been on intimate terms with at least one werewolf; she must ask whatever became of him. "It will be a relief if we face no worse during this move. Culghi, you have balcony duty during the executions; have your men check the balcony again."

"Yes, Ma'am!" Culghi headed for the door, greatly relieved. Like any good horse, he feared to charge what he couldn't see over or through. With his chief and the Regent dealing with the werebears, he could concentrate on humans.

Nimnestl would have preferred werebears.

"You know," he told Biandi, moving out, "where I come from, we have talking frogs."

"I believe that," Biandi replied. "Why'd they have to send us one? By the way, that tattoo isn't as good of luck without the red whiskers."

"I heard you did really well." Nimnestl reached for the leggings of her summer armor. That was Lamangil's voice; Culghi always fought harder when she was waiting outside.

Fully clothed (and then some), the Chief Bodyguard stepped out of her office, and nodded to her men. They set off for their places. Hers would be the balcony and, after, the Council Chamber. Each had its horrors. One of the drawbacks of her post was that she had to witness the execution of anyone she arrested, and then attend Council meetings to argue the policies under which the next ones would be caught. These training bouts were less strenuous than the double daily dosage of Council meetings, which would continue until all the details of this move were wrapped up.

She had been able to excuse herself from the most recent one on the grounds that her elite guards needed extra training. The annual moves of the court were always difficult, and this heat was all that would be needed to bring out the worst in people who were not all that good at their best. She'd need the bodyguards to be at the peak of their skills.

Three courtiers chatting on a landing fell silent as Nimnestl passed. She caught sight of the symbols they made with their fingers. She walked on. Only when general malevolence hardened into action was she required to take note of it.

Of course, there was always something going on somewhere that should be stopped, or at least looked into. Residents of the Palace Royal came in four varieties: those with power, those who tried to grab power, those who tried to borrow power, and those who tried to keep out of the way. The second group was far in the majority. Any passing crisis that offered a chance to add a single grain of power had to be exploited.

There was no real organization to the current craze of the "twelve missing Ykenai." Everyone was tossing out stories, hoping one would stick, and provide a handhold by which clout could be clutched: brown robes had been stolen, bogus meetings held just to keep people suspicious.

The Ykenai had been very literate, very methodical, keeping lists of members, enemies, and anything else they considered important, particularly their hymns. Several of their books had been confiscated, but because they had been composed by different people at different times, they did not all agree. Codes, ciphers, and plain bad handwriting added to the discrepancies.

Allowing for all that, creative arithmetic was still needed to come up with twelve unarrested Brown Robes. Only one or two names were not positively identified, and from the context, these were fairly junior members, posing no threat. Everyone else was dead now, or neutralized.

Word had spread, though, that the Regent intended to find those twelve Brown Robes if he had to kill everyone in Rossacotta to do it. He was said to fear their sympathetic magic, which took its strength from the magic of any attacker. The Army, said rumor, would be the main target of his investigation, which was ridiculous, as this was the last place anyone would go hunting the literate.

Similarly composed more of smoke than fire was the smouldering crisis of the recent rush of murders. The victims had little in common beyond the fact that all had been assigned to go north. Most likely, there was no conspiracy at all, only unconnected episodes of courtiers eliminating their competition.

Kespel was notoriously unfaithful; his wife could have killed him. Carasta's apprentice had been killed and now the body could not even be found. The one-eyed foreigner claimed it had been shipped home for burial, but Nimnestl had doubts about various of Carasta's claims.

Colonel Kirasov was in the thick of some plot, too. This was not his forte, and you could tell he was a man with a secret. But he was no fool, Kirasov; he recognized that scheming would get a man farther in the new order than his old method, gouging and stabbing. Besides, he was getting older.

Reaching the stairs, she saw General Ferrapec busy with Tyell. She giggled as he explained that in his day, young ladies wore their brooches in a more seemly fashion, to draw attention away from their bosoms rather than emphasize them. He was experimenting with a number of possible placements which demonstrated where his attention was. The general glowered at the way the girl glanced at Bonti, and even more at the way Bonti glanced back.

The general was deep in something, too; everyone knew it, and recognized his "Hoo hoo!" signal as a call to a "secret" meeting. It was considered politest not to mention this in public, though, lest the general hear of it and reveal something of your plots. Anyhow, waiting was best until you saw whether there was more profit in helping or hindering the general.

Nimnestl and Kaftus had gone farther than that. As far as they could do so, without becoming obvious, they had been furnishing the general with a supply of lucky breaks, in Council and outside. When some hint of Ferrapec's plotting came out in Council, the Regent deftly redirected the conversation. When the "Hoo hoo!" signal attracted too many curious onlookers, a diversion could be arranged. If his conspiracy looked as though it would be successful, others would join him. Since his most likely accomplices would be people who agreed with him on royal policy, the Bodyguard and the Regent hoped that by the time they "discovered" the plot, most of the radical conservatives in the Army would be entangled in it.

The aging roué was allied with, of all people, Colonel Umian, who was probably the brains behind the whole conspiracy. Ferrapec would have been just the person to spread the rumor about the coming decimation of the Army; Umian could easily have engineered the rush of murders so as to have a further cause. It might be worthwhile to prove these possibilities, and it might not; the investigation could as easily set off open revolt as avert it.

These details were more difficult than usual to come by because none of the three chief conspirators seriously trusted his allies, and passed along only the barest minimum of information to each other. They had had to resort to spying on each other to keep posted on how everyone was doing.

Two pieces of information were all that stood between the Regent and complete security in this matter. One was the identity of that third schemer. The conspirators' underlings made enough trips to the Swamp; it might be some major thug or sorcerer down there. Certainly, few would attempt to revolt here without magic backing. The other bit of information lacking was the trigger: what event would the conspirators use to set off their takeover? Something in the trip to North Malbeth? Something on the journey back?

Or nothing at all? Even empty warehouses were guarded; this Ferrapec-Umian-Whoever conspiracy might be nothing more than tiny secrets and lots of rushing around. The use of Ferrapec, known for neither patience nor subtlety, argued a low-quality organization. If the thing could just be dragged out, the general was bound to make some misstep that couldn't be covered, taking at least Umian and that flummery New Guard with him.

Nimnestl paused to let a company of dungeon guards pass, escorting the last of the prisoners to be featured in today's performance. Most of the prisoners, and the guards too for that matter, glanced up at the Chief Bodyguard and marched a little faster. One naked man, though, spied her and, ducking under the arms of the guards on his left, skidded to her on his knees.

The guards were not so very far behind; a metal-clad fist came down hard against the man's right ear. Nimnestl's raised eyebrow prevented a balancing blow to the left.

The man on the floor had sworn eternal hatred of Nimnestl during his trial, but it was no novelty for her to meet a mortal enemy; she had them all over the Palace Royal. "Anyone in this line of work who does it seriously," Kaftus had promised her, "will be murdered."

In the days of his success, Liveol had been Manager of Hay for the Army. A tip from the Undermanager had led to a surprise inspection. Of nine barns Liveol had certified as full and ready for winter, six had been half-empty, two had been emptied entirely, and one had burned down. Selling the hay he was supposed to stockpile was fraud, and the penalty for defrauding King and Army was unpleasant.

"They're going to hawk me," he croaked to the Bodyguard. "And I'm innocent."

"How wonderful for you," she told him, motioning to the guards, "to be meeting your maker while your soul is still unspotted." She looked down at the hand he'd put on her arm; he took it off.

Liveol rose, shivering. He'd been in the dungeon for six months, not because his crime called for that heinous a punishment, but because the Ykenai had been hogging the gallows all winter.

"Back to the King's picture frame for you," said a guard, yanking the chains on his wrists.

"L-let's go out and get some sun," said Liveol. He stumbled away without a backward glance. He probably hadn't expected it to work anyhow.

"No need to damage him," Nimnestl called to the guard raising one foot for a kick. "Rabioson likes them fresh."

II

THE Royal Companions were about as still as they ever got, listening to the tale of Ostrogol. The girl sang it well, considering its length and range. Ostrogol learned everyone in the village burial mound was forced by a curse to fight forever. Only one sword would strike the undead and kill them so they could rest. Ostrogol set off to find the tomb of the ancient king who had owned the weapon.

"For you must know," she added, "that in those days, all great nobles were buried with swords to use in the world next when they emerged alone into the afterlife."

Conan was startled. "Even a king in this life would have to fend for himself?"

"For kings," Nurse told him, "exceptions are made."

Nimnestl could see Polijn making a mental note about this, but she went on with the song, down to Ostrogol's own death, so that he could be buried in the village mound and properly deliver the sword. He was himself, of course, condemned to wait forever inside the grave for future arrivals.

Conan's little company followed every twist and turn of the tale, as Ostrogol ran risk after risk in his quest, losing a hand, an eye, a foot. Carasta, Nimnestl noticed, was listening intently, too, and watching the King for every change of expression. The man was definitely angling for the vacancy among the King's High Minstrels.

In fact, only a very few people were paying any attention to the action out on the gallows. The low, hoarse voice of Polijn held them rapt. But not because of the tale of Ostrogol; they knew that. The story of Polijn was still fraught with suspense.

The King was edging toward ten; it was not too soon to start planning his sexual—well, education was not the word. Agenda, perhaps. Everyone in the court, certainly, had been vaguely auditioning future queens since he had succeeded to the throne at the age of one month.

The odds on Polijn had risen drastically in past months. Two other girls, in fact, had had their hair colored to match hers, and kept it brushed well back to imitate her rather high forehead. Plucking the forehead had come back into fashion.

As far as Nimnestl could tell, Polijn aimed no higher than her current position: storyteller to the King. But the girl might well have plans that weren't obvious on the surface. She had been found after hours in the King's company. This was no doubt at the King's conniving, not hers, but it made for talk. Like Merklin, she had been honored with a robe of the same design as one of the King's. Like Merklin, she had sense enough not to wear it, but everyone knew. And now there was the business of apportioning the cookie.

Nimnestl could see Conan had meant nothing by it. Her concern of the moment was how to explain it away in terms the court would understand. Antlers were things the stag could drop; it could have been a subtle message to Merklin and Polijn not to get too comfortable in his good will. Would anyone believe it?

She looked around speculatively, and met the eyes of Raiprez, who had just raised those gleaming orbs from Polijn, herself. Raiprez looked quickly away, and began a conversation with Kodva. Ferrapec's wife had brains; so had his mother. And both had shown an interest in Polijn throughout the spring. Nimnestl wondered why. The general wanted the girl, but the women would need some goal more farsighted.

Could Polijn be the third conspirator? Ferrapec might be no more than a blind, someone for the authorities to catch, with Umian and Kodva really running things. Raiprez would be in

on it, to keep her husband in line, and Polijn would represent
a direct line to the King.

Nimnestl shook her head. Ferrapec and Umian would more
likely use the girl as their trigger. The silver panther might
be the occasion. A recent award, established by the King's
uncle, Conan II, it was awarded every year in North Malbeth
to some particularly valuable courtier. Because there was no
great weight of honor or tradition attached to it, the King was
allowed to give it pretty much where he wanted. The Master
of Horse had received it, each of the three High Minstrels
had one, and it had gone to Nurse and Nimnestl in turn. The
likelihood that either Merklin or Polijn would get it this year
was the subject of much gossip. Either recipient, but particularly Polijn, would be just the sort of thing Umian needed. A
Swamp girl, with a background none too clean or civilized, to
receive the silver panther? Would marriage to the little nobody
be next? Surely, all who valued the King's reputation would
join with us to overthrow. . . . And so forth.

The King had to marry somebody, though, she supposed. Her
eyes came back to Polijn. Below, Liveol was being marched to
the platform.

It wouldn't do. The face was hard, forlorn—not like
Tusenga's whelp, who wept a bit and made puppy eyes
when she wanted something—a face that had been hurt. It
was a face one could pity, and know that pity would be thrust
away. There was strength there, too, perhaps more than the
owner knew. The face said its owner had survived much, and
was prepared to survive worse.

All this was laudable, but not in Conan's Queen. Now was
too soon to be sure, but Nimnestl had a feeling he would grow
into an amiable but not terrifically aggressive monarch. He
did not need a survivor, but a well-fed worshipper, someone
who by her very uselessness would inspire self-confidence. A
round, stupid girl with yellow hair would do very well, she
thought. She would prefer a local candidate—a new Queen
would have enough trouble without being an outsider—though
she did not mention this to foreign ambassadors.

Her gaze fell on two dozen possibilities before she even
turned her head. Anyone without powerful enemies would
do. Royal blood was considered so exalted that nothing could

enhance or degrade it; the people would not complain whether their King married peasant, noble, or even someone from the Swamp. The opposition to Polijn would come not because of her birthplace but because she was an unknown quantity, not identified with any party at court.

She might be part of Laisida's party now, of course, but Nimnestl doubted the minstrel would promote her candidacy. The King's Minstrels seldom promoted anything but their own aggrandizement. And his wife would be sure that any future Queens he suggested would be their own daughters.

She looked over Berdais's brood with some distaste. Aperiole and Ysela were among those who were trying to fill the vacancy left by the late Lady Hopoli. More popularly known as Hopoli Feetintheair, her lips were always moist and one suspected it didn't stop there. Her popularity and her access to King and Regent had been immense, and they were trying to copy that by copying her habits. They were trying too hard. For Hopoli, power had always been a mere byproduct. She had achieved her popularity because she not only looked as if she could give her partner a good time, but as if she'd enjoy it herself. The cheerful little squirrel had even been granted access to the Regent's Chambers, a privilege Kaftus generally denied even his lovers.

It was not the way Nimnestl would have chosen to gain power, had she not found the Chief Bodyguard's position open when she was exiled from Reangle. She would probably now be part of some camp of bandits, being chased through the mountains by the same soldiers she now intimidated.

She thought suddenly of Torsun. She had interviewed an exile from Reangle who had applied for a place in the Royal Bodyguard. He had been in on the invasion of Koanta, and told of how Torsun, after that final slaughter, had been escorted to the dungeons. He stumbled; thinking it was a trick, the soldiers put eight arrows in him. Had they known Torsun, they'd have known better, but it was an entirely suitable way for him to have died.

Nimnestl did not regret Torsun. Or, rather, she did, but not for himself. The man had never been worth a nail for much of anything. But he was her first, the love of her youth, and when he was taken, so was her youth.

"Can't we do something about people in the dungeon?"

Nimnestl looked to the platform to see what had brought this on. But it was not the arrival of Liveol before the block that worried the King; it was the arrival of Polijn at that point in the story where Ostrogol was locked away in a tomblike cell. The King was not so wrapped up in the song as to forget that he was the owner of several dungeons, and that people had been placed there in his name.

Before Nimnestl could answer, Nurse snapped, "They're there for their crimes. If they deserved your pity, they wouldn't have been put in the dungeons in the first place."

The King's shoulders went up, and he said no more about it. Merklin was brave enough to point out, "Ostrogol was put in a dungeon by King Valain, and Ostrogol was good."

"Of course," Polijn put in, "King Valain was an unworthy person, and not to be trusted. If he were here now, he would be the one put in the dungeon."

"And serve him right," said Merklin.

The song went on, and Liveol was spread on the block. Someone near the platform reached up to offer him some kind of pie, or tart, as a joke. He snatched it up and hurled it into the crowd, just missing his former mistress and splattering whatever was under that crust across his erstwhile assistant. Nimnestl looked around to see if that was the signal for a rescue attempt. But no one followed up on it. Liveol had been a protégé of Tusenga, and Tusenga was gone now, in disgrace and unable to protect anyone.

The Bodyguard's eyes went to Nurse, who sat in righteousness, glowering at Polijn for bringing up a subject which troubled the King. Nurse might need protection one day. She could not be brought to remember that the boy was a King, and would be King long after he had ceased to be a boy. If at some time in the future he was tempted by Merklin or the others to try his power by humiliating Nurse, who was to say how far he would go?

Worse, he might never be tempted that way, but meekly submit to Nurse's commands until she died. That would not add credit to his name. Today the King was honored because of what he was. One day he would have to be honored because of what he did.

Liveol was having his lungs slipped out through openings in his back. The Royal Companions were weeping a bit at the travails of Ostrogol, trying one-handed to escape from his cell. Well, it was something.

The King's hands were straying toward the ornamental daggers he wore. It was his ambition to do something venturesome, something noble. Merklin had similar ambitions, though he would probably prefer to do something exciting, and have it turn out to be noble. Merklin had been at the King's side ever since the Royal Tutor had begun giving Conan lessons. Haeve had picked the boy, apparently at random but really after long consultation with the Regent and the Bodyguard. He then informed the King that, having reached the age of learning, His Majesty was too old to be punished.

"We have to make a King of you," Haeve had said. "And Kings are not to be whipped. This lump will take Your Majesty's whippings."

Conan had been inclined to treat the whole thing as great fun until that first whipping, when he discovered the Tutor had been serious: one of his friends was to be whipped for something he had done. He was not escaping punishment through his own cleverness; everyone knew he'd taken the moldy cheese and rubbed it into the tapestry. But someone else was to be whipped all the same.

The King had finally leaped at the Tutor, screaming, "Hit ME! I did it!"

"I can't do that," Haeve had told him, pushing His Majesty away with one foot. "You're the King."

He'd taken it all very much to heart. That lesson, that he had many opportunities to cause pain to innocent people, was one of the few things Haeve taught him that he had never had to have repeated. All the more reason for him not to be harnessed to a clever wife, who might take advantage of his good nature.

Nimnestl was considering the possibilities of Berdais's younger progeny when her eyes were brought back to Malamort. The Royal Iceman was in charge of summer desserts, as well as the Royal Morgue, and was serving in his preferred capacity now, ordering the placing of a large bowl of ice, in which sat a smaller bowl of flavored ices. Only the Taster benefited from this; no one else could taste the cold delicacy until the King did, and His Majesty was intent on Ostrogol, moving out of the dungeon. Malamort stood back to watch his presentation melt.

"Whee!" someone squealed. "Delish!" Nimnestl hunched her own shoulders a bit as the ruler of the pixies sped into view, stopped above the ices, grabbed her own toes, and dropped straight down into the raspberry.

Fortunately, most of Chicken-and-Dumplings's kingdom had flown to North Malbeth already, leaving behind only a half dozen or so as a rear guard. These joined their queen in the ice, picking up bits with fingers and toes and so on and flying up to spread them to less favored members of the audience. Sticky handprints and kissprints started to appear on people like Forokell, Lord Garanem, and Colonel Umian; pixies had an unerring ability to discern who was most concerned with personal dignity.

Retainers batted at the pixies with fans. This diverted the attention, and sticky embraces, of the pixies to the retainers, but that was all right, quite part of a retainer's job. Every handprint now could be cashed in for good will later.

No one was bothering to brush pixies away from Yslemucherys. First Minister, the man in charge of all foreign and domestic policy, he was theoretically one of the most powerful men in the realm. But in the days of Queen Aleia, the office had been deprived of many of its functions. And the queen had decreed that a First Minister's administration would end after five years; end permanently, too, on a silver block and with a red axe.

Death five years deferred still meant five years of life, and some First Ministers, considering that the office still had powers and salary left, had done very well for themselves. Yslemucherys, however, had been such a nonentity prior to his appointment that he had never learned to do very well for himself. Style counted as much as title here, and he was thus accorded little deference, and no respect.

Yslemucherys swung at a pixy himself, missed, and struck the naked captive Veldres had brought along for personal amusement. The blow landed low on the rib cage: not very hard, but she wasn't expecting it. She gasped, and tried to lower her hands.

Nimnestl could see the indecision in the First Minister's eyes. Was someone in his position supposed to apologize to a mere merchant? Did one apologize at all for hitting something that the merchant had bought simply for the purpose of hitting?

Veldres's host, General Torrix, tried to put him at ease. "Here, My Lord," he protested, his voice bluff and jovial, "you have the run of the Palace Royal. Go get your own."

Yslemucherys's dignity was too new for that. "I wouldn't want one!" he said, pulling himself stark upright. "That is . . . You are impertinent, sir!"

Someone sniffed. Colonel Umian's head could be seen turning away from the degrading spectacle. Torrix was too high in the Army to take "impertinent" from the First Minister if his subordinate was listening.

"My Lord's wife certainly considers me more pertinent than she considers My Lord," he informed Yslemucherys.

My Lord leaned in and hissed something Nimnestl didn't quite catch. Chicken-and-Dumplings rolled in a backward somersault, a sticky hand pressed to her forehead, crying, "With a dog that big?"

Veldres seemed to be enjoying himself. His captive looked worried. Various of Torrix's retinue were trying to catch his eye, indicating by their hands on their weapons, that they would gladly drag the man from the King's presence at first opportunity and gut him. (Gutting someone in the King's presence, without the King's command, was strictly forbidden.)

Ostrogol was nearly home. Nimnestl rose to stretch her legs.

"I do hope Your Majesty has not been upset by the behavior of these large ones," she said to Chicken-and-Dumplings, standing between Torrix and Yslemucherys as well as she could without coming into contact with the merchant's property, thin, young, and not likely to get much older.

"I know not how I can survive!" wailed the monarch of pixies, planting the soles of her feet square on her own head.

"They likely did not understand your attempt to enliven their day by starting a fight," the Bodyguard went on. "Really, though, it's warm for that kind of fun."

"All the more reason to ice them!" screeched a pixy cavalier named Tell-You-No-Lies, spraying cold water impartially on the whole group as he passed.

"For your parts," the Bodyguard went on, turning to the large ones, "I must thank Your Lordships for humoring the queen." She leaned in a bit to whisper, "One hates to force disappointment into such tiny minds."

"Ooh!" seethed Chicken-and-Dumplings. "You just watch where you sit down for the next two hundred years."

"I'll watch it for her," volunteered Porkribs, another passing pixy.

"Heh," said the First Minister. "One must have a mind to the happiness of all the inhabitants of our country." Torrix, less obedient, forced a laugh, but turned eyes on Nimnestl that showed suspicion that he was not being manipulated by the queen of pixies but by a taller woman.

Colonel Umian sniffed again. He could have done the Bodyguard no greater service. "It must be bad for the health," she said, "this moving from the drafty Council Chamber to the heat of the balcony and back so many times. I hope the colonel will not have caught a cold."

The general's eyes narrowed. His malice toward the government was of long standing, and could wait. The threat of Umian was more immediate, and hostility was best directed there first.

"It will be hot enough for him before the day is out," he promised.

"You do take such good care of all of us," purred Veldres. The merchant was very rich, and very civilized, so he was hung with rings and necklaces and thick fabric. He didn't seem to mind the heat; perhaps he saw it as augmenting his natural, and exceedingly well-bred, pallor.

"Now that your wisdom has sufficed to end the threat of the Brown Robes," he went on, "no doubt your wisdom will lead the Council in normalizing the markets once more."

By normalizing, of course, he meant adjusting them to his benefit. Basic foodstuffs were sold in the city at prices and levels decreed by Kaftus. This kept the merchants from manipulating supplies to create higher prices. Kaftus had no objection to higher prices, which meant higher profits and thus higher tax revenue, but he didn't trust them to exploit the people intelligently. Greed must lead to gouging, and a grumbling population. Kaftus wanted the population kept quiet.

"Why, the Brown Robe menace can hardly be called ended, when twelve are still missing, and up to any kind of devilment," she pointed out, falling back on a convenient, if absolutely unfounded, excuse.

"The Council may be unaware that the prices are much too high," Veldres went on, his tone declaring that, of course, none of this nonsense was the Bodyguard's fault. "We, living closer to our customers, would be better judges of how to keep them contented." He picked at a nutshell he had already emptied. "The city people are upset. There might be trouble in the Swamp tomorrow, and we might not be responsible for what happened."

That was a threat. He could be killed for it. Unfortunately, it was also true, and killing him would not change that. To even the most cynical of Rossacottans, the King was the sacred embodiment of the country, and the secular emissary of God, a divine ear one could appeal to and know one was heard. They would crowd around during the procession tomorrow, calling for cures, help for their love lives, and quick profits. A little pushing and shoving, paid for in advance by Veldres and his fellow merchants, could turn the procession into a massacre. Likely nothing would happen to the King, but dozens of other people would be killed. Six years ago, an irritated crowd had dedicated itself to killing the rich and, crying, "Kill every man with a horse!" had devastated large portions of the city.

Veldres, as if completely unaware of having said anything controversial, was running a finger down his captive, murmuring some of Iranen's tricks as if they were endearments.

"Perhaps you would not mind presenting your suggestions to the Council this afternoon." If nothing else, that would show him how hard it was to get anything approved. The general looked cheerful, too: as Veldres's host, he would get credit for this from the merchants of the city. And, the way he and his family overspent their clothing budgets, he needed credit.

"That would be excellent," said Veldres, "for all of us. Oh, My Lady, before you go, there is one more thing. Deverna!"

He glanced back to where a sleek black woman was in conversation with Fausca, one of Iraner's playthings/servants. Imidis was there, too; every word the two Diarrians said would be reported to Iranen.

"That's what can happen when two countrywomen get together, eh?" said the merchant, smiling up at the Bodyguard. Nimnestl did not smile back. As the woman came up next to Veldres, he went on, "I met Deverna on one of my trips to the northeast, working with a Diarrian caravan. I wondered if she might not find a place in your company."

Nimnestl raised her eyes to the woman's. She knew what Veldres had in mind. More than one person had gone to some trouble to import presentable young men from Reangle and Diarrio. When those failed to provide a shortcut to royal approval, it was perhaps inevitable, at least with someone like Veldres, to assume that there had been a mistake about the Bodyguard's preferences.

Deverna was muscular, sharp-eyed: a likely candidate for a place in the company. All other considerations to one side, though, did Veldres really think she'd buy meat of his cutting? Everyone knew about his "larders," how he kept women of all shapes and sizes in his employ in case he thought of some game that required a specific type.

The silence stretched; fear widened Deverna's eyes. Nimnestl's rejection would send her back to the larders, for a little while.

"Have her apply to Lord Kaftus," the Bodyguard said, and left them. Kaftus got first look at all applicants for the company, in case there was something he fancied. There hadn't been, so far, but it was a nice test of an applicant's courage.

Nimnestl reached up to wipe sweat from one side of her nose. The woman would probably be a terrible nuisance, until she could be convinced to abandon Veldres's plots and just be a bodyguard. Adimo was worse, of course, always rushing to press his qualifications any time a bodyguard was so much as bruised. At least this nuisance had some justification; in time there would have to be a Queen's Bodyguard, preferably female.

Ostrogol and Liveol had died by the time Nimnestl returned to the King's side. Mardith was supervising the distribution of sloppy ices to children tearfully telling Polijn it was the best song they'd heard in their lives.

"Let's have a cheery one now, shall we?" Nimnestl was not the only listener who cringed.

Arberth, one of the King's Scholars, was musically inclined but not musically talented. Even he was a bit startled by the chord that came from his little lap harp.

"I don't understand," he said, shaking it. "It's never been this far out of tune before."

"Cheer up," ordered the Regent. "Of course it has!"

Nimnestl took her seat. Rabioson gestured to his next selection.

III

"SO, in view of preparations already made, the route through the Swamp is the only one possible."

"No!" declared General Gensamar, throwing his hands flat on the table. "Absolutely not! Never!"

"And," Nimnestl went on, ignoring him, "since the city soldiers seem to be reluctant to venture into unfamiliar territory, we will need to have the procession led by someone who knows the Swamp: Polijn, just for example. Yes, a minstrel would be just the thing at the head of the company. And an escort of your brother's men, who are more accustomed to the threat of combat."

The redheaded general had to take a deep breath before he could even begin to answer. "It is a pity," he said, his eyes all but catching flame, "that prudence in a military man must ever be taken for cowardice. If the government is truly set on this foolhardy course, then it might at least refrain from insult. The soldiers of this city need not be humiliated by the setting of a squirrel from the Swamp at their head. In all the years . . ."

Nimnestl let him expound on the courage of his men, and their willingness to dare all dangers of the countryside. And, in the end, she would relent on the question of Polijn, as well as the escort of soldiers from his brother Tollamar's command. In the afterglow of that victory, it would take the general a little time to realize that he had somehow consented to the procession through the Swamp.

It was the old one-two: follow up on a controversial proposal with one so much worse that they would swallow the first in self-defense. Not that it always worked, but it was one way to pull on the tangled reins and make the Council move in the right direction.

Certainly no fewer than eighty people were crammed into the steamy Council Chamber. Under Kaftus, these meetings had become less a means of getting anything done than of allowing everyone to shout an opinion, so that when the Regent took action, he'd know who would be working against him. It was a matter of status to be invited to Council, however, so councillors brought aides and bodyguards, and sometimes the aides and bodyguards brought aides and bodyguards, so as to put on the best show possible. Hopeless boredom mingled with violent advocacy all around the room. Behind the bellowing Kaigrol, a servant began to juggle cheese buns. She was pretty good, too, but it was too hot to go on, so she ate them.

The chaos was only obvious to those trying to keep track of everyone up and down the massive table. Most of the councillors saw only their demands and the demands of their party, and the whole meeting could be defined in terms of winning or losing. Those trying to run the country, who had to keep track of the ups and downs, might get a bit seasick. Fortunately, by now Nimnestl knew most of these councillors, and their basic positions on almost any issue, and paid serious attention only if someone said something out of character. That person was the one who was up to some new agenda.

So she paid no attention to the Minister of Agriculture demanding that something be done about getting new boards in the King's Diving Tower, while his Underminister argued that the grass fires around North Malbeth had driven the price of timber too high. Nimnestl wondered who had passed them that information. The Ministry of Agriculture actually had nothing to do with agriculture beyond making sure farmers paid taxes. Farther down the table, the Manager of Lanterns was demanding loudly that the grilles on the third floor palace windows be replaced.

"I think I deserve some thanks for not accusing you of being bribed to say so," Morafor broke in, on his left. "If I suggested such a thing, it would get around, since there is really no other reasonable explanation for your conduct."

At the far end of the table, Kaftus was conducting an argument on several fronts, claiming that all he wanted to do was see that the next day's agenda was positively set. As a matter of fact, the agenda had been settled for weeks; what Kaftus really wanted was for the Council to think it had set the agenda and put it over on him. And he was willing to talk until past dark to get that.

"People in the Swamp are born with rocks in their hands; anything will set them off," rumbled General Kaigrol. He raised a thumb and then a forefinger. "They've got that Decency Committee roaming around. And anybody who doesn't want this university to go there will arrange troubles for us as well."

"To be sure," said Yslemucherys, "we have good, strong coaches for the King's use." Yes, thought Nimnestl, and just try to keep the King in one.

"Our soldiers are certainly stalwart enough to face peasants with rocks," the Regent declared. "As for these decency people, they would hardly expect to find any among us."

There was a little laugh, and the remark about the soldiers had drawn some nods from people back in the crowd. But those up against the table knew you couldn't agree to something the Regent said simply because it was reasonable. Kaigrol started anew. Nimnestl wiped her forehead. This trip to North Malbeth would disrupt the workings of government for more than a week. This was by no means a bad thing.

The Decency Committee was a loosely knit organization that prowled the Swamp, looking for young women imprudent enough to wear controversial undergarments, and tearing away said garments to restore the women to traditional decency. Umian denied any connection with his movement but it could not be denied that the little band of opportunists had certainly been inspired by his demands for purity among the people.

Nimnestl looked around for the colonel. He had lost his seat at the table to his superior, General Torrix, but the general had not been able to shut him out entirely. Umian was sitting in the second rank back, discussing doctrine with Robinuon, Aizon's great-grandson and head of the Royal Academy.

"All right," said the Academician, a bright-eyed scholar whose beard was as tattered and grey as his numerous robes, "let's say that someone—call him Grufus—is a saint. You say, therefore, that his parents are saints and his children are saints. Why not his grandparents and grandchildren as well?"

"That is often the case," said Umian.

"And the great-grandchildren?"

"Frequently."

"Well, now, that's the problem." The Academician spread his hands out. "If you go on promiscuously extending this sanctity, you're eventually going to get down to someone you know personally."

Kaigrol's arguments were dwindling. Ferrapec was agreeing with them, for one thing, which displeased the Lord General. And his attention had been distracted by a side argument one of his aides was having with General Tollamar over the size of the force to be sent to Ricatini. The village had been taken over by a bandit who now refused to pay his percentage to the government.

"The Army," Tollamar was saying, "cannot afford to send so many to the village at this time. There is His Majesty's procession to be guarded, and both the Palace Royal and the Summer Palace will need a company until things are settled, while . . ."

"You want to let him grow, then, man, and fortify the town?" rumbled Kaigrol. "Overwhelm him with a large enough force and you'll be back before you know it!"

"Now, now," said the Regent, also glad of an excuse to turn away from Ferrapec. "Would you have him denude our borders? Why, the force needed to subdue this hoodlum might well take the entire Army!"

Tollamar rolled his eyes. Border officials were a bit more entertained by the Regent than their palace counterparts; they had an easier time ignoring him.

Kaigrol missed the irony completely. "And if it does?" demanded the old warhorse, confident that his subordinates could survive to bring him glory out of anything he sent them into. "Would that not be better for our honor than to let this nobody dictate our course?"

"Caution, My Lord General," replied the Regent. "Better to act with caution until we learn how this nobody has been so successful."

Kaigrol snapped his fingers. An aide came up, removed the general's outermost jacket, and passed it back to a lesser aide. Tollamar and Kaftus awaited the next sally while Ferrapec droned on, completely unaware that the battleground had shifted.

Nimnestl knew, and suspected Tollamar did too, that Kaftus wanted Ricatini retaken soon. In the past sanctuary had always been provided for foreign bandits, provided they paid up and behaved themselves. A century of political upheaval, however, had allowed too many to build up personal holdings, from which they had to be removed. The last, the Paryice, had been burnt out six years ago. No sense allowing any imitators to start that all over.

Further, this would draw off the more belligerent soldiers during a period of heat and turmoil, as well as many foreign ambassadors, who would want to report on how Rossacottan troops fought. It would be a sop to Kaigrol too, who had been bellowing for years that the Army should invade someone, anyone. But he would be more content not knowing the Regent favored it, too.

Nimnestl's attention came back to her end of the table, where Iranen, inevitably perhaps, had thrown her own influence in on the side of the Swamp procession. "It is the proper thing to do," she said, with a tight and not quite adorable little smile, "since our glorious University will be located there?"

The University location argument, which had fallen to a smoulder, flared up again in four places along the table at once. Iranen sat back to watch, as two slaveys fanned her and tried not to drip sweat on their betters.

"I will stand second to no one in my regard for Morquiesse!" cried Garanem, waving both hands at Playge, the Sorcerer for the Horses. "But his every word need not be considered law. All this rushing about is no more than a drain on the Treasury. Why, Housekeeping constantly outspends its budget even without these new branches . . ."

Forokell and Maitena sat up sharp. "All the more reason," Nimnestl put in, "to choose a good Fifth Chief Housekeeper to oversee the new branch."

Iranen's eyes sparkled; she winked at Nimnestl. She saw only a new argument, another chance for mayhem. In reality, the Chief Bodyguard had set a backfire, to keep the original from burning out of control. Everyone in on the discussion now had to work both sides: the University had to be kept small, secluded, so it did not become a power, UNLESS one's own friends or family found themselves in charge, in which case it had to have everything of the best. The Fifth Chief Housekeeper did not necessarily have to be a woman, but it was a likely choice, and everyone had a daughter or sister or aunt who could use an income.

Gensamar was arguing that a University would do no harm, set away in some nice little cottage in North Malbeth, when the Lord Treasurer broke in, "I can certainly understand why some people would have it so, but if they could but look beyond their personal benefit to that of the country, they might understand that, if it must exist, the University would cost less to set up, and offer fewer opportunities for fraud, if it were established in rooms right here." Avaricious himself, Garanem was determined (and able) to check the acquisitiveness of his colleagues. Besides, his daughter, Kielda, didn't like the north.

"The Palace would be the best place for the authorities to oversee the teachings," said Aizon of the Bat, with a shrug.

"An excellent point," said the First Minister. Aizon turned a long, slow gaze on Yslemucherys, but said nothing. There was no room in the Palace Royal for the University, and people like Aizon and Garanem knew it. That suggested site was a way to block the institution without seeming to oppose it.

"Less upheaval would result from placement in the city," Laisida put in, without any apparent interest. "And it would still be close enough for palace overseers to watch." It was the most sensible of the planned sites, but Laisida's wife was one of the top three candidates for Fifth Chief Housekeeper, with Meugloth and Seuvain. So anyone agreeing with the minstrel would seem to be supporting Berdais's candidacy.

"All other branches of Housekeeping, as is right, are centered in the Palace Royal," said Lady Maitena. "So should this fifth branch, and its Housekeeper should be someone familiar with the workings of our department." Nimnestl knew she meant Lady Chymola, who had been one of Maitena's spies in the retinue of a colleague until recently.

"Far more space in North Malbeth," said Aizon, folding his arms.

"There's plenty right here in Malbeth," General Torrix put in, setting one elbow on the table. "Especially in the west. Knock down some of those broken-up shacks in the Swamp and build your University there. You'll civilize the most savage part of the city." And, thought Nimnestl, give the general an excuse to go down there more often, as Umian was no doubt about to point out.

But Lady Forokell was in first, setting out in measured tones the reasons for location of the University in the Palace Royal. Colonel Umian, Nimnestl saw, was farther back from the table, arguing with Robinuon about giving the prayer of thanksgiving on arrival at the Summer Palace. Umian's cult, not certified by the Academy, was not at all eligible, but Robinuon let him talk. He was a sensible man, the Academician: too sensible, unfortunately, to ever venture any suggestions in Council.

"The benefit of having the University in the city are so obvious that I shudder to think of my temerity in pointing it out to your lordships," Veldres was saying. "But there is always the prospect of trouble from various elements associated with . . ."

"That can be countered, though," General Torrix put in. "Build it in the Swamp and you'll be pushing dozens of scoundrels out of town."

Nimnestl nodded. "There would be a certain cleansing effect," she said. Let them think the government had no set opinion yet.

"It would be so very lovely," Iranen agreed, clasping her hands. "And I have an idea! Since she is not to be leading the procession, we can name that child, Polijn, to be Fifth Chief Housekeeper. We can bring her up as we like, sure that she is not one of the Ykenai, and thus fit her for greater things."

She was enjoying herself far too much. A dozen voices, hitherto silent because of the heat and the conviction that nothing much was going to be decided today, were shocked into giving an opinion at once. Garanem, who put his financial considerations a distant second to the support of his ego, roared about the perfidy of all Housekeepers, the folly of a University, and the complete lack of respect shown the Treasury. "As for the insistence that the University's finances be controlled outside the . . ."

"Oh, Amànamin, not that again!" cried Haeve, throwing up his hands.

"If the matter seems stale, My Lord," said the Lord Treasurer, "it is because we have handled it so often and never disposed of it."

Well, everyone at this end of the table seemed to have something to play with. That had been Nimnestl's real assignment: keep people down here occupied and out of the way of Kaftus, who just now was grudgingly allowing Kaigrol to talk him into sending to Ricatini the troops Kaftus had decided on yesterday.

Ricatini was not on her mind as she turned to the window. That village lay to the south, and her mind was headed north, to the great black lake stretching into the wintry regions of the Lossuth. The lake was claimed by a number of countries, but Rossacotta was closest to it and, inasmuch as the Lossuth were too legendary to protest and other claimants could see no real benefit in owning the lake, there had never been any trouble over it.

This was a day for contemplating that cold land where the milestones were formed of unwary travellers frozen in midstep. The lake alone was too paltry to cool the imagination on a day like today.

Heat had permeated the discussion of the Fifth Chief Housekeeper. Proper names had been suggested, but improper ones had replaced them in the debate.

"I'd expect that from somebody who let his brother rot in the dungeon for two months."

"Why not a torturer? Saplace would keep discipline."

"Saplace is better at getting information out than putting it in."

"I think it should be somebody with children."

"Well, hold off on appointing somebody for ten months and I'll guarantee I'm eligible."

"That dungshovel? After what she called me when she was striped on the gallows last fall?"

"True, wasn't it?"

"That's the point."

"No, he'll be dead before the year's out, the way Colonel Umian talks."

"Colonel Umian likes to talk."

"What was that? You want Umian for it?"

"I suppose you'd prefer a foreigner, like that eyepatched feller from the south."

Nimnestl looked to see if Carasta was here. The minstrel was way in the back, chatting up Fiera with Karabari Banglebags. There were, despite her impressions of the debate, a lot of people taking no interest at all in the discussions at the table. They were drinking or serving drinks, fanning or being fanned, depending on their rank. It was an even relationship. The retainers protected their masters from underlings; the masters protected their retainers from overlings. They gave their lords consequence; their lords gave them identity. And, with time, the protectors and protected changed places, the apprentices eventually moving to seats at the table.

Fausca tiptoed around the table with a tray for Iranen. From the way she walked, Nimnestl could tell how sore she was, and where. Well, it wasn't a perfect relationship every time.

Peleama was also moving through the crowd, to sit next to one of her underlings, a son of Yslemucherys's predecessor as First Minister. He was little more than a boy, but he was an eligible bachelor since the death of his father, and Peleama needed a husband, though as Lady Maitena's chief assistant she had both status and a steady income. So when he slipped a hand under her as she sat down, she stiffened, but did not rise.

"Disgrace will suffice to punish the higher orders, but the lower understand only pain!"

Nimnestl turned slowly. Really, this was too much. The least Kaftus could have done was kept General Ferrapec down at his end of the table.

Finding himself outside the conversation at the Regent's end, though, and catching a hint of what was being discussed up here, the general was putting himself forward as a worthy

Fifth Chief Housekeeper. At the moment, he was expounding
to General Gensamar on memories of his one major military
engagement, a brief but bloody street war between guilds. This
was a year or two before Nimnestl's time, but she had heard
about it. Ferrapec had settled the matter by sending his soldiers
out to cripple most of the participants. Oldtimers said cotton
and woolen goods had never been the same since.

Janeftox was there, too, trying to put in a word here and
there for his master. People laughed at him in a tolerant way;
they knew he couldn't help it. Ferrapec was entitled to no such
consideration. Gensamar could not fire or demote Ferrapec, as
he was the son of a genuine war hero, but he could ignore him.
He turned his head sharply away, and apparently made some
kind of signal, for one of the men on his left came around to
murmur something to Ferrapec.

"Rules! Rules!" sputtered the general. "In my day, there
were fewer rules and a man could carve a place for himself. He
could start at the bottom and cut a road to the top. Nowadays
you have to start somewhere in the middle and you need
all this reading and writing just to stay there. In my day,
all you needed to learn was which end of the sword was
sharper."

He shouldered through the crowd to where Carasta now sat
with Isanten's son. The young man was in the forefront of a
group called the Order of the Sons of Thieves, another of those
movements demanding a return to the finer, simpler days of
yore. The group was popular among the younger generation,
who needed the outlet for energy, and supported by those of
the older generation who noted with alarm that the court was
growing younger around them.

Ferrapec was certainly one of these. His underchins were
growing and the original was receding. And, flattered by the
few followers who would still tell him he was the wisest man
in the Army and egged on by his family, he had conceived a
revolt.

Who was that third conspirator? Isanten's son was too young,
really, but he was ambitious. Veldres would be an amusing
third; what a trio: Umian, Ferrapec, and Veldres. Of course,
by his use of Ferrapec, Umian had shown he didn't care how
dirty his tools were.

They must be far from accomplishing anything, though, if Ferrapec still felt it was necessary to court Gensamar, and play for the Housekeeper opening. Or perhaps the general was just hedging his bets.

Janeftox was trying to follow his master through the crowd, which did not seem inclined to humor him. He bounced over somebody's outstretched leg and sprawled against the Council table. General Gensamar reached over and jabbed him viciously under the coattails.

Across from this vignette, Garanem and Haeve had just about reached the shoving point, aided and abetted by Orna and Colonel Kirasov, who had joined the discussion. The First Minister was watching them; Nimnestl saw a sly light slip into his eyes.

"There is no need to argue it all out in Council, My Lords," he said, leaning toward the disputants. "Why not set up an independent commission, of personnel from the Department of State so there need be no charges of self-interest, to organize an equitable system of financing the University?"

Haeve and Garanem both opened their mouths to tell him why not, but he went on, "Before that, of course, we must conduct a general inventory and audit of the Palace's assets, the better to know what we have to support the noble institution. There has been none since the days of Kata, of blessed memory, and no one will expect such a move just before the transfer to the Summer Palace."

The very audacity of the suggestion made Nimnestl gasp. "Yes," said the Regent, who had caught this somehow from his end of the table. "The Bodyguard is correct. The idea of a palace audit is utterly laughable." He laughed with his upper teeth.

"Well, now," said Kaigrol, fully prepared to take anything seriously if the Regent laughed at it, "this fellow—who is it? Yslemucherys? Lord Yslemucherys is a pretty clever fellow. Maybe we'd better give this some thought."

"Ridiculous, My Lord General!" The Regent frowned at him. "Lord Garanem cannot handle so much extra work at this time. It is ridiculous to even ask."

"One moment, My Lord!" called the Lord Treasurer from his end of the table. "Why not ask me and find out? It may well

be that Lord Yslemucherys knows what he is speaking of. The
First Minister is generally well informed on such matters."

"I should think anything the First Minister suggests should
be considered because of his position alone, of course," noted
General Torrix. "But if you combine it with his personal
wisdom, it becomes even more obvious that his suggestions
should be law."

Yslemucherys was stunned. He hadn't expected this; the
audit had been a ruse to get his commission passed. All
this acclaim meant nothing if it came alone. Garanem's gruff
"Don't worry, My Lord; the Treasury can handle the audit"
flustered rather than gratified him; he had planned on something smaller, that he could handle himself.

"I would not be surprised if this audit was the best suggestion to come before this Council this year," Torrix went on.
"You may count on my support, My Lord."

Yslemucherys looked confused. He thought he'd made up
the quarrel with Torrix.

Nimnestl sat back. The difficulties of a palace audit could
clearly be read in the accounts of the last one: "Coins secreted
in hidden corridors," "Jewels in secret safes." But Kaftus was
still opposing it, even louder and more fiercely, so he must
have some reason for wanting the Council to approve it, the
old rag rug.

Yslemucherys was looking frantically up and down the table
for some chance to turn back the stampede he'd started. She
doubted he'd find it.

IV

LORD Garanem all but crowed when Nimnestl excused herself from the Council Chamber, pleading other duties. He could see that he and his colleagues were wearing down the hated Regent's resistance to the practical and really quite clever suggestion of an audit.

Nimnestl had no particular desire to sit through this "victory," and Chief Bodyguards did have other duties. She moved out to the courtyard to check the bodyguards who would be inspecting the royal chairs to be placed in the royal carts tomorrow on the off chance that His Majesty could be convinced to sit in one. On the way back, there was a tussle between Venrod and Molliam to be broken up, and Molliam to be reprimanded for losing his badge. (Pawning it, most likely.) Nimnestl could think of no reason why she should not also run an unannounced check on all bodyguards assigned to loitering in the most common trouble areas, a chore which would make for the longest delay before she returned to the Council Chamber. It was something of a walk, on a day so steamy, but it didn't raise her temperature the way sitting in Council did. By the time she returned, they might have moved to some cooler topic.

When she arrived, she was cheered to find the Council dismissed for the day, and the Regent closeted with the envoy from Keastone. She waited while the shadows grew longer. Up to a point, Kaftus loved foreign diplomacy. It gave him a chance to do what he did best: drive people utterly mad.

But his patience was not inexhaustible, nor was the Keastone envoy known for brevity. Dealing with Keastonians was a prickly business anyhow. The Keastonian "emperor" called his country Atfalas, as if he ruled the entire continent. Outsiders referred to it as Keastone, or as other names less complimentary. For centuries, the emperors had kept up an imperial front, issuing orders to "vassal kings," telling them to do exactly what they had just done. So talking to a Keastonian official required not only diplomacy but a taste for charades. Kaftus had that, of course, but not on such a hot day.

So she strolled in. Both men looked around at her, irritation and relief mixed in equal portions on their faces.

They rose. "So, My Lord," said the envoy, "what shall I say to His Imperial Highness, to give him hope?"

The Regent lowered his upper eyelids halfway. "Say that for all the long minutes you wheezed on, I sat and listened."

The envoy's mouth dropped open. "But what of my message?"

Kaftus fluttered his fingers toward the door. "I have forgotten the beginning, didn't understand the middle, and didn't like the ending. Go away."

A steaming envoy added to the heat of the room for the few seconds it took him to reach the door. "I think you damaged his imperial dignity," Nimnestl noted.

"No more than you did by entering unannounced," he told her, with a toss of his head.

She helped herself to an apple from the bowlful on a black table. "In general, you're grateful for an interruption."

The emaciated Regent reached out and lifted the flame from a blue candle. "It is not the nature of the powerful to be consistent." He set this flame inside his left nostril and waved a hand at her as she stepped forward. "And he wears more and better perfume than you do." Nimnestl stepped back again. Kaftus took the flame from another candle for his right nostril. "What you should have done, Woman, is simply batter his head in. Then I could have killed you to satisfy the Keastonians and been free of the both of you."

Hearing the gasp, Nimnestl peeked around the door and saw the Keastonian envoy hustling down the hall. "You're always so bloodthirsty when you have two Council meetings in one day," she noted, pushing the door shut. "Why not take it out on them? I have several suggestions on where to start."

"That would be pleasant," sighed Kaftus. He shook his head after a moment's contemplation of the possibilities. "But the Council serves its purpose, and that purpose is marginally more important than my comfort." His eyes came to hers to remind her that this was why she was still alive, too.

The best way to deal with this sort of thing, Nimnestl had found, was to behave as if you didn't already know it was true. "At least," she said, her face very solemn above the apple, "you are freed of the trouble the Ykenai used to cause."

Kaftus stuck out his upper lip and breathed on his chin. "You missed your calling, Woman, when you failed to become a jester. Ykenai plots are as much of a nuisance as when the Ykenai were still alive; the fact that they are figments in no way makes the plots easier to deal with. And the answer to every accusation is that the Ykenai were behind it and now that they are crushed, we should have no similar problems. It's the Council's favorite course: throw the dead overboard, blame everything on them, and sail joyfully on to the Isles of Glory." He swept across the room to what Nimnestl had always hoped was just a statue of a giant rat with a saddle. "Every copper found missing in the audit will be entered on a page headed 'The Brown Robes' Fault' and the accounts will balance exactly."

Nimnestl studied her apple. "You did want the audit to be approved, I thought."

"The audit was inevitable; someone would have brought it up one day. And to have it now guarantees that the next inventory will take place long after my time; who would want to emulate Yslemucherys's folly?" The Regent sat back against the saddle and stretched his legs before him. "And think of the lovely vistas it opens to view: people trying to remember what they've stolen over the past ten years, and wondering whether anyone will miss it."

"A little added panic was what we needed at this time," said the Bodyguard, without any expression at all.

Kaftus cracked his thumb knuckles at her. "The timing could have been improved. But when the tablet is moving, you have to write quickly. This discharges a few old scores on the part of councillors who think they've put it across against my will, and, when the audit is a fiasco, they may remember that I opposed the idea, not that they will go so far as to mention that, of course."

Nimnestl sighed. "I shall warn the guards to prepare for another epidemic of crime."

He fluttered his fingers at her. "You needn't be girding your loins for that just yet, not that you ever use your loins for anything else. There will be no audit for months to come. First, a commission will be appointed to study the last general inventory. Then, unless a commission is appointed to find out what happened to the first commission, the commission that will oversee the actual audit will have to be named. You saw Garanem exclaiming that the Treasury could handle all the extra labor, that no one else need be bothered with it? And Gensamar's face as he thought of Garanem going through the Army's books?"

"Ah." Nimnestl's attention returned to her apple. "So we've really only given them a new toy to play with while they're in North Malbeth."

"It's a nice way to make them insecure without actually having to kill any of them," said the Regent, with a nod. "And not one of them in the Palace Royal to personally supervise the hiding of assets. It may keep them so busy that they'll leave the University alone until Haeve and Laisida get it set up the way they want it."

Now that was a mild surprise. "You don't want to kill them?"

He spread out his fingers. "Oh, I want to, of course. But from a practical standpoint, it does us no good to learn how to manipulate them, and then throw them away."

Nimnestl still had reservations about the audit, but, being practical herself, knew it was much too late to register any complaint. "Well, the fun has begun. Two of the chandlers were discussing how much of their costs could be hidden under the cost of the candles the King distributes tomorrow."

The Regent winced; he hated to be reminded he was going on parade. "The boy got that out of the Annals. I doubt very much that his ancestors handed out candles just before the hottest summer in decades, but it's a nice gesture. A reputation for generosity now will serve him better in the long run than actual generosity."

"You could hand out a few candles yourself," mused the Bodyguard. "Your cheerful smile as you passed them down would no doubt . . ."

"Do not be winsome, Woman," said the Regent, an immense sneer wrinkling his whole face. "I shall suggest to His Majesty that your own popularity would be enhanced if you walked along the cart and patted babies on the head." He tipped his head back. "It might be amusing, at that, to see who would trust you within a yard of their babies."

Nimnestl nodded, acknowledging the hit. "Perhaps we could leave things as they are," she suggested. "We remain in the background, dour and unpopular, scaring troublemakers. Unless you feel the New Guard can do that."

His upper lip drew back, exposing well-separated teeth. "They'd like to, lintik black insects. They're always slipping here and there like webless spiders. Would that we could fasten them permanently to a wall somewhere."

"I might come to see that. Will it be any time soon?" This was why Nimnestl bothered to check in with the Regent at least twice a day: to find out whether their position had changed while she was out.

Kaftus shook his head and was opening his mouth to speak when a large pink leg with red hair waving between the toes popped into view. Kaftus raised a hand to it and the leg vanished.

"Occupational hazard," he said. "Ignore him."

"Anyone I knew?"

"Unlikely." Kaftus reached out a hand to an empty tabletop and lifted a cup that had been somewhere inside it. "He's dead four centuries now. And still bears a grudge."

Nimnestl considered this as the necromancer drank. As he lowered the cup, she asked, "Will you ever die?"

Thin eyebrows went up. "The oldest man who ever lived died."

"And will your bones be used in spells as you use those of others?"

The Regent shrugged and set the cup back down. "Unless I take precautions they can't overcome. It's a test of strength to match oneself against mighty sorcerers now more or less dead. And even if one wins, one loses a bit, for the bones have their effect on the spells. One way or another, I will inspire little copies of myself for centuries to come."

Nimnestl did not answer. "I know," Kaftus said. "It appalls me, too. The copies could never match the brilliance of the original."

Nimnestl smiled. "Certainly not. Who could ever aspire to your sense of duty, your service to your country?"

Kaftus could create an exceedingly nasty smile when he wanted to. Nimnestl repressed a shudder. "Do you know, Woman, what I would do with you if you weren't more use to me out there?"

"Of course not. How could my pitiful brain hope to comprehend yours?"

"I'll take the words and ignore the sentiment behind them," said the Regent. "Service to my country. Faff! What was the woman doing? Or does any woman know what she's doing?"

"She knew you wouldn't let her son's government collapse," Nimnestl replied. "And you haven't. I'd say she knew what she was doing."

Kaftus's fingers rose into the air. "I shall have to think of something lovely to do to her bones when I retire." He took a green cloth from behind a cracked mirror and wiped his chin. "This job calls for all kinds of skills I had let fall dormant in my little green castle in the hills. Who'd have thought I'd need to know so much architecture, for example? Or cooking?" He snapped the green cloth at the bat that guarded his door. The bat blinked. "But I have to know all this trivia so I can control the experts who work for me."

He flung the cloth to the ground. It crawled away. "And what fun is there in all this power? I have not touched bone or corpse, except in the way of business, for three years. I have had to spend my time raising a King. I must build better than I am, instilling in him a thousand virtues I never had any use for. That's why I have you."

Nimnestl raised an eyebrow. "Yes," he went on, with a flourish of flashing fingers, "you are the repository of everything I never had much use for." He swept back across the room. "Ah, it's always the same: the sacrifice of a great mind in public office. I used to live by whim. If I didn't feel particularly sadistic one day, I could rest up. Now all my actions and sentiments are guided by public policy. That I get to set the policy is a minor consolation."

"We were discussing policy before we went astray," said Nimnestl, who had other things to do. "You still feel Umian and his New Guard are too important to be crushed?"

"Umian's not important," growled the Regent. "He's just dangerous. His New Guard has friends and relatives through all the merchant class and the Swampites. All they need is an incident to turn friendliness into hard purpose."

"That could be the third man's duty," said Nimnestl, stepping forward. "And they've been making noises about the murders."

Kaftus raised one hand before his face and held the other one out. "Do keep your distance. It will take more than a few killings to impress a Palace Royal audience."

Nimnestl shrugged. "Culghi thinks the murders have nothing to do with the plot. He feels it's a matter of werebears."

She'd known the Regent would like that. "Werebears!" he said, clapping his hands together. "Well! That makes more sense than anything I've heard in the Council Chamber for a week."

She inclined her head, and clasped her hands in mock supplication. "May I tell him you have the matter under consideration?"

"You do that," he replied. "Say that I am using all my spells against werebears."

"Do you have any?"

"No. And I shall use every one." Kaftus tipped his head back. "Perhaps I could locate a genuine werebear and deliver the Palace Royal from the danger. Then I could promote myself as the head of a mystery cult, and give Umian some competition."

"It's a role you were born to play," Nimnestl noted, without a great deal of enthusiasm.

The Regent crossed his thumbs. "It is an idea. The thought of competition might raise Umian to such a heat that he would have to be extinguished, without actually being hot enough to take light."

"Must we discuss heat?" Nimnestl demanded, wiping her forehead.

"Oh, you're right, of course," Kaftus replied. "Much too hot to go to the work of being worshipped. I suppose we'd better show some interest, though. Why not arrest a few of their supporters on the fringe, on some charges related to an audit we obviously haven't made? Such an obvious ruse would scare the moderates into dropping out, and provoke the real conspirators into something stupid."

"There's Lord Haunau, the new envoy from Lattin," suggested Nimnestl. "Lord Arlmorin has seen him speaking with Ferrapec several times, for no apparent reason."

"All the envoys are spying, of course," said the Regent. "The Council might be properly grateful, and the unarrested ambassadors might be a bit more discreet. But, really, Haunau is the best envoy Lattin has sent us yet. I think we can use him for other things."

"You trust him?" asked Nimnestl, wiping sweat from one side of her nose and then the other.

"Of course not," he told her. "Never trust a man who shaves his buttocks. But he is so completely inept, he can only have been sentenced to this job. What other reason could there be for his attraction to Ferrapec? Oh, I shall be sorry to lose the general when this comes to an end. Harness the skilled and you have something mighty, but harness the incompetent and you have something infinite."

"I'm not sure I can bear up under all this wisdom so late in the day," Nimnestl noted, looking toward the array of hourglasses on the Regent's shelves. "I'll need to be with the King before supper. The ratbird flies after."

Kaftus nodded. "Seitun will fly after him?"

"Yes."

"Let's hope he doesn't just migrate." Kaftus snapped his fingers and a little cloud of pixies swept into the room. Taking up positions around his head, they turned their backs to the Regent and began to fan him with their wings. This was one of the most impressive things Kaftus had ever done, in Nimnestl's opinion. She wouldn't have cared, or dared, to use pixies that way.

She started for the door. "By the way, Adimo's parents are waiting outside," she told him. "I wish you'd take care of your playthings when you're through with them."

Kaftus reached up to pinch a pixy who had giggled. "Perhaps I'll give him to you, Woman. He can't be entirely useless. There's Lady Iranen, of course, but she's waiting for a gift from Veldres."

One of Veldres's servants had fled his little fortress in the city. The merchant had promised a tidy reward to anyone who would return the refugee, not to him, but to Iranen. News of this would keep his remaining servants in his larders. Nimnestl had herself heard mothers warning children to go to sleep lest Lady Iranen come for them. And a certain husband and wife in the Palace Royal had been very diligent laborers since being implicated in an affair with Kaftus's lover of the moment. The Regent had dropped hints about how a married couple might be useful to Lady Iranen. Since the man had once been engaged to Iranen herself, it would have been something spectacular at that. (No one quite knew what had become of the former lover, and no one quite wanted to ask.)

Now Kaftus glanced at his timepieces. "Yes, go now. I have an important meeting with a Treasury official, and you would be in the way."

"The Sons of Thieves business? Someone took the bait?"

He nodded. "Korielar."

"Enjoy yourself." Nimnestl reached for the door and found a plump, sweating man with fist raised.

"Lord Korielar," said the Bodyguard, bowing to the Second Lord Treasurer.

"My Lady," gasped the treasurer. "My Lord. I . . ."

"Come in, My Lord," called the Regent. "I have two signed proclamations. One announces your honorable retirement with a high pension, and the other decrees a whipping and exile for high treason. Sit down and tell me which I can tear up."

Nimnestl closed the door, nodding to Adimo's clan. It might be a nice favor to Kaftus to send them on their way, but she didn't feel like doing any favors today. And it was wrong to deny them access to Regent or Council, she supposed; as long as they saw some chance to restore the family's importance, they wouldn't try anything drastic.

The halls were packed with bustling, sweating people. This was one of those days when Nimnestl yearned for the solitude of starving in the mountains. Every single one of those people had a few axes for her to grind. It had been like that since the day she came here: so many plots and counterplots in motion at once that no one could get anything of nationwide importance accomplished. Over the years, she and Kaftus had improved that somewhat. Of course, that meant that now the plotters had a better chance of accomplishing something nationwide, too.

"My Lady."

And this was very likely another one of them. Turning, she found herself looking into the twinkling eyes of Robinuon, the Academician.

"The Academy is prepared for tomorrow's procession, I trust?" she said.

The big eyes rolled up. "It will take us the rest of the day simply to bless everyone involved."

Robinuon was the head of the Academy, which in turn was the head of Rossacottan religion. A sect, admitted to the Academy, could do no wrong. A cult, outside the Academy's approval, could do no right. Any worshipper who belonged to an identifiable sect and produced some religious writing was eligible for employment within the Academy itself. It was a dead-end proposition, for these clergy could rise only so far. Still, since the Academy protected its members, they could fall only so far, too.

Under Robinuon, the Academy's criteria had veered toward good taste rather than dogma. Blood sacrifice, for example, had been declared "uncivilized" some years ago. Such doctrinal alterations were permissible so long as ancient ceremonies, like the blessing of the King's Company, were left unchanged.

"And I'm working on a saint's life just now, too," the Academician went on, matching the Bodyguard's long strides along the hall. "Viera of Sterdam; she died at six."

"Short book," Nimnestl noted.

"Oh, no," the Academician assured her. "I have several sermons to fit into the text."

Robinuon did, on occasion, chat with Nimnestl, primarily about saints' lives in libraries in Reangle, but since her grandfather's library had held precisely one, these conversations were rather limited. She wondered what he wanted. They had not yet decided, of course, whether the Academy qualified as entertainment, which would put it under the supervision of the new Fifth Chief Housekeeper, or skilled labor, which would leave it under Iranen. But Robinuon couldn't be worrying about that; he was such a staunch supporter of Haeve and the University, though Haeve dismissed the man as a book-worker. "He never looks at anything himself," said the Tutor. "He checks to see what was written about it in five or six books, and then decides what it's like."

The University would be very useful to Robinuon. Too many people had been trying to force the Academy to teach reading and writing, and Robinuon was more researcher than teacher. And he was looking forward to dumping his more troublesome clergy into the faculty.

"Have you heard about the threat to raid the Academy's library?" Robinuon said. "A sad shame it would be, after gathering all those lives, to have them dispersed."

"No," said Nimnestl, still striding along so as to show no surprise. "I hadn't heard."

"Neither has anyone else," noted the Academician, "save Colonel Umian. He feels his New Guard should become the official guardian of our books."

"I think I will know where to find any books that are stolen," Nimnestl noted.

"So do I." The Academician folded his hands behind his back. Very few people in the Palace Royal ever walked that way. "I did point out to him certain technical difficulties in his proposal, inasmuch as his cult of decency is still classified as heretical."

"He had an answer for that."

"He did, and he suggested further that it might not be up to me to change the classification."

The Academician sounded just a little concerned with this. Nimnestl slowed her pace. "You no doubt get such threats often."

"I do," Robinuon admitted, "but never before from a colonel. And Umian seems to have a definite space of time in mind. He suggested I make my decision before His Majesty reaches the Summer Palace. I wondered if there might be more behind this than just a colonel and some tall boys in black uniforms."

Nimnestl wondered the same thing. But she looked down her nose at the Academician as she came to a halt, and said, "Why, I believe I can reassure you, My Lord. We have the utmost faith in the colonel."

"Do you really? Why, then, I beg your pardon, and the colonel's as well." His eyes showed he understood. The Bodyguard understood his concern and would take action, but didn't care to say so. "I needn't have worried at all."

"Certainly not."

"I apologize, then, My Lady, for taking up your time." He stepped in closer and added, in an undertone, "May you never have such faith in me. I aspire to sainthood only; martyrdom is too grand for me."

"I will keep it in mind, My Lord," said the Bodyguard. They bowed solemnly to each other, and moved off in different directions.

V

IN his "Tale of the Nations," a learning song of Nimnestl's youth, Flooig of Dotog called Rossacotta "the land where all the sins of the Earth claim citizenship." But he went on to speak of its great wealth and to draw a not uncommon moral therefrom. In a land choked with gold and silver, rarity was a major consideration in assessing wealth (though gold and silver were hardly scorned). Hence the value laid on civilized behavior and hence, also, the great reverence shown to glasswork.

The Royal Antechamber was filled with glass objects so large or so small as to be of obvious worth. Vast mirrors stood between wall hangings, while delicate creations filled odd spaces around the room. Here glittered butterflies so delicate that they could not be seen at all if the light was wrong. There, under glass eagles with branches of candles in their beaks, sat crystal "Seeing Eggs." Glass panthers crouched everywhere, some in coats of gold, others with collars of emeralds.

The centerpiece of the room was a gold-framed slab of glass, horizontal on six glass legs. At this, three children played Eightcastles, a card game involving much throwing of cards and even more shrieking. The Brown Robes, represented by the deck of unused cards, were losing. Beyond that, Nimnestl found the progress of the game a little hard to follow.

"Is most yes!" cried Mardith, as Iúnartar threw down a deuce.

"Oh!" exclaimed Merklin, bouncing in his chair. "Somebody ought to break your fingers!"

She crossed her big eyes at him and snapped a red bandana across the table. "I hope they slice your unders off!"

"They can shoot you a hundred times through the small parts of your body!" answered the boy. The King, bouncing in his own chair, dropped three of his cards.

Orna, the Assistant Royal Tutor, reached down to hand them back. He sat on a chair with its back to the table, acting as referee. His own back moved from side to side, blocking some of the obscene hand gestures made at the table from the eyes of Nurse, who sat farther back, glowering up now and then from the nightshirt she was mending.

Farther back still sat Malaracha, strumming a ficdual unobtrusively, ready to come forward with a song or story if the card game palled. Otherwise, he was staying out of the path of the servants passing through, replenishing the tray of bedtime snacks and checking the beverage level in the silver pitcher that sat in the great basin of ice. Mardith perched above this, his eyes alert for any abnormality that might have eluded the Taster outside the door.

Counting in the servants waiting on the King's party, and the servants waiting in the next room to escort Iúnartar out at bedtime, about twenty people were busy here tonight. Nimnestl nodded. They had kept the crowd small in hopes of getting His Majesty to bed early. Kaftus was therefore holding court in the Council Chamber, drawing off most of the people who sat in here on crowded nights. For these informal convocations in the evening, the Regent invited all the people he especially loathed, and who returned the favor, but who could not afford to turn down the summons.

Lord Arlmorin was no doubt there, among the foreign envoys and ambassadors. Rossacotta had one of the largest standing armies on the continent; Arlmorin's job was to see that it remained standing, rather than marching. The Army, whether he knew it or not, was not likely to move; too many countries along the border were paying heavy bribes to keep it from marching through them en route to somewhere else. And too many countries along the border were waiting to rush in if the Army should move out.

Arlmorin kept busy nonetheless, trying to adjust the court at Rossacotta to his liking. This spring he had imported from Braut a young man named Dalquili, whom he was obviously promoting as Kaftus's next lover, dropping hints that Dalquili could be shared with Nimnestl. To Nimnestl's surprise, Kaftus was actually paying the young man some attention.

"You do know he's a creature of Arlmorin's?" she had asked once.

It had offended him. "I do, and I do Lord Arlmorin the justice of assuming he knows I do."

"The game entertains you?"

"Say at least that I knew what the game was before I began to play."

Kaftus's one real love, she suspected, was confounding people. For his other loves, she knew little enough and had no curiosity whatever; one of the first things he taught his lovers was the value of discretion. From what little she'd heard, the job was no more harrowing than being the dependent of anyone in the Palace Royal, barring a certain fickleness that was not unknown in other quarters either. The Regent was stingy with presents, but there were endless opportunities for extortion.

No doubt the Regent was busy bewildering everyone in the Council Chamber right now. She was better off here than there, though she couldn't stay.

"Don't be diculous!" snapped Mardith, swooping in to peck at Merklin's ear as the boy tried to slip a card from the discard pile.

Iúnartar squealed with laughter. Nimnestl winced. The girl had a shriek like that of a hungry ghost and a mouth that looked as if she'd been caught in the raspberry jam.

A woman bearing cookies jumped a little to one side. These were lesser servants, not so used to waiting on the King as their supervisors (who had also been pulled away to the Council Chamber) and had kept their eyes on Nimnestl, watching for any change of expression, the flare of a nostril or a quickening of breath. They saw the Bodyguard as a great dark menace at the door, poised to crush anyone who made the wrong move.

And so she was. But after doing this sort of thing nearly every night for almost a decade, Nimnestl was also at ease. Insofar as she had any secure place in the Palace Royal, this was it. Her death was certain, her tenure doubtful. Everyone at court was willing to remind her that she was a foreigner, an outsider. At any time, matters could go seriously wrong, and she would be a penniless exile once more. She knew all these things.

But on a night like this, she could not believe them.

Once, in a half-forgotten time when she was still a human being with a home, she had sat at a table like this—a less expensive one, to be sure—screaming at her cousins and brothers, while servants sitting farther back grinned or glowered. Once she had had a station that could not, she had thought, ever be shaken by time or politics.

Remembering those days did not occlude her vision of these days. A number of things were waiting to be done. Now might be a good time to slip away and do them, while the cardplayers were intent on their game.

One could not, however, simply walk out on the King. When the time came for a redeal, and Orna was gathering in the cards, Nimnestl rose and bowed toward the card table, saying, "Your Majesty, I should check the sentries on duty at the dungeon. Your Majesty agreed that the guard should be doubled, to insure against attempts to rescue the prisoners there while so many of us are engaged in Your Majesty's procession tomorrow. If Your Majesty will permit, I will do that now and return before the lights are out."

The King's eyes came up. Merklin and Iúnartar had stopped listening in the middle of the second sentence, but suspicion showed all over Conan's face. Drat the child. How did he always know?

"Where are you going?" he demanded.

"Just to the dungeons, Your Majesty," she replied. "I might check a few other sentry posts as well. But I won't go far."

He looked down at the cards being set before him. Nimnestl hoped it was a good hand, but his head came up and he said, "Maybe I could come and check them with you."

"Oh," said Iúnartar, before the Bodyguard could respond, "it's too hot to go anywhere. She can take it; she's so . . . so strong." She waved a bandana under her little nose.

Conan sucked in his cheeks, thinking. "But maybe I should . . ."

"You ought to be in bed," Nurse observed, cold eyes pinning the King to his chair as he sought to rise. "You are far too young to go tarryvaulting around the Palace Royal in any case, and particularly on the night before a day of hot work. All this bother has been far too much for you, you know; you're tired and irritable already."

Lintik take the woman through the ears, he was certainly irritable now, if he hadn't been before. As Nimnestl watched, the royal shoulders rose and the head came down, but the King still had the nerve to declare, "I never get to go anywhere!"

Nurse set down her needle. Nimnestl was younger, though, and quicker. "Hush!" admonished the Bodyguard. "The bears will hear you!"

"Bears?" demanded Iúnartar.

Gratitude flashed across the King's face. Whatever else he was, he was clever enough to know when Nurse was tired and irritable. A distraction that might kill the argument and win him another hour or so before bedtime was more important than arguing his case.

"What do you mean, bears?" he demanded. "What's a bear?" He knew what a bear was, of course; he'd heard all the stories a dozen times.

Nimnestl rose on her toes, her arms high above her; even Orna shrank back. "A great fur-covered animal of the forests," she said. "Big as a horse when it walks on all fours, it can rise on its hind two, and tear the very bark from the trees."

The King shivered and reached for a mug sitting on a gold and glass throne. Merklin swallowed hard.

Iúnartar tossed her head. "Ridiculous! I've never seen one."

"You've never been out of Malbeth," replied Merklin, leaning over to jab her in the side. Her palm smashed against his nose to push him back.

Before the war could escalate, Malaracha had pushed his head and shoulders between them, apparently so he could address the King. "It is true, Your Majesty," he said, raising his ficdual to block a jab from Merklin. "There is just such a creature in the tale of Degungian." And with no more introduction, he struck up the tale of "The Bear That Did Not Eat the Judge."

It was a composition of Laisida's; Malaracha was surer of the words than Polijn, though she did the bear's voice better. Nimnestl lingered just long enough to be sure everyone was intent on the story, winked at Mardith, and eased her way out of the room.

She could see Mardith would have liked to come along, but the bird, for a wonder, did not argue or make a fuss. They had all agreed that until the move north was accomplished, the King would always be accompanied by at least two of the people with whom Kaftus and Nimnestl were willing to trust the King's person: Haeve, Culghi, Bonti, Seitun, Nurse, Mardith, and themselves.

Nimnestl headed for the dungeons, though there had, in fact, been no decision to increase the guard. The dungeons, known popularly as the Grey Gallows, were so ancient and fearful that hardly a soul in the Palace Royal would go there without the likelihood of huge profit. The discovery of a demon's temple deep within the dungeons had changed that not at all: anybody who needed a rescue had to come up out of the cell first.

Even guards, who after dark were posted outside the door only, didn't like the place. Only two were supposed to be on duty. Nimnestl was briefly surprised to see three.

But the third was Gilphros, Kaigrol's newest son-in-law. He spent all his days proving his courage, to show he did not owe his promotions to family relations. He flouted all authorities, bullied his wife mercilessly, and was the first to volunteer for duty that was dangerous or painful.

It was Gilphros who demanded, "Who goes there?" but Nimnestl knew Koski and Stoven were the assigned sentries, being Treasury men. "The prisoner in Scorpion-Ox is to go to the Regent," she said.

They didn't even look at the signed order she brought out; Stoven was unlocking the door while Koski lit a torch. Gilphros whispered something loudly enough for her to hear it, but no one answered him, particularly not Koski or Stoven. What the Regent did of an evening for recreation was none of their business. Nimnestl was content to let them think what they liked. The man would probably not be seen around here again anyway, and the new rumor might amuse Kaftus.

Nimnestl moved down the cold, grey ramp. Faces came to cell windows with cries for help, but disappeared when they saw who it was. The Bodyguard moved on without a glance in their direction. Prisoners not undergoing questioning were seldom treated so very badly. Many guards believed in things that cried by night from the shadows, and which would come out to avenge any brutality visited upon an inmate.

The air was cool and, at this level, dry. These had been royal apartments in years gone by. Each cell bore above it a carven symbol of a panther, with two other creatures to indicate the dungeon level and level of the cell. Nimnestl moved down to that indicated by a scorpion and an ox.

She saw no one inside. Nimnestl was not immune to the terror of the dungeons, and breathed a little faster until she had the door open. Light revealed a shaggy man cowering in the space between his slab bed and the corner of what was once a royal lying-in chamber.

"Come," she commanded.

He crawled from the corner and rose to his knees, which showed through the rags he wore. For a moment, he seemed inclined to plead his case. Nimnestl had to tap her boot just once to bring him scrambling out to the corridor.

She was careful not to speak to him or touch him, all the way up and out, and along the outer halls. The prisoner had trouble keeping up with her, but her eye was on him, and she managed to stay just a few feet ahead without seeming to moderate her pace.

They had to take the long way around; there were too many places to hide in the courtyard if Diabies wanted to risk it. But they passed no one in particular, only a few scullery men and Enaking, still seething over the number of men who had been able to help him when he lost the key to his wife's chastity belt. He prowled the halls at night, picking fights in revenge, but was too bright to pick one with Nimnestl.

Nimnestl was content; those were enough witnesses who could pass the story along about the craven prisoner and the severe Bodyguard. Her actual purpose would not be guessed.

She did hope Diabies wouldn't die of fright before she got to it.

They passed down the stairs of the gatehouse and stood finally on the great drawbridge. Halfway across it, Nimnestl stopped and turned to face the prisoner. "Now," she said.

He dropped to his knees at once. His eyes flicked from her face to the gate at the far end of the drawbridge, and then to the dry moat.

"You will not try to jump," she informed him.

"No, My Lady," he agreed. "No, no, no."

"In a moment, you will rise and walk with me to the far gate."

"Y-yes, My Lady."

"Then I will kick you and you will go home."

He couldn't even stand on his knees for that, and sat down hard. "M-my Lady?"

Nimnestl did not like being My Ladied, but did not mention it. "You know how to reach your home from here without attracting attention from the night watches?"

In answer he fell forward, hugging her boots and sobbing brief phrases about his gratitude and his wife.

That he had a wife was all they had been able to find out about him. On almost every other topic, Diabies had been forthcoming, once given a peek at the questioning room. He had been given more than a peek, eventually, but had revealed nothing about his wife. Spies in the Swamp had discovered no more; people were unwilling or unable to remember any Diabies or his wife.

"You have been very stubborn, you know," said Nimnestl, trying to keep the shudders out of her voice.

At least he stopped caressing her boots. His head turned up. "They'd have . . . hurt her. They would."

"Who? Your employers?" He started to rub his face on her boots again, and she stopped him with, "We mean your wife no harm."

"They do." He rose to his haunches, his head turned first toward the one end of the drawbridge and then to the other. His face came up to hers, entreaty in every line. But even within sight of freedom, even if she marched him back to his cell, he was determined to hang onto that one secret.

Nimnestl had seen the beggar divest himself of so many layers of dignity that she intended to leave him one. "But His Majesty, unlike his servants, is inclined to be merciful." (Conan was not, in fact, aware of the man's existence.) "So up with you now, and do not disgust me any more than you have already."

"My Lady . . ." He was headed down for her boots again.

"Up."

He rose, but didn't know where to go until she pointed to the far end of the drawbridge. With a sob, he stumbled forward.

The kick was real, so the guard on duty would hear it, but not enough to cripple the man. Nimnestl watched him go, a shadow rushing to join the bigger shadow of the old city. Diabies was moving so fast he couldn't have noticed the second shadow following him.

A faint aura of dusk still lingered at the west end of the city. The nights were growing shorter. But they were still dark enough to hide any amount of filthy business.

Morquiesse, the great painter and martyred hero behind the University of Malbeth, had been a Brown Robe, a traitor. Only a very few at the center of government knew this; it had been pieced together from many bits of evidence. But the first bit of evidence, starting them on the road to Morquiesse's death and a crisis the government barely survived, had been a piece of whispered gossip delivered to Nimnestl by Diabies. He hadn't seen; he was merely passing on something his wife had been paid to tell him.

All Diabies knew, or could say, was that the original informant was a friend of the Regency. This friend had been more trouble than any five known enemies. Kaftus and Nimnestl were exceedingly curious to know more about this friend, so as to take shelter in event of any further bursts of friendliness. So Seitun would follow Diabies for a few days, to discover whether Diabies and his wife received any reward, and whence the reward might come.

So far, all Diabies had had for his service was an uncomfortable dungeon stay. If it became necessary to eliminate his employer, Nimnestl thought, they would have to do something for the poor pawn. Find him another protector, if nothing else.

She started back for the King's Chambers, but again did not take the shortest way. She had to wash her hands first.

In the shadows within the gatehouse, a voice called, "Ma'am."

She had known someone was there, and her hand was already on her hammer. But no attack came from the darkness; only the voice.

"The general is upset. The colonel is not happy."

"The third?"

"Not known."

Nimnestl nodded. "What are they doing?"

"Talking. Arguing. Shouting."

"Let them continue to do so."

"It's dull listening."

"So much the better for us all." The Bodyguard moved on through the dark corridor.

CHAPTER THREE
Polijn

I

DAWN marked nothing in particular; the day had started early. Crowds from Malbeth had assembled at their end of the drawbridge in darkness, so as to be in on the parade from the outset. On the drill grounds, where they would not compete with the larger confusion in the main courtyard, the members of the King's Procession prepared for the grand show, bickering in a miasma of heat and horseflies over who took precedence over whom. A few pennyetke performers sang or juggled, hoping for cash and earning kicks instead. Servants scampered up and down the line with bowls and mugs, bellowed at from all directions and allowed just seconds to decide whether to obey their own masters or higher-ranking courtiers who didn't care who brought them breakfast. Mothers and daughters shrieked at each other about how many inches of spine could properly be shown.

Polijn let the eight of axes fall into the discard pile.

Aizon of the Bat passed up the line, scowling at having to waste his talents on so small an occasion. But Robinuon had him by one sleeve, and would by no means let him escape. Karabari hung back, obviously not fully awake. He stepped too close to Colonel Umian, who barked at him. Karabari's hand signal in reply brought giggles from two serving women. He winked at them, turning so the jewels on his robe glinted in the sunlight. The apprentice's jewels were said to be good luck to women but bad luck to men, particularly the husbands of the lucky women.

Everyone was gilded for this show, partly to impress the city folk, but more to impress the King, to let him know THEY trusted his choice of route, regardless of what traitors and critics might say. Dyveke, all in blue and gold, cried out, "Oh, Lord of Ten Thousand Horses!" just for the practice. Something in his delivery did not please him; he shook his head and hurried off, to be closer to Aizon when the Exorcist did the good work.

He nearly banged against Colonel Kirasov, leaning against a cart loaded with candles that bore the King's Seal. The colonel spared him a snarl, and went back to barking at those Treasury officers who would be staying behind during the parade. "Check anybody who demands admittance: anybody. Thanks to the First Minister, we've to guard against people smuggling things in as well."

He dashed the sweat from his face, nearly hitting one of his nephews. Eneste got out of the way in time, but Kirasov cursed him anyhow.

There'd been another murder in the night, to add to the confusion of the parade, the move, and the audit: Tagys, one of the parade drummers, so there could be no smoothing it over. Everyone's eyes were on everybody else.

Polijn was not happy herself, convinced that everyone's eyes were aimed at her. Such a fuss, just so the King could prove a point! And all these people eager to go gawk at those who lived in the Swamp! Polijn shifted on her seat, an upturned archery target. She had picked the spot out yesterday; from here she could watch them strap the big drums onto the horses, one on each side of the muscular Rossacottan warhorses with little ears and wide nostrils. What kind of arms did you have to have to beat one side and then the other all the day long?

She moved her right leg a little to the right, and then back. Now the seat seemed too exposed, but she could see no better place to sit. The drum horses were ready, but no one else was, so she was running the cards again. It passed the time and kept her arms moving so they didn't stick to her sides. Four threes fell into the discard in a row. She shifted her left leg to the left, and back.

A parade appearance necessitated a pile of clothes, more than Polijn had ever worn on a day like today. But they were all yellow and white: light and cool. Light colors, though, made her nervous. The light could shine through them, light to light. She wished lightning on Sielvia.

In piling on her own clothes, Sielvia had swiped those stolen panties of Maiaciara and tried them on. That was funny enough, but then she insisted Polijn try them. The humor of this exhausted, Polijn was just starting to remove them when Sielvia had slapped her hand away, allowing her white silk undertunic to come down over the stolen garment as Berdais stepped into the room.

Berdais shooed Polijn and all her daughters out early; it was Housekeeper training, Polijn supposed, to always be ready early. But there was certainly no chance in this crowd for Polijn to slip the underpants off and hide them somewhere. The best she could do was move some of her pins to the inside of her clothes, and pin the pants up. She shuddered at the thought of them slipping down during the King's Procession.

Sielvia had suggested she slip off to the garderobe and toss the contraband down a hole. It went against all Polijn's instincts to throw away anything usable, particularly something this expensive. Never having had much, she was reluctant to let anything go.

"Hoo hoo! Hoo hoo!"

Her hands dropped to her lap. But it was only noise, and not directed at her. There was no shortage of people creating noise.

"Make room! Make room!" came a call from the nearest palace door.

"It must certainly be made," Eneste replied, his uncle having departed, "for there is none left here."

But he dodged to the other side of the line when Iranen's canopy bearers escorted her into the yard. Each was smeared with a different color of obviously rancid oil, so stinging insects would take an interest in them rather than their mistress. Polijn felt it might not be so bad, in some ways, to be one of Iranen's slaveys. No one dared abuse you without her permission, so you had only one person to dread.

Dread was continued behind her, for Lord Kaftus now emerged from the Palace Royal, surrounded by the usual company of opportunists. She recognized Veldres among them, a merchant who, she knew from living in the Swamp, stopped at nothing to press an advantage. But she knew from living in the Palace Royal that the Regent was the wrong person to press.

The necromancer smiled at the merchant. "If there is any untoward noise during this procession," he said, "if anyone so much as burps out of order, we will flatten and burn your city." A wisp of smoke drifted from the Regent's collar. "And you, my friend, may be assured that I will find you and flatten you personally. So I think it had best be a point with you to be responsible, don't you?"

Veldres was nodding before the sentence was half done. "Certainly, My Lord, of course," he said. "I was only . . . I hope my words were not taken as . . ."

Kaftus didn't seem to be taking any further interest in the conversation. Veldres turned away with a furtive sneer.

"Here, man: more of that wine! Just a bit: no higher than the top of the cup!"

"Come here at once!"

Polijn watched Illefar waver, not sure whether to answer his commanding officer or his mother, who outranked the officer. Legnis the trumpeter passed around him, raising his trumpet to his lips just to make sure his mouth was warmed up.

Now a pair of women stepped from the palace, their hair pulled so far back they looked astonished. Their shoulders were bare, and their ornate overskirts were pinned up at their hips so there would be no chance of a stain or splash before the parade started. Spherical feathered hats bobbed on their heads.

Polijn wiped her mouth with the back of one hand. Pale, willow-hipped Kodva was the woman in front, with her grand-daughter just behind. Janeftox was attending them, a dagger drawn. Ferrapec's family was unpopular, and it was best to be careful when you were unpopular. The unpopular made easy targets, with murders to be answered for. The average murder in the Palace Royal didn't go unsolved for minutes, much less days. Somebody got hot and cooled things with a knife. Everyone knew where grudges lay; the culprit was known, and would pay a fine, or leave the palace for a while, or brazen it out. A well-done killing brought no shame; the only reason for concealment was a fear of vengeance by the victim's family or overlord.

But the dead in this case were all so low in rank as to be largely unavengeable. No one knew why the killer was being shy, unless it was that old demon Something Behind It. People walked very carefully when the unusual occurred, for fear of Something Behind It. They'd be happier if someone like Ferrapec could be accused of, and punished for, the murders.

Ferrapec's mother and daughter would not be here at all but for Jintabh. A hero who had, in his prime, been able to leap from the ground to the saddle and at the same time strike off the head of the servant holding the reins, he was to be fastened into a cart so he wouldn't tumble out, and displayed to the crowds. His wife would try to keep him awake but quiet, while his granddaughter rode along simply because most men felt that any public occasion that did not involve her was a mistake.

Maiaciara's attention was on smiling admirers in the crowd; Polijn kept her eyes on Kodva. The older woman's jaw was firm and her mouth, though attractive, was hard. Her eyes were half-closed, but she did not look at all sleepy. She looked formidable, and she looked irritated: one of Polijn's least favorite combinations.

The eyes met Polijn's, and opened. "Why, it is Polijn!" she noted. Maiaciara nodded, but was whispering to Janeftox.

They came on; Polijn had no choice but to rise. She set her cards down, discards facing actives so she could continue if she survived. Maiaciara could hardly help but see and recognize her own underpants. Polijn planted her feet and prepared to take the consequences.

But Kodva turned and said, "Go ahead, my dear, and accept Aizon's spells for us all. You go with my granddaughter, lest she lack for company."

Polijn watched the two move off, in case Maiaciara glanced back. Kodva, having dismissed them from her presence, dismissed them from her mind as well. "I hope the day finds you in good voice, child. So many people have told me how much they liked your performance of Ostrogol's tale."

Several people had said so to Polijn, too. They were really saying how they hoped Polijn liked them.

"Thank you, My Lady," said Polijn.

A tiny shadow appeared and vanished between the high arched eyebrows, as if Kodva had tasted cherries where she expected tomatoes, and then decided cherries would do. The eyes measured and weighed Polijn, but when no remark was made about undergarments, Polijn wondered what she was looking for. She wasn't the only one looking, either. Lord Arlmorin, the ambassador who had eyes and ears everywhere, stood nearby with his head tipped back as if he had just thought of something and was not listening in at all, at all. The pose would have been more convincing had not Iranen's chief of staff, Imidis, been standing in the same position on the other side of a cart of candles.

The men didn't see each other and Kodva couldn't see them. One thin, white hand went down to a pouch that hung at her hips, and brought out a lidless box just as long and wide as the hand.

"Girls are known to have sweet tooths," noted the older woman. "And this will be a long ride. No, take the box; it's all for you."

Polijn hesitated, her hand above the crystallized ginger. Laisida's cart would be packed with food—Berdais would have seen to that—and, in any case, she still had that lintik antler the King had given her. But the real reason she paused was that any gift of Kodva's might have conditions attached. Her mother told her, "Think twice before you give, three times before you take."

Polijn took the box. To refuse it was an insult, and that, on top of Ferrapec's humiliation yesterday, might add force to his revenge. Whereas accepting his mother's gift might offer a chance to forestall trouble.

She said only, "Thank you, My Lady." With Arlmorin and Imidis watching, she couldn't afford a word too much or a smile too long to someone so far out of favor.

Kodva's nose went up: surprised again, and a little offended. Polijn would have expected a clout on the head from anyone else, but Kodva was a frozen woman, even in this weather. Polijn caught an exotic scent, some perfume made of white flowers, she guessed, for no real reason.

"I was grieved to hear," the older woman said, her voice no evidence for grief, "that the general might have been guilty of an indiscretion that inconvenienced you yesterday."

Polijn was noncommittal. "I am sorry, My Lady, that you should have been grieved by it."

Kodva nodded. "If it is true, child, I make the general's apologies for him. If I didn't, what's a mother for?" What was intended as a maternal smile twisted her lips. "The general has been under much strain from the press of important business, and there are the usual money problems, most men being so sensitive in the pouch. When one reaches the general's level of responsibility, there is much to do, even if one is not afflicted with snake-bitten luck."

Polijn's face showed respectful attention. Behind it there was a mixture of surprise and boredom, mainly the latter. So Kodva had come only to pay compliments and forestall Polijn's revenge. The family couldn't afford to antagonize anyone at all; the only status it had left rested on Maiaciara's dimples and Jintabh's reputation. Polijn's attention began to wander; she listened to the crowd for any sign of Laisida's approach. It would also be nice to keep out of Iúnartar's way, if possible.

The Chief Bodyguard was marching out of the Palace Royal, accompanied by some of her men and Arberth, wringing his hands. "Don't let them consider my name for Fifth House-keeper," he implored. "Everyone thinks I could be useful to them there; and I'm NOT useful."

Massive and impassive, the Bodyguard strode on. Polijn doubted the woman had any intention of letting Arberth be installed as Fifth Housekeeper. Because the prince turned jester was correct: he was all but useless. The last person who had tried to use him was Aizon, the Royal Exorcist, who had long sought a legendary kettle, an artifact so potent that even the broken pieces could prolong a man's life, bring him treasure, and imprison all his enemies in glittering cages for all the world to see. Arberth came from Turin, where the kettle had last been heard of, so Aizon had hoped the jester could recall the treasure.

Arberth did know some stories, but such was his mind that he only sort of knew them, and rather mixed them up. By some miracle, his clues had led Aizon to a shard of the kettle, but his experiments had netted him exactly nothing. Either he needed a bigger piece, or more than one, or, most likely, Arberth had been wrong all along and this was just a fragment of some clay pot.

Kodva, meanwhile, had moved on into general compliments. "And such dark eyes, so like Maiaciara's, or His Majesty's! Does all your family have them?"

All Polijn's suspicions were on guard at once. "Some, My Lady." That might explain . . . no, if Ferrapec suspected she was any daughter of his, he'd be proclaiming it from the balconies.

Kodva's eyes were dark, and measuring. "It must be warm in the Lord Minstrel's rooms, with all those girls. Perhaps it might suit you to visit us some evening."

Was she really pandering for her son? Why not? Some of the stories about Kodva's past must be true, Polijn thought. If only one had wings like a pixy to fly away afterward, she might ask, like a pixy, if Kodva had really once stood out in this very drill yard as Jintabh shot off her clothes, garment by garment, with arrows that never went astray . . . accidentally.

"We are very busy . . ." Polijn began, and left it at that, since Kodva would naturally not be busy packing to go north.

The older woman was utterly nonchalant. "Not this evening, perhaps; you'll be overheated from the ride. Some other evening . . ."

"Evening," a voice intoned. "Dusk. You know when evening is nigh, Polijn? When small men cast long shadows, and night is coming."

Laisida's left crutch lashed out and caught a ratbird that had been fluttering up with a broken piece of candle. The scavenger hit a cart wheel and didn't move again.

"My Lord Minstrel," said Kodva, turning. "I was just listening to your so charming apprentice."

"She is charming," said the minstrel, condescending to approve the lady's taste. "But she should be listening to you, rather than the other way around. Lady Kodva can bring you much benefit, Polijn. Model yourself on her, and you shall reap the good of fresh air and exercise."

Someone who had been whipped on the gallows was said to have enjoyed fresh air and exercise. Polijn saw the hand coming at her and didn't dodge. To her surprise, Kodva merely stroked her cheek in parting.

"Yesssss," said the older woman. "Your elders, child, can tell you about the days before slander replaced wit. Have a pleasant trip."

Laisida watched her go, mock contrition mingling with a certain owliness in his expression. When he turned back to Polijn, only the owliness remained. "You have such an odd variety of friends."

Polijn rolled her eyes in an expression of helplessness. The minstrel snorted and turned his own eyes on Imidis, who remembered business elsewhere. Arlmorin simply bowed.

"If you are ready, Polijn, let us by all means get on with this." Polijn followed as Laisida turned away. His face was a bit redder than usual. Heat was no friend to the crutchbound. And the minstrel had been somewhat peeved ever since the King had requested Polijn's presence in the procession. Laisida was not one to share his audience, though Polijn felt she couldn't and knew she wouldn't take it away from him. Making a virtue of necessity, he had composed a two-part song that would explain, under cover of lauding, the King's purpose, outline the tradition behind that purpose, and assure the crowd that the King himself was so coming, if they had patience, like cool, glorious night after a long, hot day.

They were to ride in a cart very near the front of the parade; other minstrels would be sprinkled throughout the line behind them. Right now those other minstrels were clustered around Laisida's transport, in hopes of catching his eye or offering him a song of theirs.

The one who did catch his eye was Carasta, a foreigner. "Ah!" he cried. "My esteemed colleague! Are you going to delight us with a song, then?"

Polijn moved a little behind her master. The foreign minstrel might have only one eye, but she was sure that was looking through everything she was wearing. Carasta looked amused by the suggestion, but was too polite to admit this whole affair was beneath him.

Instead, he said, "Travel puts gravel in the voice, My Lord, as you might know. I must rest this delicate instrument for a . . ."

Trumpets blared the approach of the King, covering the rest of his sentence.

II

"NO, come on! It's easier in the Swamp. The merchandise sits still."

"I'm heading in. This place is as ugly as the sky can reach."

Not so, thought Polijn, slipping past them down the Street of the Spike; these shops only reached up two stories. For real ugliness, you had to see those ramshackle buildings down by the river. These were good, solid structures, built to last some sixty years before. The additions sometimes toppled into the street, but not the original buildings of oh-one.

She checked an alley before scuttling past it. No one was there but a few Swampers and Diabies, tugging on sleeves and whispering. If the beggar was here, then Iúnartar must have gotten the name of the man in the dungeons wrong. Polijn had worried; Diabies and his wife gave her floor space and hot beer that time the alungwe bit her, and she was too sick to make it home.

The thick, damp air was redolent of cabbage, a thing she hadn't smelled in months, and the fruit and meat pies sold along the parade route. She looked around for the vendors and spotted Lothirien, her hairdo jiggling as she fled with provocative little cries of horror. She stopped in a doorway and turned to flutter her lashes at the crowd.

137

The procession had split on reaching the western gate of the city, much of it returning to the Palace Royal via the road outside the city walls, while the Swampers, courtiers who enjoyed visiting the Swamp, retraced their steps. People who had marched with the solemn self-consciousness of those who know they are being watched with awe now became children at play, trying to catch up with those of their colleagues who had left the procession earlier on. People from Polijn's past mingled with those from her present in a somewhat bewildering blend: Torrix, Lothirien, Morafor, Pleuva, Karabari, Cithers. The only way to tell them apart was clothes: the Swampers were still hampered with layers of glory, while the Swampites had discarded neckclothes and hats, having no one to impress and being hot besides.

Well, there was partridge-shaped Ydoine, acting as an exception, wearing nothing but an eyepatch and a torn shift. She was one of the few people in the Palace Royal Iúnartar did not chatter endlessly about. Older than Iúnartar, she had attracted no patron when their mother died, and had had to go to work for Iranen. Swampites surrounded her, extending jelly-cakes, eager to find out how many of the stories they'd heard about the violent housekeeper were true.

Imidis watched from a fair distance as Ydoine leaned forward to bite into a jelly-cake without using her hands. Iranen's slaveys enjoyed life as completely as they could when their mistress was not around. (Iranen had not been invited to take part in this parade: she was no ornament to the crown, and the horses were afraid of her. She had sent Ydoine in her stead, first piercing the girl's ears, installing earrings weighing a good half pound each, and finding her a seat on the wagon with the wobbliest wheels.)

Swampers unimpressed by Iranen's playthings set off to find their own. You could do anything to anybody in the Swamp; the Swampites would do the same if positions of power were reversed. (Later, in the dark, they might be.) Order down here was kept only by local bullies who patrolled their turf and by the city watchmen, who were not taken seriously even by themselves. Something called the Decency Committee had recently begun to enforce moral standards, but this largely involved catching women who dared wear undergarments.

None of this explained Polijn's coming this way; entertainment was not her goal. She slipped along as quickly as she could, keeping to shadows where she found any, so as to reach the Yellow Dog before the first show. Torat would be peeved if harm came to someone who had been useful to the Yellow Dog, and since everyone knew better than to peeve Torat, she doubted she was in severe danger. But she might be difficult to recognize right away with all this yellow gauze, and her hair up in the clips Sielvia had lent her. "It's more civilized," Sielvia claimed. "It'll also keep all that hair off your neck. I wish you didn't have to go down there at all!"

Sielvia shuddered whenever the Swamp was mentioned, feeling that even to approach it was sure death. But Polijn knew what she was doing. Besides, this was summer, when the wilder residents headed out in search of less picked-over territory to infest, even venturing across the border to harvest Reangle or Cahoots. The rest were busy around bonfires, establishing a carnival air. It was their usual plan: let the visitors relax and enjoy themselves, and THEN loot them.

Swampers who knew their way around were heading for their favorite spots. Treasury officials tended to patronize the Rope and Irons, while Treasury guards preferred the Orange Cat. Adherents of Tollamar went to the Tall Man; followers of Gensamar sneered and went off instead to the Fallen Gown. A few grim souls were pushing into Tekel's pawnshop. A little early for that, Polijn thought, but perhaps they had spent all their money preparing for the trip north.

Coins clinked, copper ones by the sound of them. "There. Now don't tell me you're buying food and then buy diamonds instead."

She glanced back and saw Malaracha between stacks of branches at the curb, laughing at a tiny beggar to whom he had just given a few pennyetkes. He waved one hand as if chasing a bad smell, but Polijn caught the signal of greeting he made with his other hand. She responded in kind. They were to meet later at the Yellow Bottle. Laisida had returned to the Palace Royal; his former apprentice would escort the new one back. Malaracha had further orders, from his parents, to keep an eye on his brother and report. "He can watch these shows for hours," Malaracha had told her during the parade. "Come over there and we'll swap riddles until we get the three of us thrown out."

Polijn had promised, too, that she would be back in time to help Sielvia pack the family instruments, which job Berdais had assigned her. Sielvia knew the history of every instrument, and how to pack each just so. It sounded interesting.

This would not take long. Polijn wanted only to drop in and say goodbye to Glor, preferably in the presence of Torat and Karlikartis. Glor's position needed a bit of shoring. In exchange for a magic trinket Polijn had found, the Regent had remitted the taxes on the Yellow Dog. Polijn, allowing Karlikartis to believe this was the result of Polijn's clever scheming, instead of dumb luck, had gotten her mother promoted from performer to partner at the Yellow Dog. Glor had no administrative ability beyond a native talent for being nice to the help. Since Karlikartis's strategy involved keeping her employees terrified, Glor was not much use. Karlikartis's temper was unpredictable, as was that of her garottist sweetheart, but neither would harm Glor as long as they thought there was advantage yet to be had from Polijn.

So, on this hot, sticky, and altogether uncomfortable day, Polijn was going to go out of her way to visit the Yellow Dog, say farewell, and just drop the information that she would be out of the city for a few months, as she had to accompany the King to his Summer Palace. That should keep Glor comfortably employed until winter came on.

She turned off the street to slip up Chain Alley, named for the chains that could be strung there in the event of an invasion or armed revolt. At the far end, she could hear Othespins calling to other Swampers who had migrated this far, "See and hear! See and hear! An exhibition for the educated; a show for the sensitive and civilized! See and hear ladies more lovely than any on their side of the grave!"

"Which side is that?" hollered a man from the house next door.

Venedis was standing beside him on the little stage out front, her hands clasped at her throat, one tear painted on one cheek. Polijn snorted; Glor had never had to resort to painting them on.

The crowd here was smaller, less energetic: just Swampers lounging around, moving from house to house to decide whether there was anything new worth trying here.

"Last time I was here, I was looking for Lothirien. Heard Veldres got her."

"Not she. She'll have her thighs in the basket come Sepenère, and not before."

"What's the mouth on the price?"

Polijn paused to hear, but the second man didn't know. This fall was to have been Polijn's auction, too. Glor had spoken up in favor of one more year, but Ronar felt the expense of safeguarding Polijn's virginity was running too high.

Twice a year, at half a dozen gathering spots throughout the city, they were auctioned off with much ceremony and pageantry, especially at the fall auction, which was the larger of the two, since money in summer was a convenience but money in winter was a necessity. Some of the girls were bought for religious purposes, and not seen again; others were kept in stock by the rich and returned to the Swamp only after several weeks, or months. Polijn could remember names, prices, purchasers, and demeanor in the basket going back three years.

The auction was the dividing point in one's life, after all. One forfeited one's childhood work and protection. The price one brought, the purchaser's comments afterward: these set the amount and quality of your protection forever after, sometimes even who would be your protector and what would be charged for your use. A woman could overcome a bad debut, but it was very difficult.

The money was usually very good: one was expected to make back at least what had been paid for one's protection as a child. It had always been Polijn's ambition to break record prices. She was six before she learned that there were actually girls in the Swamp who didn't get to take the basket ride to the auction stage, girls in Malbeth who hadn't even heard of such a thing. She felt sorry for them, then; those girls had no romance in their lives at all. And, too, there was the money; they would obviously never have any.

Polijn had learned many things since then, one of which was the curious way money in the Swamp evaporated. When times were bad you starved because nobody had any money. When times were good you starved because everybody could afford better services than yours. Anyway, you never got any of the money you earned; it went to whichever protector you had.

Her virginity had been paid for by Ronar, who was just one of dozens of entrepreneurs who had kept the late Chordasp in business. Chordasp enforced the purity of his clients' dollymops by catching men who had threatened them, taking the culprits to as public a place as was handy, and ensuring that the offense could not be repeated by means of a simple operation he performed with his bare hands. Despite him, however, Polijn's older sister had been assaulted with such force that she later died, while Polijn had some close calls as well. Once she had been rescued only because while Lonfal was trying to drag her into an alley, Diveyn was trying to pull her into a doorway. This gave Chordasp time to intervene; he broke a few of Lonfal's bones and some of Diveyn's, and then bounced Polijn off a nearby wall a few times for allowing herself to get into such a situation.

That was this alley, come to think of it, Polijn recalled, stepping into the narrow passage on the other side of the street. But Chordasp had followed Diveyn and Lonfal into the next life, while Polijn had moved up into circles where such mass auctions need no longer be anticipated or feared. She moved a little faster. She had colleagues in her old circles who would cheerfully kill for these clothes to wear at auction.

The street where the Yellow Dog sat was still pretty quiet. Karlikartis's house had been patronized by a number of Brown Robes, and business had suffered in the aftermath of the investigation.

The Yellow Dog was a square, windowless fortress in which, it was said, one could witness displays of legendary depravity and, between shows, pay to examine for yourself the performers to be sure nothing had been faked. Polijn knew dozens of people who made civilized cries of distress when the house's name was mentioned, but, in fact, many of the horrors were expertly simulated, since the performers had to be around to do four shows daily, and nine on holidays. The worst that could really be said of the Yellow Dog was that it was ugly, filthy, filled with savage people, and stood in a bad neighborhood. And that could be said about any building in the whole city.

No line; Polijn wondered if a bunch of Swampers had left the parade early and come, moving Karlikartis to start the first show early. That didn't matter so much, now that Glor wasn't starring in the main act, but it did mean she would have to find them all in the auditorium, which would take longer.

She thumped at the door. Zhriacar could tell her where to look, and what kind of temper Karlikartis was in. The massive doorkeeper was her only friend, besides her mother, on the staff, and always willing to lend a hand, provided it wouldn't rile his employers.

He did not, however, answer. Polijn thumped again, and rattled the latch. The door swung open.

III

POLIJN peered into the darkness, her nose wrinkling. When Zhriacar had been drinking that green stuff Thergatis brewed, he liked his little jokes. But he usually couldn't afford the stuff, and he never drank this early in the day.

Shrugging, she stepped inside. No burly doorman waited to grab her. There was no doorman. Polijn shut the door herself.

The big front corridor was empty: no sign of breath or blood. Assorted rubbish littered the floor, but that could have been discarded months ago.

Polijn did not call out. You attracted attention to yourself only if you had something to sell. One hand went back to the latches and locks, but then she shook her head. She might have to use that door in a hurry any second now.

Floorboards moaned as she moved up the hall. He'd lit the torches, anyway; obviously the show was to go on as usual. Where was he, then? Everyone else might be in the aud, but Zhriacar would be stationed at the door. When he had to step out back, he had someone take his place, and he never left the door unlocked.

She knew the floorboards were not what she should be hearing. There should have been noise: if nothing else, the noise of Karlikartis or Torat rushing to confront an intruder.

Before her transformation in their eyes, Polijn had seldom
come so far into the Yellow Dog without hearing the crack of
the woman's whip, or the man's whispered reprimands. Her
throat contracted at the memory of that wire around it.

The interior of the house was known to her from Glor's
frequent tales of it. Perhaps everyone was up in the aud, with
the double-doored vestibule muffling their shouts. (Karlikartis
didn't like even the sound of the show to reach nonpayers
outside.) But the audience was in and out all during the show,
according to Glor; the four doors were never still.

Polijn paused at the door that led to backstage, but found it
locked. She was too early, then, or too late. She moved on.

Carven dogs looked down on her from the dark trim. Rumor
said Iranen and Karlikartis were partners, and surely they had
similar tastes. But this was no place for Iranen, who hated and
feared dogs. The sculpted dogs weren't shown doing anything;
they just looked. She wondered what this building had been,
before Karlikartis's day.

And she wondered where Karlikartis was. Had everyone
gone north, assuming Polijn would be there, assuming they
could do business in North Malbeth? But Karlikartis would
have rented this place out, then.

Capes and breeches had been tossed on the three steps
leading up to the aud; she kicked them out of the way, then
stooped and snatched up one of the rags. Polijn had been
in the Yellow Dog's auditorium just once, since Karlikartis
violently denied entrance to any relative of an employee. In
memory, the aud was the biggest, grandest room she'd ever
seen. Could it still be so big now, now that she'd been in
the Palace Royal? She pulled one door open, wedged the
ragged cloak under it to hold it, and moved to the next pair
of doors.

Memory was no cheat. Distantly, Polijn was aware that the
Palace Royal's great assembly rooms were much bigger. But
right now, the aud was vaster than Polijn needed. It was bright;
it blazed with torchlight. She could see every line of the high
stage and all the benches around it. Nothing was hiding here;
she saw mugs, some full, the white pots, the discarded clothes,
whips and chairs on stage. But here was nothing that was alive,
unless the flames in the torches could be living.

Polijn kicked at the cape that held the door open, and nearly stumbled on a pair of breeches. The doors of the aud shut behind her. She frowned at the long hall, and the front door at the end.

None of these clothes would be lying on the floor if Karlikartis were truly gone; someone would have known, and people would have come through and swept the place clean, no doubt the first time such a thing had occurred under Karlikartis's management, in looting it. To be sure, it was difficult to keep a place completely clean if you had the animals inside, but even for the Swamp, Karlikartis's . . .

The animals! Polijn had already passed the door, but hurried back now toward the aud, and took the little door to the right. If Karlikartis had left, she'd have taken . . .

Or maybe not. There they were when Polijn pushed open the stable door: three geese, two medium boars, seven dogs, and a small horse. They'd added a dog since Polijn had heard last.

The animals looked up expectantly, and Polijn, knowing what they did for a living, backed out of the room. Glor said they were perfectly darling, and no danger, but Glor WOULD say that. Anything that didn't kill you outright was perfectly okay. She used to sit back here and talk to them, even after she'd been moved out of their company to management.

Polijn set her back against the stable door, tapping an index finger on her front teeth as she thought. Karlikartis could have pulled out for the summer, gone somewhere else until the Brown Robe business was forgotten. The animals could have been just left; plenty of dogs in the world. Or she might have left someone to feed them: Glor, or Zhriacar.

She started back up to the main corridor. One thing Karlikartis would not have abandoned.

Her mind was still on the animals. If Karlikartis had gone, it would be wasteful to leave them to starve. Could she drive them somewhere and sell them? Fetch a buyer in here? Or get Malaracha and let him handle it?

She shook her head. Someone had lit the torches. Might be Karlikartis had taken everyone out to the Street of the Spike to drum up business, and Zhriacar had slipped away without permission to get a glimpse of the King. That wasn't like Zhriacar, though, no matter how devout a man he was. Only something serious would have drawn him from his door. Some Swamper, perhaps, who had slipped out of the procession with lots of friends, had paid a call on the Yellow Dog. Karlikartis had a bad habit of meddling in politics, looking for any advantage that would convince those above her to reach down and give her a hand up. Blackmail was not unknown to her, nor were attacks by the blackmailed.

Before she reached the main corridor, she turned off into a little hall, barely two feet wide, that formed a shortcut to the rear exit. More clothes were heaped here, as well as a white wig and a couple of bracelets. Polijn gave these a good kick; all this silence was wearing on her.

Just beyond this little hall, on this side of the door that led to the back alley: according to Glor, you had to lie on the floor, put your head and one arm into what seemed to be a rathole, and push up a jagged board to reach a big square box. Polijn took three looks behind her, four ahead, and flopped to her stomach before what she hoped was not just a rathole after all.

But the board she touched rose under her hand, and the chest was there. Karlikartis would never, never have left without her cashbox, not voluntarily.

Polijn started to come out of the hole, but then took hold of the handle nearest her. No harm in checking. The box was heavy, too; business had been better than she'd heard.

She sat back, but had to readjust her skirt and those lintik panties first. Then she looked right and left twice before raising the lid. Her face slid partway to her chest.

In the streets, Polijn had gained a working knowledge of the small coins of commerce, from the plow-faced pennyetke to the Diarrian zigil. Gold coins were out of her experience. But she needed no expert to tell her these were something special. Eight inches in diameter, an inch thick, and so heavy they could be nothing but gold, two great coins sat in the center of the box. The face of the one on top showed a woman riding in some kind of shallow boat, with ducks or something—mighty big ducks—in the water around her. Woman and ducks were looking at something above them in the sky; Polijn couldn't tell what it might be. There were words around the rim, but these were in such old letters, and mingled so promiscuously with the picture, that she couldn't read them.

No. Karlikartis would not have abandoned these. Polijn let the lid back down on the chest and pushed it into the hiding place again. Even if she did dare to touch something Karlikartis wanted, she wouldn't be able to get anything like this through the crowds outside.

She stood up. That left the back door. Once, the entire staff of the Yellow Dog had been seized by some kind of stomach disorder and spent a whole day out in the back alley. It had no doubt been an act of revenge; perhaps the original owner of those massive coins had them all writhing there again.

Between the rathole and the back door, Polijn stumbled on another stack of rags. Maybe this was Karlikartis's plan: no thief could escape without knowing where all the garbage was stacked. They'd trip and be strangled by Torat.

Her hand was on the door when it occurred to her that her foot had struck more than cloth. She turned to look, and then dropped to the floor again.

IV

POLIJN knew what dead bodies looked like in all their phases, from the moment of realization that it was all done to three years after that. She was not on her knees for the novelty of it.

The woman had been stabbed at least twice, that she could see, by someone who had twisted the knife well to be sure. And her hair was mussed. Glor hated that. Polijn reached out and smoothed a few locks back into place.

"Mother?" she said. Glor hated that, too.

Polijn looked up to the back door, to the little hall she'd just left, and to the larger corridor that led back to the aud. Her eyes hurt. Not Torat, no, not with a knife. Unless Karlikartis had suggested it to him, so he wouldn't be suspected if Polijn found out. Kind of cautious, for Karlikartis.

She shoved the body away with both hands, her teeth grinding down. Then, shaking her head, she reached out and pulled the body flat again. A sandal was loose; Polijn set it back on the right foot.

She rocked back on her haunches. What would become of the body, now? She peered at the wood around her, and the torch already lit.

She shook her head again. The torch bracket was shaped like a dog. Glor said the dogs were darling, and Polijn didn't

149

suppose she could get all the animals outside before the fire
caught.

Glor hadn't been dead long. Polijn stroked one cold, thin
cheek. She'd have had more to eat at the Palace. Polijn always
thought, once she had a truly secure spot in the Palace Royal,
she could realize Mokono's dream of bringing their mother
out of the Swamp. (Polijn did not know what Glor would
have DONE outside the Swamp; it was a question Mokono
had never addressed.)

Mokono. Mokono died so hard. This was quicker. Glor still
didn't look comfortable.

Polijn straightened her mother's little necklace. Mokono.
Glor. Then she was alone, now. Polijn stared at the ceiling.
There was Ronar; Ronar was sort of family because he'd
been there forever, since she was three. Polijn frowned. No
chance now of ever learning who their father was. Ronar's
constant refrain was how he had no idea what father could
have produced such useless, ungrateful brats.

She shrugged. Glor probably didn't know, either.

Laisida and those made a second family, but they could
discard her any time she became an embarrassment, or a
nuisance. She was a recent addition to their household, and
could be tumbled into the street again.

Tumbled into the street. Like poor, foolish Glor, the victim
of all she met. She never complained about the cold, or lack
of food; all she wanted was a little rest, which she never got.
Pity to wake her up now, Polijn supposed.

Polijn sat on the floor, and put a hand over her mother's. "Say, you'll never guess what I'm wearing. You always
said . . ."

No. A song? She shook her head again.

Her eyes fell on a heap of clothes farther up the corridor to
the aud. That was surely Karlikartis's hair on the floor. But
Karlikartis was not on the floor with it.

This was all very strange, and Glor herself had always said
what to do when things were strange. "Make sure it's wrong,
then go away."

Where WAS everyone? Where was anyone? Death was not
unknown in the Yellow Dog. Gloraida's murder wouldn't scare
everyone away, not unless . . . Well, it would depend on who'd

done it. She knew, at least, they hadn't run away for fear of her vengeance.

Polijn's face tightened. Well, somebody was going to be afraid of her vengeance. There had to be something she could do, or Laisida could do, or even the King could do.

"Hey! Hey!"

Polijn jumped to her feet. "Where is everybody?" the voice demanded.

Polijn scuttled into the little corridor she'd come through just as the door of the other hall opened and a rat-faced, red-haired man came through.

"Zhriacar!" he shouted. "How come you're telling everyone the place is shut?"

Ronar had put on weight. Naturally: Glor was making more money. He was not the person Polijn would have chosen to meet just now, or the person she'd have guessed would come so far into a building where something had so obviously gone wrong.

But curiosity, though hazardous, could be profitable. He was carrying Torat's strangling wire, a few necklaces, and what seemed to be a dried bat. A dozen bracelets were pushed up on one arm.

He shook his head as he knelt to take up Karlikartis's whip. Polijn knew what he meant. Whoever had done this seemed to have taken nothing but the bodies of people, surely the most common commodity in the Swamp.

She put a hand across her mouth. Those little piles of rags were one-person piles. Karlikartis's whip and wig were so close, and those were her clothes. Whatever had come to the Yellow Dog had taken the people right out of their belongings.

"Ah!" Ronar set everything down and went scuttling on all fours to the rathole. Glor would have told him, too. Polijn nodded when he gasped at the contents of the cashbox.

"A bag," he murmured. "Need a bag."

He looked around for something like a bag. "Glor!"

The knife wounds weren't exactly hidden. "Glor, what's the news?" Ronar went over to the body and nudged it with one foot. Then he knelt and put his arms around her.

Polijn reached back to the little heap of clothes she'd passed on her first time through. She had to look down to find the bracelets. Ronar, meanwhile, had unfastened Gloraida's earrings and was working on her necklace.

Ronar had gotten Glor the job at the Yellow Dog. Ronar had gotten Mokono that route that took her so far west, so she could wander into the path of that gang. Ronar had gotten every copper Glor, Mokono, and Polijn had earned for nine years.

That wasn't all he was going to get.

The first bracelet caught him in the right ear. He rose and looked around, as Polijn had been hoping, and the second hit the bridge of his nose, full on.

He was out the back door before she could release the third. She thought for a second of following him, to deliver it. But the sun was shining outside, and Ronar had no worse eyesight than anybody.

Better to just move out: get back to the Palace Royal and decide what to do next. Polijn stepped over for one last look at Glor. Ronar had dropped the necklace and earrings. She took them up and tucked them away with the third bracelet. There was one practical use for underpants, anyhow.

Ronar had the right idea. Something here might be of use. Polijn had no need for a garotte or a mummified bat, but she did stoop to pick up Karlikartis's wig. If she were spotted before she reached Malaracha, it would be better if people said, "Who's that?" instead of, "Why was Polijn in the Yellow Dog?"

She shook out the hair and positioned it on her head. "I wish you could see this," she said, kneeling to pat her mother's forehead. She rose and put a hand on the back door.

And was crushed against the wall as it slammed open.

V

SHE knew them, from the bully boys who had filled Chordasp's place down to Lothirien and some of the thieves and thumb boys who pulled her hair when her route crossed theirs. They had rocks and ropes and clubs and blades of all shapes, the daggers with the fashionable triangular blades, knives of cutdown swords, and the crude "farmer stickers."

Ronar probably hadn't meant to bring such a crowd into his gold mine, but he was, Polijn knew, incapable of fleeing quietly. Jampis had him by one shoulder, and shook him.

"All right, netmaker nut-taker, what was it?"

"Nobody's here . . . and everyone's gone . . . but something hit me and . . ."

Something else hit him and he went sprawling to the floor across the dead body.

"Glor's here, anyhow," Jampis said. "Where's the door-lover?"

"Hey, Zhriacar!" bellowed Lafgahon.

"Drop it!" Jampis ordered. Members of the crowd had spotted the booty lying all around them on the floor, and had begun to investigate. "It's all Mistress Karlikartis's." He raised his free hand to his throat as he looked around, and also raised his voice. "We sure mean no disrespect to anything of Mistress Karlikartis's, nor to Torat, neither."

153

"They're not here, I tell you!" Ronar called, slipping to the far side of Gloraida's body. "It's lintik magic!"

Jampis and Lafgahon rubbed their chins, while the others waited for them to hand down a decision. "Look!" ordered Ronar, throwing out one hand, "There's her cashbox, full!"

"You looked at it, nut-taker?" Lafgahon demanded.

"Why, I . . . well . . ." Ronar lifted his shoulders and put out his hands.

Jampis and Lafgahon nodded to each other. "That's it, then," Jampis announced. "If he looked and lived, there's some power here stronger than Karlikartis."

People who had been edging toward the cashbox stopped and thought that concept over. In a moment, they might start looking around for this power. Polijn knew she had just seconds to decide what to do about it.

She could, of course, just declare her identity, point out that she was known to the Regent, and stroll out. It would be exciting, at least. Her neighbors hated the Regent at the best of times, and would immediately connect the cadaverous necromancer with what was obviously a sorcerous occurrence. Blaming it on her, they would at the very least try to take her prisoner. This would naturally involve a search; once Maiaciara's underpants were seen, she'd lose any support from former colleagues in the crowd.

So a nice, anonymous escape was best. People were slipping out already, not wishing to face whatever power had claimed the violent mistress of the Yellow Dog. Somebody hollered on finding the dried bat; while people's eyes turned that way, she slipped from behind the door.

Even Ronar was looking the wrong way, and Polijn felt she had a chance as she slid to the body of her mother and started to step across. It was a long step, nearly a jump, and she couldn't think what was sliding along her leg until too late.

"Ow!"

The bracelet had hit Ronar right between the eyes, but Polijn felt less of a sense of accomplishment for this one. He stared up at her. "Hey!"

Polijn did pause. Surely a real minstrel could face down a crowd, glibly explaining her palace-made clothes and her presence in a building where the whole staff had disappeared, stolen out of their very wigs and shoes.

But she remembered she was only an apprentice minstrel. So she ran for it.

"Save yourselves!" she screamed, pushing out to the alley. "It's demons!" Two rocks landed to her left, and a knife to her right.

She heard, rather than saw, at least a dozen people following her; Ronar must have told them who she was. Breaking out into the street, she aimed herself toward the Yellow Bottle, and Malaracha, but forward progress was impossible. Bystanders, alerted by all the shouting, came together to cut her off; either they'd recognized her or just saw the size of the crowd after her and thought it might be profitable to join in.

She swerved to the west, keeping her head down, snatching up a few of the fallen rocks to toss back at her pursuers. She heard a pair of dogs barking.

Westward lay the Gilded Fly, and the Vielfrass; that perverse sorcerer seemed to have a kindness for her. But there were blocks and blocks of bad territory to cross to get there. Malaracha was closer, and more dependable. In either case, this crowd had to be lost first.

When Gloraida had taken the job at the Yellow Dog, she had investigated rather thoroughly the matter of escape routes, and had taught these to her daughters, just in case one of them had to contact her while at work and then get away from Karlikartis. Polijn twisted away from extended hands and plunged into the Iron Wolverine, the route clear in her mind: three steps down, watch your step at the bottom, nod to Nolga behind the bar, turn left, jump up and through the little half-door and you'd be in the next alley.

That was the obvious escape route. But Polijn figured the crowd knew that, too, so she turned right at the bottom, and out that door. This brought her right back to the alley she'd just come out of.

Too fast; much of the crowd was still back in the alley. And Ronar, naturally, was among them. "Hey, Polijn! Over here!"

Everybody knew who Polijn was; they all but climbed over each other to get at her. She swept along to the other end of the alley, swung left at the alley that joined it, and shouldered open the back door of the Flying Snake. The long dress snagged on a splinter; she tore it loose and ran for the stairs.

A house of assignation, the Flying Snake was loaded with emergency exits, some of which were known only to the staff. She spotted a few customers she knew, Swampers from the Palace Royal, but none of these was anyone she cared to trust. In any case, she knew only a handful of people who would even think of defending her against the mob cursing and trying to force itself through the door five or six abreast.

She reached the second floor and counted to the third window over. A short drop from the window brought her to a blackened support beam that kept the added bedrooms of the Flying Snake, as well as the front room of the Obese Cow across the street, from falling. It creaked as she landed; Glor hadn't mentioned any weight limit.

Polijn didn't like heights much. Unless you could fly, your options were very limited. Some of her pursuers had come around the Flying Snake and were tossing rocks from the street below. Others were crowding the window behind her, fortunately jostling each other too much for anyone to take careful aim. She gained the roof of the Obese Cow, cursing her palace slippers as they slid on the shingles.

A flight of irregular stairs led down the backside of the Obese Cow. Polijn felt these had their drawbacks. If she went down, the little alley would be filled with people by the time she got there. If she stayed where she was, she was a perfect target against the plastered wall.

The escape route allowed for such things; a window was waiting on the first floor of the Obese Cow. But they'd think of that. A better window was across the alley, if she could reach it. Glor's escape plans had never mentioned this window, so Polijn had no idea what waited behind it. Looked like rags. She used all the strength in her legs to make the leap.

They were rags: dozens of rags, in neatly composed heaps. It was a bit too tidy for a normal ragpicker's apartment, and, on looking up, Polijn saw that it couldn't be one.

Every imaginable edged weapon hung on the walls around her: swords of all shapes and lengths, war hammers, daggers, axes. She could hold them off at the window, maybe, if they thought to look in here for her. More likely not. Polijn had naturally used a few knives in her time, but her best defense was in her feet. Using a weapon in the Swamp, the chance was that somebody bigger would take it away and use it on you. And most everybody was bigger than Polijn.

Best to just get under cover: she saw a cupboard near the floor that would do, if it wasn't too full. On her way there, she did snatch up a punch dagger, just in case. So much for that: the lintik thing was fake, carved out of wood. The point might do a little damage, though.

Ignoring the smell of rotten leather, Polijn curled up inside the cupboard and pulled the door almost shut. A bit of rag dangled out, holding the door open; she left it. Anyone who came looking would reason that somebody in hiding would have been less careless, and move on. At least, that was the way she was going to have to bet. Heaping rags up around her, she clutched her wooden dagger and waited for the crowd.

INTERLUDE
Sielvia

THE sun was masked by a cloud, but this gave little relief to the weary souls who trudged up the drawbridge, feet dragging, faces dripping. Palace guards stood stern watch, particularly eyeing those carrying bundles.

They had left in glory, on prancing horses or in gilded carts. Now the parade was over; the King had made his ceremonial re-entrance, but everyone else had been informed that all wagons had to be searched before entering the Palace gates. They had, after all, been down in the Swamp; any kind of contraband, particularly human contraband, might have been smuggled onto a wagon.

Sielvia, watching from within the gates, had seen three Swampites already whipped from the drawbridge. Oxypt had seemed genuinely surprised at the unsavory individual who had stowed away in his elaborate wagon, but she doubted Yslemucherys's claims that the two sonsy ladies shooed out of his were no one he knew.

She was waiting for Polijn, who had promised to be back early, to help with the packing. Berdais was getting impatient.

There she was! Sielvia ran over, but found only one of Kaigrol's granddaughters, who had taken to wearing her hair in Polijn's style.

"Yes?" Lolith demanded.

"Sorry. I was looking for Polijn."

Lolith's head came up, and she sniffed. "Many of my friends think all the attention paid to that creature is quite ridiculous."

Sielvia walked away without comment. This was just the sort of thing Lolith Nose-in-a-Hole would say, and, anyhow, she was in no shape for another fight. After the King had passed through the gates, Aperiole had said something about Swampites and promises, for which Sielvia had had to bite her. Aperiole had very unfortunately been carrying a change of clothes for her employer, which included a belt.

"I'll have to teach you a few things, since no one else will discipline you," she'd said, nearly spilling Sielvia's flagon as she hauled her little sister's dress up.

Sielvia reached back to rub the bruises. At least Berdais had seen it. Not that their mother had come over to interrupt; she'd just stepped aside to have a word with Aperiole's mistress.

A few members of the parade had had the foresight, or forewarning, to have sedan chairs waiting for them at the drawbridge. This way, at least, they didn't have to do the walking. Sielvia spotted her father and ran down the boards. With one hand wrapped around the top of the flagon, she jumped up to the little step and leaned in the window.

But Laisida was not riding with his apprentice; the shadow she'd seen opposite him was Colonel Kirasov. The minstrel waved away the flagon. "Your mother sent us well provisioned."

Sielvia handed the flagon to the colonel instead. "Where's Polijn?"

Laisida shrugged. He didn't look very happy; getting down from his carriage and up into a sedan chair was no joke in this heat. "Half the procession is still in the Swamp. Most will straggle back at dawn. Or we'll get demands for ransom."

The colonel finished the contents of the flagon and laughed. Sielvia was not amused. "You just left her down there?"

Her father raised an eyebrow at her. "Malaracha is still there, with that brother of his, and will keep an eye on her if one is needed. She did live down there; she knows her way around. I believe she was going to visit relatives."

Little Polijn had never mentioned having relatives. "What if his brother grabs that redheaded dancer like last time, and Malaracha forgets Polijn?"

Laisida looked down his nose at her. "When you were little," he noted, "we could just hand you a spoon, and that would keep you occupied. You didn't have to outgrow that stage, you know. Don't fret about it. By the way, I passed your favorite uncle and he said he'd be honoring us with a visit later. You may wish to escape."

Sielvia knew he meant Morafor, probably her least favorite relative. Uncle Morquiesse had been much more amusing, though very rude, at times. This was not telling her anything about Polijn, though.

"But . . ." she began.

"They say in Keastone that staring at frogs will avert the birth of female children," the minstrel told Laisida. "I didn't hear that until it was too late, however."

Sielvia knew she was going to get nowhere with him if he was in this mood. She took up the flagon again and jumped down. The chair continued across the drawbridge. Sielvia had to dodge to avoid being kicked by the carriers of the next chair.

That was interesting: Petalec was in there, riding with the Keeper of Fruits and Flowers. Funny how people who had been so far apart in the actual parade should wind up here at the same time.

She turned and ran back toward the Palace. With everyone coming in this way, at different times, why, Polijn might well have come back already, passing her, perhaps, while she was busy with Aperiole. Even on wheels, Laisida was not the speediest in the Palace Royal, and it wouldn't have taken long for Polijn to see everything worth seeing in the Swamp.

What had she stayed behind for? Certainly, if Polijn really had relatives down there, she wouldn't want to admit it. Maybe she just didn't care to hear all Kirasov's Treasury-guarding stories.

But Polijn was not waiting in the minstrel's chambers. Sielvia set down the flagon and looked around, tapping her foot. There were certain difficulties attached to finding anybody in the Palace Royal; they really needed some official just to keep track of where everyone was. The only person she knew who might help her find Polijn was the King. And when he'd finished his triumphal entrance, Nurse had whisked him away for an immediate nap.

Sielvia let the door slam behind her as she sped back out into the halls. Nurse had, of course, told them at the far gate to watch for Polijn, and send her up to sing to the King as he slept. Nurse despised Polijn, but there was no denying she had a soothing voice when the King was inclined to be cranky.

Slipping through and around the damp, fragrant crowds, she soon arrived before the royal doorways, lower than the others so no one could enter with an upraised sword. None of the guards on duty said anything to her until she curtsied and inquired, "Is His Majesty receiving?"

Then all she got was a furtive cough. One guard reached over to knock at the door and jerked back before it opened. Culghi Mud-for-Brains peeked out.

"Come in quick!" he whispered, and opened the door a bit farther.

Sielvia squeezed past. Her questions were answered before she could ask, by a cry of, "Ha! Your blue man's on the Death Space!"

Nurse was nowhere in evidence, of course. Four boys sat round the little table, tossing dice and shifting players on a paper game. Timpre was clutching Loll, his yellow-haired doll with the long velvet tongue. He sat next to Argeleb on a low bench.

"I heard one," Argeleb said. "Why is Forokell like a foreign ambassador? Because her chest has a secret compartment!"

Forokell had lost some flesh decades ago in a knife fight with a former lover; the lover lost rather more. "Oh, that's an old one," jeered Merklin. Merklin, characteristically, sat on a sacred chest, sealed with the insignia of Conan III, containing the broken seals of previous monarchs. Conan never touched the box if he could help it. "What did the dragon say on a cold day? I can see my breath!"

The King sat astride the larger of his rocking horses, and was rocking forward to nudge one of his tokens a little closer to the glory at the end of the game while no one else was looking.

"Ho ho!" said Mardith, from his perch above the table, but was alert enough to notice a new set of footsteps entering the room. "Ho, there she be!"

Merklin reached for the tokens and the King threw himself across the paper. But Timpre cried, "It's only Siel!" and everyone sat back again.

"Whew!" said the King. "We thought you were Nurse. Where's Polijn?"

Sielvia stopped. "That's what I came to ask you. Didn't you see her?"

The King set the tokens back up into their proper places. "I couldn't, could I? She was way ahead of me."

"I meant did you see her on the way back?"

"I wasn't up to that space yet," noted Argeleb, reaching up to slide a yellow token back.

"I was asleep," the King told Sielvia, rocking back to let Argeleb make adjustments. "That's why I don't need a nap now. It was hot, and all those people were pushing all around: the skinny ones who think touching me can fix their bread problems, the fat ones who want something better than saffron for gout. . . ."

"Where is she, then?" Merklin broke in. "Isn't she back yet?"

Sielvia came up to the table to look at the board. "If she was back, I wouldn't be asking, leatherbrain."

"Lots of people stayed behind," noted the King, nudging his own token forward, and then back again.

"Polijn's no Swamper," Timpre told him. "She lived in the Swamp, so there's nothing down there new for her to see."

"She promised to come back, too," Sielvia put in, looking to see if there was an unused token she could use. "I was sure she'd be back by now."

Merklin stood up and bent across the board. "Unless," he whispered, "she's been kidnapped!"

The other Royal Playmates, as well as the King, stared at him. "Hi ho," said Mardith, a kind of sigh, and hunkered down on the perch.

Sielvia glanced back to Culghi, who was intent on Nurse's possible return, one ear pressed against the door. "He wouldn't dare," she declared. "My father. . ."

"Look." Merklin's voice was low and intense. "Lots of people don't like her—you hear that all the time—and there's this Treasury inventory coming up. Somebody could hide her and say she stole what they really took. Because she's from the Swamp: lots of people would believe it."

The King opened his mouth, but Mardith spoke. "Half-pie crazy," the bird snorted. "What name you steal somebody when killing's so easier? If you be no way 'fraid of Laisida."

Argeleb bounced forward. "It could be a plot, couldn't it? It could! You know how they kept me up under the roof for days and days! They might do that to Polijn, to make Lord Laisida do something. Or not do something."

"Maybe it's Brown Robes!" cried Timpre, slapping the game board so that a token fell off the paper.

Sielvia was solidly sick of the Ykenai crisis; Council members had been finding brown robes in each other's closets forever. The Brown Robes had done real harm, but after they murdered her uncle as part of their last thrust, the Bodyguard had killed all that were left of them.

"There are those missing robes," mused Merklin. "But it could be anybody, really."

"It could be nothing," the King put in quickly. "I'm sure it's just nothing. She just wanted to look around in the Swamp."

Sielvia had been teased about becoming queen; Eru, she felt sorry for anyone who had to marry anybody this slow. And look at that thumb heading for the mouth.

Less scornful but just as positive, Argeleb bounced forward, shaking a finger at His Majesty. "Anybody who was lucky enough to get out of the Swamp wouldn't ever go back!"

Timpre slapped his hands on the sides of his face. "What if it's Ferrapec?"

Mardith released a cry of scorn. "The lumphead! See him run yesterday?"

"Yes, but," Timpre replied, easing back a bit from the bird's perch, "but wasn't he pulling on Polijn just then?"

Sielvia bit her lip. Whatever was happening, she hoped Polijn had managed to get rid of those underpants of Maiaciara's. If Ferrapec found out about those . . .

"You know Janeftox," Timpre went on, turning to her. "Go up and ask him if his master . . ."

"Yes," Merklin put in, "and look around, too. Maybe he's got her in his rooms now."

Sielvia stood up, but didn't start for the door just yet. Janeftox would just deny it, like the time she had just mentioned, as a joke, the connection between the general and the faulty battering rams. This was serious: bad enough that the family would be split up this summer, but if Ferrapec had done something with Polijn, and Janeftox, her sister's man, was implicated (as he must be, since the general had so few servants left to blame), everyone would be devastated.

So she was glad enough to agree with the King when he said, "No, no. He wouldn't dare. Just wait. She'll be back."

Sielvia sat down, but Argeleb and Timpre were not ready to give up on the matter. "I know, I know!" said the smaller boy, still bouncing on the leather seat. "We could maybe ask one of the sorcerers to look in a magic mirror or something and say where she is. Karabari Banglebags is always around Dad's shop, and he likes me."

"But is he strong enough?" Argeleb asked him. "What about Aizon, or . . . or Himself? Or . . ."

"No!" The King, Sielvia knew, did not like Aizon Bat-Man, who was also Master of Royal Funerals, in charge of summoning back the souls of deceased monarchs. And nobody cared to disturb the Regent.

"If we're going to find her, we should look for her ourselves," the King went on, rocking faster. "Ostrogol didn't sit at home and let somebody else do the job with magic."

"In wars brave, each deed is a poem, and he writes best who engraves it on the foe's chest!" quoted Argeleb from the tale of Ostrogol, as he swung an imaginary sword in two hands.

Timpre swung an equally imaginary one-handed sword up. "The blood of an enemy is the best sauce!" he quoted. Pretty strong stuff, from Timpre Whimper.

Sielvia had been too distracted by the antics of Argeleb and her cousin to notice that Merklin was deep in thought. "Hey!" he cried, interrupting the air-sword battle. "General Patchpants wouldn't take her up to his rooms anyhow. He's so nobody these days that anyone might just walk in on him. He'd hide her someplace safe, like an empty dungeon cell."

"I'm not going down there!" squeaked Timpre.

"No, big Sir Merklin gonna do it, sure," Mardith croaked, bouncing from one foot to the other. "Big man, he knows he way around down there, ha!"

"Well, you know the way," Merklin replied. "And he does."

The King was still rocking at a perilous speed. "Oh, I've been down there a dozen times, easy." Timpre was shaking his head fiercely. "It's not that scary."

"I wouldn't be scared either, if I had people like Lord Kaftus and Lady Nimnestl with me," Argeleb declared.

A hot answer from the King was forestalled by Timpre's injection of, "And the New Guard!"

Everyone had a nice laugh at that, but Sielvia noticed the King's face falling. After a look at the door, the little monarch rocked way forward and took hold of the table to whisper, "But I couldn't go down there. Culghi won't let me out. And we might see Nurse on the way."

"Oh, come on!" said Merklin, sitting back. "All you need is a plan. We'll think of a way to go look."

"Who'd let us into the dungeons, though?" Timpre put in. "You have to have a key, or permission from somebody important."

"A key, or permission," said Sielvia. It sounded like a line from a song she knew. One of the problems of growing up in a minstrel's household was that everything . . .

"A key or permission, or ORDERS!" she exclaimed. The boys turned to look at her. "Do you remember the story of Diriel in Aro?"

"I don't know that one," the King told her, rocking back.

"Then do you remember the Spring Festival?" she said. "When you had the hiccups?"

The King rolled his eyes; he did remember. So now Sielvia gripped the game table and leaned forward to whisper. Mardith jumped down on the table to listen but, outside of one short laugh, made no comment. When she was done, everyone nodded.

Conan dismounted and hurried to a little slate in the corner of the room. "There's nothing on my schedule until late," he announced. "It's all down for naptime."

Merklin gathered up the gamesheet and pieces and carried them back to the King's Closet, a little room where Conan kept private treasures. Only Merklin and Nimnestl had ever been in there besides the King, though something Polijn had said once suggested she'd peeked inside.

"Now, what else do we need? A . . ." The King's eyes grew round.

"Your Majesty!" Merklin exclaimed. "Are you all right?"

"Whuck!" he replied. "Whuck-whuck! I'm—whuck!—okay." He tried to remount his rocking horse, but a violent "Whuck!" dumped him on the floor.

"Stars and moons!" cried the whipping boy. "Culghi! Go for help! It's the Nitrosimian Fever, just like at Spring Festival!"

The guard stepped in from the door and stared at the sight of his monarch on the floor. "I . . ."

The King tried to rise. "Never—whuck—mind. I'm o-whuck!" He slumped on the floor again.

"He needs help," said Merklin. "Don't run or tell anybody in the hall. The people will panic like last time."

Culghi showed no signs of running, or even of leaving. "Hurry!" shouted Sielvia, stamping one foot. "Go get Nurse!"

The guard rocked backward; no Playmate had ever requested the presence of Nurse. Convinced of the seriousness of the situation, he turned for the door. Once there, he remembered not to run, and strode into the hall with hurried dignity.

Mardith all but rolled off his perch, shaking with loud caws of laughter. Nurse had terrified the whole country at Spring Festival by declaring an attack of hiccups to be the onset of a mysterious fever. The Regent had allowed it to break up a debate on Corontarion politics that the King had started to participate in, but the terror of the King's illness had lingered for weeks.

"Who'd think Nurse would ever be useful?" Argeleb demanded, shaking wrinkles out of a burlap bag Merklin had pulled from the closet.

"Good move," Merklin told Sielvia, as the King crawled into the bag. "Now, when they get here, tell them we're looking for Namansi's roomdog, and didn't want Culghi along."

Sielvia stepped back, her wrists on her hips. "You're not leaving me here for Nurse! That wasn't part of the plan!"

"It is now," Merklin told her, kneeling to check the bag for airholes. "We don't need any girls along in the dungeon, screaming every time a rat goes by."

"Stars and moons! And I have to pretend we all cared about a little black pushface with teeth?" Sielvia puckered her lips at him. Merklin saw this, and swung a fist at her.

"Stop that!" the King ordered, putting his head out of the bag. "We don't know how far he had to go to find Nurse! They could be back any second!"

"She could go to her room and hide there, maybe," ventured Timpre.

Sielvia stamped her foot again. "You guys!"

"Let her come!" ordered the King. "Somebody has to carry the lights."

Merklin stomped over to the sideboard and detached two branches of an eight-candle lamp. "Should we bring some of these egg sandwiches, too?"

"Oh, we'll be back in time for supper, surely," Conan told him. "You're coming, Mardith?"

"Sure bet!" The black bird zipped down into the bag. "Lard-Nurse's face gonna look mighty white! And that Mud-for-Brains! Hee-ha-ha!"

"Even Nimnestl will be surprised," the King agreed, pulling the bag shut over his head. "We did something by ourselves."

"Polijn sure will be impressed. Ompf." Timpre took up a corner of the bag.

"Ungh," said Argeleb, taking his end. "Won't she, though, when we walk up and say hello?"

"And won't Nurse drop the Palace Royal on our heads if she gets back before we leave?" Sielvia demanded. She stepped up to the door and opened it for the boys struggling under their bulky load. The King was not the lightest of burdens, even without the heavy ceremonial robes he'd worn on parade.

"He's asleep," Merklin whispered to the guards, as Sielvia pulled the door gently shut. "Culghi's going to help us hide this." The man nearest the door nodded. Sielvia tried not to look over her shoulder as they headed for the stairs.

All they had to do now was navigate the hall, reach the stairs, descend to the kitchen level, and move back up the lower corridor to the great wooden doors three floors below, preferably avoiding any contact with Nurse or Culghi on the way. Other people might also know too much to be met with safety; the nearest stairs were unfortunately in the same tower where the Chief Bodyguard had her office (not, Sielvia reflected, that you ever knew where the woman was going to be).

They reached the tower without incident, but Gilphros was standing there, feet spread apart, obviously blocking someone on the landing from coming out into the hall. "Look!" he was saying, "You could at least think about it, y' old toad."

Gilphros would argue with anybody just for the fun of it, but Sielvia was startled to see he was confronting Forokell. The First Housekeeper sat in her Farnum chair, impassive and imposing as a peak of granite.

"You said yourself you'll need more women to cover both palaces this year. She's good blood, even if she does spend most of her days on her butt."

Forokell blinked; she didn't stand much, these days. The First Housekeeper had been known for doing her own killing until just two or three years ago, and she had plenty of volunteers eager to do it for her now. Not hard to imagine her disembowelling a lover, Sielvia thought, if you could swallow the image of her having a lover in the first place.

She merely inclined her head toward Gilphros. "Your wife is being considered for the position. There are other applicants. I do rate your wife above Adimo, for example."

One of Forokell's attendants laughed. Gilphros's wife was the youngest and least of General Kaigrol's numerous offspring. Her own father took very little interest in her, as could be proven by her marriage to Gilphros.

"There's Polijn," said someone. Sielvia looked around, but saw no sign of her.

"True," said Forokell. "I rate your wife above her, as well. I shall give the matter some thought before making an announcement."

"Well, see that you do." Gilphros pushed past the House-keeper's retinue to the stairs. One corner of Forokell's mouth crooked up.

"If the wife had half the spirit of the husband," she said, "it would be done."

The two groups passed each other now, the children showing proper deference to the Housekeeper and the reti-nue of Forokell making a little room for a group that did, after all, include some of the King's best friends. Sielvia noted Raiprez Crystaleyes toward the back, talking to Crystalcrotch, her daughter. The two women were tech-nically members of Forokell's retinue, but lately Raiprez had been eased out of most of her duties except grinding shells for face-whitener. Maiciara spent her days endlessly sewing pillows.

They were talking in competition as usual, the mother whispering irritation at the lack of serious consideration of Polijn while the daughter was interested in the case of a guard who had been thrown out of an inn in Malbeth for assaulting the innkeeper's daughter. It had not been decided yet what would happen to the innkeeper.

Two men followed at a distance, their shoulders limp and their tongues hanging out. Glasshead and Hothead, Kirasov's most trusted nephews, had little chance of courting Maiaciara, but they did like to follow her upstairs. The big stupids: they had fine clothes, while Janeftox and Jolor got only the hand-me-downs too tattered for Ferrapec's family to wear any more. Jolkoram Glasshead licked his own shoulder. Eneste was turning to say something when he spotted the children.

"Hey, um, Servia!" he called. "Your mother's lookin' for you. We just came from there. Better hurry: she's got a wooden spoon."

"Okay," Sielvia called back. Eneste moved his hand to conceal the corner of a piece of paper sticking out from under his overtunic. They'd better not have stolen that, she thought. Kirasov was a very potent protector, but not the equal of the King's First Minstrel.

The group sped up, but not toward Laisida's rooms. "What are they doing to her, in the dungeons?" Argeleb whispered.

Sielvia recognized the guards on duty only vaguely. She had an impression that they were Treasury men, which was odd. The dungeons were officially only Treasury business after nightfall. But perhaps Housekeeping had found itself stretched too thinly during the move, and tradition was being overlooked this week.

"What's with you kids?" asked the man to the right of the door.

"Just open up, can't you?" demanded Merklin. Sweat was streaming across his eyes, and he couldn't spare a hand to wipe it.

Sielvia knew this was not the way to get into the dungeons; at least not quickly. "Oh, Nurse says we have to put these presents for the King in an empty cell. His Majesty is asleep just now, so she wants it all done right away."

Both guards chuckled. "She wants it all done yesterday," said the man on the left, detaching a key from his belt. "The usual cell?"

"I suppose," said Sielvia, loudly, so as to cover a muffled "Aha!" from inside the bag. "It isn't that far down, is it?"

"I don't know if I want to go in," said Timpre.

"Are you more scared of Nurse, or the dungeon?" Merklin replied, trying to shake some of the moisture from his face. "What if she comes to check on us and finds you out here?"

"Here," said the guard, handing Sielvia a key with a dragon engraved on the shaft. "We'll tell her you've been and gone. It's just about ten paces past the quarter-mile. Stick to the center of the floor, especially if there's anything to eat in there."

"Thank you, sir; we will," Merklin said.

As soon as the heavy doors slammed behind them, the bag was dropped. "We did it!" gasped Argeleb.

"Kings do things, too!" cried Mardith, flapping free.

"Sssh sssh sssh, you guys!" hissed His Majesty, following Mardith out of the bag.

Sielvia looked over the key, which would unlock every cell on the dragon level of the dungeons, and shook her head. "I guess we could just have asked the guards if Ferrapec or Janeftox was in here today. They're Treasury men, so they wouldn't . . ."

The expression being swapped among her companions clearly said, "Girls!" so she let it go at that. Mardith swooped up to the ceiling.

"Now show everybody!" he shouted. "Now we go . . ."

The door of the nearest cell banged forward, as far as the bolt would allow, as hands and a pale face came through the barred window. "Who's there?" rasped the occupant.

"Is someone there?" called another prisoner, down the curving hall. Within moments, faces showed at every window in sight, each with a voice to call, "What's that?"

The first speaker looked up, spying movement. "The crow!" he gasped. "The carrion crow!"

"Hush you!" snapped Mardith, flying down to peck at the woman's eyes.

Doors dropped back as pressure on them gave way. Merklin looked to the King and, shrugging, started forward.

Not everyone hushed. Sielvia heard plenty of coughing, and once a cry of "Ha ha ha ha ha!" What did these people do all day? She'd been expecting a much busier place, with men in agony, and bones, bones hanging from rings set in the walls. Perhaps all that sort of thing was done in a special room. To be sure, her father'd said many prisoners on this level had better lodgings than when they were at liberty.

The corridor made tight turns, sloping down. Few torches were lit, and her candles did little to hold back the gloom. She peered at the high ceilings for a lurking spider or alungwe, but there was nothing. Walls, floor, and ceiling were bare.

"No rats," whispered Argeleb. Timpre clutched at his cousin's free arm.

Around and down, around and down: the King did his best to keep up with Mardith and Merklin, trying at the same time to look neither left nor right. That thumb was firmly between his lips now. Sielvia pulled her collar tighter. Even the larders hadn't been this cool.

This was not, she could tell, a place where treasure was buried, nor any place for little Polijn to be. It was no place for little Sielvia, come to that. She'd heard stories of these cells, stained with the crimes not only of the inhabitants but with the crimes visited upon them. The spirits that waited within wouldn't care who your father was.

"Here," said Mardith, quietly, as if even he was impressed.

They had reached the first cell with a dragon above the door, well past all inhabited cells. Sielvia looked to the King, and then to Merklin.

Merklin took a deep breath. "We better take turns looking in," he said. No one volunteered. He took another breath. "Lift me up."

Progress was slower now, as they alternated, taking peeks through the barred windows high in the doors of the cells on this side of the corridor and that. Timpre denied any desire for a look, so the searching fell to his four companions.

There was nothing to cause terror: just square, bare rooms smelling of cold old stone. Except that there was a bench in some of the cells, Sielvia could hardly tell the difference between dark cell and dark hall.

"What if she's not down here?" she whispered, after her fourth turn at a window. They just moved on without answering. It was too cold to think about such things. Maybe that was why the dungeons were so deadly: something here sapped strength and will.

Only one person ever escaped this dungeon without the help of a bribe or a friend to pass in a key. Sixty years ago, a man named Ulgoram, imprisoned for no one recalled what offense, had caught the neck of an unwary guard who had come down alone, strangled him, and stolen a ring of keys. Then he ran the wrong way, thinking to hide in an unused cell until things blew over. But there was nothing in the cells to conceal a man. When the search was made, they found him right away, just short of the three-quarter mile mark. He was crouched on the floor, full dead, the rings of keys and the hand he'd used to steal them both missing.

Twenty cells, around and down, thirty cells: they'd be running out of cells on the dragon level soon. Sielvia wondered what Nurse would do to them when they returned, not heroes, not escorting Polijn. It couldn't be anything very bad; nothing could, while you had the memory of these cells in your head.

"What's that on that door?" whispered Argeleb.

It was a stripe of red. Merklin reached the door and nodded to Sielvia, whose turn it was. Stepping up into the hands offered her, she peered inside, being careful not to set her hand on the red.

"Someone's been here," she whispered. "There's a plate and a pitcher!"

"Anything else?" called the King. "Let me look!"

She moved the candles. The shadows of the utensils stretched like black ghosts. "No," she said. "Just the plate and pitcher."

"Maybe they haven't brought her down yet," said Argeleb. "They're going to put her there and . . ."

"Ha!" Mardith, who had perched on her shoulder, darted through the window into the cell and snatched up something white. The boys jumped back, nearly dumping her, but stepped in again on seeing that it was a breadcrust.

"And not very dry," said Merklin, picking it up.

"Let's see what else is in there," said the King, reaching up with the key. Timpre stepped back, and squealed as the door came after him.

"Must not have been locked," Merklin observed, stepping around it. "Anything in that pitcher?"

"Maybe there's a message on the wall," said Argeleb. "Ostrogol scratched a message on the wall of his cell."

Watching the corners for surprises, they stepped inside. But the cell was empty, except for these few luxuries, which were generally not even allowed the prisoners on higher levels.

"Half full," said Merklin, tapping the pitcher. "Not even a cracked one. Who . . ."

A click followed a bang. "That should hold 'em 'til we're safe in the north," said someone outside. "Nobody's gonna miss a buncha kids."

CHAPTER FOUR
Nimnestl

I

NIMNESTL didn't like spending time in her office on the best of days, but she felt she ought to stay in one place, in case someone had something to report. The parade had been kind of a signal. From now until the actual departure for the north, events would speed up.

But it was hot. Riding in parade was a long, tedious business, and the post-parade argument between Nurse and the King had irritated her nerves still further. And General Ferrapec was exactly the last person she wanted at this moment.

"Let the Regent give the word," he declared, slapping both hands on the table, "and we'll have ruffles on his wrists for you!"

"I should think such a minor arrest is beneath the dignity of the Army," she noted, studying an axe hanging on the wall behind his head.

Ferrapec had four chins when he pulled his head back in outrage. "The man has made a fool of the entire government, from the Regent right down! Not only is he not from the lintik School of Minstrelsy, the man's not even a southerner! He's just another shuptit Cahotian! If the Brautian hadn't accidentally let that slip, Eru knows how far the one-eyed scoundrel might have gone!"

174

Nimnestl doubted this, particularly the part about Lord Arlmorin. The ambassador never let information slip, not accidentally, at least, and certainly not in the Swamp, with General Ferrapec close enough to hear.

"These foreigners come in here and think Rossacottans are a bunch of primitives who'll buy anything!" Nimnestl recognized this as the beginning of another of the general's setpieces, and let her mind slip from his words. How sweet it would be to have him far away, on his father's duchy. When Jintabh died, Maitena would have some claim on the land, too. But she was unlikely to mention it, and as long as she was less of an annoyance than her cousin, the Regent was unlikely to point this out, too.

The only interesting facet of this not-unexpected revelation was that the general had been interested enough to return immediately from his Swamping to report it. Was this a part of Umian's plan? Or was Ferrapec just proving his loyalty? Someone who had helped unveil an impostor who had "made a fool of the entire government" could hardly be plotting to overthrow that government, right? But most likely, she thought, he was just seizing at a possibility of reward: if the government paid him enough for Carasta, he might just turn in Umian as well.

She had no intention, however, of rewarding him with anything more than a smile. She gave him this when he paused to wipe his face. "Your loyalty is to be commended, General," she said. "It is nice to know the government can depend on SOMEBODY." She scratched her upper lip.

The general paled. Everyone knew that scratch of the lip meant the Bodyguard was enjoying a private little joke.

"But His Lordship the Regent knows many things people believe he does not," she went on. "He simply waits for the proper moment to act. And I believe he was going to use the New Guard on this matter."

Ferrapec was trembling now. Nimnestl stroked her upper lip and continued, "And he must have time to check his informants for dependability. In any case, the man is still in the Swamp, is he not?"

"Y-yes, of course," said the general. "I-I will not take up any more of your time, My Lady."

"Later, perhaps," she assured him. "We are not likely to forget what you have done."

The general stumbled out of the room. His mother was waiting for him outside; Nimnestl heard murmurs of "superlative" and "military bearing." Ferrapec regained some of his color, but muttered, "Should've stayed in the Swamp." Nimnestl got up and shut the door.

Many people had stayed in the Swamp, a lot of them heading straight for the pawnshops. The audit had frightened them. She did not like it that they were frightened, not just now. Frightened people might do something rash, and frightened people who were also hot could do things that would make Carasta's imposture a very trivial matter indeed.

"Did you HEAR about Old Eyepatch?" demanded a honey-colored being, zipping through a window.

Nimnestl had been waiting for this repository of trivial matters, but this made her no easier to take. "I heard," she said, closing her eyes for just a second.

"Whatcha gonna do to him?" demanded another voice. "Something really good? How about his other eye?"

Nimnestl opened both of hers and beheld the queen of the pixies, Chicken-and-Dumplings, and her current consort, Sir Keep-Em-Safely-Rolling. "I will consult you before we decide," she promised. "Did you follow Seitun and Diabies?"

"Yupper." The queen flittered up to lean against a spearhead just her height. "You wanna hear?"

The Bodyguard turned away to ask the male, "Is it still so hot outside?" The important thing in dealing with pixies was not to let them suspect there was anything important about it.

The little queen tugged at the Bodyguard's earlobe. "Hey-ho! We followed your boys all over the place. Don't you want to hear?"

Nimnestl watched with great interest as the royal consort flew upside-down, slapping the soles of his feet together. "Ah, feathers," Nimnestl said. "You probably lost him before he got to the end of the drawbridge."

"Fooze!" answered Chicken-and-Dumplings, giving the earlobe a kick. "We followed both of 'em! At the same time, too! The beggarman went away to a house and right to the back door. Then he sat there until a woman came out to dump the garbage."

"He talked to her," said Sir Keep-Em-Safely-Rolling, his hands over his ears, "louder and louder and louder. Then he ran away."

"What were they talking about?" Nimnestl inquired.

"Oh, some other woman," said the queen, now standing on one toe on a spearpoint, and spinning herself around. "Do you know they bust up all their eggshells before they throw them away? No good for boats at ALL!"

"Shocking," said the Bodyguard, folding her hands together. "Where did he go after that?"

"And all the broken broomsticks," said the consort, licking his nose.

"Oh, those float, at least," the queen pointed out.

Nimnestl set her thumbs together. Seitun would still be on the trail, at least. This had just been an experiment in making use of pixies. "What house was this?" she asked.

"It had a blue roof," said the male pixy, ruffling up his hair into a stack on top of his head. "Blue tiles, you know. And a big yard inside a wall, with a fountain."

"But only water in the fountain," sighed the queen.

"And where was this house?" the Bodyguard ventured.

The queen flew down to lick some dust off the tabletop. "Out in the city."

Nimnestl inclined her head. "Oh, not inside the Palace, then?"

"Do you have some?" asked the queen, looking up.

"Oh, none with fountains," the Bodyguard assured her. She licked one lip. "I did wonder where in the city, though."

The queen's nose wrinkled. "Oh, the rich part: the boring part."

Nimnestl could have deduced this without the aid of a pixy. "Past the Midtown Gate?" she said.

"Oh, yes," said the queen, checking the table legs for more dust.

"Did he turn left or right after he'd passed through the gate?"

"Left," said the queen, just as her consort said, "Right."

"Left," said the queen, flying up to face the other.

"Right," snapped her consort, sticking his tongue out.

"Don't you remember, we flew over that couple that was . . ."

"But that was on the right," said Sir Keep-Em-Safely-Rolling.

"Left!" shrieked the queen, and dealt him a resounding slap on the nearer buttock.

"Right!" he replied, responding in kind.

"Left!"

"Right!"

"Left!"

"Right!"

Nimnestl felt it was safest to wait this out. Finally, Chicken-and-Dumplings declared, "Now look what you've done! I'm all red on that one."

Her consort looked, but at himself. "Well, I'm all red on this one."

The queen and her consort raised their heads, two minds with but a single thought. Then they traded places.

"Did you have left or right?" she asked him, after a swat.

"Left," he told her, dealing her a cheerful wallop.

"Did not!"

"Did too!"

"Did not!"

On the whole, Nimnestl was inclined to believe, with Kaftus, that pixies had no uses. But it had been worth a try.

"Thank you so much, Your Majesty," she said, raising her voice to be heard over the shrieks. "I can only wish we had some sort of token that would show our appreciation, but we have only this bit of trash."

She hurled the string of blue crystal beads out the window. "Trash!" she repeated. The pixies dove for it. Would that everything that bothered her could be dismissed so neatly.

Her next main concern, she supposed, was to check with Kaftus to find out if he'd decided to hold a Council meeting, with so many councillors safely out a-Swamping. Nothing to be done about Diabies until Seitun made a real report, and the Carasta matter could wait. The only other possibility was talking to some people about the unexplained murders. To show too much interest, of course, would lend credibility to the fuss Umian was making, but to fail to investigate entirely would encourage the families of the deceased to look to the New Guard for assistance.

She hadn't made up her mind as she moved to the door. The door shook under the impact of a heavy fist, and then swung wide. A man entered, naked to the waist and smelling strongly not of the sweat running into the tangle of black hair on his chest, but of the clay he kept in tubs of water all over his studio.

"You're back, then." His voice was a boom from deep within his barrel of a body. "Glad to see it. Look at this."

Outside the window, pixies at opposite ends of the string of beads were flying into each other for the joy of collision. Nimnestl wondered if it was too late to call them back.

"Look at this, I said. Not that." The sculptor's apprentice staggered in with a big box that had little wheels at the corners.

"Oaf!" roared his master, as he stumbled. Then the apprentice tripped over an outstretched foot. Morafor caught up the box and slammed it down on Nimnestl's desk, which shuddered under the impact.

As talented and egotistic as his brothers, Morafor lacked the charm that had made Morquiesse and Laisida popular. A snarling, leering, seething, brooding bear of a man, contemptuous of lesser talents, he accorded only to high court officials the accolade of treating them as equals.

"You did not stop at the Yellow Dog, ogoti?" he inquired of Nimnestl, as he kicked his apprentice from the room.

"Ogoti," as a term of friendship, was properly used only between companions of many years' acquaintance. But Morafor's success was not his only shield; time better to teach him manners after the furor over Morquiesse's death had quieted.

"I did not," she informed him. "You did, of course?"

"Of course." He dismissed her tone of voice with a wave of his fist; so great was he that his faults were a part of his greatness. "You missed quite the different show. Completely the opposite of expectations, ogoti: clothes without bodies."

Nimnestl's face showed no interest. This was because she was, in fact, not interested: why bother her with the details of his Swamping? There were, to be sure, any number of courtiers who had acquired the habit of running to her with trivial gossip they picked up, in hopes of learning something useful in return. But Morafor was not one of these.

"And there was this box, as well," he said. A flourish of one hand knocked the lid back.

Nimnestl did not show surprise. But she was surprised. Two of the great gold coins of Eastland sat inside the box. Only about a thousand of these had been made, for royal transactions among the four quarter-nations of Atfalas; the youngest was roughly a hundred times as old as Nimnestl. The largest known collection of these coins was in the Royal Treasury right here: there were twenty. Artists from across the continent had been coming to study them since Rossacotta's borders had opened.

"The Enhar coin and the Algion coin," said Morafor, with relish. "Studied them and the other eighteen a thousand times. I do hope there are eighteen in the Treasury now, eh, ogoti? Quite the joke on Kirasov."

Now, what did all this mean? Morafor could easily have taken them himself, and was choosing this method to return them before the audit. Or, even better, he could have taken them with him this morning, so he could bring them back and accuse somebody he didn't like. Nimnestl shook her head. That would work better if he'd waited until after the audit started. The Eastland coins were usually the first things to be inventoried, because they were so seldom moved.

"But why tell you, eh? Instead of rubbing Lord Guard's nose in it? I thought you might like to know who was seen leaving the place first."

Here it came. He had a grudge against someone he couldn't kill with impunity, as he'd done with Targent when the man was paying too much attention to Kaphatari, the sculptor's best model.

"Studied her a thousand times, too," he said. "The molding of her face, those ears, the advent of lily-white swellings under her tunic. What would a Royal Playmate be doing at the Yellow Dog, ogoti?"

Nimnestl didn't know.

II

"ZHRIACAR, the doorman, a massive clot, was refusing admittance, saying the place was closed. I saw through that at once: Karlikartis wouldn't close up with that much money running around loose in the Swamp. But he didn't recognize me, so I knew he'd been doped or enchanted."

Nimnestl had requested further details, and Morafor was glad to supply these, in return for a steady supply of cool drinks. Most of his details, however, concerned his cleverness in getting into the Yellow Dog, which, though he hadn't said so in so many words, had obviously happened well after Polijn was out of the building. He seemed to have been part of a crowd chasing her, and returned to the Yellow Dog afterward.

The theft itself did not worry Nimnestl; lapses in Treasury security were Kirasov's responsibility. The sighting of Polijn was hers. Morafor could be mistaken, of course, or lying, though he had no daughters to take Polijn's place in the Royal Playmates.

She doubted Polijn could have had anything to do with the theft; the coins were too heavy. But the truth was neither here nor there. What mattered was what people would believe. And precisely because Polijn had never been implicated in previous plots, they would believe she was part of this one. Rossacottan logic: intelligent people plotted, Polijn was an intelligent person, so therefore Polijn was plotting. She had simply been too clever to get caught before.

And they feared her friendship with the King. Kaftus laughed at what he called "Polijn paranoia." Nimnestl was not amused. Even before the matter of the cookie antler, there was the skit last week, performed for the King's entertainment. His Majesty had pulled roles from a hat and assigned them to various courtiers and Playmates. Polijn had performed so well, slipping into her part so easily, that the audience forgot to applaud. If she could take on another personality so readily, who could tell when the little minstrel was lying?

"Meant to put a flea in m' brother's ear, ogoti, but thought I'd see the coins safe first. He's busy anyhow, with guess who. Kirasov, no less. The good colonel."

Morafor had obviously already decided that Polijn was some kind of go-between for the King's Minstrel and the Head Guard. Others would see it that way, too, unless they took Morafor's personality into account. The brothers were always willing to do each other an ill turn.

Nimnestl hoped that was all there was to this. The King had taken the Morquiesse business hard, and the loss of Laisida might be too much, to say nothing of Polijn. He'd want to intervene. Even among those who didn't care what the King married, this would be taken as a bad sign, a sign of weakness. His mother had been criticized for her ban on the flogging of criminals under six and over seventy-five; for Conan to try to step between the law and a traitor would start tongues wagging.

"How's about it, ogoti? Shall we have the colonel and my good brother up here, to answer for themselves?"

Morafor held his liquor well, but he'd had plenty of it: his face was all smiles. "Better to wait," she told him, "and spring it on them later. They may suspect something—that's why they're closeted—but if we keep quiet, we may lull them into false confidence. The important thing now is to see the venerable coins back to their rightful place. There must be a way to do it quietly, if only we knew some man who could hold his tongue."

Morafor seemed to feel this meant him, and he volunteered

at once. He and his apprentice could proclaim the whole box to be a gift for His Majesty, to be hidden in the Treasury until the proper moment. The apprentice agreed to all this, and to keeping quiet about it. Morafor had killed three previous apprentices for lesser crimes than telling secrets.

Nimnestl let this company get out of sight before moving off to visit the Regent. She wondered if this development would make him as uneasy as it made her, and if he'd say so if it did.

"Scullion!" someone roared, as she was locking her door. "Squirrel!"

The Bodyguard stepped out to the stairs, where she found Laisida's wife on the landing, shaking a large wooden spoon at Aperiole, the least useful of her daughters. "You and your romantics! You could've spoiled . . ."

Sullen, overpainted eyes came up and spotted Nimnestl. Nimnestl saw Aperiole's fingers flash a quick series of signals.

Berdais planted a hand on her daughter's chest. "Spoiled a whole cart of Barset livers!" The hand pushed Aperiole back through a doorway; Berdais followed. Nimnestl was reasonably certain that goose livers had not been the original topic of conversation.

She considered going after them; it was reasonable to assume, in this case, that the wife would know what the husband was up to. But the sound of many feet coming up the stairs made her turn.

Now what right had Colonel Umian to look so cool, so competent, on a hot and harried day? She could do something about that, at least.

"Well met, Colonel!" she called, moving to the top of the stairs. "Your men are in fine order!"

Five of the black-coated New Guard were coming up the stairs behind him. "Yes," he said.

"The more I see of them," she noted, "the more I feel they can be a useful addition to the Palace Royal's security."

The Colonel's eyes were wary. He stopped on reaching the landing; protocol forbade him to move on if a ranking official wanted to talk to him.

"They might serve to escort people to the dungeons, people

who are not under arrest, exactly, since we wouldn't want to worry the Palace's inhabitants unduly." She smiled a "you understand" smile. "We have been very worried about General Ferrapec."

Umian's face did not change. "You believe the general may be in danger?"

She smiled again. "That's it, yes." She scratched her upper lip. "We could take him into protective custody."

"The private guard," said Umian, in even but icy tones, "was not created for the use of those seeking to advance their personal plots."

"No?"

"No. As for General Ferrapec, you would go far before you found a more loyal Son of the Panther."

Nimnestl looked beyond him and the New Guard members to the expanse of empty stairs. "You may be correct," she said, and started down. It was important not to overdo these things. Umian and Ferrapec were now free to fret about which had dropped the bag open. One man might be sure of his own security, but neither would trust the other to be as careful as he was. Worry could make them cancel their plot, which would be nice, or speed it up, which could be nicer.

"Ah, My Lady!"

On the second-floor landing, Lord Arlmorin stood talking to a sturdy young man with clear eyes and a cleft chin. "You have met Ebset, have you not?" he asked, as the Bodyguard came down the stairs. "I have been lax in my attention to His Majesty these past days, for Ebset returns to Braut at the end of the month and must be briefed."

Nimnestl had been involved in planting lovers in the households of courtiers, and knew what the ambassador was getting at. He wanted her to assume that, since Ebset would be leaving the country soon, a dalliance with the young man could not possibly leave any worrisome political aftereffects.

"You may make up for any laxity now, if you like," Nimnestl told him. "But, My Lord, I would prefer to speak with you alone."

"Very well, but I can tell you nothing of today's plots except that they are connected with yesterday's plots. And I haven't understood yesterday's plots yet." Arlmorin nodded to his compatriot, who bowed to Nimnestl and moved on upstairs.

Nimnestl waited for the lad to get out of earshot, and looked over the Brautian ambassador. A heavyset, vibrant man, Arlmorin managed to get a great deal done without ever seeming to do much. He gave presents, which he claimed came from his king. He talked. And he listened. Of course, the more he listened, the more people talked. As with Polijn, everyone assumed the foreign ambassador was up to something. But since, unlike Polijn, he had convinced nearly every courtier that he was their very best friend, they assumed that when he did go through with it, they would benefit.

Nimnestl mopped her brow. She was uncomfortable around the seemingly omniscient anyway, and Arlmorin used some kind of soap that made him smell, even on a day like today, exactly like hot porridge with honey. Nimnestl had eaten hot porridge with honey for breakfast every day as a child.

"He really is a bright young man, not?" the ambassador asked her. "I think he's meant for great things if he has proper guidance."

Nimnestl gave him a noncommittal nod, and trained her eyes on his. "I do wish you could be more discreet around General Ferrapec, My Lord. He's at that impressionable age."

Arlmorin chuckled. "But that's when they're most useful. He can suit both Carasta's purposes and mine."

Nimnestl raised an eyebrow. The ambassador very seldom admitted that he had purposes.

The ambassador spread out his hands. "Carasta's an entertaining scamp, not? You must admire his audacity, if nothing else. I thought I would do him a favor and expose him before he becomes too involved in the creation of your University."

Nimnestl's face was grave. "I hope he appreciates the favor."

"Why, I believe he will, if it is explained to him. He hasn't been here long enough to know you all, and I have twice as many eyes, not? He was bound to be found out, but the longer this took, the more likely that it would reflect badly on the University. Lord Haeve might react violently if his pride and joy were threatened."

Nimnestl knew that. She wondered how Arlmorin knew that. But she said, "Have you explained this to Carasta yet? You have not explained it to Haeve, I hope."

"I have hinted to Carasta that, in the event that worse comes to worst, and he is banished, he may count on me for letters to my King."

"I wonder what those letters will say," Nimnestl mused, looking toward the stairwell. "There can be no doubt that he is an impostor?"

"He was drinking too heavily last night and began to sing." The ambassador's tone was dry. "There can be no doubt."

Nimnestl nodded. "Why Ferrapec, though, as your messenger pigeon?"

The ambassador set both hands flat on his velvet vest. "His Majesty takes an interest in the arts and, as I say, Carasta is an engaging rogue. So soon after the death of Morquiesse, His Majesty might take it amiss that someone had done a favorite minstrel a bad turn. Ferrapec can withstand a blow to his position better than I; he's had so many."

Something in Arlmorin's face made Nimnestl pay close attention as the ambassador spoke. His words suggested that he knew more about a number of state secrets than was really comfortable. But she said only, "It may wait until we have reached the Summer Palace."

"I'm not at all surprised," said the ambassador, in a tone of sympathy. "You have so many things engaging your interest during the move. I am a little surprised that the Royal Exorcist should be involved in arranging the supplies. But things are done differently in different countries, not?"

Nimnestl's brows came down. She looked the man up and down, but saw nothing new.

"You want me to ask what that means."

Arlmorin smiled. "It would speed things up."

Nimnestl would have been greatly irritated by anyone else who said this. But she knew the ambassador was not, in fact, laughing at her. He was simply enjoying his profession as a man of mystery, and expected her to enjoy it as well.

"Then let me inform you," she said, "that our Royal Exorcist does not ordinarily trouble himself with such matters. Have you heard something to the contrary?"

He shrugged. "I was in the Lifted Finger, in the Swamp, not? And I heard that Lord Aizon has ordered large amounts of wine. Wine to be delivered not to him, nor to any point in North Malbeth, but to a number of spots in the Swamp itself. The manager of the Lifted Finger was aggrieved; none had been ordered from him, you understand."

Nimnestl said nothing. "But perhaps this is Lord Aizon's usual custom," said the ambassador.

"It strikes you as unusual?" she asked.

He shrugged. "Wine is better than well-water for buying loyalty."

She nodded. "I shall keep it in mind."

"Much better, in some corners, than large gold coins," he went on. Now he was gazing at the stairwell.

She had not expected him to miss that story. Morafor was never noted for discretion. "Were you at the Yellow Dog, then, in your travels?" she inquired.

He gave his head a rueful shake. "A little too early, it seems. Nor was I especially venturesome, or I might have made interesting discoveries myself. But I was turned away, and there are other shows, after all. That at the Yellow Dog has not been as entertaining since the change in personnel."

"You saw other Swampers? Persons from the Palace?"

His eyes came back to hers. "Of course."

"Male?" she asked. "Or female?"

"Male." He straightened a golden cuff, and frowned at one button before inquiring, in a manner of purely idle interest, "Is there someone in particular you had in mind?"

"Female," she said. "But seen only in passing; it may have been a mistake."

She was gratified by a passing intensity in his gaze. But he went on, his voice apathetic, "I hope it was a mistake. She might well run afoul of Veldres's men. You may have been too intent on the crowds around His Majesty to note that the merchant's attendants slipped away at various times during the procession. The word is that they were searching for servants, either the one who escaped or new ones to be kidnapped. Lady Iranen or General Torrix might have had commissions for Veldres as well. An unescorted woman would be running a risk."

Nimnestl had noticed this, but had assumed they were passing the word to cancel whatever trouble Veldres had been planning in the Swamp. "Or," she said, "they could have been giving orders for the disposal of Lord Aizon's wine?"

"That I have not heard," said the ambassador. "So it couldn't be possible at all, not?"

"Certainly not." Nimnestl returned his smile.

Arlmorin sighed. "Such a hand at politics! Are you sure you couldn't find time to tutor young Ebset? Advice would mean more to him coming from one in such an exalted position. In the evenings, perhaps, when your time is . . ."

"Lord Haeve is far better suited to tutoring than I, My Lord," Nimnestl told him, "though his position is different. If you will excuse me, I have duties to attend to: more, I think, than I had at the top of the stairs."

The ambassador bowed, and Nimnestl moved on into the nearest of the three corridors that led from the landing into the main hall of the Grand Tower. Her mind was on Aizon and on Veldres, but her ears caught the sounds of combat nearby and forced her attention around to them.

No one was fighting in the Grand Tower, so Nimnestl turned back to check the other corridors back to the stairs. A little crowd was developing at the end of the corridor on the far left. She strode down to join it.

Before she reached the mob, she had caught sight of the combatants in its center: a tall New Guard, dagger in hand, was holding off four challengers. One of these was clutching a damaged arm; another wore a brown sideburn on one side of his head and a dripping red one on the other. The crowd shouted advice as the attackers moved in again.

"Get him down and feel for his eyestrings! That'll make him tell the news!"

"Kick him good! You know where!"

The New Guard wanted to go for his sword, but the sword belt had been cut, and was lying on the floor. So, when an attacker dealt him a kick, he reached down and lashed out with the loose belt. Leather curled around the extended ankle, and the attacker rolled backward.

Nimnestl would not have bothered had she not recognized all four attackers. As it was, she plowed into the crowd and demanded, "What has this man done?"

The New Guard flattened himself against the wall at the

sight of this new threat. The crowd immediately recalled business in other parts of the Palace Royal.

"Er, nothing as such, Ma'am," said the man with the wounded arm. A thought struck him. "He was making disrespectful remarks about His Lordship."

"If you intend to grapple with anyone making remarks about the Regent, you will waste much time and strength," Nimnestl informed him. "Members of the Royal Bodyguard will restrict themselves to reporting such remarks, particularly in view of the fact that it requires four of you to take one man into custody. You obviously have little strength to spare. As for your time, I suggest you report to Biandi, who no doubt has duties to fill your empty hours."

The bodyguards nodded and, gathering up such bits of themselves as had been knocked off, slipped off down the hall. Nimnestl turned to their victim.

"As for you, if you can hold off four members of His Majesty's Bodyguard, you are wasting your time and strength in the service of the New Guard. What is your name?"

"Valspar," said the guard, and added, "Ma'am."

"If it should happen that you require other employment and less somber attire, you will find I remember the name. Now go away."

By now, all but one of the crowd had gone. This one slid up to Valspar and whispered, "I bet we can take her."

Nimnestl waited long enough to see Valspar shake his head. Gilphros shrugged and sauntered away. Nimnestl moved off, too.

III

NIMNESTL had whole months in which she was sick of talking to people she loathed. She was inclined that way right now, and the sight of Kodva standing between her and the Regent's door, with an expression indicating a definite intention to speak, did not sweeten her temper.

But she did slow down when Ferrapec's mother inquired, "Have you seen Polijn?"

"Not that I recall," the Bodyguard said, coming to a halt beyond Kodva and looking back. "Should I see her?"

Kodva's nose went up. "I was of the impression that you kept track of people returning from the Swamp. I was naturally anxious that such a small child should return safely."

"It would be best to apply to Laisida for that information," Nimnestl told her, "since that is properly his concern. Is it not?"

"Lord Laisida is, certainly, more likely to have a mind to his duties," Kodva replied, and marched away. Nimnestl thought about pursuing the matter, but decided it might be better not to show interest in Polijn just yet.

She knocked at Kaftus's door and let herself in. The bat just inside hissed its warning. Kaftus glanced up from behind a table laden with small containers. He wasn't planning a Council meeting then, but intended to spend time with his mixtures and compounds. Nimnestl never asked what all this cookery was about; she had troubles enough of her own.

"You just missed your darling," he told her, reaching for the largest bowl. "His new composition is ready to present when we reach the Summer Palace. The title, I collect, is 'I Know My Sweetheart's Love is True But Unfortunately She's In Love With You.' "

Nimnestl passed a hand across her eyes. "I thought his promotion would keep him from writing songs."

"On the contrary," said the necromancer, sifting powder from a porcelain dish into the bowl. "Since all his duties are beyond him, he has twice as much time."

"Yes," Nimnestl sighed, "Arberth is rather out of his depth in Council."

"Arberth was out of his depth at birth." Kaftus moved to a wooden wall locker and took up a saucer with red crystals in it. "That's why so many people have nominated him to head the University. That would be the next best thing to having no University at all."

Adding the red crystals to the bowl threw an odor of spoiled milk into the room. Nimnestl moved a little away from the table. "That would have its advantages, of course."

"Particularly if the University were far, far from the Palace Royal." Kaftus took up a vial and emptied it into the bowl. "I think we'd do best to let Haeve and Laisida have their way for now. We can make additions and subtractions later. Speaking of which, I have presumed to hire a new bodyguard."

The milk smell grew stronger. "A new bo . . . no."

"The woman seems to be most anxious to please," he said, with an undeceptive mildness. "I told her to watch you at all times to see how it's done."

"Good of you to give her an assignment so close to what Veldres has already ordered," snapped the Bodyguard. What was the woman's name again? Deverna.

She shook her head. If Veldres was indeed involved in a scheme to overthrow the Regency, would he really pursue a time-consuming plan to introduce a spy/lover into the government? Perhaps he was just following Ferrapec's example, and preparing for any outcome.

"It's your just punishment," Kaftus went on. A wave of his hand dispersed the odor of sour milk.

"Punishment?"

"For coming in here with whatever it is you came in here to annoy me with."

"They," she said, with a sigh. "Whatever they were."

The high eyebrows arched. "So many new crises?" asked the necromancer.

"They may all be one crisis," she told him, and explained all the irritating surprises of the past hour: Aizon's wine, Veldres's search for a servant, Ferrapec's thirst for Carasta's blood, Morafor's discovery of coins that should have been within the Treasury, and Polijn's appearance after the entire personnel of a playhouse in the Swamp had been stolen out of their clothes and spirited away.

Kaftus added a pinch of this and a dash of that to his bowl. When Nimnestl finished, he glanced up. "So that's what it was."

Nimnestl folded her hands. And the Regent could do this without a twitch in his face to show he'd said something outrageous.

"What what was?" she inquired, when further explanation was not forthcoming. "You had hints of a new conspiracy in the city and didn't feel like worrying me?"

"Some of my wisdom is rubbing off." Kaftus swung a skull-topped staff above the bowl. "You are almost within a chance of approaching the truth."

She licked her lips. "Am I old enough to be told?"

Steam rolled from the bowl. When it had rolled to the height of the skull, Kaftus plunged the staff into the mixture, which bubbled and smoked. "No. But I'll tell you anyway; how else will you learn? I have detected an increase in power."

"In the city?"

"Here."

"How here? Here in this room? Did you do it?"

"That isn't my way." He dropped one white crystal into the bowl, dissipating the choking fumes. "Here in the Palace Royal. Someone has experienced an increase in power equivalent to that which would be achieved if a sorcerer walked into the Yellow Dog and absorbed the life forces of thirty to forty people, turning all their power into his own pot."

"Is that dangerous?" she asked. "For someone beside the thirty or forty people, that is?"

"Of course it's dangerous. It's just not very dangerous."

"The sorcerer couldn't attack you, for example?"

"He could, but it would be a very short battle. Not to flatter myself . . ."

"Perish forbid."

Kaftus put a hand on his chest, and inclined his head. "But the absorption of some hundreds would be necessary before he could think of competing with me. Though he no doubt is thinking of it."

Nimnestl nodded. "So he may be planning to absorb more. What becomes of the people involved?"

The necromancer shrugged, and stirred his mixture. "It depends on the method used. They may be worthless now, or he may have salted them away in mystic containers. Some people last thousands of years in one of those, and have their own powers increased if they ever escape."

"And it could be anyone on the procession, or some sorcerer who just passed through the Swamp," said Nimnestl. "Polijn might know, if she saw him. Or her."

"No," said Kaftus.

"No?"

"No to both thoughts. That little one hasn't the power or the knowledge to have done it herself. And if she'd seen the sorcerer doing the job, there'd be nothing left of her to flee: just a pile of clothing."

"Ye-es," said the Bodyguard. "Unless our sorcerer is also the third conspirator, and Polijn is some assistant of his."

Kaftus looked down his nose at her. "You are succumbing to Polijn paranoia. I think it's the heat. You need a nice, cooling vacation in the Swamp."

Nimnestl met his eyes. "To do what?"

"I am intrigued by Aizon's wine." He tested the mixture in the bowl with one finger. "The man drinks rainwater, himself. I have never before known him to take an interest in wine, or in politics. Go ask the Vielfrass about it."

She recoiled. "Why not ask Aizon?"

Kaftus tapped the damp finger behind each ear. "Besides the fact that he would certainly tell you nothing, even if his cause was innocent, he does play an important role in our departure for the north. Any move of ours against him will be taken as a bad omen, casting a pall over the whole summer's activities. Particularly if he has to sic his bats on you."

She had to admit the truth of that. But the Vielfrass! That perversely unpredictable sorcerer was as thoroughly a power in the Swamp as Kaftus was in the Palace Royal: no one ever knew what he could do, what he meant to do, or what was to be done about him.

"Couldn't you just look in a mirror or something to learn what goes on in the Swamp?" she demanded.

"That gives knowledge," the necromancer told her, pouring his mixture through a filter. "It would not give understanding."

Nimnestl shook her head. Wouldn't it be better to wait until the Swampers came staggering back? Torrix would be back late, in no condition to dodge questions about Veldres. And she could ask Karabari about Aizon, provided the Exorcist's apprentice didn't linger in the Swamp for a few days; he'd done that before and come staggering back to boast of his conquests.

Some purposes could be served by a visit to the Swamp, of course. Seitun was down there, Veldres's servants, and, if Morafor's eyesight was good, Polijn. She might be able to get some information about Polijn and her family from the head of the Prostitutes' Guild. But that woman knew more prices than names.

Kaftus was busy bottling his brew, and paying no attention. So it came down to her decision. What did she feel would do more good, on a sweltering day: making a third at the meeting between Laisida and Kirasov, or riding back down to the Swamp?

"I'll go," she said. "Most likely, the Vielfrass will be nowhere in evidence, and I won't have time to hunt for him. Some members of the bodyguard need extra training."

Kaftus glanced at her. "I take it from your tone that Umian's little company has been making inroads. Do go easy on your playthings, won't you? They can't all rise to your level. Try to be content with having a copy of yourself in wise Culghi."

Nimnestl shook her head and moved out of the room. It was Culghi's ill luck to be running down the corridor at that moment.

"Oh!" he exclaimed, perceiving his commander a second before he tried to push her out of the way. "I beg your pardon, Ma'am! Have you seen Nurse?"

"Fortunately, no. What's amiss?"

He jerked a huge hand back toward the Royal Chambers. "His Majesty's starting in on the hiccups: that fever again."

Nimnestl rolled her eyes; she knew Conan would turn that whole furor to good account someday. "It's the fever, is it? His Majesty told you so, I suppose?"

"Merklin, Ma'am, and the others."

"And who among these others is guarding His Majesty, since you have deserted him?"

Culghi swallowed hard. "Mardith, Ma'am."

Lintik blast that bird and his sense of humor; of course he'd go along with the children in fooling Culghi. "That is not the two guards I ordered, is it?"

"No, Ma'am, but . . ."

"Go fetch Nurse to him, then. Try the Wardrobe. If she leaves a square inch of hide on your body, report to me and I'll take care of the rest."

Culghi paused, trying to explain and remember which direction the Royal Wardrobe was from here. Then he took off down the hall.

Nimnestl shook her head. No doubt she should follow her own orders and go to the King now, but she had no desire to be there when Nurse arrived. Mardith was, in fact, probably enough of a guard for a few minutes. Culghi was not, however, to be thinking he could disobey orders. She shook her head again. If she could help it, he ought not be thinking at all.

IV

PAMMEL wandered from one side of the street to the other, sniffing now and again at a limp bundle of violets he'd picked up who knew where. He was starting to weave back to the original side when a hard-eyed woman wearing no more than what was essential took his chin in her hand and pulled his face down between her breasts.

She let go and strolled into one of the little shops that darkened its doorway to accommodate those who didn't care to be identified going in. Pammel's sense of smell was obviously defective; he followed her.

Nimnestl watched all this from the shadow of a braced wooden skyway that crossed the Street of Clay Mugs. She hoped the woman had nothing more in mind than obscene profit; she had neither the time nor the inclination to rescue Kaigrol's son. Pammel was not the best friend of the Regency; he had not forgiven the Regent for attempting to save his own son's life in mock battle. Obligation to the Regent was unforgivable. He and Kaigrol were loud in Council in demanding the return from exile of Kirasov's son Anrichar, who had disobeyed the Regent's order and killed the lad.

Nimnestl strolled from the shadows, moving downhill toward a little square. The meat pies she could smell had obviously been aging badly when stolen for sale today. The crowd was sparse, but since the smell was no worse than on any summer day in the Swamp, she supposed everyone had moved inside simply to keep out of impending rain. The air smelled wrong for rain, though; the night would stay hot and sticky. Her job would be the more difficult then; the Vielfrass might be infesting any one of a hundred mean little establishments. And in each there might be Swampers who would give away her identity.

Nimnestl did not like the Swamp, but she understood its appeal to the Swampers. She moved out of the way as a gap-toothed urchin fled from a Treasury guard. In the Palace Royal, a mistake could mean a shift in power, disgrace, a change of government, civil war. It was refreshing to fear nothing more than a knife in the belly.

Five men in matching overtunics that didn't quite fit pushed out of the crowd, possibly in pursuit of the guard. Nimnestl wondered who had the money in this neighborhood; the men were younger, bulkier, and rather better armed than the usual local watchmen. The big man in the lead looked Nimnestl up and down and started toward her.

Women from Reangle were not so rare here as in the Palace Royal, and, since Nimnestl had taken care to hide her hammer under an otherwise cumbersome and unnecessary cloak, he could have no idea he was facing the King's Chief Bodyguard. She was merely a large brown woman, and there was no love for natives of Reangle in Rossacotta. The two countries had set up as rivals almost immediately when they came into being in the sundering of Eastland. Each considered itself the true heir of Eastland, and the other country a nation of alien degenerates.

So there would be questions at the very least, and probably more, meaning greater delay. Nimnestl set her feet and raised her chin, waiting for them.

Before the leader could address her, however, one of his subordinates tugged at his shirttail. Everyone looked to the left and, without another glance at Nimnestl, hurried to the right. Rope pilers and beggars on the left side of the street followed them.

A column of swirling black cloth topped by a head of swirling black hair was proceeding down the street on that side, not apparently noticing the migration he had caused. The

Vielfrass paused, and stooped for something by his feet. After sniffing the violet, he tucked it behind his right ear.

The sorcerer looked more solid, more concentrated, than the other people in the market, as if he were real and the rest of the world was some misty fantasy, a belief to which he wholeheartedly subscribed. He was accompanied by an equally concentrated woman, who had not bothered with the heavy cape he favored. This was Lady Oozola, a shape-shifter of unknown origin. She pointed at something in the crowd. The crowd parted immediately as the pair stepped toward whatever it was.

Nimnestl had already begun to step toward them, but had to brace herself anew when a heavy body came flying at her. She took the brunt of the impact on her right hip, and drew a knife with her left hand.

"Th-there you are!" said a voice from the bundle of muscle, as it dropped to its knees. "R-runnin' out on me, eh? P-paid you a g-good t-t-two plows, and not to t-take a lintik st-stroll. Whatcha mean by it, eh?" The man rose to his feet.

Nimnestl held the knife in front of her. "I've never seen you before, man," she declared. "Besides, it was only one plow, and a scraped one at that. Come in here for a drink; I'll stand the cost and we'll call it even."

"I'll t-take that dr-dr-drink and we'll t-talk about st-st-standing," the man replied, clutching at her cloak for support.

She led him to the Lifted Finger, a respectable establishment as far as the Swamp went, and one which served alcohol almost drinkable. A number of merchants higher in the city ordered from the owner, but Etzner never revealed where he got the stuff, unless perhaps to his assistant bartender, Bierun.

"Two m-mugs!" Nimnestl's companion shouted, a fist landing on the countertop. "Sp-sp-p-peed it up! Ladies d-don't like to wait!"

Bierun filled the mugs and passed them over, his expression weary and wary. This was not the first fighting drunk to bang on the bar. Etzner glanced at the newcomer, but sneered and turned away.

Etzner had every requisite for being a bar-owner here: lack of interest in the customers so long as they paid and didn't damage the premises, muscle to make sure they followed those guidelines, and a tendency to break into unpredictable violence, damaging premises and customers alike. This brought him a slightly classier clientele: no two-penny uprights worked against his bar, no stranglers lurked among the barrels in back.

And customers tended to mind their own business. Even so, when they sat at the mended table in the corner, Seitun leaned forward to whisper, "I meant to report later."

Nimnestl nodded. The mention of two plow-faced penny-etkes, however, meant that important information had been uncovered about the closemouthed beggar, or his wife. "You found her?"

He nodded. "Mityrets."

"Faff! The one Veldres is looking for?"

"The same." Seitun took a drink. "It fits: with Diabies in the dungeon, he has only to get rid of her."

Nimnestl nodded. This didn't mean, of course, that Veldres was the man they wanted. The merchant might well have done all this as a favor to someone else. In which case, he would do well to be on guard. Getting rid of one's assistants could occur to other people.

"Rumor makes some connection between Veldres's household and the Yellow Dog," Seitun went on. "She could have taken shelter there, but I haven't been able to get down to that part of town."

"Better stay clear," Nimnestl told him. "She'd keep away from any place that dealt with her master." Besides, after all, who would take shelter at a theater where the shows started at nude ear-piercing exhibitions and moved down?

"Is it necessary for me to look for her now at all?"

Nimnestl set down her mug. "You have something better to do?"

He shook his head violently. "I just wondered if Veldres might be more interesting now."

Nimnestl tried to decide whether she liked the idea, and if her feeling against it was just disinclination to have Seitun thinking for himself so soon after Culghi's infraction.

Seitun shrugged to show it really didn't matter to him. "There are some unrelated matters to report," he noted. "Not related to Diabies."

"Yes," said Nimnestl, setting the mug to one side. "We've had rumors, but that's all. What have you seen?"

He checked the other customers quickly before going on. "There's some kind of feeling about the Regent," he said, his voice lower. "It's recent, or I just didn't notice it when I first came down. Carasta, the minstrel from the south, was in the Slipping Shift, and made some remark about his close personal friend. Two men called him a Swamper, not like they usually do, but as if they were angry. He just got out with his life; I got kicked in the head, just in passing."

"It's the heat," suggested Nimnestl.

"They usually won't attack a Swamper in a public place like that, not if he's spending money," Seitun replied, setting one hand on the table. "Part of it's the Swampers, too. I heard two of them nearly took apart Dindo's pawnshop when he was too slow redeeming their pledge. But most of it's because of the wine."

"Wine," Nimnestl noted, checking her mug and shooing a fly.

"Poisoned wine's been found in good bottles. They had Palace marks on them, which might mean nothing; these bottles might've been on their sixth or seventh go-around. But the story is that these bottles came from the Palace just recently. The Regent means to smash and burn the whole district, they say, after drugging anybody who might be an obstacle."

Nimnestl rubbed one thumb up and down the side of the mug. Veldres had to be involved in this, then.

Seitun took another drink. "Er, you'd . . . I mean . . . well, he isn't, is he?"

"He hasn't mentioned it," she told him, shaking her head. "I think we may find the answer if we find Mityrets."

Seitun looked as if he'd like more information, but none was forthcoming. Nimnestl watched the flies on the table. She knew more or less what was going on, now; she had only to learn who had set it in motion. Carasta, Veldres, Aizon: which, if any? Carasta could be working with Arlmorin on something, sent to make unwise remarks and upset the Swamp. Or he might just not be too bright. Aizon was interested primarily in immortality: he might drug people and then absorb them, to add their life expectancy to his own. Ferrapec and Umian might be helping him, hoping to use the turmoil that created for their own ends. Veldres, she'd have sworn, was not the kind of man who made large-scale, long-range plans. Rip out a fingernail: that's all he needed to fulfill his ambitions.

Behind the bar, Etzner swore. A tasselled dancer sitting on the bar screamed. Everyone turned to the door as a woman stumbled inside.

Naked people in flight through the Swamp were no novelty. Mutilated victims of the denizens of the alleys constituted no news. But to come into the Lifted Finger and bleed all over the painstakingly cleaned floor showed very poor judgement, to say nothing of bad taste.

Nimnestl had a good view of her: cheekbones smashed, ears all but bitten off, a few tatters of yellow cloth dangling from around her neck. She seemed intent on reaching the bar, but didn't make it.

Three customers stepped up to the body. "Dead," said one, nudging it a bit with the side of his boot. "Veldres won't pay a copper for her now."

V

THE crowd moved in, interested. Nimnestl sat where she was. This was very disappointing, to be sure, but there were ways to make up the loss. For starters, she put out one leg to block the progress of a man carrying a bottle toward the door.

"What is this?" the man demanded, obviously unaccustomed to people who had the temerity to impede his progress.

"Not leaving yet, were you, Undurom?" she inquired.

Seitun stared at the man, who drew himself up with stiff dignity. "I do not know you."

"But I know you," said Nimnestl, a little louder. "Undurom, isn't it?"

This was starting to register with the crowd around the shattered woman.

"Undurom!"

"Veldres's doorwarden?"

"Undurom's here!"

Undurom himself did not yet notice. "And if I am," he replied, his tone cold, "is that any reason I cannot have a drink like any man here, and come and go as I please?"

The crowd was beginning to turn toward this new entertainment. Nimnestl checked their faces, and saw that Undurom was not a prime favorite with them. Other things being equal, then, if it came to a fight they would support whoever looked tougher. She did the simplest thing, therefore. She stood up.

Undurom pulled back, staring at how far up she stood. "I thought we might have a friendly drink together," she told him. "I do believe that's Mityrets there. How odd that she should die while you were in the neighborhood."

Undurom took in a long breath, and tried to stand taller. He was a good foot short of looking Nimnestl in the eye, but pretended not to notice as he demanded, "What do you suggest? I have the power to order you killed here and now. I waste more time in telling you that than it would take to have it done."

Nimnestl sneered. "Where I come from, we do our own killing."

A growl of support from the crowd brought Undurom to a sense of his danger. He shrank a beat and, glancing at the heap of flesh by the bar, replied, "I . . . had nothing to do with it. I . . . am doorwarden for Veldres, yes, but I just came down here to see the King, and recruit servants."

"Kidnapper," someone muttered.

Nimnestl gestured Undurom toward the bar. He obeyed, but Seitun came up behind him just to be sure.

They looked down at the body. Working for Veldres was not likely to enhance one's well-being. Flat upper arms showed no more muscle than was essential for carrying a tray. The legs were irregular, evidence of further attention from her master. But torso and head were evidence of more recent, more concentrated attention. Bone splinters poked out at a side of the chest; blood had washed the body below a number of serious dents.

It was an ugly exhibit, and the crowd was very displeased with Undurom. "It's true!" he cried, his imagination transferring her injuries to his own body. "I came out at midday when my duties were over, just to invite anyone I saw to come take service. It . . . it pays well."

That was a stupid thing to say, with evidence of the payment on the floor right there. The crowd moved in. "I was supposed to watch for her, yes," he went on, eyes looking left and right for sympathy. "But I wasn't . . . wasn't supposed to kill her or even try to carry her back." He tried to laugh, failed, and

went on, "Why go to such trouble for lowlife scum like this
when . . ."

He swallowed hard as the crowd moved in a full foot. Most
of the people around him were lowlife scum, and knew it.

"It's a lie."

Nimnestl and those who had their backs to the bar turned.
Etzner spoke without heat, but a firmness in his voice said he
was in dead earnest, and anyone who doubted him could find
out how dead dead earnest could be.

"Been here all morning, he was. Saw him chatting her up,
saying something she might do in trade for a safe hiding place,
where Veldres'd never look. Wanted to start in right there at
the table. Might've let him, too, for it's been a slow day, but
he wanted to use one of our bottles on her. Look how he's
fingerin' that one there."

Undurom had probably picked up this bottle for use as a
weapon, if necessary. He now decided it was necessary, and
leaped at the barman with it. Nimnestl, not at all willing to
have the fight break out yet, put one hand on the elbow of
his bottle arm and the other under his chin. She lifted him a
little off the floor. The crowd drew back, recognizing her prior
claim on the culprit.

"Do stand still, Undurom," she suggested. "Your face is not
ornamental, but it will not be improved by being smeared with
honey as you stand in the pillory."

Undurom's eyes seemed to rise from his face. The crowd
was impressed, too: unfavorably impressed. Mention of the pillory identified the woman as someone on the side of the law.

"Informer!"

"What'd Undurom do to her? Pillory!"

"Probably reports direct to old Noshulla."

Nimnestl saw Undurom take this in, and open his mouth to
speak. She tightened her grip on his throat and announced, to
no one in particular, "When I speak to Noshulla, he stands at
attention."

The crowd hesitated, not certain how to take this. Nimnestl
set Undurom back on the floor, and played her highest card,
twitching back her cloak to show the hammer.

"The Bodyguard!"

"The Regent's black dog!"

"You know me," Nimnestl said to them. "Some of you may know Veldres. Or know someone who works for Veldres."

The Lifted Finger was silent for a second. Then a man said, "Aye! My sister worked there, lintik take him!"

"My brother-in-law!"

"My sister's man's father was his wine steward!"

More people were volunteering information, but Nimnestl raised a hand. "Have you ever known him to give a servant time off in the morning, before his duties were done?"

Silence fell again, for rather more than a second. A few customers slid back from the bar. "Where has Mityrets been hiding?" she demanded. "What if she had refused a request made by the man who hid her, bottle or no bottle?"

The bar-owner was no man to wait around. He leaped over the bar, shouting, "You can't . . ."

Nimnestl raised her hand again. But it had a hammer in it this time.

"You," she said, pointing to Seitun. "What's your name?"

"Pallis, My Lady," he said, dropping to his knees.

"Then you and you and you," she said, pointing at two other men, "take him to the Palace Royal."

No one moved. It seemed a pity to lose an excellent barman over a mere murder.

Nimnestl's eyes narrowed. "The Regent wanted that woman in the dungeons."

Not only did the two men she'd picked out stoop immediately to help Seitun with the body, but three more started to wrap up Mityrets as well.

Undurom had not moved. Nimnestl turned to him. "Do you feel you could spare some time from your busy schedule for the Regent?"

He licked his lips. "As . . . as much time as necessary, My Lady."

"Come with me, then. And behave yourself, remembering at all times that we are going to see a necromancer, so I am under no particular obligation to bring you in alive."

The doorwarden collapsed. Well, it might be easier to get him back to the Palace Royal that way.

CHAPTER FIVE
Polijn

I

POLIJN came to with a start. She needed a second to remember where she was, the cupboard too dark for clues. When no one had come immediately to disembowel her, she had pulled the rags up under her head for a nap. The longer she hid, after all, the better was the chance that the mob would forget her and go back to loot the Yellow Dog. The rags had a homely smell, and it had been a tiring morning.

What startled her was not that she had been able to sleep (in the Swamp, you ate, drank, and slept whenever you could) but that she had started to talk to Mokono as she awoke. Not much: just "Are you awake?" But Mokono had been dead four years; Polijn hoped this wasn't going to be a habit. Or, worse, an omen.

It was most likely just memory, she decided, stretching one leg out experimentally. They had slept in rags often, back in what Sielvia would have called "the happy times when all went well." She and Mokono had shared confidences there, while Mokono was alive, of course. Polijn didn't lack for substitute sisters now, but when venturing to confide in Sielvia once, she had so shocked the minstrel's daughter that Polijn had to pretend she was joking.

She stretched out both legs, touched the door of the cupboard, and gave it a gentle push. Chordasp never avenged

Mokono's death. The women who had done for her were Ancipo's, and, anyway, Mokono had been straying out of her proper rounds. The two strongmen had settled it all with an exchange of money, most of which Chordasp kept, passing only a few coppers on to Ronar.

The room beyond the cupboard door seemed terribly dark. Had she slept so long, or was it just getting cloudier? She crawled forward to risk one eye at the door.

Nothing seemed to be moving, so she put her head out, turning it toward the window. Clouds, then: good. If it actually started to rain, there would be fewer people out on the streets to recognize her.

She came out of the cupboard and stepped to the window for another look, down this time. There was no way down from here unless she cared to jump. Polijn did not care to jump; the way the cards were falling today, she'd break a leg. Much better to risk a walk down through the shop, or whatever it was, and hope the proprietor didn't feel like breaking her leg for her.

Whose shop was it? Polijn moved to the left of the window and then turned to examine the little room. The rags seemed to have been sorted more or less by color, but everything still looked too neat for a ragpicker's apartment. And why would a ragpicker need imitation weapons? All ragpickers were a little mad, of course.

"Ine!"

Polijn froze. She could see nothing that could have made the sound, but it had surely been in the room with her. She closed her eyes to listen for it, hoping she wouldn't hear it again.

"I-ine!"

The cry came from the darkest corner of the room, where a tall cabinet stood next to the door. Opening her eyes, Polijn saw what seemed to be a tiny white ball bouncing crazily on top of the cabinet.

Moving in, she saw it was really the one white paw of a grey kitten, who was walking . . . no, trying to walk across the top of the cupboard. It was caught, though, in the sticky filaments of a web too big and crude to have been the work of a spider.

Polijn drew back. The alungwe might have been sleeping in the cabinet with her, for all she knew. The winged webmakers were nocturnal, sleeping under roofs and in upper rooms. Being a creature of the street level, Polijn saw their webs more than she saw them: the sticky strands were impossible to get out of your hair. Some blondes walked into them deliberately, for the effect of the dark strands on light hair.

Polijn wasn't tall enough to reach up to the kitten, nor was she eager to do so without knowing where the alungwe was waiting. She walked back across the room and took a wooden spear from its place in the racks. Reaching up, she knocked a few filaments from a foreleg of the concerned kitten.

Something hissed: not the kitten.

She looked to her left and saw the alungwe not much more than an arm's length away. It was one of the white ones, with red stripes on its head and angry red eyes. These blinked in an irritated way; perhaps it had felt something meddling with its web and been roused from its own nap.

Polijn took a step back. The little white bat took its eyes off her and started to climb the cabinet.

Of course, it would have to be a white alungwe, the most poisonous kind. Not only its bite but those little climbing claws were envenomed, and could do her serious damage. It would kill the kitten at once, of course.

"They have to eat, too, you know," Gloraida had told a much smaller Polijn once, after a pair of dogs had torn an orange cat apart down on the street. "Anyway, that's how it works: they were strongest."

The alungwe was rapidly climbing out of Polijn's reach. She could not possibly watch this. Anyhow, she was the strongest one here. Provided the thing didn't fly at her, of course.

How hard did you have to whack an alungwe to knock it out? Or would trying to run it through with the spear be quicker? Fairness asserted itself; the alungwe did have to eat, after all. All she wanted was for it to find its food somewhere else.

Polijn set down the spear and reached into her pouch for Kodva's gift. Detecting this movement, the alungwe paused to study her. Polijn took a little of the ginger from the box, set it on the tip of the wooden punch dagger she still carried, and extended the point toward the animal.

The creature's nostrils flared. Then a tiny pink tongue lapped out for the ginger. Polijn watched, enthralled, as the candy vanished.

When the alungwe was finished, Polijn pulled back the dagger and set more ginger on it. But before bringing the point to the animal again, she took up her spear. Now, when the alungwe started to snack, she reached up and brushed webbing away from the kitten.

Eventually, the kitten pulled away, free but annoyed, shaking one paw that kept sticking to the woodwork. Polijn had nearly exhausted the ginger in the box, and wondered what she would do when it was all gone.

When there was just enough left for one final serving, Polijn tapped the box to draw the creature's attention to it. Then she set it down on top of the cabinet in which she'd napped. She set the punch dagger down next to it. Then she dove to the far side of the cabinet as the alungwe sailed across to finish the aromatic treat.

Now was the time to head out of the shop, whether the proprietor was friendly or not. Polijn pulled open the door and walked out into a wooden hallway.

Where she found herself facing a woman who cried, "Here she is!"

II

POLIJN was braced for a run, but saw only one person in the doorway. The intruder was not much taller than she was, but certainly older, as the white hair and rings around her eyes testified.

"Breza," the woman said, hands on hips, "I've no complaint about you kids playing dress-up in the lintik ragroom, but you've got to be getting back. There's work to be done and you've got to do it. That's the first thing you should learn. Who've you got with you, or don't I have a right to ask?"

The milestone-shaped woman peered past her. Polijn realized she'd mistaken her visitor for the redheaded errand girl over at the New Berry. Polijn put up a hand to straighten Karlikartis's wig a bit.

"No one," said the woman, her head coming back to her thick shoulders. "Playing queen, is it, because Himself passed by and smiled your way? Smiles don't come to much in cash, Breza. That's the first thing you should learn."

She turned away. Polijn, obedient in her role as the slavey, fell in behind her.

A grey gallery led to a narrow flight of stairs. Polijn slid a hand just above the railing, ready to grab it if she started to fall, but not willing to risk splinters by hanging on. A face staring up at her from the open side of the stairs made her

210

pause, but the features were too crude to fool her for long. The wooden dummy had its head and arms thrown back to simulate a dancer.

This was the first time Polijn had seen Karland's shop from inside. A massive stringless harp sat in the middle of the waterstained floor. Cats rubbed up against it and then strolled over to take a nap in a stack of hats and bonnets, or on the shelves filled with wigs, beards, and mustaches. A box of imitation body parts sat under a table laden with glass eyes. Most everything was dusty, yellowed, or both. There were windows in the shop, but most of these were little "false lights," angled so as not to give a customer too good a look at the merchandise.

All manner of garments hung on racks or hooks, or sat in heaps on the floor. These gave her her steady income. She opened in early afternoon, when her customers were waking up and finding they'd lost a garment or two in the course of the previous evening's work. Karland's big profits, though, came from supplying the better houses with costumes and props for their shows.

As an independent, Polijn had never been able to afford Karland's wares, though she did know the woman by name and by sight. She stayed to the shadows, lest Karland recognize her, too.

The woman was busy, though, pulling together a collection of garments and accessories. "She wants orange, not lintik yellow, with her complexion," she muttered. "That's the first thing she should learn." She lifted a sleeping alungwe off a stack of tunics and set it on a pile of stockings. Polijn nodded; a good security system explained many things.

Karland's shop was one of the most profitable in this part of the Swamp. Mokono had tried to get a job there, as one of Karland's scavengers. But there was no shortage of applicants for the job, and Mokono was getting a bit old by that time. Mokono was always ambitious, always made sure when the family moved, it was to a slightly better place. Polijn had always been inclined more to play the cards she was dealt, at least until Mokono died. That had shown her the world was a place where even the most basic things could not be considered secure, in which nothing was your own. You had to pile up plenty, just so you could hope to keep a little.

"Not speaking to me, Your Majesty?" demanded Karland, lifting a little box from under a counter. "Still a queen, are we? Needn't be royal around here, My Lady." She fitted a key into the lock. "I know more about you than you think I know. You're important. You've been around. You can take care of yourself. You're no shuptit old wrinklerag like me."

She lifted the lid and stuck her chin out over it. "So could I take care of myself. But you wait. Maybe you think you've only to suck up a generous friend at auction and you're set for life, hah? The taste for young girls won't end just because you've been paid for; the auction won't stop with your sale. That's the first thing you should learn."

Karland looked down into the box and started to flip one hand through the contents. "I danced at the Palace Royal, copper-slot, when I was twenty and had both eyes and plenty of teeth. Your ladies who run the houses aren't on the same street with me. Look at that Vadstena; sends orders like I was her scullion, and she hasn't been sober in ten years or had clothes on in five."

She found what she was looking for and slammed the lid down. "And you'd be lucky to make it to her street, girl," she went on, shaking feather earrings at Polijn. "It's only one of the God-knows who do. That's the first thing you should learn.

"I didn't know, then, what would become of me, that I'd have what was called for." Karland stooped and slid the box away. "That girl, Negela, my grandson's girl, now, she'll make it, if the fever doesn't take her. She's got the smile, the quick mouth. Ah, she's pretty, too, but pretty doesn't pave your street. You can paint up a dummy to be pretty. It's response that makes them come back, aye, response and durability. That's the first thing you should learn."

She tossed the earrings onto the stack of goods, and peered at them to take inventory. "I've been where you are and now I'm where I am. I commanded gold, aye, and I danced at the Palace fifty years ago: I was just turned sixteen. I took care of myself and my money by being wide awake. You have to: that's the first thing you should learn. I can grow old gracefully. I have to: I've no strength to do it disgracefully. Ha. Ha ha. Ha ha ha."

Polijn put out her arms as Karland took up the bundle and crossed the floor, still talking. "All I want from this lot is quiet, aye, and payment on time. They haven't forgotten me at the Palace. I could live up there now if it weren't a pain and a half to move everything. Young Kirasov sent around for clothes last week; I danced for his father when I danced at the Palace. That'd be when I was your age. And Umian's a decent man with a brain in his head; all my black cloth goes up to him so he doesn't have to deal with the cheats that work up there."

"So remember this about the King's smile, my chick," Karland went on, putting a hand behind Polijn to usher her out of the room. "There's nothing wrong with it: it can do you harm or good. But get his money and you know what you've got. That's the first thing you should learn."

To Polijn's relief, Karland was escorting her to the back door, and the alley. This alley opened onto a system of five branching alleys. There ought to be a safe spot in one of them.

Karland would no doubt expect her to take the branch closest to the New Berry. That would be either the first or second on the left; she hoped she would find no one there to recognize or rob her. For, being by nature more practical than Breza, she had been making plans since she'd seen the earrings.

"Tell her I expect the money quicker this time," Karland told her, adding a quick swat below the waist. "Keep your ankles crossed."

Polijn flipped a mental coin and turned into the first alley branching off to the left. Karland didn't call her back, and it was a perfect setting for her plans. Halfway along the wall to the right was a stack of broken barrels and fractured furniture, the kind of thing people stockpiled in summer for use in winter. She eased in behind a pair of barrels, so she would be sheltered from witnesses at either end of the alley.

The earrings were dangling feathers, with a long black feather in the center: the badge of the Fortune-tellers' Guild. She replaced her own with these. A light green skirt went over her shoulders as a shawl, a blue one she fastened around her waist as an overskirt. She twisted a golden scarf around her waist over that, and slipped on a pewter ring that bore the images of a fish and a pig.

From its hiding place, she drew the antler the King had given her and rubbed off the gilt. This was applied to her forehead, and daubed under her eyes, as if to cover the marks of time. Trying to look younger would communicate to her viewers that she was older.

The rest of the garments Karland had given her were balled up and slipped down her back, secured by all the clothes at her waist into a secure hump. She took a deep breath, then, murmured a few words from the song that claimed that powers above favored audacity, and stepped from the pile of trash, Polijn no longer.

This disguise might get her through the Swamp. And if there was any truth in songs, it might get her more than that.

III

THIS alley opened onto the Street of Mud Candles. Not the venue Polijn would have chosen, but she couldn't turn back: Karland might be lingering at the back door.

The New Berry was a block or two to the right, but Polijn couldn't see it for the traffic. Three men were hammering a crown to the front wall of the Gilded Grape, to suggest that the King had been served there. This street was too narrow for the procession, and the Gilded Grape was no more than a hole you stuck a mug into to have it filled. But these were not serious considerations in advertising.

Their work was hampered by the press of the crowd at the Market of Miscellanies, the largest of a dozen stores that dealt in odds and ends "lost" from the Palace Royal and the merchants' houses higher in the city. Business was brisk, thanks to the royal procession. Some of Karland's scavengers were there, and Polijn thought she recognized Breza, too, smiling up at a Treasury guard.

Swampers mingled with natives, looking for a bargain or their own property in the trays brought outside. Other customers were too proud to acquire anything by so mercenary a means as purchase. A cutpurse, dazzled by the way Karabari's jewels sparkled even on such a gloomy day, was easing on up. Not far away, a woman profited from the donations of

a literally unconscious benefactor. Cat-baiters had set up a
little arena in the street. The bets they took from passersby
were under scrutiny from a loitering pair of goblin cultists,
men who would kill a gambler for noticing their clothes. Or,
as easily, for ignoring them.

So Polijn did not turn right. The economy was less busy to
the left. Onion and garlic perfumed the air as Swampites fried
eggs in clay pans over little fires. These were the residents
willing to wait for the crowds to break up, and prey on the
strays. Cremaon strolled out of a doorway, her head cocked
this way and her hips that, so as to look less tall.

A small woman Polijn did not recognize sat in a doorway,
nursing a baby. A soldier paused in front of her, and raised
three fingers. The little mother's head jerked out in a stare
of mute incomprehension. The ferocity of her lack of understanding told the man what to do. He held up more fingers. The
woman handed her baby to her nearest neighbor and ushered
the man into the building.

Polijn strutted down the middle of the street here, her skirts
hitched back so that one leg showed well above the knee, her
head raised as if in contempt of the rather friendly aromas from
the pans. She let her eyes ride wide, and just a bit out of focus.
Her jaw hung loose, and she smiled a long smile of superiority.
And all the while she marched in obvious unconcern, she was
thinking how much better at all this Mokono had been.

Her eyes took in all the Swampites, who cast their own
appraising gazes upon the stranger. Survival could depend on
picking the right target.

She spied Darella: the very person. Gloraida had pointed
the woman out a dozen times as an object lesson in why it was
best to stay away from the Palace Royal. A Swampite who had
gone up the hill to be a general's mistress—this story said this
general and that story said that—she had fallen back down in
the days of Queen Kata. The general had been dropped from
favor, and had to divest himself of luxuries. No one else would
give her a job, so far had the general fallen. Winter had driven
her, starving, west.

She sewed playing cards to her collar to signify her minimum price. The novelty of that brought her success for a season, but she had had to change cards in the end, until just one

card would do. Her clothes tattered and tore with each change of menu, and she would never buy anything to replace them. Her palace clothes remained to remind everyone of what she had been once; she would repair them and pad them out with rags, but she would wear nothing less.

Right now she was wearing a flower in her hair and a canvas strap that passed under her arms, so she could be more easily carried. Five years ago she'd gone through the floor in the Slipping Shift where the wood was more rotten than the proprietor's teeth, and the apothecary they'd carried her to had spent her legs to save her life. On steamy days like today, her fellow employees at the Quiet Bride carried her out and set her on the curb, to get some air and to advertise the house.

Darella was the least dangerous person in sight, and also unlikely to know Polijn's face. "Good morning, My Lady," Polijn called, strolling up to her. "I hope the day finds you fair."

"So and so," answered Darella, her face not friendly but not forbidding either. "What can I sell you, Mistress?"

"I seek only directions," Polijn replied. "But I am not so mighty as to require 'Mistress' from you, My Lady Darella."

The woman leaned forward, looking for some familiar feature she had missed. "And how do you know my name, Mistress?" she demanded. "And what is yours? Do I know you?"

Polijn's hands went wide, and she dipped a bit at the knees. Her deck of cards slid from her right sleeve into her hand. "Why, I am Mokono the Magnificent. I know what you know and I know what you do not know." Her voice dropped an octave. "What you don't know is more interesting."

Bystanders eased in to learn something. Polijn continued to face Darella. "I heard the King Himself was to pass this way." She used a little palace polish in her pronunciation; Sielvia had worked hard enough to eliminate the more obvious Swampisms from her speech, though, as Laisida had pointed out, half the court talked the way Polijn did. "I thought His Majesty might have use for a soothsayer who said sooth."

Darella sneered a bit and lifted one eyebrow. (The other was scarred into a permanent position.) "You've come after the fair, card reader. His Majesty's been and gone."

Polijn shook a finger at her. "I missed one procession, but not the one to the north, for my cards tell me he means to pass this way again. I've come north myself, to consult with Quetos."

One of the listeners laughed. "You're even later for that. The old man died a year ago."

Polijn knew that, and not from the cards. "Yes, friend, he died drinking a quart, they say, to settle a bet in the Lifted Finger. I wish to go to the Lifted Finger and consult him there, for who can say when any magic-monger is truly dead?"

Her listeners decided suddenly to give her a bit more room, and backed away. Darella, unable to follow suit, chose to be belligerent. "One so knowing would know how to get there!"

Not offended at all, Mokono the Magnificent riffled her cards. "My deck is confused at so large and beautiful a city. I am from Dousand, myself, where my cards came to hand." Polijn hoped no one from Dousand had moved into this district since she'd been here last.

Before anyone could comment, she extended her cards. "Come, My Lady, with that courtesy you lived long enough in the Palace Royal to acquire, though you stayed not long enough to be corrupted, strike a bargain with me: give me directions and I shall run your cards."

"Here!" said a woman in the little collection of spectators. "Run mine!"

"I'll do it!"

"She asked ME!" Darella snatched the cards from Polijn's hand.

"My bargain is with the Lady Darella," said Mokono the Magnificent, with a gesture toward the woman. "But I am in no rush; there will be time for everyone. You, child, fetch me a drink, something cool, for Malbeth is not only vaster than Dousand, it is hotter." This was how matters were arranged in the Swamp; anyone smaller than you were was your servant unless proven otherwise.

Darella cut the deck against her chest, and started to shuffle. "Old ones," she noted.

"Ah," said Polijn. "You see where my fingers have worn the cards. You cannot see where the cards have worn my soul."

The legless woman reassembled the deck and handed it back to the gaudy hunchback. "What's coming to me when the King comes back this way?"

"Well, look at the lintik top cards!" Polijn ordered. "Eight of axes, ten of eyes. Pardon, what you would call the eight of houses and ten of cups, not knowing any better." Laisida had taught her that; the farmer-folk had different names for the cards. This would reinforce her identity as a visitor from the sticks.

"Is that a good omen?" Darella asked, running a hand down her stomach.

Mokono the Magnificent sniffed. "A good omen's nice, my dove, but each you receive means one less to come later." Without explaining further, she began to run the cards, setting her knee on the step to provide a platform for the discards. "Bad weather," she murmured, as if to herself. "You'll be rained on."

Polijn did not make the mistake of reading every card that fell. First of all, the fortune was falling very badly for Darella, and evil futures could be avenged on the foreteller. But her main reason was that she knew her audience was made up of people who had seen the cards run a hundred times, and would be evaluating her. A failing mark could prove fatal. It was much better, therefore, not to offer any readings so specific that they could be disputed.

"There's His Majesty, then," she said, as a king fell. "You will see him when he passes this way and he'll see you as well. Ah, not so good there. He passes by and you think he's not seen you, because of the rain. But the King has a tender heart and Kaigrol mentions your name. So . . . Tasak!" She slapped down a high black card. Darella jumped. "The Chief Bodyguard's hand falls on your shoulder. You are to come north with them."

Darella leaned dangerously forward. "Then what?"

Polijn was down to her last three cards. "You are given employment in Housekeeping, not in Iranen's division. But look here, you finish with the six of coins on top: who can say who might see you working there, and how high you'll rise?"

She took a drink from the mug offered her by the child she'd sent for it. "You aren't in any hurry, are you?" asked Darella.

"Not that I believe a word of it, but you can run the cards for what happens next, can't you?"

"You've had your turn!" snapped a man, shoving himself between Darella and Mokono the Magnificent. "I'll take you there myself, if you like, for a quick run of the cards. I'm . . ."

"Koquin," said Polijn, brushing a few drops of sour wine from her lips. "You're a soap and chalk artist, so you must know every beertub and wineskin around here."

Koquin stared. Darella tried to push him out of the way. "I can get money," said the woman.

"Mine's faster," said Koquin, reaching into his waistband.

Hands with pennyetkes in them were already extended toward the new cardrunner, and in some hands gold glittered, though Polijn could tell these were just the same plow-faced coins painted over. Mokono the Magnificent announced her willingness to run the cards until they were worn through, if necessary, and was soon working around the circle, just as in the days when Ronar sent her out to a party. She knew most of them at least slightly, and could guess the occupations of the others. Packframe men, who lingered on street corners offering to haul anything they could lift on the frame (the fee being slightly higher if you had left the original owner alive and likely to pursue them), naturally required different futures than the bartenders. Polijn predicted reasonably good things for all, with a few minor disasters thrown in to add to credibility.

Darella was calling out to anyone passing by that there was a wonderful new seer in town, who knew things nobody else knew. She even attracted Jentary, who was a little above this crowd. (He owned a flophouse and charged ten coppers for a blanket and floor space to sleep on. And when you were asleep, he came and took the blanket back.)

How many people believed their fortunes was difficult to say. There were the cards, anyway, and the reader was so confident and so cheerful that she must know something. Nobody remarked on it, if they noticed, that a lot of the fortunes seemed to deal with Swampers or the Yellow Dog or both. And if they thought about it at all, they assumed the fortune-teller's ability to listen to anything they said about these subjects was simply politeness, an adjunct to merchandising.

Polijn was indeed showing great interest in her customers, even to the point of asking questions about the individual's importance in the morning's affairs. How close had he been to His Majesty? Had she seen any of the really big swells from the Palace Royal? Had they really been brave enough to walk into the Yellow Dog?

So she learned many interesting things. The Swampers were up to no good. Usually no more than a source of revenue and entertainment, they had come today making demands. They wanted this or that back, things they had brought in payment months ago, even years ago. There had been fights, and the Chief Bodyguard had strangled a dozen men with her bare hands, and three between her thighs. No use counting how many she'd smashed with her hammer. And the Regent—a title spoken only after a whisper and a glance to the east—intended to hang or burn every person in the Swamp, and demolish all the buildings to make room for the lintik University.

Polijn doubted that part; when had Kaftus gone to so much exertion? On the other hand, it would be just like her to come visiting the Swamp the day it was to be destroyed.

The doorman of the Yellow Dog had been shooing people away from the Yellow Dog today, but everyone had assumed it was because the house was full. Business had been up to the rim lately; the new star of the shows was more athletic, if less of an actress, than her predecessor, bringing in more spectators. Every night, claimed Dra, the jeweller, you could see another high-ranking Swamper there, trying to extort a percentage from the owner.

"They got nowhere with Mistress Karlikartis," he said, "though she was willing enough to hear them talk, for what the knowledge they spilled might profit her." His face twisted into a pious moue. "She knows now it doesn't pay an honest Swampite to meddle in palace politics at all."

"Maybe that's all they want, up at the Palace," suggested Koquin, who stood behind him. "All their pushing is just . . . the Regent's way of asking for a piece of the profits himself."

"He has enough money from us," Dra replied, with a sneer. "And people, too. You've heard what the Decency Boys say happens to Swampites in the Palace. And then there's Polijn."

Mokono the Magnificent seemed to lose count for a second, but then went on sliding the cards. "Polijn?" she said.

"Her whose mother was at the Yellow Dog," Darella called to her. "Nasty piece of work."

"No more hips than a snake and a face to oil your bowels," said Dra. "They saw her running from the Yellow Dog with the cashbox."

"That cashbox was too heavy for a little thing like her," said Darella. "Most likely, she came down to warn Gloraida to get out of the Swamp. Let the rest of us burn, she would."

"She came for the money," Dra informed her. "She's palace-trained now. Probably knows a trick or two to astound you."

"I haven't seen the Swamp burning in these cards so far," Mokono the Magnificent informed him. "Mind, I haven't gone so far into the future. The only thing I see burning in your future is that little stove where you melt the lead. There'll be Swampers wanting you to make replacement jewelry for what they can't buy back. Naturally, they'd come to an expert."

Dra beamed at her. Beyond him, his oldest daughter was loosening her girdle to get at her money and buy her own fortune. Polijn wished she could loosen something. It was hot at the center of the crowd, and she was sure her hump was drooping as sweat soaked into it.

The crowd parted a bit as the smaller members suddenly took off, running for an alley. One or two younger adults glanced behind them and quietly slipped away as well.

"What's the fun?" a voice boomed. "A clean death to all of you, but let's have a bit of room!"

Polijn recognized the voice and bit her lip.

IV

THE crowd parted. Some of it departed: the lesser bystanders and those who weren't paid up. Two men, intent on an argument over their place in line, did not notice the new arrival. Massive hands came forward and batted their heads together, turning them a bit so as to break both noses.

Ancipo was affecting a long mustache this year, and had shaved above and behind his ears. The jewelled band across his belly looked bigger, but it still matched the ones at his wrists. Polijn watched those hands, the fingers of which had long varnished nails. Eyegouging might be considered uncivilized at the Palace Royal, but its usefulness was still acknowledged down here.

He rolled forward more than walked, smiling at the crowd. Behind him, his retinue moved just as slowly, looking happy and just a bit drunk. The dead pit was filled with people who had believed it. Ancipo's smiles were not encouraging, due to an almost complete lack of lower lip. He had taken his place in the Swamp through his demonstrated willingness to risk mutilation while he dealt out death.

Polijn bent over the cards. They'd met; strongmen knew the protégées of their rivals. Now, of course, there would be no Chordasp between them. If this disguise had any flaws at all, her fate would be predictable without recourse to cards.

"Ho ho, a lady of the cards," he declared, his bulk shuddering to a stop before her. "What's in the pips for me, eh?"

Mokono the Magnificent didn't look up, just jerked her head a bit toward the jeweller. "I've got this man to finish; keep your ottomy in." He wouldn't recognize her voice, at least; she'd never spoken to Ancipo like that.

"All's well," said her customer, with a quick smile at Ancipo. "I've heard all I need to know."

Ancipo clapped his hands together. "Come, then, My Lady! Slap a little magic on me! Shall I send my son to be Veldres's doorwarden, now Undurom's been taken off to be flayed? Or is gold going to rain on me from the clouds?"

Polijn's brain raced through the possibilities. She'd learned a few things; Ancipo might know more. But he could certainly do more. In any case, it was worth a try; he couldn't ignore a soothsayer's suggestions.

She put the cards together and handed the deck to him. "Shuffle those up, then," she ordered. "And don't let me see you palming the nine of stars or ace of axes."

Ancipo took the cards in one hand. With the other, he tapped one long nail just under his right eye. "You won't see it," he chortled, not doubting for a moment that she understood. Polijn hoped her shudder was not too obvious.

The big man shuffled with some difficulty; with great powers came great inconveniences. He passed them back. "Deal me a good hand. Ho ho."

Mokono the Magnificent took the cards without comment and began to run them. "Hmmmm," she said, as two cards dropped almost immediately.

One big hand had taken the shoulder of a woman nearby and pulled down the blouse. "Hmmm how, little one?" Ancipo demanded, running his hand up and down the shoulder.

"I see you eating salt-water fish." She looked closer. "Or is it salt fish?"

Rossacotta being landlocked, seafish were a delicacy. "And how much did I have to melt for that, hmmmm?" he inquired.

The cards slid by under her hands. "They were a gift. From your employer or your son's. Not this Veldres, then, unless he's a quite juicy man. Ah, it's somebody born in the moon of Tylon!"

Ancipo removed his hand from the bystander's shoulder, leaving nailprints, and rubbed his chin. "Ho ho!" The King had been born under that sign.

"Ye-es," she went on, as cards continued to drop. "And in the Palace Royal. It is not without its dangers."

"Ho ho ho! It takes no cards to read that! Perhaps you'd better change tunes." He leaned forward until she could smell the wine and garlic. "I don't believe I care for the Palace Royal, unless he works for Umian. Am I in danger from His Sliminess, the Regent? You did not hear that, by the way."

"No need to hit my ears to make them numb." She put out a hand to push him back a bit. The whole crowd stepped back. At least this branded her a stranger; someone who knew the Swamp, such as Polijn, for example, would never have risked that.

Ancipo just smiled. The cards went on dropping. "No," she said. "The person who means you ill is not in the Palace Royal but has been in the Yellow Dog. That's no place for Himself, now, is it? The Yellow Dog: whoever has been there and exerted power is opposed to you and this person under the moon of Tylon. Find that person, and you will certainly eat seafish."

She didn't look up, continuing to concentrate on the remaining cards. If he took her seriously, Ancipo might take care of her vengeance for her. Unless, of course, the Regent really was the one responsible.

Ancipo pulled on the remains of his lower lip. "Could you be a bit more specific, dolly? But come, a lady in your shape shouldn't have to read her cards standing. Come have a seat in the Helmet of Feathers; we'll kiss the worm and read these a bit more closely."

It was about time for Polijn to pull herself out of this crowd, but drinking with Ancipo was not the best way to do it, particularly not in an establishment he ruled. He would want more specifics, or he would want a reading for every employee in the place.

She looked up into the dark sky. "I must consult with a spirit in the Lifted Finger at dusk," she told him. "Perhaps you could escort me there?" She knew more places to hide up in that neighborhood, and there would be chances to slip away before dusk.

"I would be honored, my lovely," said Ancipo, extending an arm.

Polijn was reaching to take it when two men ran between her and Ancipo. The crowd all but evaporated in the next few seconds.

"Arlintik Eru!" growled Ancipo, losing his smile for the briefest of eyeblinks.

Someone was singing, "Ah, listen to the jitters, the flitters, and the floor, as the big fat empty barrel rolls a-rumbling through the door."

Polijn thought suddenly of writing a song triad: "The Three Loathsome Smiles." Ancipo's and Kaftus's would certainly be among them, but the chief loathsome smile had to be the Vielfrass's.

The sorcerer was decked out in an array that insulted the eye on so grey a day: clashing shades of red, blue, and brown. But it was his face that struck Polijn: that smile was the very embodiment of a universe that laughed at her. Lady Oozola trotted along behind him, sullen but serene. When he paused next to Ancipo, she strolled on to talk to Darella.

"Aft'noon, scapegallows!" cried the Vielfrass, pointing one finger at the big man's nearest elbow. "What lock are you picking today?"

The big man's smile was not so jolly. "This venerable card lady and I are away to the Lifted Finger for a drink."

"Oh, Granny," said the sorcerer, shaking his head. "And at your age. How old are you, did you say?"

"Older in winter than in spring," snapped Polijn. One of Ancipo's retinue fainted.

"The Lifted Finger's haunted by the Chief Bodyguard today, and this man-keg knows it," he told her, now shaking his head at Ancipo. "He's procuring for the Regent; I knew it all along. His Lordship will swoop down and magic you into the center of a ruby for all eternity. Such jewels are self-polishing."

"An emerald, I think," said Oozola, turning away from Darella's earnest description of Mokono the Magnificent's powers.

The crowd pulled back to make room for Ancipo to kill the Vielfrass or vice versa. "Ho ho!" roared Ancipo. "To be sure, my lady here told me I was to work for someone in the Palace Royal."

"Did she? Well, I can see you working under the Regent, at that." The Vielfrass turned toward Mokono the Magnificent. "Let's hear what's in the cards for me."

Polijn tossed her head back. "I've not finished with this gentleman yet."

"Ho ho: someone who wants to earn her money!" said Ancipo, taking a step away from the Vielfrass. "That's all right, my darling. You can run my cards again when we have that drink."

She sighed, and pulled the cards together. The Vielfrass plucked them from his hand and threw them into the air. They shot up out of sight. "What's the weather likely to do?" he asked no one in particular.

"Rain," said Polijn, in a voice perfectly flat.

"You are a prophet." He stuck out a hand and the cards fluttered down into a pile. With a little bow, the Vielfrass passed them back to Mokono the Magnificent.

Polijn was not at all anxious to take them, but they didn't seem to have changed any as she slid them under her fingers. A nine and a seven dropped. "Hmmm," she said.

"Hmmm?" the Vielfrass inquired.

"She does that," chuckled Ancipo.

"Please breathe some other direction," the Vielfrass told him.

"I see flowing water," announced Mokono the Magnificent, as a few more cards dropped. "You are down by the river, undressing for a swim, when the power that devastated the Yellow Dog casts a spell and sets your hair on fire."

The Vielfrass nodded. "Do I dip my head in the river?"

"If that's where you think the fire is," she replied. The crowd leaned in. The Vielfrass seemed to be in a good mood, and, in any case, he'd surely kill Mokono first, giving them time to escape.

"A fire-breeding dragon, perhaps," suggested the Lady Oozola.

The Vielfrass opened his mouth, but Mokono went on. "You are rescued by a small woman clad in fur, who has to hang you over a tree limb to dry out. She takes up a . . ."

"Thank you," said the Vielfrass. "That will do. My glorious future is obviously so blinding that you can't perceive it in faded cards. You do read more succinctly than most fortune-tellers I meet, kirro; you should have been a minstrel."

He reached inside his robes and brought out a shimmering coin. Extended toward the fortune-teller, it slipped between his fingers and hit the dirt.

They both stooped to pick it up. The Vielfrass's hand came down on her wrist. "Polijn," he whispered, "have you heard that Hednogge died?"

She swallowed hard, seeing the danger. Hednogge had run the cards in the Hanging Eye, one of Ancipo's houses. When business was slow, his retinue would drag her on stage, blindfolded, and dare her to prophesy what they were going to do to her next.

"Fear not," the sorcerer went on. "I shall most benevolently come to your rescue."

With that he let go of her wrist and started to walk away. Polijn rose, a little confused. Even the Vielfrass wouldn't consider that a rescue.

"Hey, my dumpling!" Ancipo called to her. "Did he let go of the coin or didn't he?"

She held out her empty hand. The Vielfrass turned. "Why, how careless of me," he said. He drew back his hand and hurled the bit of gold into the air.

Polijn automatically jumped for it. It thumped into her hand. She came down with her legs bent for impact, but hadn't expected Ancipo to try to catch her. His nails caught in her wig just as she felt her artificial hump slip.

The crowd studied her. She turned to run just a second before Darella shrieked, "Polijn!"

Now, this was the Vielfrass's idea of a rescue.

V

SHE meant to run after the Vielfrass. The Lady Oozola would be sympathetic, if he wasn't; the little woman's expression during the "fortune" had been one of admiration. But the pair had disappeared. Polijn could do no more than try to guess which way they'd gone.

As she skidded around a corner, she tore off the ersatz shawl and overskirt, and threw them down. The bandana she snatched from her waist and tied up her hair. The alley forked. Polijn plunged right.

Seconds later, she found herself on the Street of Brown Beer. Who did she know here? Who did she know anywhere that might hide her from Ancipo? She had that bit of gold from the Vielfrass, of course. That would buy her a ride to the Palace, if she could find a chair for hire. She looked around for anyone who might be useful.

She smelled the crowd before she saw it. A goodly mob of men and women had gathered around Plotchar's honeycart, which he'd parked at the Sod and Soul. What Plotchar scooped out of gutters and alleys he sold to gardeners higher in the city. "The worse it smells, the better it does the plants," they said, and everything from the Swamp smelled worse.

Some unlucky soul was probably being admitted headfirst to

the back of the cart. Polijn, having always been small, knew that cart too well herself.

She headed for it. The crowd was very nearly blocking the road completely. If she could get past the group, she would at least be concealed, and maybe Ancipo wouldn't think of coming that way at all.

Quietly, without any jerky movements to attract attention, she slipped around the assembly. Most of the women here would probably recognize her, and some of the men. She knew them, anyhow. The men were mostly young, not up to the level of Ancipo or Chordasp yet, but waiting for any opening. Kelsen there had at least three good kills to his name. He'd been a goblin cultist for a while, but now wore another uniform, with a black blazon.

He was moving through the crowd, jerking up the skirts of the women. "Here's a true Daughter of the Panther!" he'd cry, displaying someone's underpinnings to the crowd. She would slap him in a playful way, and he'd kiss her.

Looking beyond him, she saw the main attraction. Kelsen must be a member of one of the Decency Committees that had been started over the winter. They'd erected a little platform of debris wood from the alley. Tied to this, a little difficult to recognize upside down, was Sooshkind. A pair of yellow underpants was all she wore, and that had been tied at her neck.

"Three throws for a plow!" shouted Plotchar. "Three throws for decency!" Easy money: he scooped up handfuls, sold them, and once the crowd left he could scrape them all together again for sale uptown.

The men with the blazoned tunics were keeping a sort of counter together, holding the customers to a sporting distance. "There you be!" shouted a red-haired one, as a woman stepped up to throw. "This is what the Regent likes!"

"Get her!" a blackhaired committeeman urged a small boy. "Foreigners with foreign ways!"

To judge by the target, nobody here was much of a marksman, despite throwing at someone who couldn't dodge. The point, however, seemed to be to hit the broad end of a wooden paddle that had been thrust down into the prisoner.

"Filling our King with foreign ideas and ignoring the true Daughters and Sons of the Panther!" roared the redhead, picking up a missile for the woman, who'd dropped hers.

"Teach them who like foreign ways how to behave in our neighborhood!" called Plotchar. "Three throws the pennyetke!"

Polijn took all this in as she moved on, but a man pulling back for a good windup stalled her for a second. This was one second too many. She felt her skirt grabbed up from behind.

"Ha! Your turn!"

Polijn had all but forgotten she was wearing Maiaciara's imported underwear. Kelsen kicked her feet out from under her and, getting a hand in her hair, twisted her head back so he could spit "Foreign filth!" in her face.

Sooshkind wailed as the redheaded committee member yanked the paddle free and jumped over the counter with it. "Come on!" he ordered. "Get her up!"

But Kelsen was staring into his captive's face, frowning as if trying to think of something. Polijn was not at all willing that he should think of it. She bounded forward. Her head went up into his crotch as she wrapped both arms around the nearer thigh and bit down hard.

While Kelsen was dealing with that, she scrambled off on all fours. A hand caught in her bandana, but she hadn't been able to tie it tight while running, and it came away. A woman aimed a kick at her face.

The company of decent-minded people was not about to let someone like her get away, but the sound of Ancipo bellowing something made nearly everyone turn. Polijn got to her feet and ran while they were still figuring out what was being shouted.

She was nearer now to the alleys she knew well. Two more blocks would bring her to the Bedbug, not that that was where she wanted to go. She chose an alley that she knew opened onto a back square. Six alleys led out of this conjunction, not to mention four stairways and a basement window. Once she reached that, she'd have a clear choice of escapes.

In the hub of the complex, though, she stopped and stood stock still. The King's Chief Bodyguard, wearing a face of pure death, dove in at her.

CHAPTER SIX
Nimnestl

I

NO sense compromising the barkeep at the Blue Bottle by retrieving her horse. Nimnestl led them instead to the Burning Fingers, where she hired sedan chairs for herself and Seitun, and paid off those who had toted the bodies this far. Their honorarium was small, lest they think they'd done something really important and report it around. She warned them that if it developed that Veldres was involved in this business somehow, they might be called to testify against him. No one made any trouble about that; they were not ones to inform on a neighbor, they told her, but Veldres was not any neighbor of theirs. And, anyway, to deny facts unnecessarily might shut off a chance at larger rewards.

The ride back to the Palace Royal would have been tiresome even without the mutilated corpse in the seat opposite her. But she had seen worse. There were whole weeks when she felt she was no more than receiving secretary for the morgue. And there might be some purpose to this. If Undurom, riding in the chair behind with Seitun, could not tell them everything Veldres was up to, perhaps Kaftus could coax some information from Mityrets.

At length, the chair-bearers reached the gate at which town chairs had to be turned back, "I'll carry her if you'd prefer,

Ma'am," Seitun told the Bodyguard, depositing the still unconscious Undurom on the ground.

"Well, that's what we told the other Swampites you were coming along for, to be sure," she told him. "But there should be somebody . . ."

The sound of booted feet drew her attention to the gateway. Biandi and half a dozen bodyguards had come to meet their commander.

"Take these up and carry them to the dungeons, Biandi," she ordered. "We've . . ."

"Les and Tesh will do it, Ma'am, if you please," Biandi said, with a nod to two of his men. "I have orders to escort you to His Lordship at once."

She raised an eyebrow, but turned to Seitun and said, "Go with them and see that they are properly disposed."

"Seitun is to come with us, Ma'am," Biandi told her.

Seitun glanced at Nimnestl's face, but it was still. She had no idea what was afoot, but she was willing to find out before taking action.

Umian was in the courtyard, with perhaps four dozen sweating men in black uniforms. "Never mind what the amber merchants told you," he was telling a subordinate. "All the wagons, not just some of them. And when you're done, go join Panther Company in searching the stables."

He turned then and saw Nimnestl. The craggy face grew even more concentrated; Nimnestl read both hate and suspicion in the new lines. She responded with a smile and gracious nod. Whatever he thought she'd done to him, she was willing to take the credit.

"Look down upon these doors, Mighty One!" someone was crying, as they moved up into the palace. "Remove evil influences and guard all those who pass through, so they be obedient to your will!"

Aizon and Robinuon had apparently chosen today to bless the doors, a ritual they generally went into only when the King returned from the north. Aizon looked as raggedy as ever he did; the mummified bat across his chest looked better. Nimnestl knew the man made plenty of money from courtiers asking him to drive evil out of this or that new acquisition. He just spent it all on books and artifacts in his search for immortality. That shard of clay he and Arberth went after must have cost him four or five pounds of gold.

The group of bodyguards moved on up to the level of the Council Chamber. Moving through a gallery, Nimnestl heard, "I may as well jump."

General Ferrapec stood in one of the deep windows with his wife. "It's all a plot against me; I know it," he told her. "If they don't catch me in the audit, they'll stick this to me."

Raiprez turned shining eyes on him. "Then solve it, find the real culprit yourself. You're too wise to let them fool you. This is just another scheme of the Regent and his black dog."

Nimnestl was catching on. Some crisis had arisen in her absence and, glory be, for once it was as upsetting to the foes of the government as it was to everyone else. She did hope it wasn't just Nurse and the King's hiccups again.

"Why I'm so patient with you, Dear Above only knows! I've trained you as well as any bitch in the kennel!"

At the very door of the Council Chamber, Iranen was punching away facial features from an underling whose hair she gripped in her other hand. A minor crowd clustered beyond her, but it was obvious from their eyes that what held their interest was the Council Chamber door, and that only Lady Iranen's presence was holding them away from it.

The Housekeeper heard boots approaching and looked up. Her lips trembled, and she dropped her servant. "There, my bitch!" she cried, and Nimnestl saw tears in her eyes. "Everything will be all right now!"

This testimonial was unique in Nimnestl's experience. Just what was waiting behind that Council Chamber door?

It looked like a tribunal: Culghi, Kaftus, Nurse, and Haeve sat around the big table, their faces solemn. Nimnestl stopped just inside the door.

This was the end, then. Kaftus had decided to do without her, and had sent her to the Vielfrass to get her out of the way while he arranged an incident to serve as an excuse. Well, she had expected it to end, one day. Death was no problem, except that it meant leaving everything she'd done this far in lesser hands.

"This is your fault!" shouted Nurse, rising. "If you hadn't had this muttonhead . . ."

Kaftus turned to Nurse. "I am the mouth, you the ears,"

he informed her. "We shall apportion blame later." Nurse
sank back into her seat. The Regent's face came to Nimnestl.
Nimnestl could see neither glee nor triumph in it.

"We can't find him," he said.

Now, that was something she hadn't expected.

II

THE problem was quickly explained to the newcomers. This was not a Council meeting, after all, where facts had to filter through accumulated screens of personal interest. Everyone here had a grudge against someone else in the room, but was willing to acknowledge there was more important business at hand.

"Just four," said Haeve, after Culghi recited the names of the Playmates involved. "It's perfect, of course. Any more than that and the group would have been too big for secrecy."

"What did they do?" Nurse demanded. "Keep His Majesty in the middle, so nobody noticed him go by?"

The King and his friends, everyone agreed, had probably left the room voluntarily, tricking their guard to do so. The main concern was what might have happened after that. The King's sanctity would not prevent a crime. On the occasion of his naming, only Nurse and the ten most pious members of the Academy had attended on him. And his christening robes had been stolen.

Culghi murmured something, of which Nimnestl caught only "werebears." He was obviously returning to something under discussion before they arrived, for Haeve threw up his hands with a cry of "Amànamin!"

"Even the New Guard would have noticed a bear roaming the halls," Kaftus said, his thin lips turned down in sharp distaste. "And would have drawn the Royal Bodyguard's attention to it."

"And Mardith has not reported?" To Nimnestl, this could mean only that her old retainer was dead, or that he was with the King, wherever His Majesty might be. This did not mean all was well, only that Mardith felt able to handle things alone. Mardith was always willing to aid and abet his monarch, going back to the days when he'd fly in burrs, later to be hidden in Nurse's clothes.

"Nobody's seen anything!" Nurse slapped her hands on the table. "I don't expect intelligence of the nobility of this country, but I did expect eyesight! Their King strolls out among them, with no more guard than a bird and some misbegotten friends, and none thinks anything of it. Some kitchen wench says she saw brats carrying a bag, and Merklin with them, but she wasn't paying attention."

"And you're worse!" she went on, shaking a finger at the Regent. "You're supposed to be so much of a magician. Why can't you look in a magic bowl or something and see where he is?"

Kaftus inclined his head. "I have checked, dear Nurse. He is someplace dark."

Everyone waited for more. Realizing there was no more, Haeve snapped, "That's it?"

Kaftus's face was passionless. "There is a spell which would pinpoint him exactly," he noted. "It takes a week."

"All your fiddling with potions and philtres," growled Nurse. "I should think you'd have things ready for an emergency like this."

"The potions are ready. If they weren't, the spell would take a month."

Nurse was unmollified. "All I have to say," she lied, "is that a good bodyguard . . ."

Kaftus raised a hand. "The Royal Bodyguard has done what it can do, without putting the King in a cage, the way this country used to handle the matter. I don't say their leader couldn't have done better, had she been present." He turned to Nimnestl and went on, "Regardless of what I may think, that is. Did you get a chance to talk to the Vielfrass?"

She frowned a bit. "I did not."

"Pity. He'd have enjoyed this." The necromancer turned back to Nurse. "Even your conduct does not shock me unduly, though I do wish for once you had been able to hold your tongue."

The older woman turned a little red. "I expected him to be in hiding. How was I to guess he'd go so far after such a long morning?"

"He is getting older," noted the Regent.

"Fortunately, a lot of the real troublemakers are still down there, Swamping," noted Seitun.

"All of the best suspects, yes," said Kaftus. "But who's to say they aren't there to provide themselves with an alibi, while their underlings carry out their plans?"

"Was it planned?" asked Haeve, putting up two fingers to rub an eyebrow. "Most of our most diligent plotters seem to have been caught off guard. It required only a few people to see them and realize that by hiding them for a day or two, the government would look more than usual like a pack of fools."

"Would they hold the others, though, My Lord?" asked Biandi.

"To keep the secret, yes."

"Assuming," Kaftus put in, folding his hands together, "that the Playmates are not themselves part of the plan. I see no reason for Ipojn to have plotted such a thing, but Laisida, Kirasov, or Morafor could well have counted on the King being relatively unattended, and sent their relatives to coax him from his chambers. Which would be better for us, by the way, than if Timpre, Sielvia, or Argeleb turn up dead. No matter who planned it, a death like that is the best advertisement for the New Guard."

The bodyguards looked stricken. "That would explain why five such rascals would have stayed together long enough to be taken," mused Haeve. "One of them had a part in the plot."

"Where would they be put, then?" Nurse demanded. "The dungeons?"

"The guards deny anyone passed them this afternoon," said Biandi. "But they're Treasury men. They claim the usual guards, from Housekeeping, are busy preparing for the move north, but I hadn't heard about it."

"Things do look bad for Colonel Kirasov," noted Kaftus.

Culghi wiped sweat from his forehead and nose. "I heard somebody blaming Old Eyepatch, I mean, that minstrel from the south."

"Naturally, they'd blame the foreigners first," said the Regent. "Such have fewer friends. Lord Arlmorin has already asked to be taken into protective custody."

Nimnestl didn't like the juxtaposition of Carasta and the ambassador again. Nor did she care for Nurse's saying, "And I heard it was Maitena, carrying him off to make him marry one of those ill-favored girls of hers." She had hoped she'd have another year or two before that idea came up. Such a marriage was unenforceable, really, particularly with the principals underage, but once the concept was planted in people's minds, there was no telling where it might lead.

Right now it led to Sielvia. "Laisida's girl," said Haeve, sitting back. "Would that be it? I can't see His Majesty and Merklin including a girl in any adventure of theirs."

"Laisida is surely wiser than that," said Nimnestl, shaking her head. The really stupid and really daring plotters had all been weeded out in the first years of the Regency.

"He'd marry her to that Polijn, maybe," Nurse said, grinding a thumb into the palm of the opposite hand. "So he could disavow the whole thing when worse came to worst."

Nimnestl shook her head again, but paused to think a moment. Her underteeth showed. Culghi, Bonti, and Seitun sat a little straighter.

"Did His Majesty know Polijn had been seen running from the Yellow Dog?" she demanded.

Now Haeve sat up straight. "Morafor wasn't exactly discreet. You think he'd have gone to rescue her?"

"You do." It was not a question.

Nurse threw up her hands. "So all you knowing people have been able to do is narrow it down to the Palace Royal or the city. That's fine! We should have time for supper first if that's all we have to search by nightfall. I . . ."

"Will not be doing any searching," said Kaftus. His head jerked up to draw everyone's attention to him. "We need not only to hunt for His Majesty," he announced. "We need also to spread a story to keep everyone calm until he's found."

"And assure them that we have the situation under control," said Haeve.

"I think not," the Regent informed him. "We will confess ourselves mystified by His Majesty's note."

"Note?" demanded Nurse. "You said nothing of a note."

"The note he left in code," Kaftus replied, with a grisly smile. "Which only I was able to read or even recognize as a message. I haven't decided yet where I found it: in his closet, perhaps. The note said, oh, not to worry, that he would be back with surprising news. You, Nurse, will be loudly disgruntled, blaming me for deliberately concealing what the King meant to do. It will mean running counter to your obvious adoration of me, but do your best. You, Tutor . . ."

"Am ruefully proud of my student for being so enterprising," said Haeve, running a hand through his hair, "but wish he had consulted with me before doing anything."

"And the bodyguard?" Nimnestl inquired, putting a hand on her hammer.

"Will have no time to express an opinion, being too busy hunting," Kaftus replied. "You fear the King may have ventured into water too deep for him. Because you will be hunting. I count on you to remove any inconvenient persons who may wish to contradict our little story."

"We're going to look a pack of idiots," Nurse grumbled, sweat running down her long nose and splashing into her bosom.

"I think so," Kaftus replied. "But the King himself, provided he does come out of this, will be seen to have exhibited a becoming independence of our evil influence."

He let this idea sink in before going on, "I suggest our friends Kirasov and Laisida be investigated first. Then proceed to any place their wives might have stashed a number of children. General Ferrapec and Colonel Umian may be as good at acting a comedy as we, so they should be high on your list of friends to investigate. And by no means ignore Lord Arlmorin; this is not really his sort of affair, but he was very quick to apply for sanctuary."

Culghi, Seitun, and Bonti looked to their commander, who rose, looking, in her turn, to the Regent.

"We would do well to look around in the Swamp," he told her. "Perhaps Seitun could command the search here and free you to meet with your sweetheart this time."

"The Vielfrass?" she demanded.

"He sent Polijn here last year," he said. "He may well be able to do so again."

Nimnestl nodded. "You can keep people quiet here?"

The eyebrows arched. "I never could before. I may keep them busy. An emergency Council meeting will have to be called to discuss what we shall do with, oh, with those naughty Brown Robes the King has gone to locate."

"Ah, that's what he went away to investigate," said Haeve, with a solemn nod. "Won't they think it odd, when the King has said he's tired of that whole business?"

Kaftus cast the Tutor a glance of pity. "Certainly not. This is a Council meeting. Thinking would be out of place." The Regent stroked his chin. "I wonder if His Majesty found a clue in Culghi's pallet."

The Bodyguard paled. "Isn't revenge better savored for a few months?" Nimnestl inquired.

"If you say so."

"I think I will have Bonti head the search here," she went on. "Seitun can take some men to check Veldres's estate."

"Very good," said the Regent, nodding. "If I am allowed the time, I shall question those treasures you have brought me. Now: we all know the songs to sing? The King has gone off on an adventure of his own choosing. Stress that the bird is a potent guardian; remind everyone of the gouges he dug in Ferrapec's face. We are concerned, but not upset, save for Nurse, who wishes he had taken a handkerchief. And you . . ."

Culghi sank into a chair as the finger pointed to him. "Whisper of werebears," the Regent ordered. "If the Brown Robes are not enough to convince the loyal opposition, it may well develop that His Majesty is saving us all from a plague of werebears, using ancient royal powers we can only guess at."

Haeve applauded. Culghi nodded at once. He'd have agreed to cut off his toes at this point.

Nimnestl moved to the door and opened it slowly. Too thick to hear anything through, it would nonetheless have ears pressed against it.

Ears and hands pulled back far enough for her to recognize faces. Forokell was there, Kaigrol, Laisida: anyone with any authority and no interest in Swamping.

"Well?" the Chief Housekeeper demanded.

"Let the Bodyguard pass," came Kaftus's voice from inside the room. "The rest of you . . ."

"Where's His Majesty, eh? What have you done with him?"

Kaftus had reached the door, and glared wide-eyed at Gilphros, who glowered right back. Before the upstart could repeat his question, though, a hand from behind caught him by the nose and mouth. Adimo, seeing a chance to redeem himself, dragged the other man backward into the crowd.

"The rest of you will please enter," Kaftus told the assembly as Nimnestl shouldered her way among them. "We will discuss the King's message to us, and the ramifications of his efforts on our behalf."

No one attempted to stop the members of the Royal Bodyguard, not from fear but from a desire to find a seat in the Council Chamber and hear the news. Nimnestl paused only once, putting out a hand to take hold of one passerby and drag him along with her.

"You three gather the men," she told her subordinates. "I'll join you."

She dragged her captive to a small corridor and pushed him into a window ledge. "Act as if I'm about to kill you," she whispered.

"Are you?" asked Janeftox.

"It depends. Have you heard one word from your master or the colonel about this business?"

The young man shook his head. "This has been a bad surprise for the general. I expected him to surrender."

"You're sure?"

He raised his chin. "Kill me if you learn I am wrong."

"It may not be necessary." She let go of him. Janeftox was a bright young man who had been somewhat useful and might be more useful in the future. He was bold, trustworthy, strong, clean; Nimnestl thought it was a pity he had to live around here.

"In any event," she told him, "our game ends soon, here or in the north. You realize that when the general is brought up for sentencing, you must either be sentenced with him or exposed as an agent of the Regency. The Council is kindly disposed toward you as things are now, and if you join Ferrapec's downfall, you will likely suffer no worse than a short exile."

The soldier swallowed; to one bred and born in the city, the outside world was a land of death. But he said, "I understand. Whatever is necessary to shovel out the corrupt officers and restore the Army to its original purity."

"Yes." Janeftox was an idealist, so Nimnestl felt there was no point in mentioning her goal of reducing the Army to a proper state of subservience. "We can give you letters of introduction to some nobles near the border, and you will eventually return to a much altered army."

He nodded. "All I hope for, Ma'am, is to serve His Majesty to the end of my days."

Nimnestl took a deep breath. "I hope you do," she said, and moved off after her subordinates.

III

THE sun had given up for the day, blocked completely by the black clouds. These gave no relief from the heat, and the air was thicker. Odors travelled better on thick air; Nimnestl could tell she'd moved into the most westerly part of the Swamp long before she recognized any landmarks.

She had naturally made it a point to learn the major byways of the capital city, but Malbeth was still an alien world to her. Nimnestl had never been a city dweller; if there was a pattern to the streets, it was beyond her understanding. Roads and alleys branched off this way and that, apparently in a malicious attempt to mislead the unwary. That was quite in character for Malbeth.

Her plan did not require any great knowledge; it was simply to find the Gilded Fly, the most frequent haunt of the Vielfrass, and walk away from it in the direction a sane person would be least likely to take. For example, not far west of the Gilded Fly lay the river. In this district the docks were abandoned, rotting, and the bank treacherous. To venture there was certain death.

The Vielfrass would not be there. Drowning was such an improvement over life around here that the sane went that way first.

Nimnestl attracted little notice as she moved down through the Swamp, partly because she had her hood pulled up despite the heat, and partly because she was much too large to bother with on such a hot day. Large people skulking through the alleys were almost always busy with something, and Swampites who had survived infancy knew better than to interrupt them.

The Gilded Fly was a two-story building that was built ugly and then deteriorated. There were patches on the walls. There were unpatched holes in the walls. There were bits of wall that flapped in the breeze. Nimnestl stepped up onto floorboards separated by gaps as wide in places as her foot. Just inside the front door, a couple of customers were conducting a business transaction that involved combat to the death.

Nimnestl turned away from this to regard the Swamp. Her eye turned toward movement at her right.

"Spare sumpm, Mister?"

The little beggar had jagged teeth, half a nose, and only one eye. Tattoos covered a bald pate. The effect was so grotesque as to rivet the gaze. This tipped Nimnestl off, and she turned to her left.

The big man with the knife looked irritated, but made no move to hide his weapon. Nimnestl put a foot forward. Her robe fell back far enough to expose her hammer.

Three eyes widened. A voice shouted, "Take your filthy hand off her filthy arm, villain!" just as the two men leaped from the porch.

Of course, since she'd been expecting him to be elsewhere, the Vielfrass was at home. He marched onto the sagging floorboards in a swirl of his voluminous cape, crying, "Away, malefactors! Else you shall . . ."

He looked up at Nimnestl. "I could have sworn I heard someone else out here. I was going to invite them to my fireplace."

"I expect I startled them," she replied. "Sorry."

He shrugged. "Well, if they can't hold up any better than that, I have no time for them. They'll have to try harder next time." The incredible face turned to look out at the street. "I'd invite you up for a drink, but I was expecting you, so there's nothing in the house."

"This is a tavern," a voice noted, from the door.

Nimnestl turned to acknowledge the Lady Oozola. The Vielfrass did not. "Nothing at all," he said.

"Not a drop?" asked his assistant.

"Step to the left there and the floor will give you a drop," the sorcerer replied. "Save me the trouble of which shelf to put you on in the trophy room, too."

"I really don't have time to drink," said Nimnestl, as the smaller woman stuck her thumbs in her ears and wiggled her fingers. "I've come for information."

"But of course," said the Vielfrass, his eyes still on his domain.

"He's so smart his crystal ball asks him questions," piped Lady Oozola.

"I'd rent you out to a chimney sweep for a brush, but they probably put the fires out before they shove the brush in." The Vielfrass turned to Nimnestl. "What do you think Lady Iranen would pay me for her, per pound?"

"I'm sure I couldn't say," she sighed. It was like talking to pixies.

"Let me know if you find out," Lady Oozola put in, sitting down on the edge of the porch. "I'll buy me myself. I could use something cute around the place."

The Vielfrass was quite willing to answer that, but Nimnestl quickly put in, "Several people are missing from the Palace, and we hoped you could help us find them. Polijn and . . ." She lowered her voice. "His Majesty."

Lady Oozola whistled. The Vielfrass raised one eyebrow, but said nothing. Was that actually concern in his face? Nimnestl looked closer. No.

"Can you help her?" asked Oozola, kicking her legs.

"Are you suggesting that I could possibly fail to help someone in need?" demanded the Vielfrass, settling down on the edge of the porch himself. He shook three fingers at his companion. "Do not forget, pixy-puss, that I am the sole surviving practitioner of the ancient art of belkin, which I studied for decades at the feet of an ancient master and which did me no good whatsoever."

Nimnestl thought about taking a seat, too. But with Oozola on one side and the Vielfrass on the other, there was no place to sit but right on the stairs. And though she wasn't overly squeamish, she could hear some fairly violent scratching and squeaking coming from beneath them.

"My main aim in coming to you was to ask if you could find Polijn," she told him. "She has not been seen since this morning's procession."

"If I'd been part of that crummy procession, I wouldn't show my face either for a while," the sorcerer told her, kicking a mangy head that poked out from under the porch. "Where were the dancing girls? Where were the performing horses? Where was the free beer?"

"Polijn?" persisted the Bodyguard.

"Haven't seen her," he replied. "Maybe she went looking for free beer. If I do see her, I will shoo her in your direction."

"Have you tried the Yellow Dog?" Lady Oozola inquired, stroking a stray rat with her toes.

Nimnestl shook her head. "It will have been looted by now."

Oozola's thumb jerked toward the stairs. "No, it won't. He told them it was off limits."

Nimnestl's head came back to the Vielfrass. "Why?"

The sorcerer had taken a pair of maroon gloves from under his cape and was trying them on. "Oh, Karlikartis will appreciate it when she returns."

"Will she return?" Nimnestl inquired, her tone very gentle.

The Vielfrass decided he didn't like the maroon gloves and started to slip white ones on over them. "If she doesn't, I suppose she won't appreciate it, then."

Nimnestl decided to sit down on the stairs, after all. "Do you know everything that's going on here?" she demanded.

He took off all the gloves and tucked them into his collar. "Probably not." His eyes came up to hers. "What if I did? If I told you you could run along home, that your little king was safe, would you do it?"

Nimnestl thought it over. "No."

He tossed his hands into the air. "Then I might as well tell you to paint your hammer pink and go rabbit hunting."

"Is the King all right?" she asked him.

He smiled. "Maybe he would be if you painted your hammer pink."

Nimnestl rose, and walked down the stairs. "I suppose there's some reason you can't come out and tell me, like an honest man."

"Yes," said Oozola. "He's not an honest man."

"I have a feeling it's against the law in this part of town," the Vielfrass agreed. "Furthermore, if you knew everything I know, what would be the use of me? You want to know things, Giggles? All right. Your king is not safe, but he's safer than you think he is. Your Polijn has been many things, but traitor is not one of them. A fire is about to break out which will rage out of control. Lady Iranen killed a dog this morning. A pink hammer would be a definite drawback to you. And one of the things I just told you is a lie."

Nimnestl glowered. "Don't look at me," said Lady Oozola, putting her hands over her collarbones. "I have to listen to this kind of thing all the time."

Lady Iranen had, in fact, killed a dog in the Dining Room this morning. And the fact that the Vielfrass knew that could mean that he knew many things. The real reason Nimnestl frowned was that she could not think of any reason a pink hammer would be a drawback, and that was the one statement she would prefer was a lie.

"Shall we leave her with her thoughts, degenerate dumpling?" the Vielfrass asked his partner. "I'm sure there's havoc just waiting for us to wreak it."

Nimnestl was standing on the stairs, so she wasn't sure how they'd gotten down off the porch and so far ahead of her by the time she had lifted her head to look in that direction. She nearly followed them, but the Vielfrass's conversation was too much for her on a day so steamy.

In any case, the Yellow Dog was not so bad a suggestion. The King had heard Polijn's mother worked there (the mothers of rival would-be queens would certainly not have missed a chance to bring that to his attention). If he had gone in search of her, there was a chance he'd try there.

Nimnestl wasn't sure how to get to the Yellow Dog from here, but asking for directions would mark her as an outsider, and fair game. So she simply stepped up into the Gilded Fly, took the neck of the first conscious person she saw, and snarled, "Take me to the Yellow Dog."

IV

NIMNESTL kept a hand on her guide's neck all the way to
the Street of Spreading Flowers. No one paid any attention to
this, the boy was nothing to them. In fact, Nimnestl didn't see
a lot of people out and about at all, except at the little market
squares, which she skirted.

At the Street of Spreading Flowers, a victim of one of
the Decency Committees was hanging by one ankle from a
porch roof, a tattered pair of underpants pinned to her nose.
Nimnestl helped her guide cut the moaning woman down, not
because she really believed it was his sister, but because they
were close enough to the Yellow Dog for her to find the rest
of the way by herself. This would keep the guide occupied
elsewhere.

As he dragged his booty away, which fully occupied his
attention as the woman was twice his size, Nimnestl slipped off
toward the boxlike theater house, her mind on the Vielfrass's
declarations. The Vielfrass seldom told a simple lie. He thought
it a better exhibition of his genius to twist the truth.

Polijn had or had not betrayed them. The King was or was
not in mild danger. A fire would or would not burn out of
control. A pink hammer would or would not be a drawback.

She paused under the hanging picture of a long-nosed yellow dog with its ears down over its eyes. The house looked

dark. One hand unhooked her hammer as the other pushed on the door.

Most of the torch brackets were empty. One or two held torches that had already burned out, and one near the door fought against oblivion. Nimnestl checked behind the door; the doorman would need spares for lighting people out the door at night, surely. She found an unlit torch and set it afire.

Clothes and trinkets were scattered everywhere across the floor. Morafor had described piles, but the looters had been through this lot at least once. The Vielfrass apparently stopped them before they could clear everything away.

She let the door drop behind her; the thump might draw out Polijn or the King, if either was here. The response that was drawn out froze her into place. This didn't stop the sound.

It was like the barking and whining of dogs. Nimnestl peered up at the wooden animals carved on doorframes and pilasters. These dogs weren't moving.

She followed the sound down the main corridor, her head cocked to one side. It was loudest at one door on the right, but behind this she found only another corridor. She shrugged, and set off down this. Since she didn't know what she was here to find, one way was as good as another.

A glimmer of something that was not torchlight stopped her halfway down. Yet another corridor, even narrower, branched off this one. The light was daylight, coming through some small opening. Nimnestl decided it was no threat; she could check there after she found out about these dog sounds.

The dog sounds came, in fact, from dogs: six or seven of them. They were joined, as she pushed open the rough door, by the sounds of poultry and swine as well.

"All right! All right!" she called, as animals thudded against their enclosures. "I see it!"

The King hadn't been here, then; he'd have fed them. Nimnestl found buckets for the food and stuck her torch into a bracket. She was not completely new at this kind of work, and knew it required two hands.

The animals were very well kept, she thought, for having been raised indoors this far down in the Swamp. The dogs especially: her grandfather had kept dogs, and she knew something about them. She'd hunted with them in Reangle.

Rossacottans saw dogs more in terms of guards, or vermin-catchers.

And these were neither, for they were Rossacottan war-hounds, generally used these days primarily for diplomatic purposes: gifts to foreign kings. Not really hounds, since they were bred for combat rather than the hunt, they had a collar of coarse hair around the neck, but were otherwise nearly bare, with very short yellowish-white hair. A flat face was made more grotesque by short black splotches under each eye and limp, lop ears.

Nimnestl had not seen bigger warhounds even in the King's kennels. They bristled with muscle, particularly in the hind-quarters. But they were frantically friendly, for Swamp dogs, which argued the professional training that taught them to display ferocity only in combat.

While they were busy eating, Nimnestl refilled the water troughs from a barrel of stagnant water in the corner. She could use a drink, too, she thought, after hauling so many buckets. Maybe the Yellow Dog stocked something for the use of the employees, as well as the livestock. She'd have to watch for bottles with palace markings, though, or risk drugging herself.

She leaned back against the water barrel and sneered, not at the dogs. Anyone as intelligent as she was supposed to be should have checked that story by now. But there had been so many distractions, and the big man put on such a show of omniscience. It would be nice to prove a rumor that had reached him was untrue, just to show him other people were capable of thought.

If the wine really had been sent to the Swamp from the Palace Royal, the shipment would have to have been made through the Wine Steward, and signed for. That brought interesting possibilities to mind, particularly if Aizon had ordered his apprentice to handle the transaction. If the Exorcist had signed for himself, or if the steward had been too busy to get the signature, it wouldn't be nearly so useful.

The animals were content, and busy with their food, so Nimnestl retrieved her torch and moved out. The wine was a little more interesting to her, suddenly, than the Yellow Dog. Would it have been worth it to mention the wine to the Vielfrass? Or would he have thought of something even more confusing to say about it?

She found her way back to the little branch corridor, and pushed through it to a larger space beyond. This seemed to be kind of a back lobby; the daylight, growing dimmer now, came through a door propped open by the head of a naked body on the floor. Some looter, perhaps, had failed to listen to the Vielfrass. Nimnestl peeked out into the alley to make sure no one was watching, and then pulled the woman clear of the door.

The clothes scattered here were a bit richer than those inside the front door; the proprietor might have been making a run for the exit when whatever happened had happened. Nimnestl kicked at the loose garments. Was there any point in searching through this mess? There must be something for her to discover here about Polijn, or why had the Vielfrass sent her here? If he had sent her here. She supposed if Polijn had been sneaking secrets out of the Palace Royal, this could be a logical place to bring them.

She kicked her way over to the richest brocades. Some odd pieces of jewelry bounced free, with a number of knives. She followed these artifacts, kicked them again, and listened. A gilded ring dagger didn't thump against the floor just right. Nimnestl stooped and lifted it, bouncing it in the palm of her hand. Then she slid one finger through the ring at the end and gave it a twist.

A scrap of paper was rolled into the hollow handle; she eased it free. Someone had been taking an interest in genealogy, not a science one expected in the Swamp. This bit had been torn from a larger chart. Nimnestl had no trouble at all guessing who had the rest, for this excerpt clearly traced General Ferrapec's lineage back to a brother of the King's father, completely ignoring Jintabh. Ferrapec's handwriting was not so refined; this had probably been written up by Raiprez, to judge by the flourishes. Somebody had scrawled something on the back in handwriting almost as bad as Ferrapec's, but not quite.

Whoever had written this, it was at the very least a lever with which to pry some information out of the general. And if anyone in the Council saw it, it was certainly Ferrapec's death sentence. The one person in Rossacotta whose line of descent was documented and inviolable was the King.

Nimnestl felt the Yellow Dog had given her enough to think about. She stepped across to open the back door.

It just missed her outstretched hand as it banged open and a woman carrying a large pink club pushed inside. On seeing the massive dark form confronting her, she screamed and drew back. But Nimnestl had a foot against the door by this time.

"I haven't seen you for a while," said the Bodyguard, her hammer waiting in her free hand. "I don't recall ordering you into the Swamp."

"You . . . gave me no orders at all . . . My Lady," panted Deverna. "But I . . . was told to watch you."

"By whom?" Nimnestl inquired, though what she really wanted to know was why Veldres's nominee to the Royal Bodyguard was toting an artificial leg. "His Lordship the Regent, or Veldres?"

Deverna swallowed. "His Lordship, My Lady. But I . . . have never been to the Swamp, My Lady, and I . . . lost you. I went into a beer shop to ask about you . . ."

"Which one?"

"The Lifted Finger, My Lady." Deverna swallowed again. Sweat was pouring down the rounded forehead and the pretty-pretty face. "A man took hold of my cloak and . . . asked who else I wanted to kill. I didn't know what he meant and I . . ."

"Said the wrong thing."

Deverna blinked. "Broke his arm. They all ran at me, and the man behind the bar said, 'She's not the black dog; she's just another Swamper. Teach her some manners.' They had my daggers before I could turn around." She raised the shocking pink weapon she was clutching. "Some man was trying to trade this for a drink and it was lying on the bar. I . . ."

Nimnestl raised one hand. "Excuse me," she said. She stepped around Deverna and opened the back door just a crack. A good twenty men and women were arguing with each other at one end of the alley.

"The Vielfrass said . . ."

"Ah, he wants her for himself!"

"Go in and get her! How many of us could he find?"

She shut the door. "You shouldn't have been down here without training," she told Deverna.

The other woman nodded. "What's Veldres up to?" the Chief Bodyguard went on.

Now Deverna shook her head. "He only told me to . . . to stay as close to you as I could and do whatever you told me. My Lady, I . . ."

Nimnestl held up that hand again, and opened the door once more. Now forty people waited at the end of the alley, and she could hear a tumble of voices from the other end as well.

"She was a bully and your competition, but the foreigners have done her in! Will we stand for that?"

Men in the uniform of a Decency Committee were pushing to the front of the crowd, fanning the flames. There was decision in the faces of the leaders, and clubs in their hands. Blades might end it too quickly. They grumbled and growled to each other behind an invisible line they dared not cross . . . for the moment.

"Somebody cover the front door!"

Nimnestl came back around to face Deverna. Theoretically, of course, the woman was her subordinate and, hence, her responsibility. And Deverna had no chance of escaping this crowd.

"You can find your way back to the Palace Royal from here?" she demanded. "Without asking directions?"

"I-I'm not sure, My Lady," Deverna replied. "Perhaps, if I had time to get my bearings . . ."

"I will give you time," Nimnestl said. "Give me that."

She took the artificial leg. "Now your cloak. And take this."

"My Lady!" Deverna nearly dropped the hammer.

"You will report to the Regent the following message from the Vielfrass," Nimnestl told her. "Listen. The King is probably in mild danger. A young woman is probably not a traitor. A fire will probably burn out of control." There was no sense giving her more than that, not without more dependable knowledge of Veldres's plans. She did reflect, with some bitterness, that a pink hammer would have been a definite drawback.

"But, My Lady . . ."

"Here." Nimnestl handed over her own cloak. "The front door is through this corridor. Turn right when it joins a larger corridor, and left when that corridor meets the main one. When you reach the door, count off your fingers and toes before leaving. By that time, I should be well on my way."

"But . . ."

"When I return to the Palace Royal," Nimnestl went on, "I will expect to find that you have followed my orders. If not, I will turn you over to the Regent, who will put that hammer into your mouth and take it out elsewhere. You are listening?"

"Yes, My Lady."

"Put the hood up. If anyone tries to stop you, show your hands and the hammer, and they will likely let you pass. When eagles circle, quail take to the brush."

It was a proverb from Reangle. Deverna nodded vigorously. "Yes, My Lady. I am sorry, My Lady."

"Everybody's sorry today," grumbled the Bodyguard, fastening on the other woman's cloak. She raised the garish pink leg and stepped into the darkened alley.

The crowd was hushed. Nimnestl checked one end of the alley and then the other. An unthinking rush to action could only make things worse, as there were a hundred or so of them now. She had a vision of herself swinging the pink club in her good strong arms, splattering a path. It made her smile.

They saw, and fell dead silent, perhaps wondering if this woman wasn't a little bigger than the one they'd seen go in. In the moment of silence, Nimnestl put her good strong legs to work.

Her subordinates trained for this using spiked posts. The posts fell down if you failed to clear them, but new recruits didn't know that. Nimnestl cleared all but the last row of people, but the two she kicked went down just like the posts. Roaring, the crowd surged through the alley.

Nimnestl made no move for cover. Let them keep her in view and follow at full speed. If they slowed down, they might start to think. And when they stopped to think, they might stop to take aim.

She charged across the street to a wide, clear alley. That last market square she'd passed on her way west would be a good place to weed the crowd. The least determined would see enough chances to smash and grab that they'd fall behind. Any who remained could catch up to her in the Street of Giants, actually an alley so narrow they'd be able to come at her no more than two at a time.

This alley came up across a number of other alleys. Nimnestl aimed at one and saw a girl running toward her. In a moment, she had recognized Polijn and adopted pure Rossacottan philosophy: if you see something you need and nobody's there to stop you, pick it up and take it along.

V

ANOTHER crowd came hurtling up the alley Nimnestl had intended to use, so she compromised and took another. Fortunately, Polijn was no screamer or wiggler, and Nimnestl was able to gain a little time on her pursuers as the two mobs met and took each other's measure.

The result, of course, was an even bigger gang of pursuers. Nimnestl did consider, just for a moment, dropping her passenger. She could speed up and the crowd would slow down. But she just clutched the girl tighter against her hip and ran on.

Then she was in the middle of a market gathering, dodging in and out and around. Being pushed out of the way by a detached leg that was almost a glowing pink was enough of a novelty to keep the marketgoers at a distance. A few black shirts indicated the presence of a Decency Committee, but none of the members got in her way.

This was a good, thick knot of people, she thought, racing beyond it. If those following were delayed enough, she could jettison the idea of a stand in the alley, and simply make for her horse at the Blue Bottle. Nimnestl tried to gauge by ear how far behind her the bloodthirsty crew was.

There were quite a ways back, and getting farther all the time. She could hear no near footsteps.

She slowed to a trot. She looked back over her shoulder. No one had come out the far side of the market at all. She waited, and then frowned down at Polijn. The girl's face didn't move at all.

Nimnestl set her captive down. "Is there some way we can go back there and take a look without risking a meeting?"

Polijn looked up and down the street. She nodded.

"Quietly, then."

Nimnestl's hand was on Polijn's neck all the way around the block. She did not know yet which of the Vielfrass's statements was a fib. They slid through one of the more malodorous side streets Nimnestl had encountered that evening, and paused behind a stack of firewood. Nimnestl could see up the alley to the firelit scene ahead.

What she had taken for a market square had been a building once, when its walls were intact. Now, the walls no more than piles of rubble, it was half an alley and half a storm shelter.

People were gathered at a bonfire, some of them from choice, some by solicitation of men in black shirts. A few broken heads had been required to bring Nimnestl's pursuers into the fold. Some stalwarts still struggled to grab clubs away from members of the Decency Committee, but there were enough men in black to surround and subdue the mutinous.

"Get in there!" one man hollered to a couple in the street. "There's news!"

"Wait here," Nimnestl told Polijn, and started up the alley. That was a goodly mob around the bonfire, several hundred at least and still growing, most of them able bodies. This could be the fire that was going to burn out of control. If she could stop it, that might force the Vielfrass's other statements to be true.

"Get back to yer hole!"

"I got places to go!"

"You gonna use that hand tomorrow? Then keep it outa my face!"

The crowd was ominously well behaved. Nobody was selling or stealing anything. Men and women gathered into clumps, probably around various strongmen, to argue and shake fingers.

"Looka the sky! The signs are wrong!"

"It's a mistake! You don't want to kill them on the wrong night!"

"What do we care if those tax-eaters get their heads knocked off?"

"The more the better!"

Nimnestl paused to study the scene. The members of the Decency Committee actually seemed to be urging nonviolence on the mob.

"You can't go running east tonight! It's all wrong!"

"Umian says they won't be ready up there!"

"I say we go anyhow! Let him come after!"

She could see it now. Umian and Ferrapec and company had been waiting for the Swamp to rise. The drugged wine and the Decency Committees had been intended to inflame the Swampites; the audit and the heat had played into their hands. A mass uprising would furnish them either with a ready-made army, or with an excuse to call out the Royal Army. They could then subdue the rebels in the Swamp and return to the Palace Royal as heroes, quite showing up the Regent.

Or . . . but the exact scenario didn't matter once the King was missing. If anything befell His Majesty, the country would be plunged into chaos they could not combat. There were no other claimants to the throne (no one would give Ferrapec's phony family tree credence for a second), and the collapse of the dynasty meant the collapse of government, church, and the natural order.

So the Decency Committees were trying to put out, or at least bank, the fire they'd started. There must be some way to get it extinguished entirely.

A gentle cough drew her attention. "That came from back there," somebody whispered.

"Just you keep your mind on her," whispered someone else.

Nimnestl had survived too many ambushes to ever really be startled by another. She gripped the pink leg tighter. It had begun to crack at the thigh.

"It's a trick," whispered the first voice. "Or else it's not her. She'd've heard us by now."

Nimnestl turned and saw a pair of men in black jackets, knives out. "Oh!" she squeaked. "I'm so glad you're here!"

This was obviously not the greeting they'd expected. "I'm Deverna," she told them. "I worked for Veldres? I have news."

"He did have that brown-noser working for him," muttered one man.

"What kind of news?" demanded the second.

"Hurry," she said, starting for the bonfire. "We have to stop them."

Provided Polijn stayed put, she could think of only one person who would recognize her without her hammer and be likely to betray her to the crowd. And she didn't see the Vielfrass anywhere.

The two men caught up with her and escorted her forward. Not needing it as a weapon, Nimnestl used the pink leg as a flag. It attracted considerable attention by the time she reached the bonfire.

"Don't let them kill us!" she screamed.

That attracted the attention of anybody who hadn't noticed the leg. "How come the Black Jackets didn't drink any of the poison wine?" she shouted. "It's because Umian told the Decency Committees about the drug!"

This was not the kind of announcement her companions had hoped for, but she swung the pink leg, as if for a flourish, and knocked them out of the way. "I tried to tell everyone at the Lifted Finger, but they wouldn't let me."

The men got up and tried again, but found themselves held back by men without the black shirts. The Decency Committee pulled together in their direction.

"Let them go!" she screamed. "They weren't told everything! It isn't their fault! Umian wanted them to be undrugged to lead you east, to the homes of the fat tax-eaters!"

The Decency Committee paused to consider whether they were being complimented. The rest of the crowd shook weapons. Nimnestl let them, and went on, "They didn't know the Army would be waiting for us!"

"Umian's sending the Army to help us!" they roared.

Nimnestl swung the leg over her head. "Umian's sending the Army to beat your bones into the stones!"

"You don't know!" she went on, as the crowd stared. "But he told Veldres, and there I heard it! He'll kill all he can and then go back to take the castle, once he's warmed up on you!

The merchants he saved will be behind him, and make him Regent. His brand of decency will be everywhere!"

Men in black shirts started a chant of "Decency! Decency!"

"Where's lintik Kaftus's decency?" Nimnestl bellowed. "And that black dog of his: you know what she really uses that hammer for!" The crowd cheered. She knew there'd be some use for those songs Ynygyn wrote about her, before his untimely death.

"And when have they ever meddled with the Swamp? But Umian means to make you all decent! He'll close your theaters and your beer halls; he'll send our men to the farms and the women inside to weave and knit!"

Even the Decency Committee was a little stunned. One member protested, "He'd never ask that of loyal Sons of the Panther!"

He would, as a matter of fact, but they'd never believe it. A double-cross was more credible than militant morality. "Only those who aren't his special friends! The rest, those who won't follow his new rules, will go to Veldres or Lady Iranen to be played with!"

Some of them were believing this. Maybe she could bring a few more in line with an appeal to their loyalty. "The King has had all this hidden from him! He is being ignored by Umian and Veldres!"

"And that Lord Tutor!" shouted someone in the crowd. "He wants to burn down the Swamp and put up that shuptit University of his!"

Nimnestl's free hand shot out, fingers forward. "And who told you that? Wasn't it Veldres's wipers who passed the whisper?"

They thought about it. Nimnestl didn't give them a lot of time. "Life will be ruined by that University, yes! All those students buying their beer and their pleasures in your places, instead of up in hightown! All that money coming in, why, what would you do all winter, without starvation to keep you company? You see why Veldres wants it up to the east, and Umian, too. You'll do his bidding for coppers."

She gave them a little more space for contemplation now. She saw a few men slipping off their black overtunics and tossing them into the fire. One of them was one of her escorts.

"If I were you," she told him in an undertone, "I would go find a great deal of beer and bring it back here. Better leave the wine alone."

He nodded and pushed out of the crowd, pulling a few allies along as he went.

"So what will we do?" Nimnestl asked the crowd. "Toast our good fortune here? Or go east and play Umian's game for him?"

The answer was unintelligible but seemed to be tending toward the first choice. Anybody who recalled that Umian was the one who had supposedly sent word not to attack the merchants let that inconvenient memory slip away at the sight of a barrel being rolled down the street.

Somebody struck up a song on a ficdual that had not recently been tuned. Someone else battered down a door and brought out a bin of clay mugs. Nimnestl found more of these pressed on her than she had hands for, and was the recipient of more torrid propositions than she'd heard in the previous ten years. She handed the pink leg to a reasonably tall woman who looked as though she could field such suggestions more profitably, and did a reasonable job of detaching herself from the crowd. Affectionate pursuers were a bit harder to elude, and it took some time.

She slipped back down the alley to retrieve Polijn, and make her way back up to the Palace Royal. She found she would have to be satisfied with the latter. The girl was gone.

INTERLUDE
Sielvia

"I'LL have them all thrown in cells for treason when we get out!"

"What if we don't?"

The King stopped stamping up and down the stone floor and turned toward Timpre, one hand raised. Merklin stuck out an arm to stop him, pointing out, "You're the one who left the key in the lock."

"Well, I am SORRY!" The King was so mad he slammed one foot on the floor and then the other. "I didn't know anybody was behind us!"

"I fetch key back quick," suggested Mardith, flying up to the barred window.

"Yes, and get everybody into trouble!" snapped the King. "You just sit!"

To Sielvia's surprise and, apparently, the King's, the black bird flew back into the cell and sat on the floor. "What you do, then?" Mardith demanded.

The King ground a fist into his other hand. "Somebody will miss us. Those guards weren't very smart."

"And if they do miss us," said Argeleb, "how will they know we're down here?"

"The guards won't tell them," said Merklin. "No, we'll have to break out of here ourselves."

"But how?" Timpre demanded, wiping tearstained cheeks.

"We'll think of something," said the King. "If we don't, I guess Mardith can go get help. But not until the next shift. If those guys know who's down here, they might let me go and keep you, so I don't tell on them."

"But they couldn't keep us long," said Sielvia. "You could tell Nimnestl and . . ."

"I can do it myself!" snapped the King. "I can do it! I CAN!" He kicked the empty food plate, and then the water pitcher.

Sielvia and Merklin both dove for it, but it had lost nearly half its water before they had it righted again. "Do be careful," said Sielvia. "We don't know how long we might have to be here."

"Not that long," grumbled the irritated monarch. "Anyway, they bring food and water to the prisoners."

"But we're not up where those prisoners are!" Timpre told him, jumping up. "We're way down in the haunted part. We'll be here all . . ."

Sielvia broke in with, "Look!" just as Mardith called, "What this now?"

The four boys turned to look. Sielvia was pointing to the puddle of water, which shrank and disappeared.

"Oh, it's just going down a crack," said Merklin.

Mardith put an eye to the stone. "The whole damn thing."

"Going down where?" Sielvia demanded. "Is the crack that deep, or is there a cell under this one?"

They looked at each other. "Who'd put a way out in a dungeon cell?" Argeleb demanded.

"Do you serious?" demanded Mardith.

"That's right," the King put in, chewing on the end of one thumb. "I went down a secret passage in a cell once, but it wasn't this cell. And the passage was in the wall."

"Maybe this goes to the same place," said Merklin, dropping to his knees next to Sielvia, who was tracing the crack in the cold floor. Argeleb and the King took out their daggers and started to pry at the stone, and even Timpre, glad of something to do, moved in to watch.

"Here's something!" said Argeleb. He pulled back on his knife, and the stone rose a finger's width above the others.

"You going to absolutely get it!" crowed Mardith, as he

spied the handhold the dagger's tip was wedged into.

The stone had not been made for children; it required the muscles of everyone involved to pull it back just enough for a look. "Ha!" said Merklin, recognizing the use of a long metal rod set into the opening. It scraped and squealed as he pulled it up and set it into a hole in the door.

"There's a new one I never see before!" exclaimed Mardith, looking down the dark shaft.

"The other one led to stairs," said the King, setting one foot on the first rung of the stone ladder.

"We don't know what's down there," said Timpre, glancing back at the door.

"Well, you can wait here, if you think this is dangerous," Merklin told him, as the King disappeared from view.

"It's probably just a sewer," said Argeleb. "How could they handle stuff down here without a sewer?"

"It's a way out, isn't it?" Merklin replied. "And if it is a sewer, nobody's been locked up down here in tons of years." He put his own feet on the ladder.

They all climbed down, even Timpre. Sielvia came last. "I won't close it, okay?" she called. "We might need to come back, and I don't think we could lift it from this side."

"Okay!" came an answer from far below.

The torch had gone down with Argeleb, in the middle of the group. Sielvia was glad when she reached bottom, and the light. "Now where?" she asked.

They stood around the ladder at the bottom of a cylindrical shaft. Argeleb swung the torch down to a black spot on the wall. It was the opening to a low, narrow passage, with dark grey walls that stretched on in unnerving monotony.

"We could go back," said Timpre, reaching for the ladder.

With hardly a glance behind him, Argeleb climbed up into the passage. "Come on," said Merklin, going after him.

The tunnel was by no means featureless. As they moved, crouching, they found themselves tripping over steps that would go up a few feet, and then start down again, for no reason they could see.

"If it's a sewer," whispered Timpre, "we might go down to a pit."

"Everything goes down to a pit someday," Merklin informed him.

"No sewer this!" exclaimed Mardith, riding on the King's shoulder. The bird took in a long breath. "Smell like sewer, ha?"

"Dirty old bird," said the King. "How many sewers have you been in?"

"Ha!" Mardith replied. "You never had so many breakfasts as I had sewers!"

"Won't Nimnestl be amazed?" the monarch went on. "And Kaftus, too! We're explorer-heroes! Probably nobody's been here in years and years!"

"What about the guy who was in the cell?" asked Argeleb.

"He not here," said Mardith.

"How can you . . . oh!"

"What is it?" demanded Timpre.

"Nothing," said Argeleb. But he had stopped walking.

"You can tell us," Merklin told him, coming up alongside.

But Argeleb had been stating the truth. There was nothing. The tunnel ended in a flat wall, three feet ahead of them.

"It couldn't . . ." the King began to say, stepping past the others. Timpre shrieked.

Everyone jumped, but Merklin recovered first. "That's really smart," he said. "You just step down on the right stone." The King started forward again, but Merklin stuck out an arm. They watched as the door that had popped open came shut again.

"Now," said Merklin. They moved forward. "This one." He stepped down hard, and the door pulled away again.

"Eew," said Sielvia, as they stepped down. "Where are we?"

Torchlight showed a small cave with walls covered in hairy mold. Greens grew on orange and blue on green. The King put out a hand to sweep some away.

"Ouch!"

Mardith, with more room to maneuver, flew up toward the ceiling. "Rock bite you, eh, Highness?"

"Yes," said the King, rubbing his hand. "It . . . rock?" He leaned toward the wall. "It's crystal."

"In that case, it's beautiful," said Argeleb. The needlelike minerals glowed as he raised the torch toward them.

"No!" cried Timpre. The others turned to find him clawing

at the door, now shut. "There's no handle!"

"Well, this cave has to go someplace," said Merklin. He pointed to another dark opening, this one in the middle of the far wall. Argeleb took the torch to it and peered through, a knife ready in his free hand.

"Wow!" he announced.

In moments, they stood on the other side of the hole, staring at a broad corridor with a high, arched roof. Ornamented doorways opened all along either side, stretching in rows that seemed to go on for miles. It was grand, but Sielvia found the floor ominously uneven, as though many feet had worn it down over many years.

There seemed to be no one here now. Mardith flew to the first doorway on the right. Everyone followed, and peered into a shallow room. Painted on the walls inside stood tall nine-legged spiders wearing high conical hats, doing nothing in particular.

"What do you suppose they used this for?" mused the King.

"Who do you suppose is using it now?" Argeleb asked.

"I want to go someplace else!" wailed Timpre, hanging on his cousin's arm.

"We are going someplace else, duckhead," Merklin told him, turning away from the room.

Timpre wailed, "I want to do it faster!" Sielvia was going to have to slap him sooner or later; she just knew it.

The group set off down the hall, which was easily as big as any corridor the Palace Royal had aboveground. Each door led to another little room; each room had its own interesting and not particularly comprehensible pictures on the walls. Mardith was thrilled by the new sights, swooping up and down the hall to check the carven doorways and to peek at the rooms the poor wingless explorers hadn't reached yet.

Sielvia wished the bird would stay closer to the King. If anybody was down here, she doubted she and the others would serve as much of a bodyguard. She was going to mention this to Conan, but decided not to. If the trembling Timpre started to collapse, she might be able to get him moving again by telling him he was needed as a guard.

Not that she wasn't excited by the hidden passage, too. This

was certainly something her father and mother had never seen,
not to mention her sisters. Being the youngest in such a brood,
she had very few chances to impress anybody.

But she didn't like the place much, take it up one side
and down the other. Its emptiness unnerved her: this was no
dungeon, designed to be bare and unfriendly. It had been some
kind of gallery, meant to store treasures, perhaps, in the little
rooms, for the use of many people. But now it was echoingly
empty, and dead cold. Whose was it, and where were those
people now?

In the way of more immediate worries, that torch wasn't
going to burn forever. She wished whoever had made this
place had spent a little less time on decorations and more on
some kind of sign to show how far they had to go. It wouldn't
have been so difficult; they could have incorporated that into
the decorative pictures on the floor.

She stopped in the middle of one of the pictures. Maybe they
had. Maybe that was why the pictures only appeared every
twenty paces or so along the floor. They were some kind of
sign. She considered the picture on the floor—a simple design
of dogs' heads—and glanced up toward the ceiling.

Timpre did the same and, with a cry, jumped away from the
square, dragging Sielvia with him.

The others ran back to them. "Murder holes," Sielvia
explained, pointing up at the ceiling.

"Ho ho!" said Mardith, flying up to the dark rectangle in
the ceiling. "You enemy come in to see the show, and you
wait up here for him pass!"

"Come back!" called Timpre, as the bird disappeared into
the hole.

"Hokay, it don't make some difference. What name you
so leapy?" Mardith fluttered back. "No one up there, not
even bats."

"I'd like it better with bats," murmured Sielvia. The King
glanced at her, and then at the murder holes.

"Hey!" said Merklin. He dropped to his knees. "I'll just bet
you," he said, digging at the dog picture with his knife. In
moments, he had the broad stone free.

"This place has all kinds of secrets," said Argeleb, kneeling
to help him lift it.

Beneath them, no one could tell how far, was a system of uncapped corridors, like the maze at the Summer Palace seen from above, only made of stone instead of hedges. "That's . . ." Sielvia started to say. Timpre yanked on her arm so suddenly she nearly fell forward. "What is it now?"

He pointed down at the maze. A fringed yellow tail— attached to no one could see what—disappeared around a corner. Merklin let the stone drop back into place, and the group set off down the hall without much comment.

"Hoo gosh!" said Mardith, peeking into the next room.

The walls here were not decorated at all. But as the explorers started to move on, Mardith swooped inside. They all looked up at him, and pulled to the other side of the hall at the sight of an enormous owl's head.

"Oh," said Merklin, "it's one of those trick pictures you don't see unless you're standing just right. There's the corner of the room, right? You couldn't see through it like that if it was a real owl, right?"

The owl blinked.

They took off as one and dashed screaming down the hall. When it dawned on them that this was pretty silly, they stopped. It had been nice, though, to have a little noise around the place.

"Well," panted Argeleb, "what now?"

"Nobody here for sure," remarked Mardith, who had cheerfully followed them in the race. "They hear that, they be here by now."

"What are we going to do?" sobbed Timpre.

The King's party looked up the hall. No giant owls or mysterious beasts came at them. They saw only more hall.

"There must be some way to get out," said Sielvia.

"Sure," said the King, around the thumb in his mouth.

Merklin strode to the nearest doorway. "There's openings in the ceilings and openings in the floors. Maybe that's why all the rooms are so little; there's something behind them."

"Oh, look out," Timpre moaned. Merklin sneered a bit but otherwise paid no attention, marching up to a picture of leafless trees inside the room. He rapped on the trunks, one after another.

"It could be in just about any room," Sielvia noted.

"I bet there's one in every room," Merklin replied. "Some go upstairs and some go downstairs and some go to bigger rooms: treasuries and like that. You just have to know. . . . Ha ha ha!

"See?" he said, as the little door swung back. "The branches formed a pattern just like a door."

"What's back there?" Timpre demanded, trying to resist as his cousin pulled him forward.

A vast, echoing room was back there. Hundreds of pictures ornamented the walls, but the dominant feature, as far as everyone was concerned, was an immense unrailed staircase that rose out of the middle of the chamber to disappear among shadows beyond the torch's reach.

Mardith shot up toward the shadows. Timpre moaned and buried his face in Sielvia's skirts. There was just too much shadow.

"Door here, Highness!" called the bird's voice from far away. He reappeared. "No see lock or knob."

The King looked to Merklin. "One of us should go," Merklin told him. "But somebody ought to stay here and hold the door open, in case we need to go back."

"There's only one torch," the King pointed out. Everyone looked at it, but no one mentioned how low the light had gotten.

"Somebody could stand at the bottom of the steps with the torch," Sielvia suggested. "You could still have enough light back here by the door, and enough up the stairs."

"I'll go," said Merklin, pulling his belt tighter.

"No, I'm tired of carrying the torch," Argeleb told him. "I'll go."

"Quiet, quiet, quiet," said Conan as Merklin protested, pushing the torch away. "We'll spin for it." He set his dagger on the floor as the others formed a circle. With a twist, he sent it spinning.

"Cheat!" said Merklin, as the point came to a stop right before the monarch himself. "Cheat!"

"I can do it as much as anybody can," said the King, lifting his dagger and his chin.

"Not alone, though," Merklin told him, getting a grip on his arm. "You need somebody besides Mardith with you. While he was fighting off an enemy, you might fall."

"You just watch the door," the King said, pulling at Merklin's hand. "Let go!"

"Spin for it again," said Argeleb. "We don't have time to fight."

With a snort, the King set the dagger down again and spun it. "Her!" Merklin roared, outraged. "You aren't going up there with nobody but a girl to guard you!"

"Hoo hoo hoo!" cried Mardith. "What you pay not to take that to Missy Nimnestl?"

"Come on," said the King to Sielvia. "We've wasted enough time."

"You hold the door," Merklin told Argeleb, as Sielvia peeled Timpre from her arm. "I'll hold the torch, then."

Sielvia hoped Merklin wouldn't hit Timpre too hard. "Just shut up," she heard him say. "Nobody's hurting us, Whimper. Nobody's here to hurt us."

She and the King moved upstairs on all fours, knives at the ready between clenched teeth. Perhaps a hand's width of stone sat between them and a sheer drop on either side. Mardith flew to the top and back several times, calling out encouraging progress reports. "Halfway to halfway, Highness. Looking well, looking well."

It seemed to take hours, but they were by no means eager to exchange the stairs for the little ledge at the top. Only faint light reached them now from below, but the rectangle looked about large enough for Sielvia to lie down on, her hair hanging off one end and her feet off the other.

"There be it!" Mardith exclaimed. "Now I see!"

The King also saw the little hole in the door. He started to reach in with one hand, thought better of it, and slid in his dagger instead. Then he reached up and took Mardith by the legs.

"Mardith," he said, "be really, really quiet. I'm the King here and I'll decide what to do."

"You King, sure," said the bird, settling on his shoulder. Sielvia knew Mardith would not hesitate to disobey in an emergency, and was glad of it.

His Majesty reached back and took a spare dagger from a horizontal sheath on his back. "Sielvia, you hold the door while I see what's out there."

"You King, sure," she said. It was too dark to see by his face what he made of that.

He jerked the dagger in the door up and to the right. Sielvia caught it as it swung out. After making sure there was room for both the door and Sielvia on the ledge, Conan removed the dagger and stepped forward. Sielvia heard a thump.

"Not another closet?" she demanded.

"Ssh ssh ssh," said the King. Sielvia hushed. She also caught the murmur of voices.

She jerked back as something brushed her ear, and realized it was the King. "There must be another door," he said, his voice no more than a breath in her ear.

Sielvia stooped and wedged her dagger under the door. She let go with one hand, then the other, and then joined Conan in feeling the wall ahead of them.

Something went "ping!"; the wall slid to the left. Light, painful to eyes used to shadow, blazed through at their feet. The next wall ahead of them was cloth, and torn inches from the floor. They knelt to peer through.

Her mother had had some dealings with the officers in charge of army supplies, so Sielvia recognized one of the underground storerooms beneath the barracks. Some forty men were working, pulling armor out of barrels and dressing as if for war. All of them wore black livery, and helmets shaped like hangmen's hoods.

Sielvia's eyes were drawn at once to the one exception, the tidy woman with big eyes and a dress covered in tiny polka dots. "I told him he had nothing to worry about," she was telling an officer who stood perusing a piece of torn paper. "But I'm just a wife. You tell him."

Colonel Umian lowered the paper. General Ferrapec reached past Raiprez as if to take it, but the colonel crumpled it in one hand and threw it on the floor. It bounced nearly up to the tapestry behind which the King was watching.

"That's reaching too far," the colonel said. "Polijn will be of better use to us in other ways."

Sielvia heard the King take a sudden deep breath. "At any rate," the colonel went on, as Ferrapec started to object, "the location and protection of His Majesty is our first priority. All our other plans must be postponed until that is dealt with."

"We may not have that kind of time," said the general.

"We must have patience," Umian replied, raising his voice. Sielvia could tell he was trying to reassure not just Ferrapec but everyone else in the room. "The war of waiting is the hardest to wage, but it is almost always worth the effort."

"I'm sure they can do it, with YOUR guidance," Raiprez said, rolling her eyes up to her husband and then glancing to Umian for confirmation.

Umian cleared his throat and went on, "Indeed, General, you were yourself saying it would be foolish to act until we see how today's events fall out. If His Majesty has indeed gone in search of Polijn, it may help us. That will take less time than the poison that would cause Nurse to quarantine all the other girls in the Royal Circle."

"Ye-es," said the general, rubbing his chin.

"If all else fails, we will at least show ourselves as loyal and not liable to the panic that has seized other functionaries of the Court." Umian raised his chin. "The Swamp will be there tomorrow, and the Decency Committees. We need only continue as we have begun, showing all of Malbeth how our loyalty is superior to the bungling of the current government. We have still the solution of the murders to our account, and who knows what other acts of heroism may come about today?" He pointed at a soldier nearby. "Valspar, would you die for the King and the New Guard?"

The man came to attention, his armor in his hands. "Gladly, sir."

"Good. Stand right there."

They hadn't even seen the colonel draw his dagger. Valspar looked astounded. Actually, he was dead.

"He has achieved his sainthood," Umian said, wiping the blade on his knee. "You two: Cabrona, Durak. Take him to the place we spoke of, where the Regent will have stashed him after the foul murder. The rest of you, proceed to your regular duty stations. Anyone who sees the King will escort His Majesty back here, where he can safely be held until this danger passes."

The King pulled back from the tapestry. "Mardith," he whispered. "Go back down and tell them we can't get out this way. Siel, you . . ."

"I'm going to try and get that paper," she whispered, watching the soldiers filing out of the storeroom. "It'll prove Ferrapec was planning something."

"Okay," said the King. "You go tell them, Mardith, and we'll come down when you get back."

"You King," said the bird. "But we maybe could take a run . . ."

"No." The King shook his head. "There are too many, and they could just lock me up there and make the Council do what they wanted."

"You King," said the bird again, and flew off.

Sielvia, meanwhile, had been studying the crumpled paper. She was sure she had recognized it, the corner with big letters. That was the way Polijn headed her practice sheets. Which explained where Ferrapec had been able to get some paper; Janeftox had probably stolen it for him. She wondered if she really wanted that page, if it would also prove that Janeftox had been scheming.

She saw the last of the soldiers move out. The door closed behind them, and the lock clicked shut. "I'll get it!" she called to the King, and eased her hand out under the wall hanging.

She shrieked twice, once when the boot came down on her hand, and again when a heavy hand took her by the wrist and dragged her free.

"Well, the pixies have brought us a present!" roared a New Guard whose regular duty station was apparently inside the storeroom. "Got somebody there for my buddy?" He swept back the tapestry, but Sielvia had heard the door click shut. She hoped the King would have sense to go back down without her, or at least wait for Mardith.

"She's not for us, Stainface," said the other guard on duty. "That's that minstrel's brat."

The first guard raised Sielvia by the wrist for a better look. "The one that's missing, hey?"

The second guard poked her in the ribs, hard. "You missing?" he demanded.

"No!" Sielvia gasped. "That's my sister! I was looking for her!"

She was set down on her feet. "Been here some time, hey? Just looking, hey?"

"I didn't hear anything I have to tell about," she said, looking from one to the other to pick out the more sympathetic.

"Sword in a sheath's still a sword," said Stainface. "Speaking of swords." He reached down and flipped up her skirts, and she did not think he was looking for swords. "Sing, do you? We could use some entertainment."

"That's right," said his partner. "Entertain her up the hind hole and let's hear how she sings."

"Idea," said Stainface. He used one hand to turn Sielvia around and the other to unfasten his belt. "If you keep still, gosling, you keep breathing."

Laisida had not made it to King's Minstrel on talent alone, and his ingenuity had been inherited. Sielvia was in no way fooled by his promise; she knew she was as good as gutted and hanging in the smokehouse now. Her body could be planted somewhere to be blamed on the Regent, too. But she might just be able to outrun two New Guards with their pants around their ankles.

So she licked her lips and thrust her chest toward Stainface's partner, whom she had dubbed Two-Teeth. "Aperiole says she can take two at once," she said, rolling up her eyes. "Is that good?"

"Why, let's find out," said Two-Teeth, his hands dropping to his own belt.

"Over here," said Stainface, propping himself against a rack of spears. "We'll . . . aieee!"

Sielvia didn't know why he started to fall, but since he'd let go, she lunged at Two-Teeth, took hold of the obvious target, and threw herself on the floor. Four bodies kicked and thrashed on the stone.

The King rose first, a hand on Sielvia's wrist. "I got the paper!" he said. "Come on!"

He was pulling so hard, she had no choice, but took the time to snatch up a new torch from a bin on the way. They darted through the little room to the ledge, found the stairs, and started down.

The two doors clicked shut, but a sound of boots told them somebody was on the wrong side of the secret entrances. Sielvia didn't look back to see who; the stairs were hard enough to follow.

"Run!" the King shouted, as they tumbled off at the bottom, and then set an example for them to follow. Argeleb hesitated at the door, but Merklin pushed him forward, letting the decorated door snap shut behind them.

They paused in the little room to catch their breath, but ran out into the corridor when they heard the scream. Someone pounded on the door.

"Leave him there," Merklin suggested.

"We . . . we can't," said Sielvia, both hands against her chest to hold her lungs in. "L-look!"

They looked. They were four. "Mardith!" exclaimed the King.

"Timpre," panted Sielvia.

"Okay," said Merklin. "Get ready." He and Argeleb drew their weapons and moved to the door.

"I-I'm ready," the King told them, still gasping for his breath. He had one knife now.

Merklin opened the door, a blade ready. Timpre all but fell on it. Mardith flew out after him.

"All gone," the bird announced. "This man here absolutely knock old Ugly down, roll between his legs."

"But where is he now?" Argeleb demanded.

"Down," chuckled the bird.

They saw the holes in the floor only after they had lit the new torch. "I want out!" wailed Timpre.

"You didn't do so bad," said Argeleb, punching him in the arm.

"And you saved my life," Sielvia told Conan.

"There must be other ways out," the King replied, moving out to the hall.

Across the hall, up twenty paces, they found a room painted in swirls and triangles. A triangle opened to Merklin's probing, to reveal a tight circular staircase. Argeleb propped this open with his knife, and they all moved up together. Sielvia and the King explained what they'd seen.

"Why kill Valspar?" Argeleb demanded. "He's one of their best men."

"Don't you get it?" said Merklin. "Nobody's going to think Umian would kill one of his own guys. They can blame it on anybody they don't like."

"Or that doesn't like them," said the King.

"That makes reasonable," said Mardith. "You solve it!"

"Only if we get out." The staircase was similar to the hall: at every tenth step, a narrow door opened off the staircase. Or would open, had a key been available. The group went on, each member trying each doorknob they passed, without success, until they reached the ceiling.

Here the King found a metal circle that gave to his push. They climbed up into a bare, square room. A large door on their left was locked. Dark openings showed near the ceiling, too high for them to reach. They were spinning the dagger to find out who would stand at the bottom while the others climbed on his shoulders when Argeleb glanced up and gasped.

Something composed of bright stripes was oozing along the ceiling. What might have been a head turned back, and the creature moved faster, heading for one of the dark holes.

As they watched, a crested lump came out of another hole, evidently in pursuit. Timpre shrieked and covered his eyes.

"Oh, good job," said Merklin, as the object changed direction and started down the wall.

Argeleb pulled back to throw a dagger. "No, wait," whispered the King. "It might bounce back and hit us. Everyone be quiet."

Sielvia recognized it as it came closer; she'd seen these heart-shaped slugs in the kitchens. They were pure poison, and not fussy what they ate. This one was bigger than any she'd seen before, and what she'd thought was a crest was really the skeletal remains of a hand.

And jangling at the wrist was a ring of keys.

They looked at each other as the slug came to the floor. Then Merklin put out a hand. He jerked it back as the slug hissed.

"I'll take it," said Conan. "I am the King, and those keys are mine."

The slug came to a stop before the King. Conan wrinkled his nose, but reached forward.

"I want to go home!" sobbed Timpre.

"Me, too," said the King. Without a hiss, the slug turned and moved back up the wall. Sielvia had sometimes scoffed at Haeve's tales of the powers of the King of Rossacotta, knowing this particular King a bit too well. Her doubts were wiped away. The King looked astonished, himself, but turned his attention to the keys.

They were old and a trifle rusty. The fifth one he tried fit the lock but wouldn't turn. The seventh one did turn. They stepped out into a thick, damp smell.

"Parsnips," said Merklin, pulling the door shut behind them. "All this way to wind up knee-deep in parsnips."

"I hope it's not one of the underground stores," said Argeleb, stepping daintily among the aging roots.

"No," said Sielvia. "It's the quick-store they fill from the basement stores. We can go right through the kitchens."

Timpre moaned. The kitchens were as fearful, if not so mysterious, as the dungeons. Stepping from the parsnips, they looked out across huge tables to massive fireplaces where half-naked men turned long spits. Oval carts with dozens of trays and platters stood shimmering in the glare of the flames. The heat flashed into their bodies as their noses filled with the smell of raw meat mixed with the smells of baking meat, half-baked meat, and rotting meat. The noise was hideous after the silence below. All the senses were being attacked at once, in dozens of ways.

Lady Maitena strode through the half-light, calling out orders and reinforcing them where necessary with a thump on a scorched back. "More roots!" she bellowed at a greasy woman whose hands were raw from cutting turnips. "If . . . when His Majesty returns, there'll be all kinds of celebrations to supply!"

The woman peered through the smoke. "Let the brats do it!"

"You!" shouted Maitena. "Get to work!"

"We don't have to!" Timpre shouted back. "We're . . ."

There was half a chance Maitena might have recognized them, even in the murk of the kitchen, but not when she was furious. Sielvia snatched up a pan of melting sugar and threw it at everyone nearby.

The kitchen help, glad of anything outside their usual back-breaking assignments, immediately took off after the rebellious scullions. Sielvia had been through this territory before, though, and knew where the real scullions hid. She moved up, around a corner, and into a little warming room, where dishes waited until it was time to go to the Dining Room. With any luck, they could wait here, too.

Someone moaned. They turned to see a pair of men standing over a bound woman, her ears tucked between her knees and all her hairy places showing. Sielvia leaned in and recognized Adimo's sister.

"What's this?" roared Gilphros, looking back. "The rest of the clan? No end of toys around here!" He caught hold of the nearest intruder and put his grin down to the new captive.

The face was known to him. Seeing he had put his hands on the King of Rossacotta, Gilphros rolled up his eyes and quietly collapsed.

This was unknown in Gilphros. "What did you do to him, witch-brat?" roared the other man, raising a hand axe.

Mardith rolled up this man's eyes by other means. Sielvia grabbed the axe from unfolding fingers and led them from the warming room before his screams could attract attention.

Maitena's little army was scant feet away. Cross traffic made progress impossible. A blonde retainer of Lady Iranen was fleeing for the kitchens, where her mistress was not allowed, and rolled into a bundle with Sielvia and the King. The servant recovered first. She snatched up the axe and turned to face Iranen, one blonde eyebrow rising.

Iranen gleefully braced for the attack, but Maitena pushed the servant aside. Before she reached the children, a man who had been following Iranen pushed forward as well.

"Come, come, Cousin," he told Maitena. "You can't be so stupid. We come of the same stock, after all."

"Don't call me Cousin, you filthy . . ." But her filthy cousin Ferrapec was kneeling now, saying to one of the children, "Command your servant, Your Majesty!"

Before Sielvia could catch her breath, pursuit had become parade. Shouting turned to singing, cursing to cheering, and the whole kitchen staff declared itself a royal retinue. His Majesty was not, it appeared, doomed at all, and it was the Housekeeping branch of government (the only truly trustworthy one) that had found him. General Ferrapec took the lead, declaring to everyone that it was he who had rescued His Majesty, warding off possible damage from Lady Maitena or

Lady Iranen, who were telling their own versions of the story farther back in the procession.

Jubilation could not last forever. A figure of true authority broke into the celebration as it neared the Great Hall. "Your Majesty's clothes?" shrieked this official. "Well! Your Majesty must certainly be changed for the Great Banquet. As I recommend the rest of you do for yourselves; a more ragtag assembly around His Majesty I have not seen since this morning!"

The kitchen staff might have taken exception to this, but Maitena reminded everyone that Great Banquets did not simply materialize. Some scullions blended with the crowd of courtiers assembling to see His Majesty safe and whole, but very few escaped Maitena's eagle eyes.

Nurse allowed the King enough time to show himself to the new arrivals, and then whisked him and Merklin away. Sielvia could see that Argeleb had similarly been caught up, to be alternately shaken and hugged by his parents.

She spun around at the sound of Timpre's cry. There was no hugging to be involved there. Morafor dealt his son a swift kick in the nearest thigh.

She pushed between them before the next kick could be aimed. "He helped save His Majesty's life today!" she shouted.

The sculptor shoved her aside. "If you were my daughter, I'd thump you 'til you couldn't stand. And you can tell your old man that!" He snatched up his son and dragged him back to his own quarters, yelling, "And you've got all that china to paint!"

The door's slam was followed by sounds indicating there would be a lot less to paint in a moment.

"Where have you been?"

Sielvia turned to find her mother and Lotyn bearing down on her. A reply of, "I'd rather not talk about it just yet" drew the desired frenzy of demands for details. There was no doubt they were impressed, and even her father was interested in her story when they were gathered together in the minstrel's chambers.

It was all too exhilarating. But Sielvia's mouth formed a large "O" when Laisida inquired, "And where is Polijn, then?"

CHAPTER SEVEN
Polijn

I

THE Bodyguard was too far away for Polijn to be sure what the woman was doing. But the fact that an awfully lot of Decency Committee uniforms were being peeled off, and large amounts of beer being handed out, argued that she had done something. "Mokono the Magnificent" might be able to proceed to the Palace Royal at a more relaxed pace, preferably in a chair, since the sky was still threatening if the crowd was not.

Polijn jerked her head to one side. The mob had struck up a song, and the melody sounded not unlike that of a piece she'd put together for Arberth. How had that gotten down here? Laisida said songs lived forever and went everywhere; "Writing new ones," he said, "is simply adding coal to a long-burning fire." If she'd taken that seriously, she never would have written this, a humorous lament composed of bits and pieces from other songs and some filler. The singer recalled the great women of history, so upstanding and pure that they could only be tricked into bed, unlike the ones who dropped so readily today. She'd ended it with the tag line, "I'm glad they do, my friend, because/I'm not the man my father was." Arberth had had to ruin it, of course, with three completely incongruous verses about Nimnestl.

She wiped damp strings of hair from her forehead, and found metal in her hand. The Vielfrass had thrown her that coin, and she'd never had a chance to put it anywhere else. Examining it now in the light that reached her from the bonfire, she realized that there'd been no real need to run at all. This was the little amulet he'd let her carry once before, with some sort of emblem on it that apparently meant "Property of the Vielfrass." Nobody sober and sane would have molested her in the least had she shown this around. At least, it had worked that time, getting her through some of the worst of the Swamp.

Her eyes went back to the bonfire, where the Bodyguard was trying to push a path through the celebrating crowd. Then she looked to the crumbling buildings, and wondered if this was her last trip through the Swamp. Glor had been her last real tie here. She didn't really belong to the Swamp now. Did she belong to the Palace Royal? The food was colder when it got to you there, but at least you didn't have to wonder if there'd be any. And she had powerful protectors there. Even, one could say, friends.

Polijn didn't make a sound when the hand clutched her elbow. Mokono and Ronar between them had taught her to keep quiet; Ronar simply by thumping her whenever she made a sound, and Mokono by demanding, "Have I pierced your ears, that you shriek so? Scream only when the house is burning down."

She looked down into the haggard face of Diabies. He always had preferred a crouch for his nightly rounds, and he seemed to have shrunk since she'd seen him last. "Mistress Polijn," he whispered. "They killed her."

"Ah!" said Polijn. "Lintik blast them all." She stepped back a bit so the light from the fire fell on him. His bundle didn't look like a weapon, but she couldn't be sure.

"Veldres did her," he went on, following her around. "He chased her out, he did, and she went to Etzner. Etzner killed her, but it was all Veldres, who promised her a place in his mother's service if we'd do a little job for him." He held up his little bundle in shaking hands. "I have this to do him back."

"What about Etzner?" she whispered, afraid the big man might be around, waiting to kill Diabies as he had apparently done the man's wife, Mityrets.

"The Bodyguard's done him." Diabies licked his lips. "Mistress Polijn, she took you in that time you was sick. Can you take this to the ratbait that did her?"

Polijn started to open her mouth, but he went on, "They'll stop me, they will, if they see me carrying something down that way so late. But you've got the Vielfrass's good sign. They won't bother you."

Polijn had not, in fact, ever tried this amulet in the rich streets of middletown. The district was as dangerous as the Swamp or the Palace Royal, and she didn't know its ways. But she would have to pass that way with the Bodyguard.

"I guess I can throw it over the wall, at least," she said, and stepped back three feet at the expression on the beggar's face.

"That's what he said!" whispered Diabies. "He said that! I should find a lady to throw it over the wall. I'd put it under his lintik chair, myself, but he said 'over the wall,' so it must be a sign." He grabbed her hand and guided it across the lump of cloth to a smaller lump on top. "Break this, he tells me, and throw it. And then run, because it's got every kind of fury in it."

He tried to make her take the bundle, but Polijn put her hands behind her back. "Who said that?" she demanded. "Who gave this to you?"

"Sold it to me, he did," whispered Diabies. "Sold it to me and told me to find a lady to throw it over the wall. But not a lady from the Palace Royal."

"No?" Polijn continued to back away as Diabies continued to push the bundle at her stomach.

"You won't let any of them from the Palace see it?" the beggar pleaded. "He said they'd all be wanting one and it'd make his life so miserable he'd come and see I knew about it."

"Who?" Polijn demanded.

"Him! The Vielfrass!"

Polijn was even more reluctant to take the package now. "No one from the Palace Royal?"

"He said it three times, he did," Diabies assured her, his head bouncing up and down until sweat sprayed off it. "And as I goes off, he says, 'Remember: a lady from the Palace is unlucky; anybody from the Yellow Dog is lucky.' But I'm not likely to see anybody from there now, am I?"

"The Yellow Dog?"

Diabies's head continued to bounce. "Veldres always went to the Yellow Dog. They say he was there this morning, when he was supposed to be with His Majesty." The beggar put both knees on the ground when he said "His Majesty."

Polijn glanced back at the bonfire, where the Bodyguard was trying to disengage three affectionate members of the crowd without breaking any of their bones. Well, with this talisman, she wouldn't need the Bodyguard's escort to the Palace—maybe. And maybe, once things were explained, the big woman wouldn't be too irritated about Polijn's disobedience. The Bodyguard, after all, would know about the machinations of unstable sorcerers.

"Which way to Veldres's place?" she said, putting a hand on the bundle.

"The short way's back past Karland's shop," said Diabies, folding the lump of cloth into her arms. "And then around the corner to the Street of Last Sighs."

Polijn brushed the hair out of her eyes and hoped that name was no omen.

II

THIS looked like the right place: Diabies had said a big house with four ears of corn blazoned above the double doors. Hard to make out in the murk just what those symbols over the door were, though, and Polijn couldn't get any closer until that man moved in or moved on.

He was in no hurry, twirling a flower between the fingers and thumb of his right hand, and occasionally knocking with the left. The evening doorwarden might have a ways to come, though. These house complexes in middletown enclosed not only living quarters but gardens, stables, and occasionally even warehouses within their walls. The doorwarden might be escorting a guest anywhere within one of the inner buildings.

Polijn turned to check over her shoulder. There had been rustling in the shadows behind her ever since she'd parted with Diabies. Rats, she'd assumed. But why would rats be so persistent, and why did they have to follow her so particularly?

A chink of light appeared between the doors. "Master?" inquired the doorwarden.

"I wish to speak to your master, yes." Polijn peered at the man, knowing she should recognize the voice. "If there is any question of his being available, I may tell you I have a yellow dog to sell."

Yellow dog? Polijn eased closer. "Yes, Master," said the

doorwarden, opening a bit farther. "I . . ."

"Get out!" snapped the guest, jumping back.

"What was it, Master?" asked the doorwarden, looking at the ground. "A rat?"

"Some kind of cat. There!" Karabari Banglebags's face was exposed to light from inside. Both he and the doorwarden kicked at a small shadow that darted past.

"The lintik thing's playing with us!" snarled the Exorcist's apprentice. The doorwarden stepped out into the street, club in hand, as the little shadow bounded by again.

So intent were they on catching this figure that the one darting in from across the street escaped their notice entirely. Polijn saw her mistake at once, of course. She had expected a courtyard, a place to leave this package, and a place to hide herself. She stood instead in a little entryway with a dainty mosaic floor and, beyond it, a short corridor.

She should have done this the way the Vielfrass said, but she still wanted to know about the yellow dog Karabari had mentioned. And standing here would be more stupid than coming in. She stepped through the little hall to a broader one. This was decorated with a number of ornamental screens, cheaper than tapestry and so much more modern. Polijn slid behind one of these and made herself as small as she could.

"No matter, Master; it won't be in. Let me take you to Master Veldres." The doorwarden and the Exorcist's apprentice moved down the hall. They were apparently paying no particular notice to the screens as they passed.

So this was the right house. Fine: all she had to do now was figure out a clever exit to match her entrance. If Veldres actually knew anything about the Yellow Dog (which seemed likely now, after what Karabari had said) it was best to tell Laisida and let him take care of any questioning. He had the King's protection; she was just one more small inmate of the Palace, and would never be missed if things went wrong.

The easiest way out, she felt, would not be by this front door. Far better to sneak out to the stables, or the coachhouse, and find a way out come morning, when there would surely be business back there. She peered out around the screen, and darted to the next one. A secure hiding place for the night, as close to the stables as possible, was the ticket.

Polijn moved from screen to screen. If only she weren't dressed up in these parade clothes, she could hide out in the kitchens, pretending to be a scullion. But perhaps that wouldn't be safe in any case, if the tales of Veldres and his servants were true. Those servants who did escape Veldres's service tended to make him sound as bad as Lady Iranen and as clever as Lord Kaftus, just to show how daring they were to escape.

Slipping around a bend, she found another corridor, this one lined with plain wooden doors no more than four feet high. Storerooms would be just the thing, provided nothing too hazardous was stored. Polijn eased the first door open.

"Polijn! Is it the auction again?"

Polijn ducked inside, lest the woman call after her. The room was bigger than she'd expected, its walls hung with weapons, a fireplace on the far wall. In the center of the room, sitting on a stool next to a low-burning brazier, sat Hinemoa. She was peeling an egg, tears running down her face.

To be sure, Veldres had bought her in last fall's auction. She'd fetched a good price, too, with her complexion. "He kept you?" asked Polijn, her voice low. "Too bad."

"Well," Hinemoa said, jerking one shoulder up and down, "he brought me and Mother up to middletown. So when the lightning burns him, it should be gently."

Steam was rising from a pot over the brazier. Polijn moved over to look, but had an idea already what she'd see. Veldres had learned that trick from Iranen, how to fracture the shells of the eggs so they could be peeled only very slowly, and then make a slavey do it while the eggs were still blistering-ly hot.

"Warm day for that kind of work," said Polijn, waving some of the steam away.

Hinemoa snuffled. "Mother told me always to do anything he told me."

Polijn nodded; it was reasonable advice. "How is she?"

"I-I haven't seen her in a month." Hinemoa swallowed and went on, checking her egg for fragments of shell. "Did he buy you? What did Ronar get for you?"

Polijn shook her head. "I just came to deliver this package." She held up the bundle. It probably wasn't safe to tell Hinemoa much, so she explained, "Ronar said to give it to Veldres himself, but they won't take me to him, and they won't let me go back to Ronar, either."

"Oh, frogbreasts!" Hinemoa tossed the clean egg into a bowl by her feet and blew on her reddened fingers. "Unless you're somebody-somebody, Polijn, you should just wait at the door. Otherwise they won't ever let you out." She put a hand up to reach into the steaming water again, but pulled away as the steam touched her fingertips. "But if you didn't sell at the auction, maybe Chordasp will come looking for you."

There was no hope of getting any information from Hinemoa, then; she wouldn't know about anything that had happened in the Swamp since her auction. "You used to be good at getting out," Polijn told her. "Didn't you find a way yet?"

The blistered hands formed fists. "There isn't one." Hinemoa bit her upper lip. "M-m-m-mamma tried to find one but they caught her and . . ."

"This way," called a voice from the corridor.

"They'll come in!" said Hinemoa, much too loudly.

Polijn clapped a hand over her mouth and whispered, "Mityrets got out; they talked about it at home. Tell me where I can hide until I find out how she did it, and I'll come back and tell you."

One red hand shook toward the fireplace. "There's a ledge," said Hinemoa, as Polijn darted over to it. "Don't blame me when they find you."

The inside of the chimney was large, and strangely clean. Polijn figured it out when she climbed up on the ledge formed of crisscrossed iron bars. Directly in front of her were little chinks of light. Iron plates covered holes through which someone's arms, legs, and neck could be stretched. She slid one of the armholes to the side.

"We'll be safe from the ears of that wine pitcher in here," Veldres told Karabari, escorting his guest inside. "And the servants have orders not to enter these rooms unless they care to stay."

He strode across to Hinemoa, took one of her ears in each hand, and twisted her head back to where he wanted it. "Correct?"

"As you say, Master," Hinemoa replied.

His face came down to hers. She wasn't reluctant to the

point of pulling away, because she had her orders, but her
wish to be elsewhere was writ in every line of her face. The
heels of her hands pressed into the back of the stool.

"And she won't tell anyone, I suppose?" said Karabari,
closing the little door behind himself.

"Oh, Hinemoa's a good little hamhock. Never makes a
sound." Veldres took a spoon, fished up an egg, and brought
it over to Hinemoa. Using his free hand to tip her head back,
he dropped the egg down the front of her shift.

The chin came down as soon as he let go. Her hands stayed
where they were. She closed her eyes.

"You train them so very well," Karabari noted, leaning
against the wall next to the door.

"Yes, I do." They were watching Hinemoa's face. Polijn
could see by the way she arched her feet and wiggled her toes
that she was not entirely numb.

"But am I reassured?" the Exorcist's apprentice went on.
"She may talk to someone less well trained."

Veldres's face was forgiving. "No one comes into these
rooms without my orders. And none, having entered, leave
in any condition to talk."

Hinemoa's eyes opened wide. Her lower lip went in. "Did
no one tell you, my chicken?" Veldres folded his hands and
looked grieved. "Yes, it's a thistledown seat for you. But you
have a few days. Perhaps I'll bring in a churn and let you churn
sand for the rest of the month. Won't that be exhilarating?"

"M-master, even you wouldn't . . ."

"Even you?" Veldres caught up a pair of tongs from a hook
on the wall and used these to lift a coal from the brazier.
"Never speak ill of your hairdresser, lambchop, for curling
irons may slip."

"If things are going to get messy, I'll leave," said Karabari,
reaching down for the doorknob. "You'll likely stain my
robes."

Veldres tossed the coal back in with the others. "Oh, yes,"
he snapped. "I know how you like to stain them yourself."

Karabari straightened. "I'd take that as an insult, if I could.
But, of course, insults only apply between equals."

Hinemoa choked. "Something funny?" Veldres demanded.
"You see, magician? I can't let up. Women lack a rational

brain; they are creatures of nature. Like other animals, they become too free and easy with men through long acquaintance, forgetting their lessons." As he spoke, he was doing something with the tongs that made Hinemoa squirm, but he was blocking Polijn's view of exactly what it was.

Karabari watched without expression. "You'll be valuable to the new government. Tortures that leave no exterior marks are always valuable."

Veldres let go, and set the tongs on Hinemoa's lap. Polijn would have tipped up the hot water on him at this point, and made a run for it, but Hinemoa did nothing as her master strode over to his guest and breathed, "When?"

The Exorcist's apprentice dusted off a few of the gems on his lapel. "Now, when I told you about the King, you were complaining it would be too soon."

The merchant marched back to Hinemoa. "It can't come too soon," he grumbled. "But it won't come at all if you rush it."

He turned to face Karabari, shaking the tongs at him. "Why didn't you consult me, at least, about that wine business? I'd've told you what that would lead to. We're not ready."

"Oh, now you're talking like Ferrapec," the taller man replied. "And he's so boring he shall have to be dropped from the government at the first opportunity."

"You still need a voice in middletown," Veldres replied, clutching the tongs with two fists. "And you're not up to striking strength yet."

"I think I'm the best judge of that." Karabari took an egg from the bowl at Hinemoa's feet, and, after looking it over, took a bite. "And it was someone whose name sounds like Veldres who botched the business with Mityrets and her miserable husband."

"Well, how was I to know they'd let the piece of hamfat go free?" demanded Veldres, rapping the tongs down on Hinemoa's head.

"In any case, it has alerted the government," Karabari told him. "We must act before they can."

The tongs came down and caught at Hinemoa's neckline. "Think you're ready to face that aligjat, then?" Veldres demanded. "Pale as a parsnip you were at the Yellow Dog, after sucking up the staff. When that bacon rind came in out of the alley, I had to do her before she could yell. And we never did find your lintik coins."

Polijn's gasp could not be heard for the tearing of cloth as the tongs ripped down Hinemoa's shift. "Perhaps if you hadn't been in such a hurry to stick your blade into someone, we would have found them," Karabari pointed out. "Both in power and in value, they'd have smoothed out the road. In any case, you will be gratified to learn that the coins have found their way back to the Palace without a clue as to how they left in the first place. And since the New Guard was good enough to add the Treasury guards who let me take them to the list of mysterious murder victims, no one remains outside our circle to tell how I had Karlikartis change them for honest gold, not knowing I meant to have them back from her."

"There's one left outside the circle who knows." Veldres tore away more of the shift in little jerks that nearly pulled Hinemoa off the chair.

"I'd have thanked you more if you'd knifed him and let the woman live." Karabari stepped to one side for a better view of Hinemoa. "The one-eyed fool had a cat with him; you know what that does to my spells."

Veldres's head came up. "Knife him? The man's a minstrel!"

"Minstrel or not, he's the kind of scum who'd smuggle a cat into a house like the Yellow Dog, to release it on stage." Karabari sniffed. "I want no such creature in my government."

"Our government," said Veldres, "will need minstrels."

"Then you'd best see he doesn't drink himself to death." Karabari motioned toward the door. "And see that he knows nothing about the King. That's why I came: to tell you Umian's shutting down everything until the King's business is resolved. I don't want any minstrel interfering with Umian's plans; we have enough trouble with shuptit Ferrapec."

"Let me but take care of a bit of business here and I'll come out with you." Veldres grinned at Hinemoa. "Someone has been neglecting her eggs."

Hinemoa started to weep out apologies. Veldres hauled her

off the stool and backward toward the fireplace. Polijn pulled back, just in case he glanced up.

"Now," said Veldres, rising from the metal cuffs set in the hearth, "once those eggs are good and hot, I'll come back and put them where you can't help but pay attention."

Hinemoa's nose was bleeding. Polijn watched the blood run until the door had thumped shut. Then she eased herself down from the metal shelf, being careful not to step on her colleague.

"Oh," Hinemoa moaned. "Where are you going?"

"Out." Polijn eased over to the door to listen.

"You can't get out." Hinemoa tried to rise, but was fastened flat on her back, her arms outstretched, her heels under her buttocks. "You have to help me."

Polijn stepped back over the shreds of the shift. "If I can't get out, I'd better not help you. Mityrets got out."

"You can't." Hinemoa did raise her head. "Polijn, it may be my turn tonight, but you'll be next."

"In that case, take your time." In the old days, Hinemoa had been competition, working just two streets over, on corners that were Mokono's once. Mokono had liked her, though, while she was alive.

Hinemoa thumped her head back on the hearth, practically the only way she could register frustration. "Get Mamma. Maybe Mityrets told her . . ."

"You know very well your Veldres has killed her." He'd killed Gloraida, at least, so why should anybody's mother be safe?

The head of the captive thumped harder and harder against the stone hearth. "Polijn, you have to!"

Polijn didn't think she did. But she nonetheless got down on all fours and tried to turn the screws Veldres had twisted into the floor. Once they came loose, she boosted Hinemoa up to the ledge in the chimney.

"I'm going to come back for this if I can," she said, with complete untruth. "If they come for you, break this and then try to run. It's wizard's work; the Vielfrass's." Hinemoa slid as far to the end of the shelf as she could. "Now, how can I get into the courtyard from here?"

Polijn moved from screen to screen and corridor to corridor. Veldres did not crowd his house with as many people as cluttered the Palace Royal, and she found her way into the darkened gardens without incident. Now what she needed was a hiding place. With any luck at all, they would find Hinemoa, get the Vielfrass's little trap set off in their faces, and raise such a ruckus that she could get out, vengeance completed and none the worse for wear.

Any of these leafy bushes would do; she hadn't the strength to do much hunting. The afternoon had been long and hard, with little food and much panic. Anything that offered cover . . .

"Well, the hole for taking it in's so much b-b-bigger!"

Polijn turned to see the door to the gardens open. Turning, she stepped in something that slid. Knowing what it likely was, she spun and tried to roll back away from it. One leg went up in the air and did not come down.

"Well, now," said the one-eyed minstrel, using his other hand to take one of her shoulders, "Veldres never said he had a p-pretty little thing like you."

III

"AW, now, don't do that," said Carasta, as Polijn twisted in his grasp. "If you come to this playground you're bound to get knocked around a bit, but if you're nice, you might not get hurt so . . . ow!"

She had pulled her foot free, and kicked it up at him. He dropped her, but lashed out with his own foot.

"Is there some problem?" inquired Veldres, coming to the door.

"A little poison ivy among your honey creepers," the minstrel replied, grabbing a big handful of Polijn's hair.

"Who is this and how did it get in?" the master of the house demanded, coming to help.

Polijn tore free of the minstrel and threw herself on her knees in front of Veldres. "Please let me stay, Master!" she wailed. "I hid during the day, when they were chasing me. They said I was Polijn from the Palace, but my name's Mokono! Keep me safe!"

Carasta sniggered. Veldres rubbed his chin. "I heard there was some noise about someone in the Swamp," he said. "What do you think they . . . No, how would you know?"

"Mistook you for Polijn?" demanded Carasta, exhibiting his teeth and breath in a close-up smile that made no pretense of friendship. "The minstrel's wiper?"

Polijn nodded. "You do have the look of her," said Veldres.

Carasta spat, just missing her face because he wasn't sober enough to aim. "I can tell the difference with just one eye." He turned and started back for the house. "If I were you, I'd throw her back. She's too small."

"Not much meat, is there?" Veldres agreed. "Well, we'll find you some other snack."

"Oh, must I go?" Polijn cried, holding clasped hands up to him. "Is it safe?"

"There's no one out there now. Come." Veldres took her wrists and an ankle. "Over the wall for you." He was bigger than Carasta, and her weight was not so much of an awkward burden. His chin came up, and his face took on that solemn expression the King's did whenever Conan wanted to make an especially important pronouncement.

"You will live to tell your grandchildren you met Rossa-cotta's next Regent and First Minstrel," he said. "Here you go."

The grass was worn away where he stopped; evidently, he'd done this before. Well, it wasn't the way she'd wanted to leave, thought Polijn, but it was a way out.

"Onsah!" he said, swinging her back. "Dosah!" he said, as she went forward and came back again. Polijn braced herself for flight.

But he didn't make it to the third swing. He let go of her wrists and shook the ankle he held. "Well, it's a naughty little meat pie."

Polijn tried to think why she was a naughty little meat pie. Those lintik underdrawers! "Those aren't mine," she sniffled. "When they first caught me they made me put them on and . . ."

"No, no, Mokono," said Veldres. "Some of us can read." He put a finger down to the embroidered letter. "M does not stand for 'Not Mine.' Perhaps you're right; you'd best stay the night."

She flailed for a grip on something, to pull away, but he started back toward his house. Beyond the outer wall of his compound, she could just see the tops of the Palace Royal's four corner towers. That made it worse.

Veldres was a good host, at least. She was soon set up in

a private room. "We'll just see what other surprises you may have under your skirts, my dumpling," he said, locking a cuff to her right wrist.

"I have this," she said, using her left hand to dig out the Vielfrass's amulet.

It did make him pause. "You may keep it," he said. He stood back for a second, and then locked the other end of the chain to an iron circlet in the floor. "I think the Vielfrass will not be passing through here, to see what becomes of you. I have never counted him among my guests."

"There." He caught up both ankles. "Now we can examine this problem from all angles."

"Mercy!" she exclaimed, as her head hit the floor. It was more an expletive than a request.

"Mercy is indeed a sign of power," Veldres noted. "But so is withholding it." Dropping her feet, he took hold of her hair and dragged her upright. The nail of one finger slid down her cheek. She winced.

"It's so nice to discuss one's hobbies with someone who really cares," he cooed. Using her hair as a handle, he brought her over to a shelf along the wall. The chain at her wrist pulled back just as he got there. Polijn declined to complain. The time for thinking like Hinemoa and calling the result Mokono was over. The imposture was a discredit to her sister and, anyhow, Mokono had always told her never to show enthusiasm or revulsion. "It gives them a handle."

Veldres had picked up a long, long pair of tongs. "This is an invention of my own. I can pinch you in places you don't even know you have." But he used them to open a drawer under the shelf instead. "And have you ever worn a straw girdle? My sugarcookies swear by them, especially on the third or fourth day."

He wanted sobbing, gasping, as a sign of how clever he was. As he pointed out implement after implement, he really reminded her of the King, showing off his treasures in the closet, looking to her after each item for comment. Even the little drawers were like the King's, places he hid things from Nurse.

For the King, Polijn made all the proper sounds of interest. She didn't feel like accommodating Veldres. Her mistake, she realized; Veldres noticed.

Both hands caught in her neckline and hauled it down, pinning her arms against her sides. "You can at least act like you're having a good time," he said, catching an inch of skin and squeezing it hard between his nails. Polijn had been given every opportunity to get used to this sort of thing; it hadn't done much good.

"That's better," he said, as she ground her teeth. "But not quite good enough. Maybe you've been outside so long you're numb from the cool summer air. A few hot coals . . ."

The door of the little room opened. Veldres turned to glare at the intruder, but let go of Polijn and stepped back a little behind her.

"Veldres," said a woman Polijn had never seen before, "that eyepatched person is becoming . . ." Cold eyes fell on Polijn. "Another one?"

The merchant's head pulled back between his shoulders, and his right shoe traced a pattern on the stones. "It's a trespasser, Mother."

"Then you should have thrown it over the wall instead of dragging it in here," the woman told him. "Will you look at me when I'm talking to you, sir? What your father would have thought of some of the trash you bring in, I hesitate to think. This 'minstrel,' as you call him, was found in the wine cellar just the now, and when I ordered him ejected, he said I dared not, so close was your friendship. Tell me to my face I dare not, sir!"

"Maybe you misunderstood," murmured Veldres, wiping off the toe of one boot with the toe of the other.

"I believe I understand the words 'dare not' well enough," declared his mother. "I did not expect to hear them addressed to me in my own house. Are you going to have this fornicator with sheep thrown from the house or not?"

"I'd better talk to him, Mother," said Veldres, starting for the door.

"I'll just come help you do so," she said, moving after him. They stooped under the door and were gone.

Polijn was taking a deep breath when the door opened again. "You!" snapped Veldres. "Kneel right there until I return!" Polijn dropped to her knees at once. Not that it would mollify him; there was slow dismemberment in his eyes.

After the door had slammed, she rose and walked around the room, testing the limits of her chain. Then she knelt to try the bolts that held the iron loop to the floor. No good: these hadn't been designed to be taken up and then refastened, the way Hinemoa's bonds were.

No way to run, nowhere to hide: she understood Hinemoa's feelings a bit better now that her two best strategies had been taken from her. Now what? Explain to Veldres that she was Polijn, and suggest that there would be a reward if she was returned to the Palace Royal? Only if she could convince him she wouldn't tell anyone about his mother. And the merchant looked hard to convince.

Her eyes went to the chains and forceps and funnels Veldres had shown her. There might be something there she could use as a lever. She eased on over, and heard the door again just as she reached the nearest shelf.

Veldres had not, however, returned. A kitten had wandered through the door and sat considering her. Polijn frowned.

"You're the one who was at the door, aren't you?" she whispered. "Are you Lady Oozola?"

The cat continued to stare, unblinking. It was interested in her, then; Polijn had noticed that cats blinked at you if they wanted you to know they were looking through you, not at you.

"Did someone send you to help me?" Polijn went on.

The cat rose and walked out the door. Polijn shrugged. So much for that. She went back to the shelf of Veldres's toys.

Glor had taught her the four basic groups of props: openers, closers, holders, and hitters. Polijn had been taught the sub-groups, too, but that brought up visions she'd rather do without just now. There was not a thing here she hadn't seen before in some version or another. Most of them, though, she'd seen at a distance, and never in use. She had no desire to remedy this gap in her knowledge.

Except, perhaps, for this. By stretching her arms to the maximum, Polijn was able to catch hold of it. She'd seen men using crossbows at the Palace Royal. This was a much fancier one than theirs, shaped like a naked woman lying on her back. One put a short arrow in here, and pulled it back . . .

how? And where were the arrows? If she could find them, and pull one back, and if Veldres stood still long enough, and if he came close enough for her to get the key off of his body . . .

That was a lot of ifs. Polijn took hold of the bowstring and pulled.

"Oh!"

Polijn turned to the door. Really, for such secret torture chambers, these were the commonest rooms in the house.

"I heard them say Master had a new one and I was afraid it would be you!" cried Hinemoa, bustling in. "Oh, Polijn . . ."

The woman took hold of Polijn's dress, pulling the torn neckline down again and scraping Polijn's sore shoulders. "What are you doing?" Polijn demanded, drawing back. "Go back and hide!"

"I can't," whimpered Hinemoa. "I . . . oh, Polijn, I broke it! What's going to happen?"

Polijn had to recall what Hinemoa could break in the chimney. She threw down the crossbow. "I don't know. Get out quick!"

"There's no way out!" Hinemoa wailed, dropping to her knees.

Polijn thumped her on top of the head. "Then get as far as you can from the house. The stables, maybe."

"You come, too!"

Polijn rattled her chain. "I can't." She could squeeze her hands out of some cuffs, but Veldres knew his business.

"Oh, Polijn, I'm so . . ."

"Get out!" ordered Polijn, giving her a push toward the door.

The sobbing woman rose and stumbled to the door. Polijn wasted no more time on her, but grabbed up the end of a heavy whip. The stock looked solid; it might serve. She moved back to the center of the room.

"Not kneeling, my bay leaf?"

She whirled to face Veldres. Hinemoa was nowhere to be seen. So someone might escape, anyhow.

"Master!" Maybe if he were told about the Vielfrass's bundle, she'd have her chance. "I . . ."

He raised his right hand, and put his left on a metal bar. "Please don't apologize now, my little caraway seed. You will have ample leisure for regrets in the days to come."

IV

POLIJN retreated; her skirts had drooped so much since he'd loosened the neckline, though, that she could pull back only two steps before she tripped.

The metal rod came up and back. Then it hit the floor.

"Yaybunnies!" screeched something whizzing past Veldres's head. Polijn stared. A pixy rode an alungwe above her, a steaming hardboiled egg raised in one dainty hand. To judge by Veldres's remarks, the pixy had had two when she came in.

"Here 'tis!" called the pixy, no less than Chicken-and-Dumplings. She swooped and shoved the second egg down the front of his waistband while he clawed at the back.

Veldres swatted the air where the pair had been, and danced forward. Polijn stuck out a foot. He snatched at her as he fell, but she brought the wrist with the cuff on it against his head. He hit the floor. His head came up. She hit it again.

"I thought he might be going to do something interesting," called the queen of the pixies, "and it would have been very sad if it was something you didn't want him to do, but interesting, only when I saw he was just going to hit you I thought we ought to do something right away."

"How did you find me?" Polijn asked.

Chicken-and-Dumplings was riding the alungwe up along the array of pain-producers, having lost interest in what Polijn was doing to Veldres when she saw it involved simply removing a ring of keys. "What? Oh, well, your King sent me, because I am the one he trusts out of all those silly subjects of mine, to look and see if I could find you, because he can't get away from that noisy creature with the big nose and, anyway, there's the party. So I came down and as long as I was there I thought I'd drop in and see Karland, who's always got pretty clothes and fun things around. And who should come in but Sugarlump, looking for a winged webmaker to help you."

Polijn tried to remember a pixy named Sugarlump. The second key on the ring unlocked her cuff. As she let it fall, though, she saw a furry form, and grabbed the chain back so the manacle wouldn't land on the kitten.

"Are you Sugarlump?" she demanded. The kitten sniffed, though whether at her or at the name, Polijn couldn't tell.

"Karland's friends look after each other," said the queen of the pixies, considering some armor with spikes on the wrong side. "And she said you helped her out once."

"Did I?" Polijn put a hand out to the kitten. Sugarlump gravely checked out the fingers and moved close enough to be stroked. Polijn couldn't swear this was the same kitten she'd found in the alungwe's web, but she supposed it must be. "But if they're all friends, the alungwe wouldn't have eaten the kitten, would it?"

"What makes you think so?" asked the pixy, patting the head of her mount. "He'd eat me if I got caught in his web. The thing is, they just don't know what to do about anybody that isn't caught."

Polijn shook her head, and rose from the floor. "Are you sure the Vielfrass didn't have something to do with this?" Surely only he could have produced a rescue so confusing.

"Ooh, don't mention his name!" said the queen, shaking both hands at her. "He might appear, and I owe him at cards."

Veldres moaned. "We'd better go," whispered Polijn.

"Why? If you can't think of anything else to do to him, I can." Chicken-and-Dumplings picked up a pair of forceps.

Polijn curled her fingers. "But you'll want to show His Majesty how well you did. And did you say there was a party?"

"Oh yes! Do you know Tyell, the one with the bottom that twinkles? Well, she went into one of the general's rooms, like she does, you know, and got herself up onto that wooden horse he's got, with her clothes off, right, and she didn't know he thought she'd do that and put wheels on the horse, so when she had her feet in the holders, he 'accidentally' bumped it and she goes rolling out into the hall, just bawling. It's a great party. You'll love it."

Polijn had picked out one of the bladed implements on display, and was easing open the little door. "Wait for me!" shouted the pixy. "I'll get some more eggs. I'm glad I heard her tell about them. Come on; I'll show you where they are."

The kitten was somewhat more practical, moving ahead of the group and apparently keeping an eye out for members of the household. What the kitten would have done had it seen any was not revealed to Polijn, because they met no one until they reached the guard at the door.

"You'd better let us out, fellow," said Chicken-and-Dumplings, as his mouth dropped open. "We're strange."

He picked up a club from the table next to him and swung it. Polijn could have told him that would do him no good.

"Well!" said the queen of the pixies. "Life is life to certain people!" She made the alungwe dive straight in at his face. He was a solid guard, and did not flinch; if he knew where they were going, he knew where to aim. But he did not know where the kitten was.

Kitten, guard, club, and table tumbled to the floor. Torches and other supplies on the table clattered around him. "Clumsy, clumsy!" called the pixy. Polijn pulled on the bar across the door.

Seeing this, the doorwarden gave up on his smaller assailants and grabbed at her. It was a bad grab, for one of his knees was on the floor and the other on an unlit torch. He rolled backward onto the upended table.

"Help!" he shouted. "They're getting out!"

A hand caught her shoulder. Polijn thrust her knife back without looking. It stuck in something soft. She left it there.

Then she just about hit the pavement with her face. Hitching her skirts back up, she charged forward. The first nook she saw for hiding was the narrow alley leading back to Veldres's stables. She took it. There was no way she could get all the way home tripping on her hems. She reached down for some pins to secure the neckline.

"What do you think he was going to do to you when he was done hitting you?" demanded Chicken-and-Dumplings, bringing the alungwe to a stop above her. "Or is that as creative as he gets? I think . . ."

The pixy had been paying too much attention to Polijn's disordered clothes to notice the broom coming down. She and the alungwe flew against the inside of the canvas bag, but could not escape.

"Now," said Veldres. The hand without the bag in it was inside her dress again, twisting the whole top of it into a handle at her waist. He pulled her up to him. "I will see your tears run red!"

Polijn had no reply prepared, and no time to deliver it. The sun, long obscured and somewhat set, exploded into view over the alley.

Veldres turned to stare at red rolls of flame and white clouds of heat spreading above his house. Polijn realized it was Hinemoa's doing: she'd left that bundle of fury in the chimney, and it had chosen the easiest route out: up.

They recovered at exactly the same moment, Polijn trying to pull away and Veldres throwing an arm around her neck. This was all either of them had time for before a scream of, "There's Veldres!"

"There's the one we can have!"

There was no escape: the alley was lit as bright as day by the flashes overhead, and two people who knew exactly whom they wanted—Diabies and Hinemoa—stood at the head of the mob. Veldres dropped his bag.

"Oh, bitehimbitehimbitehimbitehim!" shrieked the queen of the pixies, flying free. The alungwe flew out after her, and they both proceeded to sink their teeth into the merchant.

Veldres took off at once. Polijn paused only long enough to pick up the dress that he had let fall around her ankles. The homeowner pushed through the doors of his stables. A hand reached out from the stable doors of his neighbor to take hold of Polijn's elbow.

V

"GOING my way?" inquired the Vielfrass, pulling her into the doorway.

"No!" Polijn replied, pulling away.

"Good," answered the sorcerer, taking hold of her again. "Neither am I."

And Polijn had to stay with him, because the crowd was there, pushing in Veldres's stable doors with no apparent effort, pouring into the compound.

"They seemed a little forlorn after they were talked out of tearing down the government," the Vielfrass said. "So I suggested a little recreational violence as a way to work up an appetite for breakfast."

Polijn supposed he knew what he was talking about. She pulled free of him again, but only to yank her dress up over her shoulders again. Gloraida had not raised any children to run all over the Swamp showing off a pair of underpants.

"There's that pixilated monarch," murmured the sorcerer, his words completely clear to Polijn right through the roar of the crowd. "She has debts to pay. Let this be a lesson to all of us: never play strip games with someone who flies around naked."

Polijn jabbed the pins into place, stabbing her fingers over and over and not really fastening the dress very well. He was so lintik cool, so completely unflustered. He probably didn't sweat at the height of summer. Nothing could disturb his calm; nothing could hurt him. She had seen him tear people into equal portions without really even getting his hair any untidier. He could have walked her home through all the dangers of the Swamp and middletown as easily as he could thumb his nose.

And he hadn't. Polijn knew there was no reason in all the world that a sorcerer should take care of her. But it seemed very hard that anyone with so much power could not at least come out and tell her whether he was her friend or her enemy, instead of acting like both. There was no reason for him to be afraid to tell her.

"Did you know what would happen to me?" she demanded, giving up on her neckline.

He rolled his eyes down toward her. "More or less." He turned back to watch the crowd still shouldering and elbowing its way into Veldres's compound. "I didn't know what you'd do about it. I felt sure it would be entertaining, though."

"Enter . . ." Something her mother had told her about the worst house in the Swamp came back to her, as if in explanation. "Do you drink that stuff they serve at the Gilded Fly?"

"The idea!" The Vielfrass tossed one hand up in the air. "You just wait 'til you're my age. Once you have a few thousand years on you, you'll start to understand things."

"Do you?" Polijn persisted.

"I do not." The Vielfrass sniffed. "I simply brew the stuff. It might dull my senses for my more delicate divinatory procedures."

"Good," said Lady Oozola, stepping into the shallow doorway, a kitten in her arms. "A little dullness might help."

"She doesn't like sharpness," the Vielfrass whispered to Polijn, "ever since she got those splinters in her . . ."

"Why don't you do something about all the things you know?" Polijn demanded. "With all your divination?"

"Chair," the Vielfrass went on. "Why, if I did everything, child, what would be the use of you?"

"And if you don't do anything," said his partner, stroking the kitten, "what's the use of you?"

"Guess where you're going to find splinters next time," the Vielfrass warned. "Oh, infant so ill at smiling, we workers of wonders see more people in a millennium than you can count. We can't do good deeds for them all, no matter how deserving they all feel they are; we'd have no time to stop and smell the bunnies. So we do only what we really need to do or what might be amusing in passing. This way we save our powers for that really big emergency."

"What's that?" Polijn demanded.

The Vielfrass exchanged a glance with his partner and said, "You won't worry about that; it may never happen. Which means I can conserve my power forever while I continue my research into methods of pixy-abuse. It's so relaxing."

Polijn reached inside her clothes and drew out the bauble he'd given her. "Maybe you want to conserve this," she said, holding it out.

The Vielfrass turned to Lady Oozola. "She's pouting. Isn't that cute?"

"It's your masterful touch with women," Oozola told him.

"You'd know. Infant, let me tell you a few things about living with a shape-shifter. On second thought, don't let me. It would curl your ears, and then you might start shifting shapes in envy. No, take it back, take it back. Wear it around your neck."

"There's no chain," Polijn began to say, and then held still. There was a chain on it now.

"There," said the sorcerer, dropping it over her head. "You never know when you may need that."

"But you do," she said, eyes narrow.

He smiled. "Maybe."

"No reason you have to tell me," she muttered.

"Of course not," he replied. Both hands went up in the air. "Everyone wants me to tell them things tonight, but when I start to explain about how I, personally, all alone, faced down the purple dragon of Philomathea, will they listen? Just for that, I won't tell you about the wild party waiting for you at the Palace. Off you go now."

Her eyes came up to his, but didn't stay long. "Off?" she demanded.

"No need to look at me like that," he told her. "You're safe as houses." He glanced at the bits of stable door lying at his feet. "Safer, at this rate. This crowd may get greedy and start on the next building over when they're through with Veldres. And Veldres's neighbor owes me money. I'm going to see that the burning is limited; they need my supervision more than you do."

Polijn's chin came up. It was just an excuse to send her on her way. He could say what he liked about a party waiting for her at the Palace; he knew whether or not she'd get there.

"You really shouldn't have trouble with anyone," said Lady Oozola. "Everyone's here."

"Just so," said the Vielfrass. "And remember: no matter how many days in a row you wear them, they're still just yesterday's socks."

That was as close to a word of wisdom as she was likely to get from the Vielfrass. Polijn set off up the alley.

CHAPTER EIGHT
Nimnestl

I

CLOUDS completely hid the moon and stars; Nimnestl thought she almost heard thunder. It matched her mood perfectly, despite the cries of "His Majesty is well!" that greeted her as she reached the drawbridge.

The courtyard was in hysterical glee, palace women hiking up their skirts in a spirited rendition of "Shallow River" for the amber merchants. Merchants and performers alike were draining jug after jug in the national game of Rossacotta: last one left standing got to loot the others.

One celebrant, near collapse and stinking of sweat and cheap alcohol, bounced quite close to the Bodyguard's horse and laughed up at her. "Bet ya din't even know's Majesty's safe!"

Her expression did not alter. "Yes, so the Vielfrass said." She urged Meriere forward to whispers of "The Vielfrass!"

Inside, they were all but dancing on the walls and, being of a somewhat higher class, had generated a very fog of perspiration with their heavy festival garb. Wine was being passed out of the Great Hall, and wedges of melon the same delicate shade as Maiaciara's back. The rinds were hurled onto the floor, or at whoever was standing in the way of more wine.

Two minstrels had set up a puppet show just inside the Great Hall, but three pixies were interfering with the show, improvising dialogue that had caused a great crowd to assemble. Chymola was at the back, where Nimnestl entered. Her hair was stuffed with wool to make it fuller, her dripping arms were bangled with golden bracelets, and her hands were inside the tunic of Garanem's oldest grandson, who was no more than fourteen. He was blushing a little; Lestis, in a grandiose wig of orange feathers strewn with grey gemstones, had her hands down the back of his pants. He studied the floor, trying to keep up a conversation with both women, thus missing the glances of murder that passed between them as they vied for his compliments.

Nimnestl pushed on. New alliances and enmities were developing every second in the Palace Royal. And she had to keep track of every one, not only for information, but so as to manipulate them. An insult here, a sudden smile there: all so no one could establish a more secure position than the government.

She spotted the Regent standing on the platform around the throne, and moved through the throng. Some of the celebrants made way for her, but there wasn't room for others to move, even if they hadn't been too drunk and gleeful to notice.

"Long live th' King, I say! Brave li'l King, anyhow!"

"There's a King does more'n what Lord Aligjat tells him. B-brought b-back a signed confession, I heard."

"Listen, I say the Regent knew where he was ever' second. He acts like some care-for-nobody, mindin' his own pleasures, but don'tchoo let him fool ya."

"If he had the power to turn his enemies to stone, Morafor Chiselhand would never need to make another statue."

"Doesn't that blowpipe ever breathe?"

"He must. I see th' lace move on his chest."

Someone was singing. The closer Nimnestl got to the minstrels' stand, the less she heard about the King's greatness. "The ship of state sails 'cross the land, plucking the fruit of every house," the singer intoned. "Leaping through all impassable obstacles, quietly majestic as he shouts the victory at every pause in his relentless gallop on the throne!"

She was glad that becoming a government official had dulled none of Arberth's peculiar skills. By the faces of his listeners, the song had been going on forever, as many of

Arberth's songs did, given a chance. Spying her, the ex-jester waved. His audience growled; he was too important to knock off the stage these days.

Overheated, with nerves rubbed raw by the song, courtiers in this corner of the assembly weren't nearly so joyful. A Treasury guard was having his head banged on the floor for having offered his friend a swig from the bottle he carried, without first wiping it. Beyond this tussle, an ashy young woman spat at a colleague, "He's my husband, isn't he? And if I say he can have a mistress, whose else's business is it?"

A hand caught in the loop of her left earring. "And who said I needed your permission?" Gilphros demanded, yanking her off her feet. His father-in-law, General Kaigrol, raised an eyebrow and stepped over her to refill his mug at the wine table.

"The very idea curled my blood! His Majesty's friends leading him astray! They should have someone like Umian to watch over them!"

"Ah, Iranen's the only one with any sense. You can live without friends, but not without servants."

Nimnestl slowed her progress to regard the speaker. General Ferrapec's back was to her as he stood in the center of a crowd of lesser officers and women. "She wastes some, of course," a soldier said.

"Let her take her slaveys from the city, then," Ferrapec replied. "Those rabble are born to die, just props with which we higher orders can do our deeds of greatness."

His listeners were actually nodding; the general's stock must have gone up while she was absent. Nimnestl pressed forward to have a word with him, but he saw Biandi at the same moment. Excusing himself from his circle of admirers, he tugged at the younger man's sleeve.

"Listen," he said, when Biandi, glancing at Nimnestl, came to a halt. Ferrapec was obviously trying to speak softly but still be heard over the music. "This prisoner who basely attempted to hold His Majesty: is he a tall felon with a scar just here?"

Biandi studied the general for a second. "Yes."

Ferrapec nodded fiercely. "Ah! Ah! I gave him that. In revenge, he may well claim that I had something to do with this business. Foul, is it not?"

Biandi blinked. "Yes."

The general's hand covered Biandi's. "Here's a little something. See that he's quiet."

"No one could hear much in all this noise anyway," said Nimnestl. She gave him a smile that showed all her upper but none of her lower teeth.

The expression on the general's face before courage put a smile over it told her nearly everything. "Quite a crunch, My Lady Bodyguard, eh?" he said. "A pity it isn't in your honor."

She liked him better nervous. "May I suggest that when His Majesty puts in an appearance, you not be in evidence?"

Ferrapec's face was expressionless now, save for one nostril raised in a sneer. "She must be frightened who begins to threaten."

"A warning only. Biandi, you wished to see me?"

"His Lordship asked to see you as soon as you returned, Ma'am."

Nimnestl nodded assent, and followed her subordinate. She glanced back just once, though she was sure Ferrapec would now remain in the Great Hall for hours, to spite her. Umian had pushed to his side to say something. Ferrapec's face went fierce.

"My Lady?"

A knife was already out to counter the glint of metal approaching from the left. "Ma'am, His Lordship says she's to be one of us."

Nimnestl set the knife away, pleased to see that Deverna had held her ground. "Your h-hammer, My Lady?" the younger woman said, holding it out.

Nimnestl took it, her hands automatically sliding up and down the wood in search of cracks or traps Veldres might have put there. "You returned without undue trouble?" she asked.

"Yes, My Lady." Deverna executed what might have passed for a curtsy. "I have your cloak as well, My Lady."

The corners of Nimnestl's mouth went down. "Members of the King's Bodyguard address me as 'Ma'am.' "

"Ma'am?"

"That is correct." She turned to Biandi. "Seitun's company is short one, is it not?"

Deverna glowed as Biandi led her away to find Seitun, perhaps at being accepted into the bodyguard or at having fulfilled the first stage of her real master's orders. Nimnestl was somewhat impressed by her ability to make it back from the Swamp; even if most of the troublemakers had been busy in one place, it was a long, hazardous trip. But Veldres would have to be neutralized if she was really to be of any use.

As Nimnestl mounted to the Royal Platform, Kaftus stepped past a leather curtain that hung before the King's garderobe. She followed. The curtain fell rigid behind her; no one else would pass through until Kaftus willed it so.

A dark missile flew at her head. Knowing what it must be, she didn't duck.

"Missy!" cried Mardith. "I would come to you that time I could, but you say stay by King!"

She ran his tail feathers between her fingers as he settled onto her shoulder. "Who's with him now?"

"Nurse and Culghi," the Regent told her. "They deserve each other."

She looked up into his face. "All is well, isn't it?"

He handed her a mug. "I do wish we could avoid any occasions calling for a song from Arberth," he said, "but everything else seems to be under control."

Nimnestl checked the contents of the mug before taking a drink. "Is the whole song as bad as what I just heard?"

"Oh, no. The first half hour was almost tolerable."

"You, Missy?" Mardith demanded. "You no break something?" The bird's head bobbed up and down, checking her for fractures.

"Nothing of mine." She hung her hammer at her belt. "So," she said, taking a breath, "where was he?"

"Below, according to Nurse and Merklin and your loyal vulture there. I have not so far been vouchsafed an audience with His Majesty. Nurse wasn't quite through speaking to him. Arberth's song was marginally preferable."

The necromancer explained briefly, with rambling footnotes by Mardith, what the King had been up to, and how he came to be locked in while doing it. "The Treasury guards are in custody, being given an opportunity to explain why they were guarding the dungeons in daylight. So far they claim they were accommodating the Housekeepers."

Nimnestl snorted. "One of them is the man with the scar I heard about on my way in?"

"No," Kaftus told her. "That hero enters our saga later, with the New Guard."

Nimnestl's mug was empty by the time she'd heard the full tale. "So," she said, setting it on the floor. "And what policy decisions have come out of this?"

Kaftus ran a hand across the few strands of hair adhering to his domed pate. "There are still bits of information I don't see. Treasury men have never particularly shown an interest in assisting the New Guard, the latter being so thoroughly Army. Nor do I see how Housekeeping fits in, if it does at all. I do dislike to tighten any screws until all of them are in place."

Nimnestl nodded. "What about the Playmates who went with him? Do we punish them, reward them, or leave them alone?"

"Their parents have a variety of ideas on that matter," he replied. "I think it can be left to them. Nurse, of course, will remind the children of it for the rest of her life."

"Yes, that might be enough," she said. Mardith cackled. Then he tugged at her ear.

"You, Missy? What you do?"

"Yes," Kaftus put in. "Did your little vacation do you good? I can't say that I detect the rosy glow of health in your cheeks."

She outlined what she'd seen of the turmoil in the Swamp and what she'd done about it. "A check of the wine order should be all I need for verification," she said. "Do I have the time before His Majesty puts in an appearance?"

The Regent folded his hands. His features took on a worshipful cast. "Nurse will let us know when His Majesty is ready to see us."

Nimnestl set a hand against the leather curtain, which did not move. "How much of this does everyone know, by the way? Is there an official explanation?"

"Ah, yes." Kaftus's face became even more solemn. "His Majesty was hunting Brown Robes, and found evidence of someone hiding in the dungeons. This may or may not be related to a piece of paper which I have not so far been allowed to see. This incriminates someone, not Ykenai, in this summer's murders."

"Everyone believes this?"

The skullish head tipped back. "Credulity is a social obligation. But I'm afraid the name Polijn is being passed from mouth to mouth. We were too late to keep the Playmates from talking to their parents, and their parents from talking generally."

"Lotsa talk, Missy," Mardith put in.

"And you can't get Nurse to show you the paper?" she asked.

The Regent's hands came up. "Even Nurse has not seen the paper, or had not, when I took flight. Even threats of her special nerve tonic did not move His Majesty. He says the paper is for you or for me. You are honored to be ranked so high, I presume?"

Nimnestl let the jibe pass. "He did rather well, didn't he? In any case, I don't see how this adventure can hurt his reputation."

"Don't you?" Kaftus waved a hand, and the leather hanging swung back a bit. "Well, at least he made an impression. A king will be forgiven nearly anything so long as he isn't boring."

II

"I WONDER who was in that cell," Nimnestl said. "You saw no signs?"

"Not a damn." Mardith ruffled his feathers at a housekeeper who approached too near.

Nimnestl wondered just how much there was to this wicked old pile of stones. She knew three or four ways into nearly every room on the first three floors, and more were being found every month. This could, of course, make the place more daunting to an invader in time of war (or give one side an advantage in case of a civil war, which might have been in the minds of some of the designers). Only recently had they discovered that the dungeons were nearly as bad, with a secret exit in at least every third cell. The upper dungeons had, of course, been the royal apartments in the bad old days. But the Palace was even older than those days. Who had built this place? Who could have dug so far?

She smiled. Who could go lower than a Rossacottan?

A few more steps, and her ears felt the glorious decline of pressure as she moved from the tumult of the Great Hall to the merely raucous main corridor outside. She passed a pair of pixies singing a little song in honor of a feather that had just floated past, and wondered where their little queen was.

Queen? She nodded. That was what Kaftus had hinted. She

315

and the Regent certainly understood that Conan's adventure had been a matter of misplaced enthusiasm. Children could get so worked up about a plan and then go through with it without evaluating it. She recalled painting her grandfather's horses once. Only her grandfather had saved her from a whipping. She'd been startled and a bit offended that anyone could take her beautification program amiss.

She liked the King's initiative in the matter. But it would do him no good to have people know he had done it all while hunting Polijn. And it would do Polijn even less good. No one would see her as an excuse for the King to do something exciting; they would all envision her under the Queen's Coronet.

"Watch self, Missy," said Mardith.

"Hush." She had already spotted the little clump of black-shirted New Guards.

"We have a right to advise the King," one of them was arguing. "The colonel says we proved it today looking for His Majesty. Did the Regent and that black dog of his exert themselves to the point of inconvenience, even, for the King?"

"Rights are all very well," said another, "and I'll serve His Majesty whatever comes. What I want now is my money. That was in there with all that stuff about what we proved: that we'd get our palms metalled. Where is it?"

"The Paymaster's supposed to be coming," said a third. "I heard . . ."

"Sssh sssh sssh!" They had spotted her. Two slipped down the hall one way, a third the other way. Those remaining simply stood at attention as she passed.

"No cells yet?" sighed Mardith.

She shook her head. She would have liked to take a few off to the dungeons, but they couldn't be arrested right away. Without some overwhelmingly good excuse, any arrests would be seen as part of her embarrassment at not being the one to find the King. She would have to see if his precious paper gave her any good excuses.

"Ah, My Lady!"

Kirasov was surrounded by his retinue, and parts of other people's, as was only to be expected since his son had shown himself a fellow adventurer of the King. The colonel was resplendent in assembly clothes; he'd always had an eye for color remarkable even among Treasury officers, long known for gaudy costume. Even his pipe, which gave off a noxious smoke proving he used sweet tobacco mixed with berries, was slung with gold chains.

He stopped a few feet in front of her, his retinue rumbling to a halt around them. His nephews were closest to him, in case he needed protection from the Chief Bodyguard, but relations between her and the Chief Treasury Guard were cordial at the moment.

And, in fact, Nimnestl was almost glad to see him. Colonel Kirasov was an old-style courtier, a plotter almost incapable of long-range schemes. Immediate revenge or gratification were his goals; he was easy to stay one step ahead of.

"Hear you've been down to the Swamp, My Lady," he said, sucking on the pipe. "A lot of unrest down there."

"It has quieted considerably, Colonel," she replied. "I'll be making a report in Council."

"Very easy to say so, but the damage is done," he replied. His followers nodded almost in unison. "We hear the mob tossed Tirbain into a ditch and then threw his horse on top of him."

She raised her eyebrows. "And how comes it that a Sixth Tax Collector can afford a horse?"

Kirasov took out the pipe and licked his pointed front teeth. "He may have well deserved it, I'll say that. We know what a job it is, picking up taxes. But there's still going to be bad feeling down there, and I expect His Majesty still means to leave the city by that route. Now, what I suggest is we get up a company to clear a path; just check to make sure the way through the Swamp isn't obstructed. Then they spread out, just to see if rumors of His Majesty's disappearance are growing into bad stories among the peasantry."

Nimnestl inclined her head. "I presume these men would be taken from among those stalwartly loyal Treasury guards?"

Kirasov raised his chin. "I have need of all my guards where they are. Send a company from the Army."

She looked down her nose at him; until now, it had seemed like a plot to get guards out of the Palace Royal before their comrades in custody confessed. For him to suggest such an

escape for his rivals in the Army was out of character entirely.

He understood her lack of response. "In this heat, I can't
have them attacking my men all over the Palace. There are
hotheads on both sides, and this weather just makes 'em hotter.
Get together all the soldiers you don't want my men mutilating
and get them out of the way. They can go to Ricatini after
they're through the Swamp; that's the place. Put Janeftox at
the head of them; he's reasonable enough. Almost wish he was
Treasury."

Nimnestl saw it. "Janeftox? You aren't suggesting him just
to gratify General Ferrapec, I suppose?"

"I am not. A fine thing when a man can't do honor to
a promising young man in another branch simply because
his . . ."

"Then it must be Laisida," she broke in. "What hold has the
Lord Minstrel got on you, Colonel?"

"Nothing!" Kirasov snapped, while his retinue grumbled,
and Eneste looked murderous, only to draw back when Mardith
returned the favor. "Lord Laisida is a gentleman. Not but what
we owe him something, or his family. You'll not forget that
apprentice of his, that Polijn, pulled my boy Argeleb's chest-
nuts out of the fire. And here today it was one of his girls
took part in His Majesty's grand adventure, and who's to say
she didn't do something of the same for the boy? Argeleb
needs good company, what with me so busy and his brother
in exile."

"So this is your way of showing gratitude. I think you will
find the Regent open to your suggestion, and even Kaigrol may
consider it worthy, provided he doesn't hear the suggestion
came from you. I'd advise you ask Lord Kaftus whether the
company could not be sent out tonight, which would test
whether the Army is as combat-ready as its generals always
claim it is."

The colonel was much struck by that suggestion, as General
Gensamar had more than once pointed out that Treasury guards
had an easy job, living close to their permanent post, while
real soldiers had to be ready to move out in any direction at
any moment. He moved off, his retinue following in a cloud
of congratulations. The colonel was not a bad sort, Nimnestl

thought, for an old reprobate who had gouged out more eyes in his time than she'd seen in hers.

But a Chief Bodyguard couldn't be too friendly. There were only two people in the Palace Royal she had sworn not to kill. Friendship with any of the others might slow her hammer at a crucial moment.

She was not often tempted, at least. As she neared the kitchens and spotted the man she sought, he fell silent at once, as did the woman he was addressing. Their faces slid into masks of mingled respect and hostility.

"What now?" demanded Maitena. "No birds in my kitchen!"

"Thank you, Lady!" Mardith replied. "No time to chase rats now, anymeans."

"It is a matter for Hoöshkian, and need not involve entering the kitchens," Nimnestl replied, implying in her voice that she was glad it need not. "The Council is still discussing the faculty of the University. . . ."

"No!" declared the Wine Steward. "How could I transfer my bottles?"

"We could never dispense with your services, Steward," the Bodyguard told him. "It is just that the question has arisen as to whether Lord Aizon knows how to write. No one has ever seen him do so, but since anyone ordering a large quantity of wine . . ."

"Yes!" said the Steward, his hands slapping together. "He had that wagonload of Southern. Rogowta! The book!"

"We knew keeping records would be useful one day, no matter what the Council said," Maitena declared, relaxing a bit since it was not another problem for her. "I wager he doesn't write any more than he bathes."

"Ha!" cried Mardith. "Bet he does more than you bath yourself!"

Hoöshkian was less interested in this debate than in seeing his records used by the Council. "Rogowta!" He unhooked a silver cup from his belt and banged it on the wall. "Rogowta! Ah, he's probably in there by the minstrels, talking them into singing another of his lintik . . . Ah! No, forget it. Forget it."

"Forget it?" Maitena demanded, turning away from Mardith's scornful gaze. "I have money riding on this now, Steward."

The Steward threw up his hands. "He didn't sign for the wine; who ever saw Aizon Bathead come down this far from his tower? He sent his shuptit apprentice, of course."

Nimnestl nodded. "I was afraid of that. Karabari's the obvious person to ask, of course, but we haven't seen him tonight, Has he been here?"

Maitena snorted. "I doubt I'm pretty enough to have him visiting me. It's a bed check you'll be needing."

With a shrug, Nimnestl turned away. "I not forget you bet, no!" Mardith called back. Maitena answered him with a hand signal.

It was what Nimnestl had expected: Aizon wouldn't have bought all that wine, probably couldn't have. All his money went for those books, except for the lot he'd squandered looking for that shard of Arberth's.

A beak tugged at her ear. "What we just do?" Mardith asked her. " 'Sides grease old Maitena, ha?"

"We . . ." She paused, looking for a way around the brawl building up on the left side of the corridor.

Someone shouted, "Knock out his other eye!" and she looked for a way into it instead.

"Let's see how he was trained in dancing!" bellowed someone else.

"Shuptit fake!"

Carasta was warding them all off with a lacquered wicker shield he'd picked up somewhere. "The sword," he panted, "is an instrument of service . . . to one's master, and should not . . . be drawn except in his service."

A knife shot past him. It was not as well aimed as one he hadn't noticed stuck in his leg padding, but struck the hilt of his gleaming sword. The hilt hit the floor.

"It's a clip-on!" someone roared. "Even his weapons are fake!"

This was no friendly party massacre; these men wanted the minstrel's blood. His crime, of course, was not imposture but exposure. Had he admitted earlier on to someone that he was a fraud, he'd have had adherents in what he was plotting. But now it was too late.

"It's his fault the King . . . aiee!"

But the brawl was more talking than fighting at this stage, so only a few swings of the hammer were required to calm things down. A few of the more energetic combatants were inclined to strike back, Bodyguard or no Bodyguard, until Nimnestl noted, "Rabioson will do a much more thorough job, after all."

"Let Sausagefinger have him!" snarled one of the men.

"No!" called another. "Lock him in the kennels with Iranen!"

"Give him to the Regent and see how he likes that!" suggested a third.

It was as close as Nimnestl ever got to popular approval, arresting someone the courtiers disapproved of. "You'll be better off in a quiet cell," she told Carasta, pulling him along with her. "At least until they calm down."

"I think so, My Lady," said the minstrel, glancing back at his assailants and walking all the faster. "My thanks for the ready rescue."

"Where's your friend, Karabari?" she asked, as the cries of "Stripe him! Dot him!" faded behind them.

The minstrel's eyelids came together and then fell open. "Drinking at Veldres's," he said. "I left early before I could be outpaced in the contest. You Rossacottans and your capacity!"

His breath told her something different, but either his own capacity was pretty good or the fight had sobered him. "How long ago?"

Carasta shrugged. "Veldres was being taken in by some chipmunk who claimed she was Polijn. He took it personally when I refused to believe her and, rather than argue, I took my leave."

"He throw you out, ha?" Mardith deduced.

As they would throw Carasta out of the country, Nimnestl reflected: not so much for his pretense, which would be admired for its audacity, but for hanging around with Veldres and Karabari Banglebags. "She called herself Polijn?"

Carasta sneered. "No, it was the old double fake. She said she'd been mistaken for Polijn, but she wasn't. I hope a graduate of the School of Minstrelsy has enough training to see through that, though, which I, perhaps unwisely, told them. I . . ."

"A moment." Nimnestl reached out to a couple hurrying

toward the Great Hall, the state of their clothing suggesting that they had lingered over their errands to Ferrapec's chambers.

Jolor opened her mouth to speak, but Nimnestl held up a hand. "You," she said to Janeftox, "are to report to the Royal Platform. Lord Kaftus and Lord Kirasov want to see you at once."

The lovers exchanged a glance. "The general is worried tonight," Janeftox said. "He . . ."

"He will be more so, but you won't see it," Nimnestl told him. "Report now."

Jolor's upper lip trembled. Nimnestl moved on, pushing Carasta ahead of her.

III

THE quickest route to the dungeons took them past the King's Chambers. As they passed the door, Nimnestl heard an exclamation from Nurse and a cry of alarm in answer from the King. Nurse had never worked herself up to the extent that she might strike her monarch, but it had been a very long day. Nimnestl used Carasta to push the door open.

She was thus just in time to see Nurse turn a vase of flowers upside down on the head of the hapless Culghi.

"Werebears!" Nurse exclaimed.

"But in truth . . ." Culghi started to say. Nimnestl cleared her throat.

"As for you," Nurse said, whipping around, "what do you mean by inflicting the criminally stupid on His Majesty?"

"I'm beginning to wonder," Nimnestl replied. She thrust her captive toward her subordinate. "Culghi, escort this gentleman to a reasonable cell. He may be attacked on the way; see that he is not injured."

"Yes, Ma'am," said the bodyguard, taking hold of the minstrel.

Nimnestl turned to Nurse and, before the older woman could start, said, "I thought you should know Kaftus is picking at the hangings on the Royal Platform again. You know how he does, without thinking."

323

"I have told him and told him . . . and today, of all days!" Nurse stalked away, nearly beating Culghi to the door.

Nimnestl looked to the King as the door slammed. "Whew!"

"Whew!" replied her sovereign. Mardith flew over to take up a post on his shoulder.

The King was sweltering in yards of his finest velvets and furs. Nurse had pulled out all his really grand garments, either to awe the crowd or to prove she didn't need to whip somebody to punish him.

"You had an adventure, I hear," she said, coming forward and holding out one hand.

He caught it and brought it up to one damp cheek. "There are so many people plotting against us," he murmured.

"Well, most of them aren't against you so much as they're just for themselves."

The King looked up into her face. Nimnestl and Kaftus were the only adults he could be sure hadn't killed his parents; they weren't even around the Palace then. Everyone else above a certain age was suspect.

"You saw a lot of new territory, too," she went on.

"Oh, yes." The King looked to Mardith. "It was really interesting, wasn't it?" But there was a lack of excitement in his voice to show his mind was somewhere else.

"I also heard you discovered something important. Did you give it to Nurse?"

The King's underlip started out, but then came back in. "Sielvia found it. I wouldn't let Nurse have it. I'm still the King."

Both feet came down hard on the floor as he stood up and pulled a torn sheet of paper from deep within his robes. Nimnestl felt his eyes on her face as she looked down at the page. He had trusted her at once with the paper he wouldn't give Nurse. They were two, united against the plotting world. It couldn't last, of course; there was room for only one on the throne.

"Is it true?"

She started, and looked at the words on the page, one side and then the other. The main exhibit was a long family tree, in Raiprez's elegant hand, tracing Polijn to a woman named Gloraida and Conan II, Queen Kata's older brother. Nice try, but the last king had been dead these nineteen years. Conan III was a little hazy on the death dates of his immediate predecessors, an understandably ticklish subject to teach him.

"No. No, it's not."

The King nodded. "Good. Then it's all just evidence. General Ferrapec had it, and handed it to Colonel Umian. Raiprez was with them."

"Let me see." Nimnestl moved to a nearby table, pushed aside a stack of gold chains, and set the paper down. She took out a scrap of her own and fitted it into the page. "I found this in the Yellow Dog."

"Hoo hoo!" exclaimed Mardith, hopping down to the table for a look.

"The place where everyone disappeared?" the King demanded.

"I'm afraid Ferrapec and Umian and their friends have been very busy," she told him.

Conan studied the page. His right hand came up toward his mouth, but at the last minute veered off to smooth a lapel that didn't need it. "And is . . . is Polijn one of their friends?"

They looked at the page together. Beneath the family tree, this time in Kodva's handwriting, were several lines of "quotes" from Polijn, most of which were swipes from old songs, and notes on her resemblance to characters in history. Oh, this was dangerous, even in a court full of illiterates. Perhaps especially here. How many would believe it? How many, not believing it, would find it convenient to blame it on Polijn?

The King so worshipped by his subjects had one aspect of godhood, certainly. He was very dangerous to be around.

"I don't think so," she said. He turned to her, needing more than that. "She'd have been able to talk to Laisida, you see, and wouldn't have made this silly mistake about the date here."

She pointed out his uncle's name and explained the problem. "That's right. She knows lots of old things."

Conan turned to regard himself in a standing mirror. Oh, thought Nimnestl, the closer the target, the harder it is to see. But she said, "Yes. This is the work of someone too busy planning for the present to consider the past."

The King adjusted an emerald at his neck. "Did you find Polijn, too, in the Swamp?"

"Not yet." She tapped the incriminating paper. "It might be better for her if she didn't come back, once people see this."

Mardith looked up at her. The King demanded, "What? Why?"

"A lot of people will believe she's guilty of forging this." She flipped the page over to show the verses Polijn had written on the other side. "Some who know she's not guilty won't say so."

"But it isn't her fault! You just said she wouldn't have . . ." His hands made fists. "I know why they don't like her. It's the way she sits and listens and looks at you but doesn't ever say anything. That's like putting an arrow to the bow and not shooting. But you're not like them; you wouldn't . . . arrest her and . . ." The King knew how thoroughly people were killed for treason.

"I think it's because she's not from the Palace," she replied. "They can believe anything about her, the way they did about Carasta. This wouldn't have had a chance if they'd put Iúnartar here, or Masalan."

He shook his head. "But she's just as innocent. And Siel wouldn't have picked up the paper if it hadn't been about Polijn. So if it weren't for her, we wouldn't have this paper at all!"

The paper might make life easier; Ferrapec might confess to save his life if confronted with it. A pity he hadn't just done this job on himself, and left Polijn out of it.

"Well, I'll speak for her, certainly," she said. "If it comes to a Council discussion."

"I sing, too," Mardith assured the King.

He came up to take both her hands in his. "I knew you would."

Nimnestl pulled back just half a step. "But if I do, you know they'll assume she's going to be your queen." And, she did not mention, would make the connection Nimnestl-Polijn-Kaftus. Anyone who saw that would see the Regent in control of the government for decades to come. On a hot and bewildering day like this, that connection might trigger an explosion.

Conan shook her hands up and down. "You could keep her safe, though, the way you do me. She doesn't want to be queen. I don't even WANT a queen!"

"I watch little girl, Missy," Mardith volunteered.

Him, too? "Mardith, hush. I see three choices."

"Yes?"

"Yes. But remember: just because you have a choice doesn't mean any of the choices are good."

She pried loose of his grip and set a hand on the paper. "First, we can just burn this and pretend it never existed. Polijn won't be in any trouble."

"But it's evidence!" The King put one of his own hands on the loot from his excursion. "Anyway, everybody knows I found something."

"And if we show them nothing, they'll be suspicious. Your second choice is to proclaim that all this about Polijn is false, and you refuse to have her arrested."

His head came forward. "You said it was false."

"It is. And you say you don't think she'd do such a thing."

He nodded. "I know she wouldn't."

"Not that one," Mardith agreed, head bobbing.

Nimnestl nodded back at them. "And everyone will say you're doing it because you plan to marry her someday." She raised two fingers. "No, it's the way they'll be thinking. This was written on the back of one of her songs. People will be convinced she had a part in this plot, even if we just use this piece." She held up the fragment dealing with Ferrapec's lineage. "They might pretend, for a while, to believe you when you say you don't think she'd have done anything like this, but deep down they will continue to think she took part, only to desert Ferrapec and Raiprez, and that you have some particular reason for shielding her."

It hurt to go on meeting his gaze, but she managed it, and went on. "The Regent and I can pretend to be furious with you—and Nurse won't have to pretend—and that would at least win her some friends. But half the court will still be trying to kill her, while the other half tries to get her to do them favors."

Conan breathed deeply. "She wouldn't . . ."

"She's human. I think I can take care of her, if that's what you choose. The third choice is to have her arrested for involvement in treason."

Conan stamped one foot. "You want her to be killed!"

"I don't. I'm sure she's innocent, and I shall say so to the Council." Her hand slapped the paper. "But because of what this paper claims about her, if the Council gets involved at all, it will require that she be punished, lest some people believe it's true and we're treating her leniently because of that."

He closed his eyes. "But it's a death sentence for treason!"

"I said involvement in treason," Nimnestl told him. "Someone who assisted in treason, not knowing what was going on, is guilty of a much lesser crime. And she has powerful friends: Lord Laisida, Lady Berdais, not to mention you and me. She might be banished for a few years."

The eyes popped open. "Banished? Years?"

Nimnestl put out one hand as if to lower the volume and pitch of his exclamations. "Then she'd be safe out of the country until people find other scandals to consider. Maybe she'd come back after you've married your queen, so they won't suspect her of that."

"Oh, not that long!" the King protested. "And it's not safe outside the country: who knows what might happen to her out there?"

"Nothing worse than would happen to her here," Nimnestl said. "But you decide. We can't keep Polijn out of trouble altogether; which way would give her—and us—least trouble?"

The King kicked the table leg. "I don't know. What should I do?"

"You tell me." She looked away, toward the door. "As King, you will find people very anxious to make your decisions for you. And you will be surprised how often you're willing to let them. Because then, no matter who gets hurt, it won't be your fault. And deciding is such hard work."

A small voice asked, "But a real King has to do it?"

"Yes."

They stood in silence for a second. "Missy," said Mardith. "Now?"

Nimnestl looked at her old retainer. "Right now?" the bird demanded.

Nimnestl spread out her hands. "He's right," she told the King. "You needn't make a final decision right now. Other things may happen; Ferrapec may make some other slip tonight. He's in the Great Hall now. He may say something unwise, as he's done so many times before."

Conan didn't seem to be listening. His eyes came up to meet hers. "Nimnestl," he said, his voice a sigh. "What good is it being King?"

"I don't know," she told him. "It is your job, though."

IV

NURSE returned at the head of a small army of bodyguards and, after an inevitable amount of fussing with lapels and misplaced emeralds, the Lord and Master of Rossacotta, the Mines of Troppo, the Great Black Lake, and Anything Else He Could Grab moved out toward the Great Hall. Nimnestl was just behind him to the right, Nurse to the left. The company was massive, grand, and just short of terrifying. Passersby flattened themselves against the wall to let it pass.

Except one. A soldier stood one step out from the wall and said, "My Lady Bodyguard, if later you could . . ."

Nurse turned on him. "Armed? In the presence of His Majesty?"

The soldier stepped back. "I'm sorry." He lowered his head. He had done this too late. "Nimnestl!" whispered the King.

"I see," said the Chief Bodyguard. "You see how serious decrees of the court can be. Go on. I will rejoin you later."

The company moved ahead, collecting courtiers as it went, until the company of bodyguards could not be seen for cheering subjects and stumbling New Guards. Nimnestl was left behind with the offending soldier.

"I did not mean . . ." he began. "I was . . ."

"Not what you were," said Nimnestl, reaching out to remove his helmet, "but who you are."

The man was pale, but he made no attempt to run. He was, as the King had seen, Anrichar, the banished older son of Kirasov. Exiled for killing a man in mock combat after the Regent had declared hostilities ended, he had become much more popular in his absence than he had been while at court. Hot blood excused the killing (as it did most anything in this lintik country), and Nimnestl knew he was admired for the contempt he'd shown Lord Kaftus.

He licked his lips. "My Lady, those men who guarded the dungeon were friends of mine."

"So much the worse for them." She put out a hand.

"Surely nothing will happen to them," he went on. "They didn't realize it was the King."

She shook her hand at him. "Your scarf."

Anrichar reached under his armor for it, and drew it out slowly, aware that the Bodyguard's hammer was unhooked and ready to be swung. Every exile was issued a scarf on which was embroidered the first safe date of return. Pictures were added for the illiterate: five suns for five summers, or three clouds for three springs, and so on.

Nimnestl regarded the scarf. "I do not believe your time is up," she told him.

"There's no place for a Rossacottan, once you pass over the mountains," he told her. "A Rossacottan's a beetle or a rat, to be killed when you see it. Or a dog, to kill for you. I'll kill for myself or for His Majesty. But I'm no servant of any foreigner."

He said this without any self-consciousness or apparent awareness of the fact that he was answering to a foreigner right now. Nimnestl let it pass. "So you came back. How?"

His eyes seemed to focus, and his chin came down some. He hadn't rehearsed this bit. After a look left and right, he murmured, "Met a man who said if I could tell him how to get along in the Palace Royal, he'd take me on as a servant until I could reach my father."

"A man," said Nimnestl. "What man? No. Carasta, was it?"

"Yes, My Lady."

"You were the servant he reported murdered?"

Anrichar nodded. "Father hid me in the dungeon until he could get this uniform made. Through somebody in the Swamp, so no one here would be asking questions."

Nimnestl let the head of her hammer swing in little circles. "You were in the cell His Majesty found had been occupied?"

His hands came together in a knot. "They didn't know it was His Majesty! They thought it was just Merklin, playing at one of his adventures. I told them they ought to go back and let the kids out, but by that . . ."

"And they brought you food and water, too," said Nimnestl. "A pitcher. A plate. How did they get those from the kitchens without comment?"

"Father . . . had help." Lips snapped shut.

"Lord Laisida," Nimnestl told him. "Lady Berdais."

Anrichar's head sank. He nodded. "One of their daughters brought it. I forget which one. I was gone already, from the cell, when His Majesty went down there, but they didn't have time to take away my things. They figured they had time. Maybe . . ."

He was really very much like his father, Nimnestl thought. "And you were to pose as a soldier? You were going to escape with this expedition Kirasov suggested?"

"Yes, My Lady." He licked his front teeth and went on. "I was to hide in Ricatini for the rest of my term, if I could manage it, or find a place in North Malbeth. But my friends, My Lady? They meant no harm, or even disrespect, to His Majesty. Can't you do something for them?"

"You are in no position to make any plea on behalf of someone else," she informed him. "You're in trouble enough on your own."

"His Majesty wouldn't . . ."

"Quiet! It is not for you to say what His Majesty would or would not do."

"Yes, My Lady. I'm sorry."

The Chief Bodyguard glowered at him. His crime was worse than Polijn's; the girl had done no wrong beyond existing, as far as she knew. But to bring Anrichar to anyone's attention right now would mean an end to that peacekeeping company headed out and, thus, no escape for Janeftox.

"Your friends will likely suffer no worse than reassignment to the Summer Palace for the winter, if what you say is true," she told him. "As for you, I do not wish to have you interfering with His Majesty's triumph tonight. We shall decide your fate at some other time."

"Yes, My Lady."

"Later."

"Yes, My Lady."

"In Ricatini. Report to your father."

The hanging head came up, its mouth open. But Nimnestl had already turned away and was marching toward the Great Hall.

V

THE King was already on the platform when Nimnestl reached the Great Hall. He didn't look very happy, but he did look grand. Nurse had an eye for impact, even if she did disregard such details as comfort.

Nimnestl betrayed no sign of her own discomfort. Very bad for her reputation as a person of iron to put her hands over her ears as screams of approbation pounded through the air. People's hearts were so full that they emptied everything out of their lungs to make room. The King's return meant a return to natural order, a return to (relative) peace and tranquility. It meant the country would not be plunged into unremitting fire and blood today.

It also, though this was farther back in their minds, meant probable profit. Such a gala celebration could end only in presents and honors. Power went hand in hand with wealth; loyalty was based on the receipt of gifts. Courtiers were thumping each other on the backs, not only from jubilation, but because it might be their last chance before they were promoted to a more dignified and formal post.

The King raised his arms for attention. "Children of the Panther!" he shouted. The crowd was stilled, temporarily. It broke out into cheers again and again throughout the little speech that had Kaftus's finger marks all over it. The speech

334

said nothing beyond "Nice to be back," but it said so over and over, and in such a way that everyone present felt personally responsible for the niceness. Nimnestl paid very little attention to it, pushing through the throng.

She passed the minstrel's stand, where, praise be, Arberth no longer stood. Malaracha was there, probably interrupted by the King's entrance. As Nimnestl worked her way along the stand to the Royal Platform, however, he gave up his place to his former master, Laisida. It was only fitting that the King's First Minstrel be in the stand when His Majesty finished speaking.

At the corner of the stand, she turned and looked back at Morafor. There was more to the sculptor's grin besides glee at the King's return. What did that gleam of mischief portend?

The King had concluded his remarks, and was accepting more ear-blistering cheers. Laisida was tuning up. Morafor glanced at him, one hand plunged into a heavy bag. Morafor's servants, in the background, seemed to be breaking a chair into its component parts.

Nimnestl caught sight of Culghi, and redirected her feet toward him. They needed to be ready for whatever was in the air.

The cheers ebbed a bit, and Laisida struck an opening chord. "Hail the return of our blessed King!" he called, and winced as the crowd hailed it, at full volume.

"It brings to an end so many woes," he went on. "The deaths of friends, the joy of foes." He paused, in case people felt like yelling some more. But the crowd was yelled out for the moment. Nimnestl moved away from the wine tables; they'd be heading there for something to soothe the throat, and progress would be easier across the floor.

Laisida started in on a list of woes the King had remedied, spelling out first the names and family relationships of all the victims of the unsolved murders. Nimnestl understood everything when he sang, "And Valspar, once so tall and brave." She pointed out strategic points to Culghi and sent him hurrying to tell the other bodyguards what they were to do, and where.

Valspar had been dead bare hours, killed in full view of the King. And of Sielvia, of course. Laisida would have heard the whole story from his daughter by now. Laisida was not one to hesitate, either. Men of the New Guard had laid hands on a member of his family. And revenge was no good if it was not publicly flaunted.

Nimnestl looked to the platform. The King didn't seem to be paying attention, particularly, but the Regent had caught on. The set of Kaftus's lips told her he was amused, lintik blast and burn the man.

The minstrel showed absolutely no consciousness of what he was doing; it was just a song. And he had mentioned neither the New Guard nor Umian in connection with the murders. But references to black shirts and black pants had had their effect on the sober. A circular clearing was developing around Umian. Even his guardsmen were pulling away.

The colonel's rocky face was pointed at the minstrel. He would not betray himself. He would not. Even when the first rock sailed past his head, his expression did not move. The sneer seemed to settle over it gradually.

The Regent rose on the platform. "Enough!" he called.

And it was, too, because everybody who could be expected to get the point had heard all that was needed.

"They killed our Nemly!"

"Lecture us on what's civilized, ha?"

Knives appeared and then disappeared, only to reappear red. Bits of chair and broken pottery flew at Umian. Jewelled pitchers, imported at great expense from calmer lands, became clubs. The crowd, already in the throes of strong emotion, was ready now to turn its mind to destruction.

But this was not at all Nimnestl's idea of a celebration. Bodyguards stepped from their places and thumped New Guards and their assailants alike. Nimnestl stepped up to Umian.

"His Majesty has already ordered an investigation of this matter!" Kaftus called from the platform. "I will see to the guilty myself! I will also see to those who would mar His Majesty's triumph with violence!"

The announcement was easily as effective as the muscles of the bodyguards. Umian did not resist as Nimnestl took him by the arm.

"The good minstrel has the right of it," he said, as Nimnestl led him away. He didn't bother to brush away the marshmallows hurled at him by pixies. "I have feared for some time that the younger members of the New Guard were becoming restless in this heat. I should have investigated at once instead of waiting until we'd reached the Summer Palace. I accept full responsibility, of course, for their errors."

"I'm glad to hear that," she told him. She knew what his plan must be, of course. He had only to hold out in the dungeons until his partners took over the government and brought him out. He probably knew as well as she did what the chances were that Ferrapec and Karabari would decline to retrieve him, but it was all he had to go on.

Biandi and Seitun took charge of him, adding him to a number of other captives, both New Guard and belligerent bystander. Nimnestl beckoned to a number of Treasury guards in the crowd. "You will follow these men's orders," she informed them, pointing to the two bodyguards, "until the prisoners are bestowed. Colonel Kirasov will note your service in this respect." She did not like to send too many bodyguards out of the Great Hall, but she couldn't have Umian's underlings outnumbering their escort, either.

"We will not," she added, to soothe any Treasury man's objection, "trust the Army for this errand."

In fact, she decided, turning back to consider the crowd, it was time to irritate the Army just a little bit more.

"Some party!" said Mardith, zipping down to peck at her ear. "All the time fun fun fun. You needing this?"

She took the object he'd plucked from her hair, a bit of debris that had hit her on her way to Umian. It was Morafor's, a bit of the scrap pottery Timpre painted as a love token for Polijn. Pity those two were too young to be married and end the . . .

She tossed the piece of pottery up into the air and caught it as it came down. Morafor was master of many plastic arts, so as to be ready to satisfy the demands of the King. Or any paying customer. And Karabari had been frequenting his studio over the past month.

Just now, though, it was Ferrapec she wanted. Umian's reputation was damaged, but not beyond repair. He had ordered the killing of people without major connections. And Sielvia had suffered no serious damage. In days to come, the Council might easily remember his high moral tone, and overlook the murders of some expendable underlings.

But let it be known that he was allied with Ferrapec, and there could hardly be any rescue. Few crimes were worse than failure, in the eyes of this court, and the use of Ferrapec was to court failure.

She had to step over Aoyalasse, who was being given one of the table legs Morafor's servants had left over. Aoyalasse did not appreciate the gift, and shrieks of pain drew Iranen's attention.

"How interesting," said the Housekeeper, who never, ever let any of her slaveys be tortured without permission. "I think you must come to work for me. He could teach me something, don't you think?" She turned to Nimnestl for reinforcement.

"Indeed," said the Bodyguard. "I think you will find his former master more than willing to give him to you."

"Ho ho," said Mardith, as the man collapsed on top of Aoyalasse.

"You're friendly tonight," Iranen told the Bodyguard. "Does it mean you're going to have me killed?"

"Your contribution to the gaiety of all celebrations is always appreciated," Nimnestl told her. "I may well have other gifts to pass along later tonight. If you will excuse me, My Lady?"

Iranen did not excuse her, but trotted right along behind her as she moved to join a circle of soldiers who had joined Ferrapec at the wine table. The general was telling them all how he had rescued the King, but fell silent as Nimnestl, Mardith, and Iranen came into his view.

"You really must have your story recorded in the Diary," the Bodyguard told him, reaching to take up a drink. "His Majesty is keenly interested in the recording of history, particularly in the words of those who made it. The Tale of Silver-Spurred Ferrapec would be a fitting addition to his collection."

"Why, My Lady, I . . ." He paused. Everyone knew the general's silver spurs were long pawned.

He apparently felt it was just an oversight. "I believe history is a fitting study for young men of His Majesty's age. That way they can learn about the glories of the Army in the days before it was shamed by the antics of such as Umian. Can you believe the old fraud was having his New Guard paid with funds from Veldres, down in the city? That's what I've heard. All these modern movements in morals and civilization are just a blot on our noble history. The . . ."

Nimnestl was spreading a torn piece of paper out on the wine table. "And to add to our noble history," she said, smoothing the two pieces together, "we have this royal chart, found in all the furor of the day."

"Something like this you see before I don't think," Mardith promised onlookers. Everyone, including General Ferrapec, leaned in for a look, tales of treasure maps on their minds. Kodva recognized it first, and looked a warning to her daughter-in-law, but Raiprez was trying to see around Iranen's shoulder.

Nimnestl took in all these moves, but her main attention was on Ferrapec, who had gone very white. "It's all just a forgery, of course," she explained to him. "Someone trying to rearrange our noble history and sort out the succession."

His head was shaking. He mouthed the word "No" several times.

Nimnestl turned a little so everyone who wanted could get a look at the paper. At least two of the people in the first row were literate, and no friend to the general. "It looks," she said, as if these ideas were just occurring to her, "as if, once the King was disposed of, whoever it was meant to make you Regent by means of these lines on paper, for a ruling queen with a false claim. I suppose Umian was meant to head the Army. He had this paper."

"No!" said Ferrapec, out loud. "Not a ruling queen; she was to marry . . . I've never seen this paper in my life! It has nothing to do with me!"

"It has your name on it," she pointed out, putting up a hand to keep him from snatching up the document. "And the person who found it . . ."

"Lies!" Ferrapec snatched out his short sword. "I never . . ." The hand holding the sword trembled; the point was aimed at the floor.

The crowd pulled away to give the combatants room. Ferrapec's mother, stricken, reached to the wall for support. But Culghi was there, preventing her access to the wall, and to the torch burning just within reach.

Raiprez laughed, a high, forced gaiety. "Why would he plot to take over? Does he not have all a man could want, having me?"

"Why don't you come explain to the Regent that His Majesty lied about who handed this paper to whom?" Nimnestl suggested. "Unlike me, he can be very hard to convince."

The sword continued to tremble. The point touched the floor. "I am loyal!"

"To Ferrapec." She would be very surprised if he attacked. Still, Umian had surprised her by not fighting; who was to say Ferrapec might not also do the unexpected? She glanced behind him and said quickly, "Of course, it may not be your handwriting. We should not act hastily when making accusations of this gravity."

He fell for it, jerking his head back to see what she'd seen, and was now trying to keep him from noticing. Her hammer was out and down before he'd fully turned. The blade shattered and flew among the spectators.

"You can't do this!" he screamed, looking down at his broken sword. "I . . . we have . . . I can . . ."

He looked to his wife and mother for suggestions. Then he looked around for support. Only Iranen was smiling.

He knew. Nimnestl could see that he knew, his eyes widening to take in all the mistakes he'd made to reach this point. How far back he had to look, she couldn't guess. He didn't have very far to look forward.

"Missy!" cried Mardith, darting down.

Ferrapec fell backward under the bird's assault, but his target had not been the Bodyguard. The sword hilt had been turned in on himself. "Not the gallows!" he shrieked, as the jagged remnants of the blade tore in under his ribs. "Not the gallows!"

They watched until the spurts of blood subsided a bit. "Huh!" said Kaigrol, lumbering away. "One less fool in the world."

Nimnestl beckoned to a pair of her subordinates. "Culghi, take . . ."

Iranen's gasp brought her around. Raiprez was stepping barefoot through her husband's blood. Dropping to her knees beside the general, she put a finger to his wound and then to her tongue. Had the little intrigante really loved the general? How ill-judged. How silly.

One bodyguard stepped up and took her by the shoulders. Culghi knelt on the other side of the general. He frowned, looked up at Nimnestl, and looked down again.

"Ma'am," he said. "If we hurry, I think he'll live."

Nimnestl closed her eyes. Trust Ferrapec to botch even that.

CHAPTER NINE
Polijn

I

POLIJN stumbled on the hem of her dress again. It tore some more. She hiked it back up and shoved the dripping hair back off her forehead.

Panting, she stared at the dark bulk of the Palace Royal. It was just too lintik far! The heavy amulet had protected her from all threats except two: the heat, and her own failing strength. The weather wasn't going to break; she knew the air of those nights where you hoped it would rain, and it never did. She sucked sweat from her upper lip.

The Palace was her safe place, though; there could be no stopping before she reached it. This was no place to sleep. The land outside the walls was prowled by all manner of vermin at night: animal, human, spirit. Then, too, there was all that about Veldres and Karabari to be told. They'd said something about the King; it might be important, urgent.

So she urged herself onward, reciting the names, making each syllable a step forward. Anybody could take one more step, last one more syllable. Then she'd start the next name before she had time to think.

"Veldres. Umian. Ferrapec. Tell Bodyguard. Karabari."

She was saying them out loud as she staggered up on the drawbridge. The guards had obviously been celebrating something; they shifted in their sleep a bit as she dragged herself on.

"Veldres. Umian. Ferrapec. Tell Bodyguard. Karabari."

"That looked like Polijn! Hey!"

An amber merchant lurched after her, but he'd been celebrating, too, and his aim was off. He caught hold of her dress. It tore some more. Polijn just stepped out of it.

"Veldres. Umian. Ferrapec. Tell Bod-y-guard. Kar-a-bar-i."

She was moving slower. She willed herself to keep moving forward, no matter who shouted or tried to catch her. She'd been running since noon, trying to get here. If she had to run from here, where would she go?

"Vel-dres. U-mi-an. Ferr-a-pec. Tell Bod-y-guard. Kar-a-bar-i."

And here was the Palace Royal! She climbed the stairs almost on all fours, and crawled out into a back corridor. There were people here, wide-eyed people she was sure she knew, if she could just think of their names. She rose to her haunches, swinging the golden amulet with the Vielfrass's mark on it, sweating in the extravagant undergarment marked with the initial of Ferrapec's daughter.

"Vel-dres," she murmured. "U-mi-an. Ferr-a-pec."

She couldn't seem to rise. Every hand she reached to for help up was pulled back, afraid to touch her or afraid she would touch it. Stupid of her to expect any assistance, she thought. There were cries of "Polijn!"; she couldn't tell whether or not they were hostile. Better keep moving. Which way was Laisida's suite from here? Where was here?

She dropped to all fours again just as a boot came in at her stomach. She rolled down the corridor a bit, glad she'd had so little to eat since the parade.

"Who is it?"

"Isn't it Polijn?"

"What do we do with her?"

"Those are Maiaciara's; she showed them to me when she got them."

"She was calling for Ferrapec."

"Royal Companion, isn't she? Better call for Nurse."

There seemed to be no point in moving until they made up their minds. Polijn closed her eyes.

The water was cold, but it burned. This was not so much
of a surprise when she opened her eyes and found the Regent
himself before her.

She had been propped up in a chair in the Council Chamber.
The only other person present was the Regent, unless you
counted the skull he was stroking. Polijn would have wished
for the Bodyguard, who might have been more sympathetic,
and was at least more human.

They sat along the wall to the left of the great Council Table,
with nothing between them. Polijn looked up into the Regent's
eyes, and wished she hadn't.

"I see you brought souvenirs from your afternoon in town,"
he said, thin lips snaking up into a smile. "Nothing for me?"

She was suddenly cold. All this trouble to get home safe,
and now it was obvious that she had done something wrong.
Too tired to be ashamed of the tears that started in her eyes,
she wondered if she couldn't just ask him to kill her now and
save her any more effort.

But he apparently intended to kill her by throwing questions
at her: Raiprez this, Ferrapec that, did she know thus-and-such
about Kodva. Her brain came back from the humid haze it had
melted into on the way here, and cold disbelief was building up
beneath it. Was all this trouble about these lintik underpants?

She pulled herself up a little in the chair. She did know
something about Ferrapec, one thing to barter for her life.

"Karabari's plotting to take over," she told him.

"We know."

Had the Regent or the skull said that? "He's working with
Umian and Veldres and . . . and I think Ferrapec."

"We know."

"He has a spell that sucks people out of their clothes."

"We know."

"He stole two ancient coins and sold them to Karlikartis."

"We know."

She could make up something more exciting. But he'd catch
a lie. The truth wasn't doing her a whole lot of good, either,
though.

She was opening her mouth to try again when there came a
heavy thump on the door of the chamber. The Regent raised
one hand and the door swung open.

"Ah," he said. "Come in, Lord Aizon."

II

THE Royal Exorcist stepped into the room, nose lifted, beard rustling, or perhaps it was the bat on his chest. "We hear that Polijn has returned," he said, voice stiff. "It is true?"

The Regent folded his hands and inclined his head in Polijn's direction. "As you see."

The Exorcist was the last person Polijn would have expected to express concern about her. His next words, however, explained his interest.

"That little one has caused us all a great deal of trouble." Lord Aizon stepped farther forward. "Are we to be allowed to hear what she has to say, or see what she has brought?"

"Why," said the Regent, as Polijn put a hand up to the Vielfrass's amulet, "I believe you both should be allowed to see what she has—do come in, both of you—and hear what she has to say, particularly what she has to say about you, Lord Aizon."

"About me?" Aizon came forward some more, and Polijn could now see Karabari standing just outside the door.

"I was skeptical about it, My Lord," the Regent replied, "but the Chief Bodyguard agrees with me."

Aizon would gladly have stepped back now, but his apprentice had followed a bit too closely. Karabari's eyes were on the Regent, burning with the desire to find out what his

345

master was being accused of. But Polijn, whose eyes were pointed the other way, could see the Bodyguard stepping to the door, followed by Lady Forokell and a number of others. She thought Berdais was among them, but couldn't be sure.

"We are all in agreement, are we not, Polijn?" The Regent smiled at her; she didn't like it. "We wonder what you mean by concealing a national treasure. Anyone else would have flaunted it, for not everyone can afford an original piece of Morafor's pottery."

The Exorcist glowered. "I have no notion, sir, what . . ."

"Did your apprentice tell Morafor what he was copying, or did he simply take him the piece and have him duplicate it?" The Regent's eyes were turned down toward the skull as he considered the question.

The change of attack was swift, and Aizon was not slow himself. It seemed to Polijn that more than two arms came around as the Exorcist, crying, "The shard! My shard! You stole the real one and made a copy!" lunged at Karabari's throat. Just one arm—blue, and thick as a man's head—pushed out at Aizon's chest and knocked him to the ground.

The Bodyguard, inside the chamber now, raised an eyebrow at the Regent. But the necromancer didn't move.

"Paranoid old fool!" snarled Karabari, standing above the body of his master. "Crumpled my lapel." He ran his hands among the gems on the cloth, apparently oblivious to the approach of Nimnestl and the others. But Polijn saw his lips moving as he smoothed the velvet.

No one else seemed to be doing anything about this. So she meowed.

Karabari jumped six inches into the air and two feet back. She realized she hadn't fooled him when the knife came at her. "Brat!" he snapped.

The heavy blade stopped in the air, twisted, and thudded to the floor. The Regent's head was up now. His face lost any warmth it had assumed. "Your trouble is with me, youngster."

"Not so!" exclaimed the apprentice, spreading his arms out in the air. "Yours is with me! The magic shard will imprison you all!"

He raised the arms slowly, and his face blushed bright orange. Lips and eyes burned bright red, and the room shuddered, moving the immense Council Table a hairsbreadth to the left. None of this seemed to interest the Regent much.

"You are mine!" roared Karabari Banglebags, as his hands came together.

Then he vanished. Gaudy robes hung in the air for a moment, empty.

Then they exploded in flesh. A wave of humanity rolled from the robes: feet and navels, dimples, nipples, and knees. Hair and skin, bruises and bald spots: everything seemed to be mixed together.

This column of humanity pushed chairs and spectators back as it fell into its component parts. Polijn recognized Torat and Zhriacar at once, but Karlikartis took longer. The woman looked younger, somehow, without her clothes and wig.

"On your lives!" someone shouted. "Don't move!"

It was the Regent, wading knee-deep in naked Swampites, most of them too disoriented to complain as he kicked them aside. The tall necromancer pushed to the center of the pile and lifted out Karabari's gaudy garments. "Ah!" he said, passing his hands over them.

One long hand slid into them and drew out a piece of clay not as big as his hand. It had some kind of design on it, but Polijn was too far away to see.

"And the culprit?" inquired the Chief Bodyguard, stepping on Torat's hand as she entered.

"Here." Kaftus raised the lapel and tore off one gem. Light flickered across its surface but, leaning forward, Polijn could see that the movement was not entirely caused by the light outside. Someone was inside.

"Very tidy," the Bodyguard told him. "Did you do that?"

"I did not," he told her. "I was plotting something far messier. His own spell was bounced back on him."

Nimnestl looked back to the crowd at the door of the chamber. "Then," she said, her voice low, "someone here must be an Ykena."

"Probably." The Regent thrust both jewel and clay artifact inside his robes. "But I believe we have disrupted our little household enough for one evening. Unless . . ."

He whipped around to Polijn. "Unless you have any more surprises for us?"

His smile now was simply too much after so long a day. Polijn fell off her chair, landing on Karlikartis.

III

CONSTRUCTION on the gallows was fully visible through the window. Polijn turned her back on it, and raised her flute to begin again.

The more Polijn learned about music, the more there seemed to be to learn. She had dared once to ask Laisida whether it was all necessary. "Can't you make a good song with just a tune and a rhyme, without all the attention to interval and rhythm and tempo and key?"

"Of course," he had told her. "And most audiences will enjoy it readily enough. But it will earn you no prizes from the experts, and those are the gentry who compile the books."

The manuscript was an old one, and she had to draw a candle a little nearer. It was morning, but clouds still hung over the Palace Royal, admitting no more light than could burn through the dark masses.

She had slept late. When she rose, only Fiojo had been there to hand her some breakfast and tell her she was to stay in and practice. "Master says in case somebody decides killing you is the patriotic thing to do." Sielvia had wanted to be there, too, Fiojo said, but Berdais dragged her off to work.

"And Lord Laisida?" Polijn had asked.

"In Council," the servant told her, and ran a hand through her hair. "You won't fret? He'll do it; you're one of ours."

Polijn had been working for Laisida thirty fewer years than
Fiojo, so she hoped the older woman was correct. On being
brought back to the First Minstrel's suite and revived, she had
had explained to her, about eight times, everything that had
gone on in her absence: the King's quest, the New Guard's
disgrace, and, most ominously, Ferrapec's paper.

Ouch! Either the flute needed tuning, or she'd read that mark
all wrong. She set the instrument in her lap, her fingers running
along it.

They couldn't be meaning to do anything too terrible;
Karabari's captives had all been sent back to the Swamp
this morning, told that they owed their rescue to "the
King's mercy and Polijn's information." They wouldn't
have mentioned her name if she was to be carved for
treason in public later in the day. It might have been
no more than a conciliatory move, something to keep the
Swamp happy. The Yellow Dog was to be refurbished, most
of it with the proceeds from what was left of Veldres's
lands and property. (The merchant himself had not been
seen for some time, and was not expected to return.) Their
captor was to be executed the day before the King left
for the north. He would not be the only traitor on the
platform.

Dozens of people, it seemed, had been found expendable, or
at least punishable, in the wake of the turmoil. Among those
to be discussed were Morafor, Ferrapec, Raiprez, Umian, the
Wine Steward, some people from Treasury, the higher-ranking
Mew Guards, and, because of Ferrapec's paper, Polijn.

She licked her lips, and set the flute up to them. But there
wasn't much power in her to produce sound. She was innocent, and most of the people who mattered knew it. "But
once connected with Ferrapec, there's no luck at all," Laisida
had told her. "An appearance on the gallows is probably
inevitable. But I've been up there myself; if you can walk
down by yourself, you can make a recovery. Some of us
will just have to see that your stay there is brief and boring."

She wasn't sure quite what to expect. The Paryice had liked
her, but she and Mokono had been kicked out after Mokono
had used the Paryice's coat to put out a fire at table. The flames

could have done damage; not Mokono's fault it was the man's lucky coat.

Polijn set the flute down again, and turned the manuscript over. Perhaps if she started from the vocal part at the beginning, and then tried the flute part, it would flow more readily.

It seemed to do so, to her. She was not alone in her opinion, either, for a voice remarked, "You have so much talent, child, in your little finger."

She hadn't heard his crutch thumping on the floor. "Now, if we could only do something about the other nine," Laisida sighed, seating himself next to her.

"You have the right tone, however," he went on. "Too many apprentices try to sing this with a rich, full, lush voice. It requires a piping sound like a lone breeze on a clear night in the dark plains."

"Songs!" exploded another arrival.

They both looked back to where Sielvia had been intending to hide. "Eavesdroppers must show patience if they wouldn't show their faces," her father told her. "Come in, then, and we'll discuss whether we couldn't disguise you and turn you over to the Council for Polijn."

Sielvia stepped into the room and sat on the floor next to Polijn's chair. "What's going to happen?" she demanded. "Are they still arguing?"

The minstrel set his wooden ankle up on the real one. "Well, now, His Lordship assembled the most thorough Ferrapec-haters and Polijn-loathers he could call together."

His listeners nodded. Polijn twisted her hands around the flute.

"And then he wouldn't let them talk. He told them what he thought of you and of the general. He wanted your blood seven ways. He described you, particularly, in words that would have shaken down any walls but those of the Council Chamber."

"What did the King say?" Sielvia asked him, putting a hand on Polijn's leg.

"He wasn't there."

Sielvia rocked back as if struck in the face. That had been their best hope.

"It was all choreographed, child," her father said, with a roll of his eyes. "There sat His Lordship, telling us what to do, in very clear and occasionally crude phrases. We must do this to Polijn, we must do that to Polijn; the most basic laws of great and glorious Rossacotta would be a mockery if we did not do thus and so to Polijn in full view of the people. Kaigrol's ears pricked up at the first use of the word 'must.' As soon as he got a chance, he declared that you were a fetching little thing who deserved protection. Jontus, who had orders from his wife to see that the Council turned you over to Iranen at the very least, started to blow out smoke about your youth and tender years. 'Sweet innocence' was the phrase bandied about."

Master and apprentice raised an eyebrow at each other. Sielvia was less entertained. "But . . ."

"They all but drew arms in your defense," the minstrel went on. "Umian was consigned to the pit without demur. Ferrapec's half dead, but there's a little life they can take from him yet; they agreed to take it in a quarter the time it took Tollamar to declare what an ornament to the court you were. Polijn this, Polijn that; the penalties suggested grew lighter and lighter."

But he said nothing about the penalties being waived, she noticed. "Thank you," she told him.

He waved this away. "I did very little. My sole contribution was to swing the crutch up between Arberth's legs as he rose to sing a little lyric in your honor. That would have been a sorry setback."

"But how light?" demanded Sielvia.

Laisida set his crutch back to push himself out of the chair. He stepped away from Polijn, his back to her. Sielvia was breathing hard; Polijn could feel the younger girl's tension in the way Sielvia kept moving closer and closer, trying to bring as much of herself into contact with Polijn's leg, as if to anchor her there.

For her part, Polijn was content to wait. Let the man have his drama; it was his livelihood, and it probably became habit after a while. She expected he had something unpleasant to tell her: some moderate beating on the gallows, a small brand, broken bones, and then display on the stocks, pillory, table. They could string her up like a goose on the gallows, as long as they didn't feel it was necessary to remove her giblets. Laisida was correct in that: if you were alive when they finished, there was always a chance to recover.

"They couldn't declare you completely innocent," he went on, his back still turned. "Not as long as you had those undergarments that were so obviously a gift from the general. No!" He raised a hand as Sielvia sputtered. "I know. The idea of Ferrapec giving gifts might have been humorous enough to prevail in a reasonable atmosphere. I wonder if the Council Chamber is cursed. Lady Maitena was arguing that you still deserved death, if a quick one, for your association with him when precisely at the right moment, the Bodyguard entered the chamber."

Polijn and Sielvia both leaned forward.

"She'd come from the King, she said. His Majesty would not listen to reason, she said. She would try to show him how much of an affront it would be to law and order if you were allowed to live, she said. Nurse would help her, she said, and it would help if the Council would make a recommendation."

"And did they?" whispered Sielvia.

The minstrel turned. He had a small black ficdual in his hands; it was the one Polijn used in practice, and needed a new string. Polijn saw he had strung it for her.

"Of course not," he said. "They were too busy abusing the Bodyguard for daring to bully His Majesty that way. Lord Kaftus let this go on for some time and then demanded a decision. Any councillor along the table who suggested death for you after that would have been hawked and hanged himself."

Sielvia's clutch on Polijn's leg was all but cutting off the flow of blood. "But what are they going to DO?" Laisida's daughter exclaimed.

Laisida took two steps forward and paused, his eyes running over Polijn. She sat back, and he took the ficdual by the neck.

"This," he said, as it landed in her lap, "will not fail you. Fortune may. If it does, come back and we shall try again."

"No!" said Sielvia, shaking Polijn's leg. "Not banished!"

The minstrel came back to his seat. "Anrichar was banished, child. Perhaps we can simply say it is time for this young singer to set out as a journeyman."

"Am I ready for that?" asked Polijn, as Sielvia sobbed into her thigh.

"No," came the unexpected answer. "But sometimes one learns more that way."

He put one hand on her wrist and another on the ficdual. Polijn looked up at him and then to the window, where she could see the gallows, and the outside wall of the Palace Royal. And, beyond that, a thin strip of green beneath a heavy grey sky.

EPILOGUE
Sielvia

YSLEMUCHERYS, soused and silly, was capering outrageously for Lord Arlmorin, who had got him that way. Bilibi and Kohoontas, more professional fools, eyed the First Minister gravely and made criticisms that made the foreign ambassador bellow with laughter, and Yslemucherys jump the higher.

Beggars and pickpockets from the city identified reasonable targets, and moved in. Servants who were supposed to be busy on last-minute errands sidled up to the wagons of the amber merchants while trying to keep an eye out for both the weather and their masters. They were chased back with curses or whips, depending on the status of those masters.

Colonel Kirasov knocked down a Treasury guard who was doing a little dance in mockery of the First Minister. The man rolled back into the path of a serving girl ducking under the whips of the amber merchants. Berdais leaned out of a carriage nearby, but whether she was scolding Kirasov, the guard, or the girl, Sielvia was too far away to make out.

The noise and fuss were all but unbearable. The Chief Bodyguard rode back and forth through it, high and hard on her horse, her glowers going everywhere impartially.

A vast chain of wagons, newly gilded and recently polished, stretched back across the bridge to the very courtyard. The fringes were mostly new, and the wheels shone. Even the wagons for carrying supplies were bright and grand. Shining banners tall enough to tickle the low clouds rose above it all. The parade had been simply grand setting out.

Then the wine coach had broken a wheel not ten yards from the gatehouse. Rather than split the parade at that point (which would have made for less of a show), the whole company had halted. It stood garish and incongruous against the grey of the Palace Royal and the growing blackness of the clouds. People in processional array sweated to keep animals and servants in line, so as to be ready when the signal was given to begin again.

Sielvia sat sweltering in a carriage that hadn't even made it out of the courtyard yet. A half dozen favored Playmates, under the supervision of Orna, would ride just behind the King's Coach, on call in case His Majesty grew bored during the trip. Masalan was drowsing in a corner of the seat, ignoring the argument outside as Argeleb, Timpre, and Irleston demanded to be allowed to ride on top, with the driver. Orna's voice was louder every time Sielvia heard him speak; the new Tutor was easier-going than Haeve about geography and reading, but his temper was touchier, and he had a good, solid backhand.

"If Polijn were here, we could at least tell fortunes," Iúnartar pointed out.

Sielvia had not known she even had nerves until Iúnartar's excited but mournful chittering started to get on them. Not for the first time, she wished Ferrapec and the others had chosen this girl instead of Polijn for their plotting. Of course, if they had, they might have succeeded after all. But would that have been so bad?

Iúnartar would have screamed on the scaffold, of course, if Ferrapec had failed after all. But she'd screamed on the balcony anyway, closing her eyes at every stroke and then reopening them immediately to ask what had happened.

Sielvia sighed, and turned to leave the window and sit down. But this brought her eyes around to that other wagon, the dingy grey one. So she didn't leave the window after all, despite her resolution not to look.

Twenty-six men and seven women were crowded onto benches in the rough cart. One of the men was already dead, draped over the side, having apparently forgotten in the course of conversation with the others that he had been stripped of his armor. No one looked at him; it would have been illegal to dump him out of the cart. His companions studied the sky, as thunder followed soon after every flash of lightning. They had been provided with no canvas canopy.

Polijn sat toward the rear, her pack on her lap, her hands folded on top. She had her instruments there, a change of clothes, her cards, some money. Sielvia had been saving six coins for illicit excursions into North Malbeth from the Summer Palace; she had forced these on Polijn, crying at how few they were. Polijn had been nice about it, saying if she had to carry more, she'd be robbed before she passed the gatehouse.

Polijn was off, off to the west, to the haughty cruelty of Lattin, the mindless violence of the Northern Quilt, to face the horrid, foreign ways and places with no one to watch over her. And she had wanted to go south, to see the civilized people there, to visit the ancient School of Minstrelsy. But Lord Arlmorin had given one or two of the exiles letters of introduction to his king, so all had to move west. There was a time limit, after all; Polijn could not be allowed to wait around for a wagonload of exiles that was headed south.

The cart sat, not allowed to set off ahead of the King's Entourage. An escort of sufficient size to be sure no one left the cart stood guard. In accordance with tradition, the exiles would be taken to the border, and there given "the wink," a parting gift that was both contempt and consolation, an expression of "Huh, you got caught and I didn't." Each would be given a scarf embroidered with the first safe date of return, a purse containing five coins (at least one of which would be counterfeit), and a boot in the backside. The escort would enjoy that last, particularly those who had been assigned to the North Malbeth trip until pulled out for this duty.

They would not run short of food on the trip, to judge by the amount thrown at them. People were getting bored, waiting on that wheel, and hurling something at the exiles was the best way to show you were not in sympathy with them. That would be to risk being dropped at the last moment from the northbound caravan. Sielvia barely stifled a cry of warning as something large and dark flew at Polijn's head. It fell short, though, and hit someone two benches ahead of her.

Others paid no attention to the exiles at all. Losers were beneath contempt. To be sure, the King had started to ride over that way twice. But he had turned back both times. Sielvia looked around, but didn't see him now. No doubt Nurse had scolded him in out of the weather. Thunder rumbled again.

If only they could have left yesterday! Yesterday it might have been possible to hope. But there had been too many things to be done to the wagons before setting off, and the great executions held to celebrate the failure of one more plot against the pale, tearstained King.

Rabioson Sausagefinger hated wholesale slaughters. He had said more than once that if the treason trade continued to expand, he'd need to take on a partner. His concentration was fragmented with as many as six people dying at once. A few chores could be ticked off to apprentices, but in matters of treason, the law required him to give each of the condemned his personal attention.

This applied even to those in the less visible parts of the platform, set up for sideshows involving those traitors whose punishment did not involve eventual demise. Raiprez had been given her life; her brother had spoken for her and gotten her a light sentence. Stripped to the waist, with her ears stapled to a whipping post, she had been lashed until she tore loose and dropped off the platform into the crowd below.

It wasn't fair! Sielvia punched the windowframe. Polijn should have been allowed to escape so easily. Raiprez had been salvaged, dragged dripping and naked from the crowd by her brother's men, and now lay in a wagon behind them, headed north. Kodva, as widow of one war hero and wife of another, had gotten off all but free. She, Jintabh, and Raiprez would go to the Summer Palace for one day, and then move on to the little castle in their little duchy, forbidden to come within a day's ride of His Majesty ever again.

But Polijn had no castle and, so far as Sielvia knew, was related to no war hero. Avid applause had greeted her appearance on the platform. Her sentence had been twenty stripes "and no more, because of her youth" and five years' exile from her homeland. Yet Morafor, a grosser and less pleasant person, and probably more guilty, had been sentenced to nothing at all!

His only penalty was to be required to tend the comatose Lord Aizon. If the Exorcist died, the severity of Morafor's misstep would be reconsidered.

Sielvia had seen progressively larger bribes leave her father's hands regarding the frills and accessories that were open to Rabioson under the wording of the sentence. Bribes from other courtiers had been heavy to see that Polijn was permanently crippled, disfigured, or otherwise removed from competition, in case she was able to sneak back from exile. Laisida had even dipped into the University's bribe fund. Rabioson, with one of his rare smiles, remarked that this was the most lucrative nonfatal sentence that had ever been handed down.

When the time came, he chose one of his less lethal whips. Little Polijn was only tied to the post. After she had stood a while, white and naked in the steamy heat, an assistant had stepped forward with clamps, but had been waved back by his master, who had spotted him in time.

The amateur hackwork displayed in thin scars scattered across Polijn's back made Sausagefinger wince. He had created an exquisite crisscross pattern, made the more piquant by a few beads of blood here and there. Lauremen had fainted, which put Iúnartar in a sorry dilemma, not knowing whom to watch.

Removed from the post, Polijn had been stretched across a table for display. A target for more than jeers, extended across rough planking in the heat for a good four hours while the rest of her supposed accomplices were tortured to death, Polijn had done what only Polijn could do: she took a nap.

Sielvia had to laugh, even now, thinking about it. They had all thought she had merely fainted, but when the assistants came to undo her, she had jerked up, immediately awake, just as if she'd been lying in the hammock.

"Oh!" Sielvia jerked back as a whip cracked. Then she remembered where she was.

"Away back there!" someone bellowed. She put her face to the window again just as the cart lurched forward.

"We need all the road!" the whipcrackers shouted, as drivers tried to get the exiles' cart out of the way. The motion all but threw Polijn off her bench. But Carasta had a hand under her shift already and was thus able to catch her. The exiled minstrel lifted her up to his lap.

Sielvia growled. "What is it?" Iúnartar demanded. "Uh-oh. Listen!"

Rain began to spit onto the roof and sides of the coach. Intermittent taps were quickly replaced by a rhythmic drum, water slashed in at the window, dashing the fringed curtains aside.

"Oh, wonderful!" Iúnartar cried, jumping up to pull the shutters over the windows. "That is ALL we need right now."

Snarling, Sielvia pushed the little girl back and punched the shutter back open. Through the veils of rain, she could still see the wagonload of exiles, but their faces and heads were only grey ovals now. She did not resist as Orna reached past her to shut the window again.

Seigniorage: The profits resulting from the difference between the cost to make a coin and its face value, or its worth as money and legal tender. Most coins cost less to make than their face value; when it becomes too expensive to make a certain coin, its size, weight and composition are often changed.

Series: Related coinage of the same denomination, design and type, including modifications and varieties.

Slab: A rigid plastic, sonically sealed holder, usually rectangular, especially one used by third-party grading services.

Specie: In the form of coin, especially precious metal coin; paper money redeemable in coin. From Latin meaning "in kind."

State coinages or notes: Refers to coins issued by one of four state governments (Connecticut, Massachusetts, New Jersey and New York) between the Declaration of Independence and the ratification of the U.S. Constitution when the states' rights to issue coins were suspended. Among paper money, refers to notes issued between Declaration of Independence and Civil War by state governments.

Stella: A gold $4 pattern never issued for circulation.

Subtype: A modification of a basic design type that leaves the basic theme intact without major revision. Examples include the Bison on Plain and Bison on Mound reverses for the Indian Head 5-cent coin and the three reverse subtypes used on the Capped Bust half dollar from 1836 to 1838 (the same Eagle design was used with and without E PLURIBUS UNUM; the denomination appears as 50 C., 50 CENTS and HALF DOL.).

Surcharge: An extra charge placed on an item, the revenue of which is usually earmarked for a specific fund. It has been the recent practice of the Congress to place a surcharge on commemorative coins, sometimes to benefit a worthy organization.

Trade dollar: A silver dollar coin produced for overseas markets. The U.S. issued a Trade dollar from 1873 to 1885 for use in Asia.

Type: A basic coin design, regardless of minor modifications. The Indian Head and Jefferson 5-cent coins are different types.

Type set: A collection composed of one of each coin of a given series or period.

Uncirculated set: Set of coins issued by the U.S. Mint, consisting of one of each coin issued for circulation. Also called Uncirculated Mint set, or unofficially, a Mint set.

Upsetting mill: A machine that squeezes planchets so that they have a raised rim, in preparation for striking.

coin denominations. Often called "private gold," which is correct for many but not all of the issues, and "territorial gold," which is incorrect since none of the coins were struck by a territorial government authority.

Planchet: The disk of metal that when placed between the dies and struck becomes a coin. Also called flan or blank.

Prestige Proof set: A special U.S. Proof set, containing regular Proof coins plus commemorative coins of that year.

Proof: A coin struck on specially prepared planchets on special presses to receive the highest quality strike possible, especially for collectors.

Prooflike: An Uncirculated coin having received special minting treatment and a mirror surface for the benefit of collectors, with minor imperfections due to the minting process permissible.

Quarter dollar: A 25-cent coin of the United States.

Quarter eagle: A gold $2.50 coin of the United States.

Reeded edge: The result of a minting process that creates vertical serrations on the edge of a coin.

Registry set: Two grading services, Numismatic Guaranty Corp. and Professional Coin Grading Service, allow participants to register their graded and encapsulated coins as sets. Collectors "compete" to have the highest-ranked registry set in terms of quality and completeness. The concept has led to very high prices being paid for "grade rare" coins that in terms of total mintage are common, but are rare in ultra-high grades.

Restrike: A numismatic item produced from original dies and by the original issuer, but later than original issues. In the case of a coin, the restrike usually occurs to fulfill a collector demand and not a monetary requirement. Sometimes "restrike" is used in a broader sense to refer to coins restruck at a later date, but not from original dies or by the original issuing authority.

Reverse: The side opposite the obverse; usually but not always the side with the denomination (the denomination appears on the obverse of the State quarter dollars, for example). The side opposite the side containing the principal design. Informally, the "tails."

Rim: Raised border around the circumference of a coin, not to be confused with the edge.

Ringed bimetallic coin: A coin composed of two parts: a holed ring into which is inserted a core. The two parts are often different colors and compositions. The only U.S. ringed bimetallic coin is a 2000 commemorative $10 coin honoring the Library of Congress, composed of a platinum core and gold ring.